PRAISE FOR *BEFORE YOU FOUND ME*

"Brooke Beyfuss has written a raw, real[...] about healing and forgiveness, recovery[...] deeply heartfelt without being sentimental; this is a beautiful, touching, and hard-hitting story that is ultimately, wonderfully redemptive."

—Kate Hewitt, *USA Today* bestselling
author of *The Secrets We Keep*

"Can there ever be sympathy for a kidnapper—no matter how forceful her case? Don't decide until you read *Before You Found Me*, Brooke Beyfuss's complex, compelling new novel that dissects the tangled psychology of right and righteousness in a story of true love."

—Jacquelyn Mitchard, #1 *New York Times* bestselling
author of *The Deep End of the Ocean*

"*Before You Found Me* is a heartrending story of empathy and courage. Beautifully crafted, it was impossible not to be carried along as Rowan and Gabriel raced to stay ahead of the danger that was chasing them, opening their hearts, healing, and becoming a remarkable family along the way. An emotional page-turner I couldn't put down."

—Suzanne Redfearn, #1 Amazon
bestselling author of *In an Instant*

"A richly imagined story celebrating the healing power of love as Rowan—herself an abuse survivor—fights to protect a young boy trapped in a similar circumstance. *Before You Found Me* is sure to appeal to book clubs and readers of standout family drama."

—Christine Nolfi, bestselling author of *A Brighter Flame*

"A powerhouse of a novel, a literary masterpiece shaped out of heartbreaking prose, a moving examination of trauma, sacrifice, and the true definition of family. *Before You Found Me* grips readers from page one and delivers on every front."

—Terah Shelton Harris, author of *One Summer in Savannah*

"I cried both happy and heartbroken tears through this story of love and family bonds created out of tragedy. *Before You Found Me* is utterly unique and moving, terrifying, funny, relatable, and life-affirming. It will leave readers on an emotional high."

—Annie Ward, author of *Beautiful Bad* and *The Lying Club*

BEFORE
YOU FOUND
ME

A NOVEL

BROOKE BEYFUSS

sourcebooks
landmark

Published by Sourcebooks Landmark, an imprint of Sourcebooks
P.O. Box 4410, Naperville, Illinois 60567–4410
(630) 961-3900
sourcebooks.com

Library of Congress Cataloging-in-Publication Data

Names: Beyfuss, Brooke, author.
Title: Before you found me : a novel / Brooke Beyfuss.
Description: Naperville, Illinois : Sourcebooks Landmark, [2023]
Identifiers: LCCN 2022061853 (print) | LCCN 2022061854
(ebook) | (trade paperback) | (epub)
Subjects: LCGFT: Novels.
Classification: LCC PS3602.E945 B44 2023 (print) | LCC PS3602.E945
(ebook) | DDC 813/.6--dc23/eng/20230109
LC record available at https://lccn.loc.gov/2022061853
LC ebook record available at https://lccn.loc.gov/2022061854

Printed and bound in Canada.
MBP 10 9 8 7 6 5 4 3 2 1

For Brandon and Tess

AUTHOR'S NOTE

Dear Reader,

My debut novel, *After We Were Stolen*, led both the characters and the reader on a dark journey. I felt strongly that a trigger warning would be more than appropriate, as I wanted to give every reader the option of traveling that path or not. After the book's release, I received dozens of messages from people who have experienced darkness in their own lives. After reading the trigger warning, some were able to read the book, and some were not, which only strengthened my resolve to give readers all the information they need before stepping into this story.

I began drafting *Before You Found Me* many, many years ago, and the characters are extremely close to my heart. As opposed to *After We Were Stolen*, this story was not quite as emotionally difficult to write, because it is, at its core, a love story. However, the characters have to kick and scream for every inch of happiness they earn, and because of that, I would like to share a few things about what you can expect when reading *Before You Found Me*.

Portions of *Before You Found Me* deal with domestic violence, child abuse, child abandonment, traumatic injury, traumatic death, and emotional distress that may be difficult to read. A far larger portion explores hope, healing, unconditional love, and the true meaning of family.

As is the case in this story, I'm hopeful the good will outweigh the bad.

With love and best wishes,

Brooke

CHAPTER ONE

WHEN SHE FINALLY LEFT, SHE LEFT WITH NOTHING.

She could have gone home. Packed a bag and grabbed the very few things that meant anything at all, but she didn't. There wasn't a single thing in that house worth facing all the blood on the floor. Her neighbor—the same one who'd called the police—had delivered her car to the hospital a few days earlier. As soon as she had her discharge papers in hand, Rowan made one phone call and followed Route 13 up the coast, leaving Virginia behind in a blue-and-white blur.

She was exhausted, but she wasn't worried about nodding off. Her entire body was a slug writhing in salt, a freshly skinned knee bathed in alcohol. Thirty staples forged a metal path from her left hip to her right shoulder blade, along with God only knew how many stitches. The pain wasn't foreign…just different. Over the past two years, she'd been on the receiving end of countless slaps, frequent backhands, and many, many closed fists. But shattered glass had a finer touch; it paid personal attention to every inch of her body. The glass had coated her, clung to her, impregnated her until she was so sharp, no one could touch her without bleeding.

It took the surgical team hours to free every shard from her skin. She swam up from a leaden fog to a parade of doctors and nurses, all of them dying to tell her how lucky she was. That it could have been so much worse.

It was an interesting statement, and it always came without elaboration. So Rowan asked everyone who said it how much worse it needed to be before she was allowed to get upset. What was the invisible threshold she needed to reach before it became acceptable to grieve the body she'd lost? No one had an answer, so they sent in specialists with expensive watches and eager hands, full of ideas about reconstructive surgery and laser treatments and skin grafts. She hadn't listened because it didn't matter. Even if they could erase every blemish and every scar, she would never be the same again.

Driving kept her focused, quieted her mind, but after she'd spent five hours on the road, the sun set, and her energy went with it. Rowan flexed her hands against the steering wheel and tried not to veer over the yellow lines as she approached Wilmington, Delaware. She braked at a red light, wincing against the pull of the seat belt.

Her fingers floated toward her left eye, probing for pain and tenderness in small, curious strokes. It was sightless and still closed, her eyelid puffed tight against the line of black stitches that crossed her temple like marching ants. The patchwork of bruises coloring the rest of her face was yellowing around the edges, but a few knotty bumps remained stubbornly purple.

When the car filled with green light, Rowan could barely lift her foot from the brake. Sore or not, she was tired—far too tired to pull the all-nighter she'd been counting on. With more than three hundred miles in front of her, she turned onto a local road and parked under a tree that cast enough shadows to hide her face.

Bedford Memorial Hospital had released her with a plastic bag of bloody clothes and two accessories: one old and one new. The new one, a thick white hospital bracelet, still circled her wrist. The old one gleamed from the third finger of her left hand. The diamond sparkled in the dim light, throwing rainbows across the ceiling as though it had nothing at all to do with what had happened.

Rowan slid the band over her knuckle and rolled down the window. She tilted her face toward the sudden rush of cool dampness, but the late-spring breeze did nothing to soothe her skin or quiet her mind. She closed her fingers over the ring, forcing the stone into the center of her hand. In the next breath, before she could decide not to, she tossed it out the window in a glistening arc and threw the car into gear. She drove with her foot to the floor for perhaps ten seconds before a passing streetlight lit her broken face. Her hand felt empty on the wheel, too light, as though she'd severed some vital part of herself. She reversed and flew fifty feet backward without a single thought or glance; the brakes screamed and so did her back as she tumbled out of the car and began combing through the grass and gravel.

The smashed remains of drunken littering turned the road glittery, and Rowan's scrabbling hands closed on every bit of shine that caught her eye. Passing headlights threw her bloody fingers into sharp detail, effectively arresting her search. She took a deep breath and braced her forehead against the bumper of the car.

Ethan walked toward her, all lit up in rolling waves of blue and red. His steps were easy, a saunter that belied the fury in his eyes. Shattered glass covered Rowan like confetti, forming glistening rainbows that trembled and danced with every breath. The sirens were getting closer and so were the lights; they skimmed across the side of the house, and the trees, and the blood that painted her shape in the wood. Ethan leaned over her, and he said...

"Do you need some help?"

Rowan spun around, her right eye wide and terrified—a sharp contrast to her left, which barely resembled an eye at all, puffy and weeping pink tears. A small man in jogging clothes stood ten feet away. Rowan dimly realized he was offering the space so he wouldn't scare her. She had scared him instead. She knew what she looked like.

"No, no, I—well, maybe. Maybe I do." The words cracked with leftover tears, and she lifted a hand absently to her hair, the only thing about her that wasn't a mess; it fell down her back in a bright curtain that shimmered in the breeze. Her smile felt broken.

The man took a few steps toward her. "Are you having car trouble? My wife is home. I can call her if you need a ride somewhere."

"No, it's just—my ring. I dropped my engagement ring, and I can't find it."

Another car passed, lighting the surprise that flashed across his face. "Oh. Well, I can offer you an extra set of eyes if it'll help," he said. "They're a little older than yours, but they work."

She offered a weak note of thanks as he dropped to the ground and began edging along the asphalt. Rowan joined him, praying her ring wasn't barreling down the road as a fifteen-thousand-dollar adornment in someone else's tire.

"This probably isn't polite," the man said as he crawled all over the blacktop, caring not a whit about the health of his bare knees, "but aren't you a little bit young to be engaged?"

It was a terrible question, but not as bad as the one he could have asked. Rowan shrugged. "I can vote. I can drink. Isn't it a little bit late for a jog?"

He smiled. "I worked second shift for years. It turned me into a night owl." His head disappeared behind the rear tire. "You don't happen to have a light, do you?"

Rowan tossed him the tiny flashlight she kept on her key chain, and he aimed the beam under the car. "I think your troubles are over, my dear." He flattened himself against the ground and wiggled under the bumper, grit and pebbles dimpling his skin. A moment later he dropped the ring, grimy now, into her waiting hand.

"Thank you so much," Rowan said, finally embarrassed. "I'm sorry. I know I look…" She shook her head. "Thank you."

"Glad I could help." He got to his feet, glancing at his watch as she rubbed the ring with the hem of her shirt. "You're right. It is pretty late. Does your fiancé know where you are?"

Rowan finished giving the ring a hasty polish. After a moment's hesitation, she slid the band onto her right ring finger—the one with no connection to her heart. She regarded her unexpected savior with an expression that was no longer pleasant and no longer grateful.

"I hope not."

Rowan surrendered the night at a motel with a deeply slanted roof and a row of red exterior doors. Trucks clogged the parking lot, but the lobby was deserted. When she got to her room, she dropped her bag onto the floor and forced down her dinner: french fries chased with a chocolate milkshake melted into soup.

The air conditioner whirred to life as she stared at herself in the blank face of the television. The woman at the front desk had refused to meet her eye, but as Rowan turned to leave, a voice at her back had whispered that lavender oil was good for scars. Sage advice, something a mother might say, though Rowan had never known that privilege. She only knew Celia.

The thought of her sister—who hadn't even bothered to visit, let alone offer organic remedies—shattered the remains of an old promise. She cursed her racing heart as she picked up her phone, and a moment later, a sleepy voice was in her ear.

"Hello?"

Rowan gritted her teeth. "Hey, Ceil, it's me. Were you sleeping?"

"No," Celia said, clearing her throat. "I'm awake. I've been waiting for you to call."

"Phone works both ways."

Celia ignored that. "Where are you?"

"Delaware. I'll be at Laine's tomorrow. Did you kick the squatters out of my house yet?"

"No, I did not. They have two months left on the lease. I'm not going to throw them out because you're too proud to sleep in my spare room."

Rowan gripped the phone tighter. "I told you I'm not staying with you. Why should I?" Her voice faltered and broke. "Six days in the hospital is a long time when no one comes to see you."

The change in Celia's own voice was subtle and tense. "You were a thousand miles away. I couldn't possibly be gone that long. I have a lot of people who depend on me, you know that."

Rowan let out a bark of laughter. "Right. Silly me for thinking I'd get some priority, huh? By the way, did the doctor tell you how many blood transfusions I needed? I think it was two, maybe three. I don't remember. I was so out of it. And I have one of those rare blood types, but you know that, right? 'Cause you have the same one? See, right there, you could've helped me out, but it's okay—your patients are far more important than your sister." Celia started to speak, but Rowan wouldn't let her. "I will be at Laine's for the next two months, just a phone call away. When *my* house is ready, please be kind enough to let me know."

She hung up and tossed the phone onto the bed. It ricocheted off the mattress and landed facedown on the floor next to her hospital bag, which was spilling its contents across the threadbare carpet. As Rowan sifted through packets of ointment and rolls of gauze, the phone came to life again, a harsh buzz that felt like a punishment even before she saw the screen. When she did, she sat frozen, clutching the phone as it screamed his name again and again, the air between her hovering finger and the glowing glass the only space between them. Every vibration echoed in her heart, quiet and trembling, in a room that was all at once too big and too bright. Eventually, the phone went still, leaving a silent corpse in her hand.

Ethan

Missed Call

Rowan placed the phone on the floor again, gingerly this time.

It wasn't the first time he had called—she'd picked up the first time, fresh out of surgery and too groggy to understand that bail hadn't been enough to hold him.

She got up to check the lock on the door, and then she fumbled through the bag again, poking and searching until her fingers found the amber bottle, currently her most prized possession.

The pill melted against her tongue, sharp and bitter with the promise of release. She tried to breathe as she rested against the pillow, expecting a greater yield considering how heavy her head felt. But there was no peace behind her eyes. Every image was red and dripping—jagged memories from a place that was always dark.

———————

The curtains were edged in pale yellow light when Rowan was wrenched from sleep by the thundering fist of the cleaning woman. After cracking the door open to defend her checkout time, Rowan stood under a warm shower. The soap scraped against her staples, and the knotted ends of plastic thread poked her fingers. Rowan tried not to prophesize on the scars that would follow. She brushed her hair until it was barely damp and then looped a skein of it around her fist, finding no comfort in the pale marriage of red and gold. She loved her hair. It had been her favorite thing about herself until the first time Ethan had used it as a leash, snapping her head back and laughing. She twisted the bright length on top of her head in defiance.

Her head ached from the weight by the time she drove across the Massachusetts state line, sucking down the icy dregs of her third Coke. Two hours later, she rolled into the westward town of Ellisburg where Laine Mae, her best friend, had offered Rowan the use of her house, currently unoccupied while Laine spent the summer visiting her grandparents in Seoul.

It was more than generous—Rowan hadn't seen Laine in years. The two of them had met shortly after Rowan was placed in her final foster home, a hurried and messy transaction following her second failed stint with Celia. Her new family was parented by a pair of retired teachers who housed a tangle of kids in their rambling New Hampshire farmhouse. Laine lived down the road. They were both thirteen, with birthdays a week apart, but aside from that, they had nothing in common. Rowan was on her ninth foster placement and well past jaded; she wore defiance like a badge, while Laine barely spoke above a whisper. But their differences balanced, and they fit together without friction. Where Laine was gentle and calming, Rowan was fierce and protective, and it wasn't long before they became home to each other. They stayed joined at the hip until Celia stepped in once again to rip Rowan from the happiest life she'd known in a long time, herding her onto an airplane to Virginia for her next fresh start. Rowan hadn't seen Laine since. Celia was always too busy to orchestrate a visit, and then Ethan showed up, scissors flashing, ready to sever every relationship Rowan had.

But despite Celia's indifference and Ethan's best efforts, they never fully lost touch. And when Rowan had needed help, Laine was the first person—the only person—who gave it to her.

"You're doing me a huge favor," Laine said when Rowan called her from the hospital. She sounded great; her voice buzzed with an energy Rowan couldn't fake. "The neighborhood's pretty quiet, but I'll feel better having someone there."

"Are you sure? Celia said I could stay with her, but—"

"It's yours," Laine had replied.

Rowan navigated half a dozen tree-lined streets before reaching a tight-packed row of houses separated by thin strips of grass. Her temporary haven sat at the far end of the road, quaint and unimposing behind a slightly weathered picket fence. While Laine's house needed a little work, Rowan could see huge potential. The beautiful arched windows were surrounded by grimy patches where the shutters should be—the result, Rowan knew, of a recent renovation snafu. The missing shutters gave the house a crooked appearance, like a face with no eyebrows.

She walked to the side yard, where a terra-cotta flowerpot was perched in the grass next to a low basement window. Rowan reached inside, digging through dead stems and wilted petals until her fingers found the key—a flash of bright metal twinkling like a promise in the dirt.

CHAPTER TWO

GABRIEL WAS READING WHEN THE SHADOW CROSSED HIS LAP.

It was nothing, really—just a blip on his radar—but he glanced up as the shape blotted out the dusky light. A well-worn copy of *Robinson Crusoe* was balanced on his knees. In the moment before the pages had gone dark, he'd been thinking that he would gladly battle cannibals if it meant he could go outside.

But his own island was dangerous enough. It was damp and moldy, with a cold floor and gray cement walls. He had one window, almost too high for him to reach, and every spring and summer, ants and spiders and mosquitoes crawled through the holes in the wire mesh. Winter was better because there were no bugs, but it was also worse because winter was cold.

Gabriel really didn't mind the bugs that much—at least the

ones that didn't bite. There were plenty of worse things to hate. Like eating. He didn't get to eat every day, but he still hated it because the food he got was always cold, and sometimes it was so dry and stale that every bite hurt his mouth. His showers were cold, too, but that was okay. The laundry soap he washed with burned his skin.

Most of all, he hated the kids across the street. They played outside every day just because they could, flying over the sidewalk and chasing the ice cream man. They screamed with voices that were clearer than his and never faded. Gabriel used to scream, too, but he stopped as soon as he learned it only made things worse. It took him a long time to learn—long enough for his voice to match the way he looked: thin and gritty and weak.

But this interruption, the alien shadow, was something new. He dragged his chair to the window and stood on it, pressing his nose against the screen. The shadow fidgeted and paced until his eyes adjusted to the light and showed him a girl. Not the girl who usually lived there; she'd been gone for days. This was someone different. She bent suddenly, and Gabriel jerked away from the window, curling his fingers against the rusty edge of the metal frame.

She didn't notice. Her eyes were fixed on a flowerpot, her fingers rooting inside and spilling dirt down the orange clay. Gabriel studied her carefully. Her hair was bright coppery gold, and she had a ton of it, all looped on her head like a bow on a present. When she stood in the sun, her entire head looked like it was on fire. It was warm outside, but she had on big, baggy clothes and dark glasses that covered half her face. The skin he could see was blotchy and red, like she was getting a sunburn or had just finished crying.

Once the girl dug up whatever she'd been looking for, she unlocked the side door and disappeared into the house. Gabriel watched her go, a small bubble of excitement taking root in the pit of his stomach.

Then the door to his own house slammed above his head, and heavy footfalls pounded the ceiling. He moved away from the window, walked to the corner of the basement, and curled into a ball, as far from the stairs as he could. His hands shook. They always did when the door slammed.

His father was home.

CHAPTER THREE

ROWAN LAY IN BED WITH THE SHEETS PULLED UP TO HER EARS, COWER-
ing in the quiet comfort of Laine's guest room. The moon was full,
shining cool light through a window Rowan couldn't shutter. Her
phone was next to her. During the day, it stayed dark, but her nights
were filled with the constant buzzing reminder that Ethan was not
about to let her go that easily.

On the first night, she'd blocked his number, but her resolve
hadn't lasted long. It was like standing with her back to a loaded gun.
The fact he was calling her at all meant he didn't have the means
to do much else. It was also evidence. She sent screenshots of the
missed calls to her lawyer every day. If the phone kept Ethan busy,
she was content to let him dig himself deeper.

But that didn't make it any easier to hear. Rowan had no tethers to her old life, no sentries to call for updates, save for the attorney who assured her that no, Ethan couldn't leave the state, so he was right where she'd left him. It didn't matter. Ethan liked getting inside her head as much as he liked tossing her across the room, and it would take a lot more than eight hundred miles to stop him.

———————————

Rowan tried to open her eyes one morning, but they felt like they were full of sand. She'd been at Laine's for two weeks, and she still didn't feel safe enough to sleep behind those wide-open windows. The makeshift curtains she fashioned out of bedsheets were of little comfort and always landed on the floor before morning. As usual, she'd barely managed to grab a few hours before the sun woke her. In the kitchen, she drank cup after cup of coffee and searched neighborhood sites for local painters, anyone who might be able to close the eyes on this house. Once the caffeine kicked in, she couldn't sit still, so she wandered into the garage, where the weathered shutters lived, flakes of red paint dotting the floor.

Rowan knew the story. A few months earlier, Laine had hired a guy off a grocery store bulletin board to strip and paint her shutters following a particularly nasty winter. After a signed contract and a hefty deposit, he appeared one morning, yanked the shutters off the house, and piled them in the driveway. Two days later, Laine's check was cashed, his phone was shut off, and the shutters were nearly hijacked by a group of overzealous curbside scavengers. Before Laine had a chance to threaten legal action, her grandparents had surprised her with a plane ticket, leaving the house in its present state—blank white and startled.

Rowan was pretty startled herself. Far from enjoying a peaceful respite, she'd fallen into a pattern of behavior that was disturbing even by her standards. In the hospital, when she wasn't drugged, she'd been remarkably lucid—when the police took her statement, she threw Ethan so far under the bus, it felt like she was driving over him. But since arriving at Laine's, important details had begun slipping away, despite the evidence carved in her skin. The selective amnesia was so sudden that Rowan began carrying around a copy of the police report, anticipating those desperate, panicked moments when she needed to know if it had happened at night or during the day, the name of the arresting officer, the color of her shirt. Twice, she grabbed her phone to answer one of Ethan's many calls, and her only thought was that she hadn't talked to him in a while. She was so blinded by her mind's attempt to shut off, so completely distracted, that she didn't notice when her stitches finally dissolved and her left eye no longer puckered and drooped. After her staples were removed, she barely registered the long puffy scar where the glass had split her in two.

It sounded like healing, but it wasn't. It was a trick, and she was playing it on herself. She stared straight through the scars she'd wear for the rest of her life while her mind tucked away every bad memory, as though hiding them were enough to make them disappear. It was exactly how she'd stayed with him for so long. She had to notice. She had to remember. She had to do anything she could to keep her anger from fading to that once-upon-a-time when Ethan had been the only one there for her. She needed to harness that energy before it consumed her—cash it in before it drove her even further away from what little peace she had.

Rowan danced her fingers along the wood, chips of paint clinging to her skin. The shutters were long, each with a half-moon carved on top to fit the arched windows. They were also old, original to the house, and awkward as hell. They folded of their own free will, something she discovered when she nearly severed her fingers on the first pair she tried to lift.

She ignored the sharp pain shooting from her left hip to her right shoulder as she dragged the shutters toward the side of the house. She was barely through the garage door when a voice cracked the air like a whip, so sudden and so loud that Rowan jumped. The shutters slipped and landed right on top of her foot.

"Whoa, whoa, whoa!"

She looked up and saw an absolute giant of a man hurtling toward her. "Is this your first day on the job, or are you just desperate for a hernia?" he asked, grabbing the edges of the wood.

"What?"

"You're lifting with your back. Bad form." Before Rowan could say a word, he pulled the shutters out of her hand and hoisted them up, balancing the wood on top of his head. "Where do you want them?"

"Um…over there," Rowan said, pointing to the stretch of siding next to the kitchen door. The man propped the wood against the house and headed back toward the garage.

"Did you buy this place?" he asked, grabbing the second pair.

"No, I—"

"Renting?"

"Just for a few months. You really don't have to—"

"It's no trouble. My name's Lee," he said, setting them down in the grass and offering his hand; it swallowed hers, his grip tight enough to hurt. "Lee Emerson." He jerked his thumb toward the house next door. "I live here."

"Nice to meet you."

"What's your name?"

For a moment her reply was caught behind her tongue, snagged on something she couldn't see. "Rowan."

"Rowan." His eyes were very blue—charming but not sweet. They raked her from head to toe. "Sorry for busting in on you, but you didn't know what the hell you were doing."

Rowan laughed, one quick, nervous bark. "And you do?"

"Damn straight. Check out the van," he said, pointing to his driveway. "Emerson's Masonry. I haul rocks all day long; these are toothpicks to me."

He leaned the second pair of shutters against the house. Flecks of red twirled like snowflakes in the breeze. "Are you going to strip them?" he asked.

"I'm going to paint them."

"If you don't strip them first, you're wasting your time. Come inside for a minute," he said, starting toward his house. "I've got some solvent, I think—"

"I'll buy my own."

"It's right in the garage—"

"I met you three minutes ago," she said. "I'm not going in your house." She smiled tightly, her fists clenched at her side.

Lee laughed. "Cautious to a fault, huh?"

"No. Just smart."

"Smart-ass, you mean," he said, disappearing into his garage. A minute later he returned with a rusty can and a flat-edged scraper. "Here you go," he said, handing them over. "Don't say I never gave you anything."

"Thanks."

"And don't go hiring anyone to get those shutters back on the house if that's your plan, neighbor," he called, climbing into the white van in his driveway. "I can probably spare a few guys for you." He stuck his head out the window as he backed out. "If you're as smart as you say, you'll take me up on that."

Rowan watched him as he drove away, the can and scraper still clutched in her hands.

The solvent had a noxious odor and was as thick as condensed milk. It took her forever to pry off the lid, and she was rewarded with a chemical burn when the solution exploded from the can. She forced her pinched and blistered hands into a pair of gardening gloves and began covering the wood with wide, sweeping strokes.

While she waited for the chemicals to dissolve something other than her skin, Rowan turned her attention back to Lee's house, surreptitiously judging the state of his shutters. Structurally, the house was similar to Laine's, but it had been polished to a shine. The perimeter was framed by a short brick wall and impeccable landscaping. The lush shrubbery and tumbling flowers made the tiny house look like a little kid playing dress-up.

When the paint began to blister, Rowan pushed the scraper across the slats, sending a crimson blizzard swirling in the breeze. She worked steadily, if not competently, to lay bare the weathered boards, gouging tiny nicks into the wood with every pass.

It wasn't long before her arms were burning from the effort, but that wasn't what made her stop. There was something stirring in the space around her, some kind of weight in the air, as palpable as a shout. For a minute she thought Lee had come back, but his van was still gone. She looked down the driveway, as though someone had called her name, but the street was still and silent.

Rowan's heartbeat picked up as she pressed the scraper against a stubborn patch of red paint. She half expected her phone to buzz in her pocket, but it too was quiet. She turned suddenly, and her eyes caught a dancing shadow darkening Lee's basement window, something small and quick that vanished the moment she saw it. She returned to the shutters and glanced over her shoulder again. The shadow retreated. Her voyeur was matching her movements, ducking out of sight whenever she looked up. They were good at it, too; they hadn't made a sound. Rowan pulled off her gloves. "I can see you, you know," she said. "It's not nice to spy on people." The shadow scurried away.

Rowan shook her head and turned back to the battered wood.

"I wasn't spying."

It was a quiet voice for such a loud shadow, low and husky. The speaker was young—there were no more than ten years there—but something about the tone sent a chill up Rowan's back.

"I was just looking out the window."

He sounded like a little boy, but his voice was all wrong. It lacked…childishness. She'd never heard someone so young sound so spent, so completely drained. He sounded as tired as she felt.

Rowan bent down to peer at the screen. It was speckled with red paint, but there was nothing but darkness beyond. "Sorry," she said. "I guess that means I was spying on you."

He didn't respond.

She tried again. "What's your name?"

Long pause. "Is my dad gone?"

"Who, Lee?" she asked. "Yeah, he's gone. Why?"

"I'm not supposed to…I'm grounded."

"Oh, I gotcha," Rowan said. "Don't worry, I spent half my life grounded, I won't tell. What's your name?"

"You promise?"

"What?"

"You promise you won't tell my dad you saw me?"

"Cross my heart."

Two small hands pushed the screen up, and the boy suddenly appeared—at least the top of his head did. "Gabriel," he said quietly.

"I'm Rowan."

"I know," he said, pacing from one end of the window to the other. "I heard you talking."

"How old are you?"

"Eleven. How old are you?"

Rowan smiled. "Yesterday was my birthday. I turned twenty-two."

"That's old."

"Yeah, it's really not." She heard metal being dragged across concrete, the stamp of two small feet, and then the boy rose into view slowly and shyly, squinting against the light.

His face bore no resemblance to the gravel in his voice. He was beautiful. The sweetness she'd sought in Lee's blue eyes was bright and shining in Gabriel's. His skin was very pale—almost sickly, she thought—and smudged with dirt beneath his wavy mop of dark hair. Something about his face was familiar to Rowan for no reason she could pinpoint. Gabriel blinked up at her.

"Hi," she said.

"Hi."

"Want to come out and help me? I bet your dad won't mind if I put you to work."

He hesitated. "I can't."

"There's twenty bucks in it for you if you do."

"No," he said quietly, staring at the grass. "I'm grounded."

"Well, that's a standing offer," Rowan said, picking up her brush. "This is going to take me days. What are you doing down there?"

Gabriel stretched his hand through the window and grabbed a fistful of grass, twisting the blades into ropes. "Be careful," he said. "That stuff burns."

"I know. It took half my skin off. Why are you in the basement?"

He shrugged. "I like to read down here. Or draw." He pointed suddenly, his finger jabbing the air. "It's dripping."

"You read and draw?" Rowan repeated, adjusting her stance. "Shouldn't you be glued to YouTube and addicted to video games?"

"Why?" he asked, without a trace of sarcasm. He sounded confused, as though he'd never heard of such things.

Rowan nodded. "An Amish existence. I get it."

Gabriel frowned up at her. "What's Amish?"

"Off the grid. You know, horses, buggies, lots of straight pins and puppy mills." She was smiling when Lee's van pulled into the driveway. "Uh-oh. Red alert."

"What?"

"Your dad's back."

She barely got the words out. When she turned to the window, she got a final, fleeting look at Gabriel before he vanished, as though he'd been snatched into darkness by a hand she couldn't see.

CHAPTER FOUR

TWO DAYS, A GALLON OF PAINT, AND EIGHT SCRAPED KNUCKLES LATER, Rowan propped the freshly painted shutters against the house, covered them with a tarp, and decided she had helped enough.

Her gaze bounced from the red wood to Gabriel's window. He'd been conspicuously absent since their chat, and she wasn't sure if she should be worried about him or not. She'd seen Lee plenty of times and even talked to him once or twice, but true to her word, she hadn't said a thing about Gabriel. Lee never mentioned him at all. Rowan found herself sneaking glances toward the window as she sanded and painted, her eyes catching on every glint and every shadow.

Now she checked the driveway. The white van was gone. She kneeled next to Gabriel's window and saw her own face mirrored in the glass. She rapped on it lightly.

There was no response. She knocked again, hard enough to send ripples through her reflection.

Sunlight glistened on the dusty pane, and she thought she saw a stir in the shadows, some fleeting small shape. There was no answering call. She kept one eye on the window as she gathered the cans and brushes and went inside.

————————

At two o'clock in the morning, something pinged against the kitchen door.

Rowan was standing at the counter, rubbing butter into flour for blueberry scones. She hadn't even tried to sleep. Her lawyer had called that afternoon, and instead of telling her that a court date had been set or responding to her many reports of harassment, he had different news to share.

"Three years?" she whispered. "Three years, Barry?"

"Yes. He'll be on probation for five after that."

"But I thought—you said he could get twenty, how—"

"He took the plea deal."

"But that's nothing!"

"It's something, Rowan. If it went to trial, it really could have been nothing. I told you from the beginning that it would be hard to make a first-degree assault charge stick. He didn't use a weapon."

"He threw me through a glass door!"

"It's not a weapon," Barry repeated calmly. "There were no previous assaults—"

"There were plenty." She choked up.

"No reported assaults," he amended. "We went over this. There
was no evidence, no hospital reports, nothing. You don't even have
pictures."

"So it's my fault?" she asked tightly.

"I didn't say that. I'm saying he had a clean record, and this was a
single instance of domestic violence. The plea deal was the best way
to ensure he got at least some time behind bars."

"If that's true, why didn't he take it to trial?"

"Because it's a bigger risk for him too. I know it doesn't sound like
it, but this is the best possible outcome."

"He's been calling me," she said. "He calls me every day, dozens
of times. I told you, and I told the police, and you've done nothing."

"Once he's in, he won't be able to contact you, and if he does it
when he's out, it'll be a parole violation."

"For five years."

He was silent for a moment. "Yeah."

"And what," she asked, "am I supposed to do after that?"

He hadn't responded.

The door pinged again. Rowan stood stock-still, her hands worrying the cold butter. The kitchen window was dark; all she could see
was her own face mirrored in the glass.

Ping!

She groped for the light switch, smearing the wall with grease and flour, but she managed to snap the floodlights on. There was movement in the grass, something wiggling wildly, and when her eyes adjusted, she saw Gabriel hanging halfway out the basement window, one arm poised to throw. When she opened the door, something small and hard bounced off her good shoulder; bits of shine littered the grass around her feet. "What are you doing?" she asked. "Why are you throwing pennies at the door?"

"Shhh!" He waved her forward, rosebud lips pushed into a defiant pout. "Turn the light off!"

Rowan did. The shadows returned swiftly, and she crouched in the doorway, lowering her voice to a whisper. "What's the matter?"

"Why were you knocking on my window?"

"What?"

"This afternoon. You knocked on my window. You can't do that. I'll get in big trouble."

"Why would you get in trouble?"

"I told you. I'm grounded. What'd you do that for anyway?"

Because you look like I feel.

"I don't know," she said, her face burning in the cool air. "I guess I wanted someone to talk to."

His expression didn't change. "Don't do it again."

They stared at each other over the strip of grass. Gabriel had pulled back from the window, partially shrouded in darkness. But there was enough light to see something was off; he was fidgety, constantly moving, like he didn't want her to get a good look at him. His face was just as smudged as it had been a few days ago, but now it didn't look like dirt. Her mind kept clicking, flashing memories of her own face, her old face, welts and bruises, one after another, until the picture was whole, and she realized exactly what was in front of her. And it was like discovering a nest of rats, something vivid and horrible enough to make her scream.

She crawled over to him, her eyes never leaving his face. "What happened to you?"

"What do you mean?"

She took his chin in her hand, tipping it toward the moonlight. "Your face…"

He twisted away. "It's nothing."

"It's not nothing, you're a mess." Bruises bloomed along the line of his jaw. The bridge of his nose was swollen. A gash split his lower lip in two. "What happened?"

"Nothing!"

Rowan stared at the play of colors on his skin, bruises that were old and new, and his mottled features suddenly made sense. It was the same complexion she'd had to hide for the better part of two years. Gabriel tried to push her hand away, but she cupped his cheek and didn't let go.

He sneezed.

A fine mist of blood exploded into the air, red droplets blooming against her skin like poppies.

Rowan froze, still clutching his cheek. Gabriel's hands flew to cover his nose.

"Bless you," she whispered. "Move your hands."

"No."

"Yes," she insisted, tugging his arm. A thin stream of blood slid down his wrist and made a sticky trail around her fingers. Rowan jerked away, but the shape of her hand stayed behind, outlined in red on his skin.

It's your own fault. I told you a million times—learn to protect your goddamn face. Get an ice pack on it. And if anyone asks...

She drew back. "I bet you fell in the bathroom, right?"

"What?"

"Or maybe you tripped coming down the stairs," she said, her voice rising. "Or walked into a door?"

"Shut up!" he hissed. "My dad'll hear you."

"Good!" she said. "You should tell him you're losing a pint of blood. Or does he already know?"

His mouth snapped shut.

"Does he?"

Gabriel pressed the hem of his T-shirt against his nose.

Rowan rocked back on her heels. "Right," she said, getting to her feet.

"Where are you going?"

"To call the police," Rowan said over her shoulder. "Since you don't want to talk to me, maybe you'll talk to them."

"The police?" Gabriel repeated, more amused than someone who had been beaten and trapped in a basement had any right to be. "Why?"

"What do you mean?"

"Why are you calling the police?"

"Why are you in the basement all the time?"

"I like the basement."

"But you have your own room, right?" Rowan pressed. "A regular room you sleep in every night?"

"Yes!"

"Could you go there right now?"

"If I wanted to."

"Okay, go turn on your light and wave at me through the window."

Gabriel wilted, his head drooping between his shoulders. "No," he said quietly. "I don't want to."

Rowan deflated a bit too. "If you tell me what's going on," she said in a softer tone, "I can help you."

He lifted his head. His eyes were bright, shining with unshed tears. "No, you can't."

Rowan crouched again before wiping blood from his nose with the sleeve of her sweatshirt. "Your dad?" she asked. "Your mom?"

"My dad," he whispered.

She saw Lee's face, his wide solicitous grin, and her fingers itched for his throat. "Does he—Jesus Christ, Gabriel. Are you locked down there?"

He nodded.

"Since when?"

He thought for a moment. "Since my mom died. That was when I was eight, so I guess three years? It's hard to remember—"

"Three years?" Rowan cut in. "You've been down there for three years, and nobody noticed?"

"Nobody sees me."

"What about school?"

"I don't go to school."

"When was the last time you were outside?"

He looked at her evenly. "When I was eight."

"Come out now," she said, grabbing his hand. "Come on, you can fit. I'll help you."

"I can't!"

"Why not?"

"Because I'm...because..."

"Because you're scared."

"I'm not scared!"

"Then what are you waiting for? The day *he* decides to let you out? Or the day he kills you?"

"He's not going to kill me."

"How do you know?" Rowan demanded. "He only needs to hit you the wrong way once, trust me. Let me call the police. They can—"

"No!"

She still had him by the hand; he squeezed her fingers, hard enough to hurt her blistered skin. "No," he whispered again. Another trickle of blood ran from his nose, but he made no move to wipe it away. "Promise me you won't tell anyone. Please."

She stared at his hand in hers. They both had fine filaments of blood staining the lines in their skin. He tightened his grip, and Rowan nodded. "All right. I promise."

CHAPTER FIVE

GABRIEL DIDN'T LOOK OUTSIDE AT ALL THE NEXT DAY.

He sat on his bed reading *Tender Is the Night*, one of his mother's favorites. It wasn't one of *his* favorites, but there weren't many books he'd managed to keep hidden from his dad. If Gabriel were caught with one, his father would tear out a chunk of pages from the end. Gabriel had a whole pile of books without endings, the characters trapped in fights and sadness and trouble forever. Those same books had once been wrapped in birthday paper or piled under the Christmas tree, his name written on the tags. His mom always told him nothing would make him smarter than reading, and she'd taught him long before he started school. By the time he'd been in second grade, his teachers were feeding him middle school assignments and returning his carefully printed book reports with an A on top of each.

He ran his fingers over the worn cover, creased and softened by his mother's hands. Her touch, like her face and her voice, were starting to fade from his memory. It scared him. There were still tiny moments when he could feel her arms around him or her hand in his, but she never stayed long, and time kept pushing her further away. Once she was too far to reach, he'd have nothing left to hold and no one to hold him. He hadn't understood that until last night, when Rowan rested her hand on his cheek and held his bloody hand tight. It was the first touch in years that hadn't hurt. He'd felt it for hours. His eyes drifted to the window, pale sunlight streaming through the grimy glass.

He returned to his book. He hated Rowan. Hated her for stirring him up and making his mind wander where he didn't want to let it, hated her for talking to him, for even caring.

The light was getting deeper. He'd have to stop reading soon, but he didn't mind because after it was dark, she was going to come back. She'd promised to come back.

And he couldn't wait for that.

———

Rowan stood under the shower, letting the water work the kinks out of her neck and shoulders. She'd spent the entire day in the kitchen, pulling batch after batch of cookies out of the oven and spooning chunks of sugary dough directly into her mouth. She'd eaten nothing else, and now her tongue tasted tinny and bitter. She filled her mouth with hot water until she gagged on it.

She traced her fingers over her torso, feeling the raised lines of her scars until they twisted out of reach. She closed her eyes, but there was no peace there. She saw Gabriel, his face white and scared under a camouflage of bruises. She saw Lee and his wide flat hands, big enough to haul rocks. She saw herself, twisting under the glass that pinned her like a butterfly to the splintered deck. She jerked her head twice, quickly.

Rowan wrapped herself in a towel and lay wide-eyed on top of the rumpled covers, her wet hair soaking the pillow. Despite what she'd told Gabriel, she really didn't want to call the police. She knew what happened to kids like him; she knew exactly what he'd be in for. Rowan had spent more than half her life in foster homes and group homes, shuffling from school to school where she was always temporary and always new. She had no right to sentence him to that.

Somewhere amid the folds of the sheets, her phone began to vibrate, writhing and hissing like a snake.

Seventy-six missed calls—seventy-seven—seventy-eight…

When the phone rang for the seventy-ninth time, her resolve shattered into a million pieces, coating her in jagged shards for the second time. Her anger rose, and she jabbed her fingers at the screen. She lifted the phone to her ear, and all that terror and fear bubbled up her throat until it exploded in a single word.

"What?"

Silence. A heavy, expectant silence that banished every illusion of freedom and told her to sit there and behave herself.

"About time," Ethan said. "I was beginning to wonder if I'd killed you after all."

Rowan clutched the phone tighter.

"They showed me pictures from the hospital. You'd be better off if I had."

Her vision swam; if she hadn't been lying down, she would have fallen. "What do you want?"

"I'm glad you asked. I want to express my displeasure that I'm about to be locked up for three fucking years because of you and your bullshit. And I want you to know that I will be spending that time deciding exactly what I'm going to do to you when I get out. That's lots of time, Rowe," he said, his voice going silky. "Lots of time to be creative."

The phone went slick in her hand. "You won't find me," she whispered.

"You won't find me," he repeated, high-pitched and mocking. "Please. You're either holed up with that head cunt Celia at the familial estate, or you're with fucking Laine."

"And you," she said, willing her voice not to shake, "don't know where either of those places are. I always made sure of that."

"I'll find out. It's hard to stay hidden nowadays." He dropped his voice. "So you better stay on your fucking toes. Make no mistake, Rowe—the next time I call you, you'll be close enough to grab."

Her jaw was clenched so tight, it hurt. Before she could bring herself to hang up on him, he hung up on her.

———————————

It was after midnight and the moon was high when Gabriel pushed open the window. A warm breeze flowed over his face, and the smell of grass and burning wood overtook the dampness of the basement. He could see Rowan bobbing around in the kitchen, and when she finally stepped outside, her arms were loaded with foil-covered plates. A picnic basket hung from the crook of her elbow.

"Hey, kiddo," she said, easing to the ground. "Are you sure this is okay?"

"He never comes down at night. I think he takes pills to sleep."

"Well, I hope you're hungry," she said, unwrapping one of the plates.

Gabriel's eyes widened as she set it on the grass. "You made me cookies?"

"Don't you like cookies?"

"Yeah, I just…I haven't had one in a long time."

"I figured. Eat," she said, unwrapping another plate. "I didn't know what you'd like. I made a batch of chocolate chip and one of peanut butter… You aren't allergic to peanuts, are you? I didn't even think about that. I don't want to kill you." She opened the picnic basket. "I have snickerdoodles, and lemon iced, and turtles. I brought you milk too. There's no point eating cookies without milk. That's just torture if you ask me."

She smiled and offered him the plate. Gabriel hesitated for a moment. Then he took a cookie and bit into it.

It was still warm, soft and buttery and stuffed with melting chocolate. The taste brought him back to school, like the smell of fresh pencils. The last cookie he remembered had been tucked inside his lunch box by his mother, all wrapped in waxed paper with a red heart crayoned on the outside. For a minute he felt like he was going to cry.

"Good?" Rowan asked, handing him a plastic cup of milk.

Gabriel nodded, swallowing around the lump in his throat. "Thank you."

She fiddled with the handle of the basket. "I packed you some sandwiches and juice too. I want you to take this and hide it somewhere. I'll bring you more tomorrow." Her eyes fell on his. "He doesn't feed you much, does he?"

Gabriel shrugged, staring at the cookie in his hand.

Rowan pressed a hand over her eyes. "I have to call someone."

"Don't," he said thickly. "You promised."

"I know!" she said, her voice high and tight. Somewhere in the distance, a dog started to howl. "I know. But I'm not going to be here much longer. I can't just leave you like this."

"Why didn't you call the police?" He didn't know why it was important. "Why did you listen to me?"

"Because you'd probably end up fending for yourself in a group home, and kids get beat up in those too," she said, rolling onto her stomach. "Believe me, I know. I was a foster kid for years."

"You were?"

"Until I was fifteen." Her eyes were the color of the ocean, and they never left his face. Her left eye drooped a little bit; a thin pink scar tugged at the corner and stretched all the way across her temple.

"My parents died when I was three," she went on. "They were on a charter plane, and there was a crash. I don't remember it. Then it was just me and my sister. Celia was older, almost sixteen, and she was placed in some kind of boarding school. I went into foster care. We had no close relatives. There was no one to take us."

Gabriel lowered his eyes. "My mom died too."

"I'm sorry."

He shrugged.

"What happened to her?"

He traced the edge of the windowsill with his thumb. "We were in an accident," he said slowly. "Crossing the street before school. She wasn't—the car came at us really fast—all of a sudden, it was just *there*. My mom pushed me out of the way. I didn't even know what happened. When I got up, she was lying underneath it. I tried to go over to her, but then the police got there, and no one would let me see her. An ambulance came, and I thought that meant she'd be okay, but she wasn't. She died before she got to the hospital."

When he looked up, Rowan's eyes were fixed on the moon. He could see her throat working. "You must miss her a lot," she said quietly.

"I do."

"Was your dad—Did he hit you before she died?"

"No," Gabriel said quietly, reaching for another cookie. "He used to be different."

Rowan waited a moment before asking, "How did he use to be?"

"I don't know," Gabriel said. "Like a real dad. He used to do things with me. He would take me to work and let me climb on the rocks, and he coached my soccer team. He never hit me, not once. But after she died, it was like he didn't even want me anymore. One time we were in the supermarket. He kept saying he didn't know what groceries to buy. He was just throwing things in the cart. I asked him if I could pick out a cereal, and he said yes, but as soon as I turned to look, he hit me on the side of my head. It knocked me out. I fell into a rack and got all scraped up. The police came and took me to the hospital, and there was a lady there who told me my father was sick and couldn't take care of me, so she would find a family who could."

His stomach twisted at the memory. "I said no," he whispered. "I never thought he'd do it again. They made us talk to a therapist together instead, every week. The social worker would come to the house and talk to us too. My dad didn't hit me again, not once, and I thought everything was going to be okay. But it wasn't. After a while they stopped checking on us. Then my dad moved us here. The day we moved in was the last time I was outside."

"Did he ever tell you why?"

"Because I killed her."

Rowan shook her head once, quickly. "What do you mean *you* killed her?"

"She was there because of me," he said. The words came easily; his dad had said them thousands of times. "A big dog jumped on me while I was waiting for the bus the day before. I was scared it would happen again, so I asked her to come with me. She never would've been there if I hadn't."

Rowan pressed her fingers to her temple like she was trying to rub away her scar. "So, okay. You're telling me your dad keeps you down there because he blames you for a car accident?"

"It was my fault, I—"

"No," Rowan interrupted. "It wasn't."

"Yes, it was," he insisted. "She died because of me. I killed her."

"She died because someone hit her with their car. Not because of you." She rose to her knees and picked up her phone. "Can I see into that basement, please?"

Gabriel looked at her. He'd made a mistake; he shouldn't have talked about his mom. "No."

"Why not?"

"I don't want you to."

"I'm trying to help you."

"You can't," Gabriel said. "You can't do anything."

Her face went hard, almost angry. "Don't say that to me."

"It's true." He shoved the plate away, and cookies tumbled into the grass. "Leave me alone."

Rowan's eyes were wide and unblinking. "Why won't you let me help you?"

"Because there's nothing you can do! There's nowhere for me to go—you said it yourself. I *know* that…" His voice caught. "Go away," he whispered. "I don't want to talk to you anymore."

Rowan pressed her lips together. Then she put everything back in the picnic basket and left it sitting in the grass. Gabriel watched her walk back to the house. "It's your window, Gabe," she said just before she went inside. "Use it."

———

Rowan closed the door behind her. Her mouth felt ice-cold and lined with metal. She slid to the floor with her back pressed against the wall.

She fumbled for her phone. She was done playing around; she was going to call the cops and wash her hands of this entire situation. She wasn't going to listen to a brainwashed kid who had absolutely no idea how much danger he was in. Rowan mumbled that to herself as her head filled with horrible churning images—Gabriel trapped and alone in that dark hole; his blood splashed across her hand; her own blood staining the wooden deck. She pictured red and blue flashing lights, Gabriel being led to a police car, but there was no peace in the thought. Just memories of her own scared small self every time she was handed over to strangers.

You can't do anything.

She tapped her fingers against the cool tiles. In the hospital, the doctor had asked her where she planned to go. He could call a shelter, he said. A safe house, somewhere secret and hidden where no one would be able to find her.

No, she'd told him. She didn't need that because she had her own safe house, and once she got there, she would disappear forever. Ethan knew it existed, but he didn't know where it was—nobody did. It was the one tangible thing her parents had left her.

A big empty house in the middle of nowhere. A haven.

Rowan picked up her phone and pressed nine. Then she pressed one.

She put the phone down.

She tilted her head until it hit the wall. She just needed a minute, just one minute, and then she would be able to do it. She counted it out loud, sixty seconds, and then she picked up her phone again, punching at the screen, leaving damp fingerprints behind.

She expected a harsh jab to voicemail—it was after midnight—but Celia picked up. She even sounded happy to hear from her. "I'm glad you called. I was going to try you in the morning. The tenants found a new place."

Rowan let out a massive sigh that offered no relief. "When can I move in?"

"They'll be out in a week, but just give me a few days to get the place cleaned out for you." Celia paused. "You're driving?"

"I have to. I need my car."

"It's fifteen hundred miles, Rowan. Are you sure you want to do that alone?"

Rowan's knuckles went white as she got to her feet and stared out the window. "Don't worry." She didn't elaborate until well after she hung up, delivering her next words to the space beyond the blackened glass. "I'm not going to be alone."

CHAPTER SIX

GRUDGES WERE A LUXURY NEITHER OF THEM COULD AFFORD. THE
following night, under a wash of damp air and broken moonlight,
Gabriel winced as Rowan applied an ice pack to his cheek. His skin
was taut and swollen, the first tender stage of bruising. "What was it
for?" she asked, pushing his hair away from his forehead—he felt hot
and dry, almost feverish.

Gabriel shrugged, keeping his eyes down. Then he bent, fumbling
for something at his feet. It was a book, a well-worn copy of *Tender
Is the Night*. The last few chapters had been torn away, and the spine
was cracked so badly, the remaining pages clung to the binding like
loose teeth.

"He tore up your book?"

"He ripped out the ending. He always rips out the endings."

"Why?"

Gabriel looked at her like it was a silly question, something she should know. "That's when all the good things happen," he said. "At the end."

"Oh." Last night's words had been so angry, she didn't think she'd see him again, but when she'd stepped into the dark air, he'd already been at the window, waiting. "I'm really glad you came back," she went on. "I thought you were mad at me."

"I didn't mean it," he said.

"Good. Because I want to talk to you about something."

"What?"

"I was thinking about what you said," she began. "Last night. And I think there may be a way for me to help you without calling the police."

His eyes were guarded but curious as she pulled her phone free. "What?"

"I have an idea. I'll tell you about it in a minute, but is it okay if I take a picture of you first?"

"Why do you want a picture of me?"

"In case we need it."

"Need it for what?"

She glanced at the phone in her hand. "I told you. I have an idea."

He looked wary but not scared. "You won't show anyone?"

"No," she promised. "Can I?"

He lowered the ice and gingerly probed the bruise on his eye. "I guess."

Rowan held up the phone. "I'll be quick."

She took pictures of his entire face and then close-ups of his black eye, split lip, and the yellowing stain across his jaw. The light flashed again and again, lighting up the finger-shaped welts circling his upper arms, a near-camouflage pattern of bruises on his torso.

"Here," Rowan said, handing him the phone. "Take pictures of the basement, too, just press the circle. Everything. Where you sleep, where you go to the bathroom, the floors, the walls." She watched him walk around the room slowly, every flash giving her a tiny glimpse into the shadows. When he was finished, she took the phone back and leaned in through the window so she could get pictures of him inside the room. Then she switched from camera to video, put on the flash, and motioned him closer to the window. She flicked the red button. "Tell me your name," she whispered, "and how old you are."

Gabriel's blue eyes blinked against the glare. "You already know."

"Tell me anyway."

"My name is Gabriel Emerson," he said. "I'm eleven years old."

"Who are your parents?"

"My dad is Lee Emerson. My mom was Caitlin Emerson."

"What is your address?"

He shook his head. "I don't know."

"I'm recording from 214 Cambridge Way," Rowan said. "Ellisburg, Massachusetts. How long have you been down there?" she asked Gabriel.

"Three years."

"You haven't been outside in three years?"

"No. I'm not allowed outside."

"Does anyone know you're down there?"

"Just you."

"Why are you down there?"

"My dad makes me. He locks me in."

Rowan drew a deep breath. "I can call the police," she said. "Do you want me to do that?"

"No!" he yelped, voice rising in panic. "You promised you wouldn't!"

"I will help you right now," she added.

"No!"

"Why not?"

The light caught the tears trapped in his eyes. "I'm scared," he whispered.

Rowan nodded and ended the recording. When she was finished, she cleared her throat and leaned forward on the lawn, balancing on her forearms. "I'm sorry," she said, trying to smooth the book's torn cover. "But that was important. It has a lot to do with what I want to talk to you about."

"What?"

"I'm leaving soon."

He blinked up at her. She couldn't read his expression.

"I'm going to Oklahoma," she went on. "I was born there. My family moved to New Hampshire right before my parents died, but they still had the Oklahoma house. It's mine now. Well, mine and my sister's. All their money, everything they had, was split between us." She fixed her eyes on his. "They had a lot of money.

"And the thing is, I've been kind of lost, lately. What I really want to do is go far away, get a fresh start." She leaned in closer, looking him straight in the eye. "And I was thinking," she said slowly, "maybe you could use one too."

Gabriel didn't move for so long, she began to wonder if she'd said it out loud. "What?"

"Come with me."

"What?" he repeated.

"You heard me," Rowan said. "You heard me."

Gabriel's mouth opened and closed. "Wh... How?"

"It's easy. You come outside, and we leave."

"What if someone sees?"

"We'll go in the middle of the night. If your dad never comes down at night, then we'll be long gone by the time he notices. It's not like he can call the police. You said it yourself—no one knows you're down there."

"But he knows you. You talked to him. He'll figure it out if we both disappear on the same day."

"All right," she conceded. "What if I leave first? I'll wait a few days and then come back for you."

He shook his head again. "He could still see you."

"What if—"

"It won't work," Gabriel cut in.

Rowan sat up and drew her knees to her chest. A late-afternoon thunderstorm had dropped the temperature by ten degrees, and the sky was still rolling with leftover clouds. "Why not?" she asked quietly.

His eyes were swimming. He looked like he was sitting in front of the biggest gift in the world with his hands tied behind his back. "What if we go there," he said, "and you change your mind?"

"I wouldn't—"

"You would just keep me? Why would you want to do that?"

Rowan fell silent, trying to put a reason behind the want. His resistance wasn't unfounded—he was a person, not an object, and despite the colloquialism that suggested otherwise, she could not just wrap him around her finger. She didn't want to tell him about Ethan, didn't want him to know she was just as beaten up as he was, that she understood. She wanted him to trust her, and you wouldn't sit in a chair if you knew it was broken.

"I haven't seen Laine since I was fifteen," she said finally. "I could have rented an apartment, or stayed in a hotel, or moved in with my sister. But I didn't. I called her, and I came here." She leaned in closer. "Think about it. I can take you so far away, he'll never be able to touch you again. You'll have a life again, a real one. Who else can give you that? I can help you, Gabe. I want to."

"Why?"

Her heart hammered against her ribs. She was glad he couldn't hear how loud it was inside her head. "Because you don't deserve this. I'll figure everything out, I swear. Just say you'll do it. Come with me."

Gabriel's fingers were pressed against the metal ridge of the window. He stared at his hands for a long time. Then he nodded.

———————

That night Rowan slept fitfully, her dreams harsh and punishing and dark. Her hands were itching to snatch Gabriel from that black cement hole, but the more she thought about it, the more impossible it became. Every time she woke, she was greeted with another problem, another unknown, another scenario that ended with both of them trapped. She had a passing familiarity with sociopaths—they weren't easy to trick. In the morning she sat at Laine's kitchen table clutching her coffee cup and flipping through the pictures she'd taken the night before. They'd only be useful if they got caught—there was no guarantee she wouldn't get in trouble, and even if she didn't, the police would definitely take Gabriel. Her grand plan had seemed so simple and so smart in the cool night air, but it crumbled to dust the moment she opened her eyes.

Rowan was walking to the sink when someone rang the doorbell. She jumped, and cold coffee sloshed over her hand. She stayed where she was, praying they'd go away, but a minute later, the knocking started, a steady drum of knuckles on wood, every blow a shock to her nerves. Rowan peered into the living room. Through the rippled glass, she could see Lee, one hand rapping on the door, the other clutching something bright and pink.

She grabbed the fireplace poker on her way to the door.

Lee greeted her with a wide, warm smile, but all she could see was the purple bruise on Gabriel's cheek, the ruined paperback lying in the grass. Her fingers tightened around the poker. "Morning, Rowan!"

"Good morning, Lee."

"Did I wake you?"

"Almost."

"Sorry, sorry. I just wanted to give you this," he said, holding up a sheet of pink paper. His smile grew bigger. "Block party—Saturday night. We have one every year."

Rowan scanned the sheet. MUSIC! GAMES! BARBECUE! FIREWORKS! "Saturday?" she repeated.

"Yup. Whole street'll be there. Tons of food, booze—I do a big fireworks display after dark. It's a great time. We keep it going all night."

She slowly met his eye, her own smile just starting to touch her lips. "Really?"

"Yup. Neighborhood tradition. You should come."

Rowan nodded and smiled for real, holding the paper close to her chest. "You know what? Maybe I will."

———————

The week that followed was frenetic, lined with excitement and nerves, and while the street was buzzing with anticipation for the upcoming festivities, Rowan was cementing her plan to abduct Gabriel.

Her first step, the worst one, was to disappear.

It was horrible and necessary. She needed to put at least a few days between her departure and Gabriel's. Lee was disappointed the morning he found Rowan struggling to haul her suitcase down the driveway. She'd burst out the front door the minute she spied him getting into his truck to go to work, and she made as much noise as she possibly could, huffing and cursing and letting the oversize bag drag her to the ground. Lee was at her side in an instant, and she smiled inwardly as she handed over the suitcase—it held every-thing Gabriel had pushed through the window in anticipation of their escape.

Lee asked Rowan if she would at least stay for the party, but she said no. She was going to college, she told him, and she needed money to fix up her dorm room and buy books. Her cover story put her on the South Carolina coast, where she planned to spend the summer waitressing at a high-end resort before the fall semester. Then she smiled, thanked Lee for everything, and drove away, watching him fade to nothing in her rearview mirror.

Leaving Gabriel alone with him felt like leaving her skin behind.

But Rowan didn't leave him with nothing. The night before she left, she'd given him a burner phone and strict instructions to call her every single day, along with a set of clothes that actually fit him and enough food to last until the party. She spent the next four days planning a route that was direct—but just a little bit unpredictable—and loading up on supplies. She bought Gabriel shoes, and books, and two suitcases full of clothes. She traded her car for a brand-new pickup truck in midnight blue.

Now it was Saturday, nearly nine o'clock, and the sky was losing the last of its inky purple hue in favor of full darkness. Rowan heard the party long before she saw it: music and laughter cut with the high-pitched whooping sounds kids only make in the summertime.

She parked behind the line of traffic cones blocking the street. Gabriel's house was the last one on the block; it would take her seconds to get him in the truck. People swarmed the grills fifty feet away, their voices and laughter oddly muffled in the smoky air. There was another set of cones beyond the grills; caution tape had been stretched around them, marking a clear circle of asphalt. Rowan could just make out Lee in the middle, standing head and shoulders above two other men and sorting through a huge pile of brightly wrapped tubes and packages. Rowan kept her eyes on him as she walked backward toward his house, dipping deeper into the shadows with every step. When she was fully out of sight, she ran to Gabriel's window and dropped to her knees, a terrified, slightly hysterical smile teasing her lips.

He wasn't there.

Rowan blinked and tried to peer inside. "Gabe?" she said, as loud as she dared. There was no response. Beyond the blackened square, she could see the basement door was open, light spilling down the steps.

There was an odd, lumpy shadow at the top of the staircase, like a bundle of rags had been piled up to prop the door open. As her eyes adjusted, Rowan saw something else: a sneaker-clad foot dangling limply against the top step. She knew the sneaker. She'd bought it herself, four days earlier.

He wasn't moving.

Rowan cursed under her breath and stuck her head through the window. She called his name again, this time as loud as she could, but he still didn't move. All at once there was a tremendous *pop* above her head, and a burst of light briefly turned the night into day. The crowd cheered, and Rowan didn't wait. She slid her legs through the basement window and dropped to the floor.

Her feet hit the ground with a dull thud; the shock sent pain shooting through her ankles and up to her knees. Over her head, fireworks flashed like lightning, and each colored burst revealed foreign shapes in the hulking shadows. Everywhere she looked something was watching her. Next to the washer and dryer, there was a half-deflated air mattress covered with an old blanket. On the other side of the room, she saw a toilet and a rusty showerhead hanging over a drain. The floor and the walls were cement, the temperature at least ten degrees cooler than the air outside.

The shadows clung to her back as she ran up the stairs; they were narrow and cracked, and they screamed as her feet pounded the wood, one after the other, until she reached him.

"Jesus," Rowan breathed. "Oh my God…"

Gabriel was sprawled across the kitchen floor, surrounded by bright, garish splashes of blood that looked too fake to be anything but real. His hands scrabbled against the tiles, leaving long red streaks, but when he tried to speak, the words died in his throat.

Her vision doubled and then tripled. Rowan leaned against the basement door, balling her fists into her eyes until the nausea passed. She stamped bloody footprints across the floor as she stepped around him and dropped to her knees. "Don't talk," she said, taking Gabriel's head in her hands. "Stay perfectly still." The back of his shirt was slashed to ribbons, torn in parallel pairs as though he'd been clawed by an animal. A two-pronged barbecue fork lay on the floor next to him, threads of reddened cloth dangling from the tines.

Blood bubbled over Gabriel's lower lip as he tried to speak, the bitten flesh puffed fat on one side. "The window… I climbed out—to see if I would fit…he…" A violent shudder tore through him.

"I'm right here."

"Please…"

"I'm here. I'm not leaving you." Her words were calm, but her voice rose and fell in rhythmic terror as she sat back on her heels and tried to estimate the distance to the truck. She slid one arm behind Gabriel's shoulders and the other under his knees before lifting him slightly off the ground. He sucked in his breath.

"Sorry," she whispered, letting his body fall gently back onto the ground. The bloody fork glistened wetly under the harsh light; she could see faint crimson fingerprints smudged on the handle. Rowan yanked open drawers in the kitchen until she found a trash bag. She turned it inside out and used it to cover her hand as she lifted the fork and pulled the plastic over it.

She tied it shut with trembling fingers. Gabriel's gaze was starting to lose focus. "Ro…" he whispered. "I can't get up."

"I know." Rowan put her arms around him again. "I'll carry you."

"What?"

"I can do it," she said, not even convincing herself. There was a side entrance, but it would put them on the wrong side of the house.

She was going to have to carry him right out the front door. There were stairs at the front door. She clutched the plastic-wrapped fork so hard, it hurt. "I'm going to carry you to the car, but listen to me, Gabriel—you have to hold on. Okay?"

She pulled his arms around her neck; his grip was stronger than she expected, but the fear didn't leave his voice. "Don't drop me," he whispered. "Please."

"I won't. It'll only take a little while," she said. Her knees shook, but her feet held, and she stood, cradling Gabriel tightly in her arms. "I can do anything for a little while."

Rowan didn't look at Gabriel as they started their slow departure from the house. She tallied their progress by degrees: *get to the door, down the stairs, end of the walkway, into the truck.* Her arms trembled and burned, and the plastic bag grew slick, but she didn't stop.

The air was thick, filled with burning matches and colored smoke. The crowd of people that concealed his father was no more than twenty yards to the left, their collective voice rising and falling in the warm night. Rowan was halfway down the cobbled walkway when Gabriel's hold on her neck loosened, and fresh blood began dotting the pavement. Before she could adjust her grip, his supporting arm slipped from her shoulder, and his entire body went limp. His dead faint threw her off-balance so badly, her knees buckled, and she lost her footing, twisting her ankle at a painful angle.

The crowd cheered. Another explosion shattered the darkness, illuminating Gabriel, still and lifeless in her arms. Rowan hoisted him higher and stumbled toward the sidewalk, making low soothing sounds he couldn't hear. When they got to the truck, she climbed on the runner and hoisted Gabriel up into the passenger seat.

Fireworks screamed above their heads. Blood dripped down the leather seats in long, thick streams. Gabriel didn't stir, and Rowan didn't wait. She jumped into the truck as trails of whistling smoke exploded into fat colored orbs, and they sped away from the glitter-filled sky into darkness.

CHAPTER SEVEN

THE MOTEL ROWAN FOUND AN HOUR OVER THE NEW YORK STATE LINE
looked clean and decent. After lying about her name and paying cash
at the desk, she parked the truck in front of their door and turned
back to Gabriel.

He was pale. So pale that she was seconds away from ending the
entire charade and taking him to the hospital, kidnapping charges be
damned. With the last of her strength, she dragged him into the room
and hauled him onto the bed, leaving him there while she brought
in the three plastic bags she'd filled at the drugstore. She pulled the
curtains closed and twisted the locks.

The bed was hidden beneath a blue-and-red patterned coverlet, busy and synthetic enough to handle any blood that might fall.
A round table and two chairs—in addition to the requisite wooden

sideboard with a television on top—completed the room. She flicked on the TV for background noise.

The blast of sound roused Gabriel from his stupor. He writhed on the bed as Rowan knelt next to him, the stiff carpet needling her knees. "Gabe," she whispered. His eyes rolled to her face. "Listen to me. I know it hurts. I'm going to give you something for the pain, and then, um…then I'm going to fix you up. Okay?"

"Okay," he said tightly, burrowing into the coverlet.

"Okay." She reached for her purse, fumbling for the amber bottle that held her Percocet. When her own pain had been at its worst, she'd taken two pills, twice her prescribed dosage. But Gabriel was tiny, even for eleven. Rowan probably had forty pounds on him, maybe more. She looked him over, said a quick prayer, and snapped one of the yellow pills in half.

In the bathroom, she padded the toilet with towels and covered the whole thing with the plastic shower liner from the curtain rod. Then she half carried, half dragged Gabriel inside. She set him down facing the tank and pressed the pill into his hand. Without awaiting further instructions, Gabriel shoved it into his mouth and bit it, screwing up his face against the bitter fragments.

"Wha—No! Don't chew it! You have to swallow it in one piece." Rowan cupped her hand under his chin. "Spit it out."

He spit into her hand, tiny pieces of yellow shrapnel. A second later he gagged, and the next thing she caught was a wave of vomit that shocked them both. Rowan grabbed another towel and wiped his face. "Are you okay?"

"No…"

"Well, that would make anyone throw up. Can you try again?"

Gabriel shook his head against the plastic. "I don't know how to swallow pills."

"It's easy. Just put the pill under your tongue and take a drink of water. When you swallow the water, you let the pill slide down with it."

He shook his head again. "I don't want to."

"You don't want to take the pill?"

"I don't want to throw up again."

"Fine." She wasn't going to argue with him about a stupid pill. The exterior corridor was lined with vending machines. Two minutes later she was back with a can of ginger ale. She poured an inch of soda into the bathroom glass and used the bottom to pulverize the other half of the pill. She scooped the powder into the cup and handed it to Gabriel. "Here. Drink."

He drained the glass, his eyes heavy and wet. Rowan dragged one of the straight-backed chairs into the bathroom and sat behind him. "How do you feel?"

"Hurts…"

"I know." His T-shirt was in tatters, stiff with dried blood. "I need to look at your back, okay? I'll be careful."

"Okay."

"Stay still." Her fingers were clumsy against the plastic latch on the sewing kit she'd bought. Fumbling with the scissors, she slit his shirt from hem to neck, slid the fabric aside, and nearly gagged. "Oh God…"

He'd been slashed half a dozen times—long angry gashes in eerily uniform pairs. She could see puffy white tissue hanging between the red lips of every cut. Gabriel caught her reaction in the mirror before she had a chance to wipe it from her face.

"Is it really bad?" he whispered.

"No, it's—"

"It hurts." Tears made clean tracks down his cheeks, and his hands scrabbled uselessly against the wall. "Please make it stop," he said, his voice hitching on every word. "Please…"

"No, no, shhh." Rowan leaned in close and hooked her arm around his waist. "Listen to me. You're going to be fine, okay? You're going to be perfect. That was the last time he will ever hurt you, and it's almost over. Can you do it?"

The mirror told a more accurate story than the one she was selling. Gabriel's face was sunken and bloodless, with a purplish bruise crawling across his cheek. Rowan was flushed, hectic, splashes of pink coloring her neck and collarbone. A low sigh parted Gabriel's lips. Not an expression of defeat but permission to continue. To fix him. "Yes."

The alarm clock blinked innocently next to the bottle of Percocet lying sideways on the bedside table. Rowan prepared another pill, bathed it in soda, and held the glass to his lips.

Fifteen minutes later she sat with her forehead pressed against the nape of his neck, tears streaming down her own cheeks as Gabriel slept, slumped over his terry cloth pillow. His skin was clammy, but his breathing was even and deep. Even when she shook him, he didn't wake up.

She allowed herself to count to ten before she sat up and threaded the needle.

––––––––––––

Gabriel's eyelids felt too heavy to lift, but it didn't matter. He wasn't ready to wake up. He didn't know where he was or how he'd gotten there. For a minute he didn't know *who* he was. The air was cold, but he was all bundled in something warm and soft. Sounds reached his ears—laughter and music, people talking—but it was like trying to hear underwater. He opened his eyes.

He was lying in bed, flat on his stomach. The lights were off, but the television was on, filling the room with flashes of color. Someone was stretched out next to him; it took him a full minute to realize it was Rowan. She was staring at the ceiling, her eyes wide and blank.

"Rowan?"

She jumped at his voice, like he'd screamed instead of whispered.

"Gabe?" she said, leaning in close and pressing a hand to his forehead. "Oh my God… Are you okay?"

"I don't know." There was still pain, a lot of it, but it felt like it was in a cage. His back was wrapped so tight, the pain couldn't get out. Through the damp motel air, he could smell soap on his skin. "What happened?"

Rowan's gaze covered every inch of his face. "You scared the hell out of me."

"Why?"

"You've been out cold for hours. I couldn't wake you up." Her eyes were bright and shiny. "I put you in the bathtub, and you didn't wake up—"

"You gave me a *bath*?"

"I had to—you were covered in blood."

Gabriel groaned into the pillow.

"Are you going to throw up again?" Rowan asked. "Because I'd love it if you were over the toilet this time."

"I'm not," he mumbled.

Rowan fiddled with the gauze near his hip. "How does your back feel?"

He stretched a little. "Hurts. The bandages are tight."

"I know. I had to give you stitches."

Gabriel lifted his head. "I thought only doctors could give stitches."

"When there are no doctors, there is always Google." Her smile trembled at the edges. "I'm sorry. The cuts were too deep. I had to." She poked at him again. "I did the best I could, but you'd probably have prettier scars if I'd taken home ec."

His thoughts flashed to his father and the hiking trip they'd taken a few years before his mother died. Gabriel tripped on a chunk of rock and split his skin wide open. His dad drove him to the hospital, and the doctor put six stitches in a neat line on the bony part of his knee. They went out for ice cream afterward—three scoops in a chocolate-dipped waffle cone. It had made him forget it hurt.

He blinked himself back to the room so hard, he could see stars. "Where's my box?" he asked Rowan.

"What?"

"The big box I gave you. Did you bring it?"

"It's in the truck."

"Can I have it?"

"I want you to eat something first," she said. "Are you hungry?"

"I'm thirsty. Can I sit up? What time is it?"

Rowan helped him to his hands and knees and eased him over. "Three thirty."

"In the morning?"

"Uh-huh. There's a convenience store across the street. I got some stuff." She handed him a bagel stuffed with cinnamon and raisins and a bottle of apple juice.

His torn lip throbbed, but the first bite told him he was hungrier than he thought.

Rowan pushed his hair back and examined his eyes again before getting to her feet. "Be right back."

She returned with the white box that contained all his mother's things, everything he had left of her: old pictures, odds and ends from her nightstand, and whatever else his dad had stuffed inside. Gabriel opened the lid and grabbed a handful of photos. Rowan picked up a big envelope with *Gabriel* scripted on the back. "What's this?"

"Stuff from when I was a baby, I think."

Rowan lifted the flap and pulled out a handful of papers. She was frowning at first, but then her eyes got big, moving from the pages in her hand to his face.

"What's the matter?" he asked.

"No, nothing," Rowan said. "Nothing."

"Don't lose that envelope," he warned. "My mom wrote on it."

Rowan looked at him again; then she tucked the papers back inside, carefully. "I won't. Is that her?" she asked, nodding toward the photo in Gabriel's hand.

"Yes," Gabriel said. It was his favorite one—his mother was sitting in the grass with her head thrown back, smiling up at the sun. She had a bunch of pink flowers in her lap.

Rowan scooted behind him so she could see it. "She's beautiful," she said. "You look just like her. What's on the back?"

"One of the flowers," Gabriel said, turning the picture over. "She used to save all kinds of flowers. I don't know what kind it is." The flower had been pressed to the photo and covered in clear tape; the yellow center and the pink petals almost looked like a face.

"That's a daisy." Rowan ran her finger over the curled edges. "But it really shouldn't be loose like this. We'll have to frame it."

"Really?"

"Of course. We can frame all your pictures as soon as we get home."

Gabriel nodded silently. He could feel Rowan's heart beating against his back, and when he looked at the picture again, a rush of tears came to his eyes—hot, burning tears he couldn't blink away.

Rowan touched his hand. "Are you okay?"

He tilted his head back, staring at the ceiling. It was the way she said "home." Not *the house*, or worse, *my house*. It was the thought of seeing his mother every day in that photo without being worried his father would tear her up or snatch her away. It was the past few weeks, the past few *years*, hitting him all at once.

Gabriel wanted to tell her that, but his throat was too tight. He turned toward her instead, resting his head against her shoulder. He was afraid she might push him away, but she didn't. Her arms came up around him, and he couldn't figure out how she could pull him so close and hold him so tight without touching anything that hurt.

After a while he forgot about the pain.

The television sent flashes of color over the bed as her heart pounded against his ear. He hadn't been hugged since his mother died. It was as foreign as the room they were in, as Rowan herself. And as strange as it should have been, it wasn't. In that room, at that moment, he knew he'd never felt safer in his entire life.

After five days on the road, the adrenaline that had fueled them for more than a thousand miles evaporated, and the worst of their fears went with it. The idea they might get caught had always been abstract, and it faded into giddiness as the trip wore on. If she'd had her way, Rowan would have done the drive in twenty-four hours flat, but with Gabriel's back the way it was, even five hours was pushing it. So they crawled along, sleeping late and stopping often.

No matter where they stopped, Rowan made sure the box came with them—the white box with the envelope Gabriel's mother had written on. And every night, after he went to sleep, Rowan pulled out that envelope and sifted through it.

At first glance it wasn't much. Report cards. Elementary school awards with gold foil seals. A kindergarten class photo.

But behind all that, creased and folded from being shoved inside with real anger, there were more precious gifts. Gabriel's birth certificate—not a copy, the original, signed and notarized. A sheet of card stock with his social security card still attached. Savings bonds.

His mother's death certificate. All of it bent and crumpled, as though they would cease to be facts if the proof was hidden from view.

Out of everything in that box, those sterile documents brought the only pity she felt for Lee.

As they drove through the last stretch of Arkansas, Rowan eased the truck around a slow-moving vehicle clogging the left lane and glanced at Gabriel. She'd cut the last of his stitches that morning, and the bruise on his face was fading. Now that he had some pink in his cheeks, it looked like a more innocuous injury, something he might have gotten falling off a bike. For the moment, he looked wonderfully normal.

Darkness was crawling up the horizon when they crossed the Oklahoma state line to Route 70, which would bring them to Durant, the university town south of the capital, where Rowan had spent the first three years of her life. It was well past the time they should have stopped, but she didn't; they were close now. Rowan could feel the house tugging her forward, and she kept her eyes on the twin beams of her headlights as the hours wore on, bringing with them a night unlike anything she'd ever seen. The darkness was intense, velvety and alive, and the flatness of the land created a strange illusion of endless black—a sea of nothing that stretched in every direction. Next to her, Gabriel slept curled in a ball against the seat.

Her parents' house sat on the outskirts of town, quite literally in the middle of nowhere. The GPS dropped them between two fields, and Rowan drove up and down the same road three times before she found it. White rocks rolled and bumped around the tires as she parked in the driveway and cut the engine, leaving the headlights shining over the porch. A bench swing rocked in the breeze, dancing slowly to the musical offerings of summertime insects.

The house was much bigger than it looked in the pictures Celia had shown her: a rambling white Victorian stacked like a wedding cake. The roof rose in peaks and arches straight out of a fairy tale, right down to the rounded turret with tall windows. The porch wrapped around the entire house, hugged by white rosebushes in the shade of a pink magnolia tree. Rowan stared out the window, trying to find some inner pull of familiarity, a link to a past version of herself.

There was none. There was only a house and a tree and a driveway made of smooth white rocks. A small part of her had hoped for ghosts—the long-forgotten whisper of her mother's voice or the feel of her father carrying her sleepily up the stairs. Neither came.

Gabriel hadn't moved; his sleeping face was calm in the darkness. Rowan leaned down and spoke quietly into his ear. "Gabe," she whispered. "Wake up."

He rolled toward her. His eyes were tired and glazed in the moonlight but still wide, still wondering. "What's the matter?"

"You're going to be a lot more comfortable sleeping in your own bed," she said, smiling as he lifted his head and took in their surroundings, finally waking up. "We're home."

CHAPTER EIGHT

A<small>FTER A LOT OF FANFARE SEARCHING FOR THE KEY</small> C<small>ELIA HAD HIDDEN</small> too well, Rowan and Gabriel climbed the porch steps amid an orchestra of chirping creatures. Rowan stuck her phone under her chin, trying to aim the flashlight at the door; behind her, Gabriel shifted his weight from foot to foot.

"Gabe, please," she said, "if you have to go that bad, just go in the yard." She wrestled the key into the lock and stumbled into the pitch-black foyer, where she immediately tripped over a table and sent a heavy rotary telephone crashing to the floor. A rush of footsteps sounded on the porch, and then Gabriel smashed into her like a ton of bricks.

"Jesus Christ!" she hissed. "You scared the hell out of me!" She kicked the receiver across the floor.

"I thought you were in trouble!"

"I thought you were peeing in the yard. Don't move."

Rowan felt her way into the house, fumbling along the walls until she bumped into a light switch. The sudden illumination shattered the darkness, revealing the reality of their new home in a single gasping breath. Rowan turned in a slow circle. "Whoa…"

The front hallway alone was big enough to hold the entire first floor of the house she'd shared with Ethan. The right side opened into a formal dining area lined with the same tall windows she'd seen from the outside. On the left, a pair of French doors hid a sunroom with blond wood floors and white wicker furniture. A wide archway led to a living room full of cream-colored furniture and a framed family portrait she had never seen before. The Rowan in the photograph smiled from her mother's lap under a cloud of pale auburn curls. Her father stood behind them with his arm around Celia, who looked like she had a stick up her ass even at fourteen. Rowan walked deeper into the house, waking up the rooms as she went.

Just past the dining room, there was a curved staircase, and then the house branched out again, revealing a den with a brick fireplace and oversize furniture that looked more comfortable than any bed she'd ever slept in. The kitchen was in the very back of the house, a monstrous affair with marble countertops and a row of windows overlooking the yard. She approached the back door and flicked on the porch lights—moonlight bounced off the surface of a pond just beyond the yard.

She doubled back down the hallway. Gabriel was exactly where she'd left him, stooped over in the foyer. His eyes were owlish as he took in the height of the ceiling.

Rowan smiled. "Not bad, huh?"

"I've never seen a house this big."

"Well, now you live in one. Come on, I want to see the rest."

They climbed the stairs to the balcony on the second floor. Rowan approached the first door she saw and pushed it open. Gabriel peered over her shoulder.

The room was big and airy, but its anonymity was not unlike the many motel rooms she'd seen the inside of lately. The bed had a gauzy white canopy draped over the posts, and a plush, cream-colored rug covered a large patch of the wooden floor. It was all very bland and tasteful.

"No wonder Celia didn't want me coming here," Rowan said. "She'd never want me to be this comfortable." She turned to him and smiled. "So?"

"What?"

"Which room do you want?"

"Oh," he said, going pink. "It doesn't matter."

"Pick one," she insisted. "Do you want this one?"

"No, you take it."

"It makes no difference to me. Go ahead, look at the rest—you can choose two if you want."

Gabriel wandered down the hall, peeking into rooms as he went. After a minute he came back before disappearing into a dark rectangle two doors down from where Rowan still stood. "I like this one."

Rowan joined him by a row of windows overlooking the magnolia tree. He hadn't bothered to turn on the light, but it didn't matter— she knew this room. "This was mine."

"Did you want it?" he asked, silhouetted against the window.

"No," she said. "I mean it was mine before. This was the nursery."

"How do you know?"

"If I tell you, you may not want it anymore." She flipped a switch, bringing the room to light. Gabriel stared at the carpet.

"Oh," he said. "Pink."

"Yup. Celia has pictures of me in here as a baby."

His finger caught on something in the windowsill, and he stared at the wood, rubbing it back and forth. "Can I have this room anyway?"

"Of course. We can paint it, get new carpet, whatever you want. The closet is here," she said, pulling open a door. "And this door goes to the bathroom."

Gabriel nodded and sat on the bed. For a minute, Rowan just looked at him; she had no idea what to do now that they'd realized their only goal. "Why don't you get cleaned up for bed?" she said finally. "I'll go down and get our stuff."

When she returned with their bags, Gabriel was bent over the bed, wincing as he tried to peel the adhesive tape off his side. Rowan straightened his shoulders and pulled it free herself. She soaked a washcloth in warm water and wiped away the film of dried blood perpetually on his skin. "Pajamas are in here," she said, handing him a blue duffel. "Are you having any pain?"

Gabriel shook his head and lied through his teeth. "Not too much."

Rowan put a bottle of Children's Tylenol on the nightstand, her sad attempt to wean him off the tiny bits of Percocet she'd been feeding him. "I guess I'll take the first room—I'll leave the door open," she said. "If you need anything, just yell."

"Okay."

She nodded, but she didn't move. They'd spent the past five nights sleeping in the same room; he hadn't been out of her sight all week. Her newborn fear of failing him, of making a mistake, was very bright and very alive. She tried to push it down, but as she said good night and turned to leave, she couldn't shake the feeling that she was missing something.

The next morning Rowan realized, perhaps belatedly, that falling asleep on the second floor of a house in Oklahoma in the middle of July was a bad idea. It hadn't seemed all that hot when they'd gone to bed, or maybe they'd been too tired to notice, but she'd woken up completely cooked. Gabriel wasn't in his room, which led to a brief moment of panic, but when she stumbled downstairs, she'd found him slumped over the kitchen table with a wet towel on his head.

He pressed his forehead against the table as Rowan guzzled her third glass of water. "Keep drinking," she told him. "We're not dying of heatstroke on the first day."

"It's so hot," he moaned.

"It's horrible. I can't believe Celia left ten pages of instructions on how this house works and didn't mention a thing about air-conditioning. I can't find it anywhere." She scrubbed her hand over her face. "I should make breakfast. Are you hungry?"

"Uh-huh."

"What do you want?"

"I don't know."

Rowan wasn't expecting much by way of groceries, but to Celia's credit, the kitchen was stocked. The refrigerator held milk and heavy cream, a jug of orange juice, fresh butter and eggs, and a tub of strawberries that smelled sweet as candy. Stacks of plates and bowls filled one cabinet. A second had about eighty pieces of Tupperware. In the third she found a loaf of bread and baking things: flour, sugar, and a tub of lard that was so big, it would have frightened a less capable cook.

"Okay," she said. "We can have eggs, or French toast if you want something fancier. I can do crepes or biscuits with strawberries and whipped cream. If there's a blender, we can make smoothies. Do any of these options sound interesting?"

Gabriel lifted his head. "You know how to cook? Real food?"

"Yes, real food. I bet I can put ten pounds on you in a week. Go watch TV for a little while, and I'll make you something. It'll be a huge exciting breakfast surprise for our first day here."

Gabriel nodded and shuffled into the den.

Rowan decided to make pancakes. She felt good in front of the stove; she was competent there. When she'd been around Gabriel's age, she lived with a caterer who always needed someone to help chop and grate and knead, and after a year, Rowan had been as seasoned in the kitchen as any grandmother. She gathered her ingredients and set half an inch of water over low heat before adding sugar and two handfuls of chopped strawberries.

With her hands busy measuring and sifting, Rowan's thoughts turned to her sister and the hell this situation was going to bring. Celia wielded her big-sister sword like Excalibur, and Rowan had nearly been beheaded many, many times. On the plus side, Rowan had a lot of cards to use against Celia, but they were old cards by now. They were creased and folded, and Celia had had lots of time to think of new ways to play.

Even so, Rowan still had plenty to throw down.

When she'd been nine years old, a social worker pulled Rowan out of class in the middle of a geography lesson and led her down the empty hallway to the guidance office. Having gone through five different foster homes already, this was not a new drill, and Rowan shuffled along, accepting her fate with dull surrender. As expected, there was a stranger waiting for her in the tiny room: a tall woman with long dark hair, a tentative smile, and a visitor badge clipped to her shirt.

The social worker smiled, squeezing Rowan's hand tight. "Sweetheart, I want you to meet someone very special," she said, tugging her forward.

"Another foster mom?"

"No. This is your sister. This is Celia."

Rowan stared into the face of the woman in front of her. Celia's eyes were a bright bluey green, just like Rowan's, but the rest of her was wrong. Sisters were supposed to look alike, and Celia didn't match her at all. Rowan clutched the social worker's hand and let a long strand of silken hair fall from her mouth. "You are?"

"Yes," Celia said. "I know you don't remember me, but I've been waiting for you. You're going to live with me now."

Rowan glanced at the social worker again. "What about Jeanne and Bill? And the other kids? I like it at their house. I want to stay with them."

Celia clucked her tongue like Rowan had said something silly. "They're not your family, Rowan. I am. Your real family."

Rowan thought about that word: *real*. Her whole life, she'd never been a real anything to anybody. The families she lived with were real, with real mothers and real fathers and real kids. And they were so real, they made her forget most of the time that she wasn't. But she knew anyway, and when her kindergarten teacher had read the story of the Velveteen Rabbit to the class, Rowan had needed to be led to the nurse's office as she cried and cried for what looked like no reason at all. Because she'd known, even then. The other kids in the family, the *real* kids, were already on their way to having their fur loved off. And Rowan knew if they had to choose one to throw into the fire with the rest of the things that were dirty and sick, it would always be her, no matter how plush and beautiful she was.

But if Celia was real, that meant Rowan would be too—real sisters, real family, something she hadn't even allowed herself to hope for. If Celia took her, she'd never have to move again, and Rowan's face exploded into a grin as she hugged her sister fiercely, tighter than she'd ever hugged anyone, because Celia was her first real thing, and she already loved her for it.

They flew to Virginia, where Celia had a room all set for Rowan in a house by the ocean. She told Rowan stories about their lives before their mother and father died, how happy their family was, how much their parents loved them. Rowan started a new school where she proudly told her teachers and classmates how she lived with her *real* sister who loved her so, so much, and for the first time in her life, she didn't feel like she was less important than anyone.

Four months later, Celia decided to attend graduate school for nursing at the University of Virginia—something that required far more time and energy than someone raising a nine-year-old alone could offer. And with a smile and a pat that barely rumpled Rowan's billowy fur, Celia had packed her bags and sent her off to be the new fake thing for a new real family.

"Something's burning."

Rowan jumped, scraping the spatula across the griddle. "Sorry," she said to Gabriel, dropping the charred pancake into the garbage. "Everything's ready." She brought her makeshift syrup to the table and made plates for both of them, piling butter and fruit on the pancakes and sifting powdered sugar over the whole thing.

They ate in silence. Gabriel looked a little shell-shocked, and Rowan was too busy formulating a cover story to chat. They'd just finished washing their dishes when a posh and all-too-familiar voice echoed through the house. "*Rowan?*"

"Oh my *God!*" Rowan hissed. Her hands flew like birds, and she pulled Gabriel away from the sink.

"Rowan, where are you? Did you actually purchase that monstrosity in the driveway?"

"Fuckfuckfuckfuck*fuck!*" Rowan whispered. She ran to the first door she saw and pulled it open. "Quick, get in there, and don't come out until I tell you!"

Gabriel peered inside. "I'm not going in the basement!" he shrieked. Rowan clapped her hand over his mouth.

"Shhh! Sorry, sorry!" She steered him toward the back door. "Go around the porch, come back in the front, and go upstairs. Be very quiet, don't come down until I tell you, and don't let her see you!"

"Rowan?" Celia called. "Are you upstairs?"

"No!" Rowan shouted. "I'm in the kitchen!" She pushed open the door. "Go!" As soon as Gabriel disappeared around the corner, she turned and found her sister frowning at her from across the room.

"What are you doing?" Celia asked.

"Celia!" Rowan exclaimed, pressing one hand against her heart. "I wasn't expecting you."

That was an understatement. Rowan hadn't laid eyes on her sister in four years; seeing her in the flesh was a jarring experience. Celia was as tall and willowy as ever, blessed with both their father's height and their mother's olive complexion. Her dark hair was twisted into a knot, with a few loose wisps framing her face. She wore a taupe pencil skirt with an immaculate white T-shirt—silk, from the look of it.

Rowan tugged at the hem of her shorts. She often thought that she looked like a drawing of Celia that had been erased, leaving nothing but ghostly pencil strokes behind, pale and undefined.

"I just got out of church. I brought you some things," Celia said, crossing the room to hug her. "I didn't think you'd be here for another few days."

Dimly, Rowan thought she could hear footsteps on the stairs. Celia stepped back and appraised her with narrowed eyes. "You look thin."

Rowan pushed her away. "I'm fine."

"You're pale too. And you need to cut your hair."

"Did you come here purely to give me shit, Celia? Why don't you make a list and come back tomorrow?"

"Don't be ridiculous," Celia said. "Or vulgar, for that matter. Come and sit with me. I haven't seen you in years. I don't want to fight."

"Could've fooled me," Rowan muttered, but she joined Celia at the table, fiddling with the sugar bowl.

"How was your trip?" Celia asked.

"Long."

"And you're feeling all right? You're feeling…better?"

Rowan prayed Gabriel wasn't hanging off the banister listening to them. "I'm fine."

"May I see where they operated?"

Rowan heaved a sigh and stood, lifting her shirt. Celia tutted and frowned, examining every inch of broken skin. "Staples?"

Rowan nodded woodenly.

"I see. And I'm sorry," Celia said, tugging Rowan's shirt into place. "I would have been there if I could."

Rowan felt her resolve slip. "You could've."

"I could not. I had a huge patient load, and it was still flu season."

Rowan snorted. "Flu season, wow. Thank God I didn't die—who knows how many seniors I might have taken out."

"Don't even joke about that. I prayed for you every day. And there's no use dwelling on it. You're here now, and everything's going to be just fine."

"Just fine," Rowan echoed.

"Have you thought about what you'd like to do?"

Rowan couldn't sit still a minute longer. She stood and wandered over to the refrigerator. "Yes," she said finally. "I was thinking of becoming a foster parent."

Celia's eyes widened. "Really? Since when do you have experience with children?"

"I don't. I just—It seems like a worthy thing to do."

"Well, I'm sorry to burst your bubble," Celia said, "but you would never be approved. You wouldn't even pass the background check."

"Why not?"

"Why not? You rolled into town five minutes ago, you have no job, and you have a criminal record."

Rowan threw her hands in the air. "I do not have a criminal record!"

"Really?" Celia replied, ticking off points on her fingers. "Arrested at fourteen for underage drinking. Arrested at sixteen for drug possession—"

"Oh, for God's—I *hardly* think getting caught with Boone's Farm in the middle school parking lot and smoking pot with Ethan are grounds for juvenile delinquency."

"Speaking of Ethan—"

"Which we are not."

"Why are you still wearing that ring?"

Rowan regarded the ring, her hand hovering near her waist. "I like it."

"You *like* it?"

"What's not to like? It's a bauble," she said, wiggling her hand.

"It's a gruesome reminder of someone who tried to kill you."

"Jeez, Ceil…"

"I'm serious. It's morbid."

"It's mine, okay? Who cares where I got it?"

Celia sighed. "Fine. Wear the ring if you want. I'm not here to fight with you. I'm worried about you. You need to go back to school; that's the most important thing. I'm not going to let you sit around all day."

"You aren't going to *let* me do anything. I'm out of your jurisdiction, remember? I can do anything I damn well please."

"Language," Celia said, massaging her temples.

"Shit, Celia, am I upsetting you? Fuck me."

"Rowan!"

A muffled swooshing sound interrupted what might have evolved into an epic sparring match. Rowan's gaze flew to the heavens as Celia's eyes grew even darker. "Rowan," she said slowly. "Who else is here?"

Rowan looked from the ceiling to her sister. "What?"

"Who's here?"

"No one."

"The shower didn't turn itself on."

Rowan said nothing.

"Tell me," Celia demanded.

Rowan eased back into her chair. "Um, Celia," she said. "Are the phones in this house turned on?"

It sort of worked; Celia looked confused. "Are the *phones* turned on? No, why?"

"Can I see your phone?"

"For what?"

"I just—I want to see it." Rowan pressed her hands to the table so they wouldn't shake.

"I'm not going to ask you again," Celia said. "Tell me what the hell is going on here."

Rowan shook her head. "Language."

Celia looked like she was one second away from slapping her across the face, and Rowan honestly didn't blame her. She had to tell her. There was no point trying to hide him now, and as demented as it sounded, she was dying to tell *someone*. She held up her hands. "Okay. I'll tell you. But you have to promise me, *promise,* you won't freak out."

"I'm not promising you anything. Not after an intro like that."

"You owe me, Celia," Rowan said. "You know you do. Now promise."

Celia smoothed her hair and folded her hands on the table. "I promise."

So Rowan told her the entire story, starting with the shutters and the day she found Gabriel. She detailed their escape and the drive down, how well she'd already taken care of him. Celia looked straight into her eyes, maintaining a mask of casual indifference, and when Rowan was finished, Celia fixed her with a cool gaze.

"I don't believe you."

"What do you mean you don't believe me?" Rowan asked. "Why would I make something like that up?"

"Forgive me, but you've never needed an incentive to make things up," Celia said.

"I don't know what else you want to hear. It's the truth."

"You're telling me you *kidnapped* a child, after making a completely irrational plan, and drove him fifteen hundred miles away, nursing wounds severe enough to require stitches that you yourself put in. Can you see where I'm having trouble?"

"Honestly, no. Why would I make that up?"

"You tell me. It's a fascinating story, but I need more proof than that."

Rowan looked at her for a moment. Then she silently produced her phone and pulled up an album. She slid the phone across the table.

Celia picked it up. Her eyes got bigger and bigger as she sifted through every bruise, every scar, every dark corner of the basement.

When she got to the video at the end, she watched in silence before moving on to the photographs of Gabriel in the bathroom, crude stitches mending the ragged edges of his bloody skin. She put the phone down.

"Want to see the fork?" Rowan asked.

"Tell me this is a prank," Celia said slowly. "Those are the only words I want to hear. Please tell me that."

Rowan stood and marched to the foot of the stairs. "Gabriel!" she shouted. There was no reply. "Gabe? It's okay. Come on down." She turned back to Celia. "Don't you dare scare him. He's been through hell."

Celia's face had gone ashy, all traces of her tan gone. "Rowan," she choked out. "Tell me you didn't…"

Gabriel walked into the kitchen. His face was pink and scrubbed, his damp hair almost black against his bright blue eyes. Rowan put her arm around him, and together they faced Celia.

"Well, here he is," Rowan said. "Isn't he cute?"

Celia stared at them in slack-jawed silence.

"So, now, what were you saying, Celia? About me lying or something?" Rowan prompted.

"You can't be serious," Celia whispered.

"How are you this surprised when I just sat here and told you everything?"

"I didn't think…"

"Yeah, that's a big problem for you. You never think." Rowan turned to Gabriel. "You can go back up. She needs a minute." Her arm around his neck tightened. "How's your back?"

"It's okay," he said quietly.

"I'll take a look at it in a few minutes. Go ahead up." Rowan pressed a kiss to his temple and nudged him toward the stairs. She and Celia stood there in silence until Gabriel's footsteps faded away.

It was about ten minutes before Celia finished gnawing on her perfectly manicured nails and became capable of conversation.

"You're not calling the police," Rowan said.

"I won't. I said I wouldn't," Celia said, pacing the kitchen. "You'll have to call them yourself. Tell them you found him on the side of the road, or hitchhiking, or in a ditch somewhere, but you can't keep him here, Rowan. You just can't."

"Why not?"

"Why not?" Celia screamed. "That child has been severely neglected, and you are in no position to help him! He was kept in that house since he was eight?"

"Yes."

"How old is he now?"

"Almost twelve."

"Rowan," Celia moaned into her hands. "You have all that proof—why didn't you just call the police?"

"He didn't want me to."

"And you listened? Do you realize what's going to happen if you get caught? Oh my God, you crossed so many state lines. What if there's a search?"

"How? It's not like his father can call the cops to look for a kid nobody knew he had."

Celia paced the kitchen again. "That's why you need to call them. You have proof if you need it. Maybe they'll—"

"No. I'm keeping him."

"What do you mean you're keeping him?"

"I mean I'm keeping him," Rowan said. "I'll raise him myself."

"We're not talking about a puppy, Rowan! He's a human being, and he needs a lot more help than you can give him."

"If I call the cops, he'll get taken by the state, just like we were. He'll be put into a house with a family he doesn't know and thrown into a school with kids he's never met. Do you remember what that was like? I do. It happened to me *nine times*. He's safe with me, and I'm more than capable of taking care of him. I have the space and the money."

Celia's eyes softened to sadness, as though Rowan suffered from some fatal flaw she was woefully unaware of. "It's not about money."

"I know that. I—"

"It's about support," Celia went on. "It's about being emotionally equipped to deal with the responsibility of caring for another person. You're not ready for that. Not after what happened to you."

Rowan's entire body tensed. "Nothing happened to me. I'm fine."

"No, you're not. You're using this boy as an excuse to ignore your problems. Does he know about Ethan?"

"Of course not! I'm not going to tell him something like that."

"Why not?"

"He doesn't need to know. Why should he have to deal with my problems?"

"Have you asked yourself why you should have to deal with his?"

"Because he needs me!" Rowan cried. "He's not going to be bounced from one house to another and wallow every day about what a victim he is. It's not saving him if he goes from getting beaten up at home to getting beaten up by kids who are a lot nastier than he ever learned how to deal with. I want to give him a life, Ceil. I want him to be happy."

"So your grand plan is what? To be a mother to this boy?"

"If that's what he needs me to be."

"Yes, Rowan, that's exactly what he needs you to be. And we're not talking about an infant. He's been through years of physical and emotional damage. You have no idea how difficult that will be. Being a mother means putting his needs before yours for a long, long time. You won't be able to go to school, or date, or do much of anything without considering how it will affect him. You are twenty-two years old. If you take responsibility for this child, he is always going to come first."

Rowan leveled her eyes on Celia. "Is he? Because I didn't."

Celia went beet red.

Rowan leaned in closer. "Do you really think you have room to talk after what you did to me? You threw me away twice, Celia. Twice. The minute I got in your way. I would never do that to Gabriel because I know how it feels. You're damn right he's going to come first. I'm going to do everything I can to take care of him, and that's a hell of a lot more than you ever did for me."

Celia steepled her fingers under her chin. "That's enough," she said. "I'm not going to sit here and be attacked. We're not getting anywhere, and we're starting to say things we don't mean. I think the first thing we need to do is take a look at this boy and see what kind of shape he's in."

Rowan nodded. "Fine. I'm worried I took the stitches out too soon."

"How long did you leave them in?"

"Five days."

"You took them out too soon. I'll see what I can do. And, Rowan?"

"What?"

"My helping you does not mean I support this. At all."

Rowan's head ached with heat and emotion as she climbed the stairs and tried to wipe the argument with Celia off her face. White noise echoed through the hallway like the hum of an insect. "Gabe?"

"In here."

Gabriel was sitting on the floor in his bedroom. A metal box fan whirred in the window. Every now and then, a magnolia blossom would get pulled in, the shredded pieces floating like confetti, pink petals on the pink carpet. "I found it in the closet."

"That's great," she said, forcing a smile. She sat next to him. "Are you okay?"

He shrugged, dropping his gaze to the floor.

Rowan tipped his chin up. "Don't worry," she said. "Everything's fine. I talked to Celia, and she's—well, she's not happy, but she's not going to do anything."

Gabriel nodded, but his eyes were scared. Rowan couldn't bear his face; she leaned into the stream of blowing air and wrapped her arms around him. "I'm going to take care of everything," she whispered, pressing her cheek against the top of his head. "No matter what."

Gabriel said nothing, but he held her just as tight. They stayed that way for a long time, and it was like they were being recharged, the contact setting them right again. "Would you mind having Celia take a look at you?" Rowan asked when she pulled back. "She's a nurse practitioner, which is practically a doctor. She wants to see what a terrible job I did."

"I guess so," he said. He stared at her for a moment, concern taking over the fear in his eyes. "Are *you* okay?"

"Don't worry about me," Rowan said, rubbing his shoulder. "You don't ever have to worry about me. I'm a rock—haven't you noticed?" She pulled him to his feet, and they started down the stairs, leaving the whir of the fan and the scent of magnolias behind them.

CHAPTER NINE

I T WAS TURNING INTO A BAD DAY.

Gabriel lay sprawled across the kitchen counter, trying not to scream as Celia nudged and poked the sorest parts of him. In the past five days, he'd fainted in Rowan's arms, thrown up on her, bled all over the truck, slept through a bath, spit in her hand, and cried. Twice.

He was not going to scream.

"What did you say he used?" Celia whispered to Rowan.

"A barbecue fork."

"This is terrible. What kind of thread did you stitch him with?"

"I don't know, sewing thread? Black thread?"

"That's not—did you put *glue* on him?"

"You can do that for smaller cuts!"

Gabriel had known they were going to fight, but he hadn't expected to get caught in the middle. Celia wasn't nice like Rowan. She didn't ask him if things were okay before she did them. The minute he came downstairs, Celia stripped off his shirt and lifted him on the counter, mumbling about infections and blood poisoning.

"Gabriel," Celia said. "On a scale from one to ten, how much pain would you say you're in?"

"Um, six? Or—four?"

"Which is it?" Celia pressed.

Rowan rubbed his head. "Be honest, Gabe. You've been lying to me all week."

He shoved her hand away. "Five."

"Fair enough. How are you feeling otherwise? You're going to need to eat better; you're very thin."

"Eat *better*?" Rowan repeated. "He was starved, for Christ's sake."

"I understand that, Rowan. I just meant he'll feel better once he starts getting proper nutrition." Celia poked him again. "Are you allergic to penicillin?"

"I don't know."

"That's okay, Gabe," Rowan said.

"It's not okay. We still need to give him something."

"So do it! You're talking a lot, but I don't see you doing anything."

"There's not much we can do, except let it heal." Celia pressed a cloth against his side, and the next thing he knew, she was pouring something on his back that burned like fire. He sucked in his breath and grabbed Rowan's shirt in his fist.

"Celia, stop!" Rowan shrieked. "What is that?"

"Antiseptic."

"Why didn't you warn him?"

"The anticipation would have been worse than the pain," Celia said, taping fresh gauze to his back. Her touch was more professional than Rowan's; it wasn't as warm. "Help him sit up."

"Slowly," Rowan said, glaring at her sister.

"I'm going to the pharmacy," Celia announced with a look just short of disgust. "Do *not* give him any more Percocet. I'll be back with an antibiotic and an *appropriate* painkiller for an eleven-year-old child." She turned to Rowan, her eyes narrowed and icy. "You could have killed him, you know. It wasn't enough to hack him to pieces— you also turned him into a drug addict."

Gabriel narrowed his own eyes as she marched out, understanding better why Rowan hated her sister.

Rowan helped him off the counter and eased him into a chair. "Don't listen to her. She missed the day they taught compassion in nursing school. Are you okay?"

"Do you think she's going to tell anyone?"

"She can't for now," Rowan said, holding up a silver case. "I stole her phone." She traced a line on the table, her face screwed up in thought.

It was hard not to be nervous. Rowan's brain didn't work like other people's. It was full of plans and tricks and cookie recipes. He knew he was smart, but he was pretty sure she was a genius—the mad kind who blew things up and laughed about it.

"I don't know what she'll do," Rowan admitted. "But don't worry. If she says a word to anyone, we're out of here."

Gabriel nodded. He didn't have the energy to worry; it was too hot, and he was too tired. Rowan noticed. She led him into the den and helped him lie down on the couch. As his eyes slid shut, he thought he felt her lips on his forehead again, but he was asleep before he could be sure.

Celia returned in full fury an hour later. She stomped into the kitchen and let the screen door slam behind her. "Give me my phone."

Rowan pulled the purloined phone from her pocket and pressed a finger to her lips. "Gabriel's sleeping."

"Wake him up. He needs to take this," Celia said, slapping a prescription bottle on the counter.

"Celia, please," Rowan said. "Will you sit for a minute? There's something I need to say."

Celia looked wary but deigned to sit, folding her hands primly in front of her.

"Okay, look," Rowan began, wiping a sheen of sweat from her forehead. "I want to apologize. It wasn't fair of me to bring Gabriel here without telling you, and I shouldn't have spoken to you the way I did. You have every right to be angry, and I'm sorry."

Celia raised an eyebrow but didn't respond.

"And while I'll admit I may have been wrong in the…execution of all this, I don't think I was wrong to take him."

"You were wrong," Celia protested. "He's an abuse victim. He needs—"

"No," Rowan interrupted. "He's not. He's an eleven-year-old boy. Yes, he went through a horrible experience, but that experience does not define him. *That's* how you become a victim. It's not a label that gets handed to you the first time someone swings their fist. It's a mask you wear until it festers, and then you aren't you anymore—you're just this *thing* that something happened to. I'm not going to let that happen to him."

"He's not the one I'm worried about," Celia said, covering Rowan's hand with hers.

"I appreciate your concern," she replied, pulling away. "But I'm fine."

Celia's eyes searched Rowan's, the sadness in her expression adding lines that hadn't been there before. "No, you're not," she said. "You're not. Why did you do it?"

Rowan stared at the wood table for so long, the grain began to reveal secret dwellers: a smiling dog's snout, a man sitting on a bench. The images vanished as she lifted her head to speak, and her voice emerged small and cracked, barely a whisper. "Because I couldn't leave him there." She stared at her sister with a new level of desperation. "You did it, right? You left—you *had* to leave me," she amended. "Do you remember how it felt? Please, at least tell me it was hard, and then tell me again that I did the wrong thing." A single tear slid down her cheek.

"Of course it was hard," Celia said, floundering. "You're the only family I've got. It killed me to give you up."

"If you could do it again, you wouldn't have left me, would you?"

"No...no, I—You know all this, Rowan!" Her knuckles were white. "I didn't want to leave you the first time. I tried to tell you, but I couldn't make you understand."

"Because I was just a kid, right?"

The cracks were forming—gossamer threads that started in Celia's eyes. "It wasn't a choice I wanted to make, but I was young too." Her mouth was pinched as she fought for control.

Rowan leaned forward and nodded. "You were. I know you were, and I understand. But now you know better, Celia. Now we both know there are some things you shouldn't do, no matter what. So let's call a do-over, okay? You can make up for it right now. It's just a different kid this time."

With that, Rowan's ace on the table, Celia bit her lip, regarding Rowan carefully. And she nodded.

"What did you say to her?" Gabriel asked as Rowan dug around in the bottom of a paper bag.

"Nothing that didn't work, so don't go worrying your pretty little head about it."

They were sitting at the kitchen table, surrounded by white take-out containers. Celia had gone home an hour earlier, but not before providing Rowan with a terrifying list of dos and don'ts.

"Keep his back clean, and make sure he takes the antibiotics three times a day," Celia had begun. "Check the gauze when he goes to bed tonight. If it's dry and there's no blood, you can leave it off, but I want you to call me if he gets a fever or seems sick. He needs to gain weight. Give him lots of protein, whole grains, and as much milk as you can. Don't feed him junk." Celia's fingers worried a lock of her hair. "Have you set up an alert for his name?"

"There's not going to be a search."

"You don't know that. You need to come up with a real, plausible reason for having him here because people are going to wonder. We need to think of something," she said before heading toward her car.

"Celia, wait!"

Celia had jumped and nearly fallen down the stairs. "What's the matter?"

"How do you turn on the air-conditioning?"

Now, twenty degrees cooler, Rowan and Gabriel traded white cardboard containers across the table. Rowan took huge portions of everything, victory awakening her appetite. Gabriel examined the food on his plate like it might come to life and bite him. "What is this?"

Rowan peered over the table. "It's rice."

"No, I mean what's in it?"

"It's pork fried rice. Pork, rice, eggs—"

"*Eggs?* Why?"

"I don't know, that's just what's in it."

"I don't like eggs."

"So don't eat it."

He continued to poke at his plate. "What's this?"

"What's *what?*"

"*This,*" he said, spearing a piece of sweet-and-sour chicken with his fork.

"It's chicken, Gabe. I don't—Can you see all right?"

"It's all puffy."

"Well, I don't know what to tell you."

He pushed his plate away. "I'm not hungry."

"Yes, you are." She dug a piece of pineapple out of her carton and put it on his plate. He ate it without question. "What'd you think of Celia?"

"She's scary," he said.

"That is true," Rowan replied, handing over a few pieces of her own chicken.

Gabriel cut into a piece with the edge of his fork, frowned at the result, and put it in his mouth, chewing slowly. "She kept talking like I wasn't here."

"Yeah, her bedside manner leaves something to be desired. Try this," she said, passing him an egg roll.

"What is it?"

"It's an e—a roll."

As they rinsed their dishes, a rising wind shook the screen door, bringing the smell of rain along with it. The air that rushed in was sweetly scented and deliciously cool. She motioned for Gabriel to turn off the water. "Leave it. Let's go outside."

They sat together on the porch swing. The dense darkness had returned, and Rowan could see movement in the shadows—dim and liquid forms that morphed before her mind could force them into solid shapes. Gabriel pushed the swing back and forth, keeping one foot on a loose board that rose from the rest of the line. The sound of crickets grew until it turned into a full-fledged orchestral arrangement. "Rowan?" Gabriel said, bringing the insect chorus back down to white noise.

"Yes?"

"I forgot something."

"What did you forget?"

"I forgot to say thank you," he said, staring straight ahead. "You know, for…" He met her eye. "You know."

Rowan took his hand. "Yes. I know. And you're welcome."

CHAPTER TEN

ROWAN HUSTLED OUT OF THE HOUSE, PUSHING GABRIEL AHEAD OF her. "We're late," she said. "Get in the truck. I'll be right there." She circled the porch to the little herb garden she'd set up on the back steps. The mint was drooping, but the basil leaves were green and lush, reaching for the sun. She rotated the clay pots and misted them with water.

Gabriel had commandeered the driver's seat, twisting the steering wheel back and forth. Since his back had healed, he'd spent a lot of time eyeing the truck with great interest, not quite grasping the fact he wasn't allowed to drive because it was illegal, not because Rowan wanted him to be bored.

"Don't do that," she said. "You're going to destroy the tires."

"Can I back out of the driveway?"

"No."

"Why not?"

"Because you're eleven."

"How come I'm old enough to save you from monsters in the middle of the night but not to back out of the driveway?"

"Gabe, I swear to God, if you bring that up one more time..."

The past four weeks had been blessedly calm and uneventful. Their willingness to be seen didn't extend past the driveway, so they stuck to the house, venturing to the small grocery store at the end of the road only a handful of times. Being new, they attracted a few stares, but on the whole, the locals were sleepy. She and Gabriel seemed to be the only bright spots in a neighborhood covered in dust.

The only incident of note had happened a few nights earlier, when Rowan was jarred awake by a monstrous thunderstorm. The sheeting rain knocked the power out two minutes after she opened her eyes, and the thunder sounded like an attack. She stumbled downstairs and felt her way to the kitchen, fumbling for the flashlight near the basement door. The stairs creaked beneath her feet as she swept the light in a wide arc around the pipes and windows to check for leaks. A basement, Rowan had learned, was a rare luxury in Oklahoma—something to do with soil or frost—and she'd promised Celia she would be vigilant about maintaining this one. It was really more of a rec room than a basement, and it was so quiet that Rowan seriously considered crashing on the couch and watching TV until the storm passed.

But then she saw the snake.

It was no more than twelve inches from her bare foot, its narrow head rising to strike. She dropped the flashlight and jumped three steps at once, screaming so loud that Gabriel came running downstairs.

"What's the matter?!" he shrieked as she burst into the kitchen and slammed the door shut. Rowan clawed at her head, practically ripping her cheeks. "Rowan!"

"Theresasnakeinthebasement!"

"What?"

"A snake," she wheezed. "In the basement! There's a snake in the basement, a SNAKE…"

Gabriel's face lit up. "I want to see it!"

"No! Get your shoes on. We're going to Celia's. I can't stay in this house with a snake—I can't!"

"I don't want to go to Celia's. It's raining—"

"I don't care!" she screeched, gripping his shoulders. "Put your shoes on!"

"What kind of snake is it? I'm going to look."

"No!"

"Just for a minute. I won't go down the stairs."

Rowan tried to catch her breath as he opened the basement door and disappeared into the dark rectangle. There was silence, and then Gabriel started down the stairs. "Gabe!" she screamed.

"It's okay!" A minute later he stepped back into the kitchen with his arm extended, illuminated by the storm outside. "Is this what you saw?"

The object in his hand was rigid, not particularly snakelike. "What is that?"

"It's a stick." He laid it on the floor, and it looked like a snake again, head rising and body twisting behind.

"A stick?"

"Uh-huh." He kicked it toward the door. "Are you okay?"

Rowan let out a breath that sounded like a sob. Then she grabbed Gabriel by the shoulders, hugging him so tightly, she could feel his heart beating against hers. "Thank you," she whispered.

"Why are you so scared of snakes?"

The thunder roared, and lightning lit the kitchen as she pulled away. "I don't know," she said. "I just am." She tried to smile, but it felt borderline gruesome.

Lingering adrenaline dashed any hope of sleep. Rowan pulled two containers of ice cream from the freezer, and they grabbed pillows and blankets from their bedrooms before piling onto the couch in the den. They sat there together, spooning up melting dollops as the storm raged and watching the rain make patterns on the walls.

Rowan didn't think about it then, but when they woke up the next morning, still cocooned in blankets on the couch, she realized Gabriel had blindly, and without hesitation, gone back underground that night just because she was scared. And for that, she'd started to love him a little bit.

"Make sure you eat," Rowan said. "I don't care what she makes, just eat it."

Gabriel huffed. "Is she going to weigh me again?"

"Yeah, probably."

"Why do we have to go there?"

She tapped her fingers against the steering wheel. "I'm not sure." She'd been wondering too. The sudden invitation to Celia's house felt sinister, like they were being lured into a trap.

Rowan had fully expected Celia to all but move in with them following their arrival, but in the past four weeks, she'd only made two visits, apparently too disgusted with Rowan to function. On her second trip, Celia brought a scale and a color-coded chart, instructing Rowan to track everything Gabriel ate and mark his height and weight every week. She then handed her a massive document that turned out to be the course catalog for Southeastern Oklahoma State University.

Rowan hadn't opened it yet, but she had stood on it a couple of times to reach the cabinet over the refrigerator.

Gabriel pulled his knees to his chest and yawned, squinting against the sun. "I don't want to go," he mumbled.

"Why not?"

"She doesn't like me."

Rowan glanced at him. He tired easily, which wasn't surprising since he barely slept. Every attempt brought nightmares that held him captive, with him crying out until Rowan could rush down the hall and rescue him. Gabriel never said what the dreams were about, but Rowan alone seemed to chase them away. If the fear didn't leave his eyes, she didn't leave him. They spent most nights sleeping side by side, their hands loosely clasped.

"She doesn't like anyone," Rowan assured him.

Celia lived thirty minutes away in a redbrick ranch tucked into a cul-de-sac, as safe and idyllic as a child's drawing. A weather vane perched on the roof, a bugle-blowing angel in place of the usual rooster. The pressed-metal cherub achieved only a vague semblance of piety.

"Lord, would you look at this place," Rowan said wryly. She parked the truck and turned to Gabriel, whose appearance had not improved much in the past thirty minutes—or even the past thirty days. He'd gained a few pounds and gotten some color back, but he still looked small and exhausted. He sat sideways, resting his head against the leather seat. "Maybe we should have stayed home," she said, pushing his hair off his forehead. "You look so tired."

"I'm okay."

"Okay," Rowan said, unconvinced. "Let's get this over with. Are you hungry?"

"I don't know yet."

Gabriel tried not to make a face as Celia slid a plate in front of him. He recognized nothing. He glanced at Rowan, but there was no help there.

"Heirloom beet salad," Celia announced. "With goat cheese medallions, yellow tomatoes, and avocado."

Gabriel's throat cinched shut.

Rowan frowned at her plate. "I hate beets."

Celia handed her a basket of rolls and sat down. "Just try it. This is the type of meal you should be making. It's very healthy."

"The first time I ever ate beets was with you," Rowan said. "You made them on Thanksgiving, and I gagged so hard, I threw up. Did you really forget that?"

"I guess I did. But thank you for the appetizing reminder."

Rowan made a face and pushed the beets to one side of her plate. Gabriel couldn't remember if he'd ever had a beet; he was more worried about what cheese from a goat would taste like. He tried to distract himself by begging Rowan for a roll using the powers of his mind.

While he waited for her to respond, he poked around in the salad. The beets were covered in some kind of oily black stuff. Earlier, Gabriel had heard Rowan on the phone telling Celia to make something plain for lunch. She'd said he didn't have an "adventurous palate."

It was pretty obvious Celia didn't care about his palate.

He'd tried to be nice to her when they got to her house, but Celia barely looked at him. As soon as they all said hello, Celia pulled Rowan into the kitchen, leaving Gabriel alone.

His eyes wandered the room. The furniture was all beige and brown, and the walls were crammed with pictures of rosy-pink angels and golden cherubs shooting arrows at each other. He picked up a framed photo of a younger Celia holding a baby, and then he moved to examine a large print hanging over the brick fireplace. He was still staring at it when Rowan and Celia returned. Celia's face was flushed as she hurried to his side. "Don't touch that, please."

Gabriel yanked his hand away from the wood. "Botticelli," he blurted.

Celia blinked at him. "What?"

His cheeks burned; he hadn't meant to say anything. "The painting. It's by Botticelli. That's the angel Gabriel."

Celia looked almost comically stunned. Out of the corner of his eye, Gabriel saw Rowan lift her head and smile. She stayed back, moving to the scale Celia had set up near the front door—she stood on it and frowned at the green number.

"That's right," said Celia. He could tell she was trying very hard not to sound impressed. "How did you know that?"

"We had the same one in our house. It was one of my mom's favorites. She—my mom—studied art in college." He looked at the floor. "My dad got her this picture when she was pregnant with me. That's where she got my name."

No one spoke. Rowan moved beside him and squeezed his shoulder.

Celia had cleared her throat. "Lunch is ready. And we have some things to discuss."

Any respect Gabriel had gained from identifying Botticelli over the fireplace was slipping away as he continued to poke at his salad. Nudging the goat cheese aside, he carefully selected a beet and speared it with his fork. It was mostly free of black oil, so he put it in his mouth and chewed. It tasted exactly like what he imagined actual dirt would taste like. He swallowed the piece whole and took a huge gulp of water.

Celia was talking to Rowan; neither of them seemed to notice how close he was to throwing up. "So," Celia asked. "What have you been up to?"

Gabriel and Rowan exchanged a guilty look. They'd mostly been watching television and taking turns riding around on the lawn mower. One night they tried to make a raft out of a pallet they found in the garage, but when they threw it into the pond, it had sunk.

Rowan selected a green wedge from her salad and popped it in her mouth. "Not much. Getting settled."

"Have you met any of your neighbors?"

"We have neighbors? Where?"

"Not in proximity, no, but there are a lot of families nearby who would certainly remember you if you let them know you're in town."

Gabriel took a bite of goat cheese, dancing on the thin line between bravery and stupidity.

"What should I do, just go around knocking on doors?" Rowan asked. "No one's going to remember me. I was a baby when we left."

"They remember me."

"You weren't a baby."

Gabriel's only thought was that he had to remove this thing from his mouth, and he had to do it immediately. The napkins were cloth, so he couldn't spit into them. His throat clenched so tightly, his eyes teared.

"I just want you to be prepared," Celia was saying. "Someone is bound to get curious about you two, and you better have your story straight."

"What are they going to do, run a background check?" Rowan asked, polishing off her goat cheese with much more enthusiasm than he had. "The neighbors can't be that nosy."

"No, but the school board is. You can't just waltz in and think they're going to take your word for it. You need legal documentation that says he's yours to care for. He needs health insurance and a pediatrician too."

"Okay, Celia, I get it. He's not ready to go back to school yet anyway."

"Maybe not, but you are. I don't want you to waste any more time. You could have graduated already."

"Could not. Who was it... Oh, it was you who wouldn't let me apply as soon as I finished high school."

"You were barely sixteen when you graduated. I only suggested you wait a year."

"Why'd you graduate so early?" Gabriel put in. It wasn't polite to talk with your mouth full, so all he had to do was keep talking.

"I'm a genius," Rowan said. She popped a beet into her mouth and immediately spit it into her napkin, staining the cloth with red juice. "Celia, these beets are hideous. Can you make me a grilled cheese?"

"Who said you're a genius?" Gabriel asked.

"Yes, Rowan, please tell us, because I love your use of that word," Celia said, glaring at the half-chewed beet in Rowan's napkin.

"I skipped two grades in a row."

"You weren't knocking them dead with your aptitude. You were a terror, and they needed to keep you busy," Celia said with what could have been a smile.

"Not like you were there to know," Rowan shot back.

"No, I wasn't," Celia said. "I was in school myself, if you remember."

"No, I don't. I hadn't met you yet, if *you* remember."

Gabriel didn't want them to go at it again. The last time they sounded like this, he'd been stripped and tortured. He pushed his plate away, the glass screaming against the table.

"This is really bad for my palate. Can I have a grilled cheese too?"

———————

"How big are the burgers here? Are they really big?" Rowan quizzed the waitress who stood with her pencil poised.

"They're pretty big," she said, indicating with her hands.

"Okay, I'll have a cheeseburger and whatever comes with it. Gabe?"

"I'll have one, too, please."

As soon as the waitress was gone, Rowan reached over and patted Gabriel's hand. "You," she said, "are an *outstanding* partner in crime. That was amazing."

"She made us leave."

"And I couldn't have done it better myself." She leaned back and threaded her fingers into the braid at the nape of her neck. "But she was right about one thing."

"What?"

"The doctor. I need to find a pediatrician so I can get you checked out."

"I'm not sick."

"You're also not sleeping," Rowan said. "I spent five out of seven nights in your room last week."

Gabriel shrugged.

"So what's going on?"

"I don't know," he mumbled.

"Bad dreams?"

He shrugged again.

"Because if you tell me what they're about," she added, "they might go away."

His blue eyes were wide, devoid of any readable expression. "I don't remember."

The waitress came back with their food, and the discussion was paused for about ten minutes, which was all the time it took them to devour everything on their plates. Rowan wiped ketchup from her fingers as the waitress returned. "Can I get you anything else?"

"Gabe? Are you finished?"

He nodded silently.

"Just the check, please." She gripped Gabriel's arm as the waitress walked away. "What's wrong?"

He shook his head as he slid out of the booth. "Nothing."

The cashier was an old woman with fire-engine–red hair and lipstick to match. The color bled into the creases around her lips, but her smile was warm and friendly. "Cash or card, honey?"

"Card."

"Chip reader's broken. I'll have to swipe it."

Rowan handed her the card. The cashier slid it through the

register and started to hand it back, but then she stopped, holding the plastic loosely between her fingers.

"Is everything okay?" Rowan asked.

She waved the card. "Is this you? You're Rowan McNamara?"

"Yes."

"Celia's sister?"

Gabriel inhaled sharply.

Rowan put her hand over his and tried to smile. "Uh-huh."

"Good Lord, I'm gonna smack that girl silly next time I see her. I had no idea you were in town! We prepare meal carts for some of Celia's patients. She talks about you all the time!"

"Oh God, really?" Rowan said weakly.

"Oh, yeah, she's a doll. She does so much for the folks under her care. A lot of them don't have family around."

"That's nice of her," Rowan said. She took a step forward, nudging Gabriel behind her.

"I haven't seen you since you was just a baby," the cashier went on as she changed the tape in the register. "I knew your parents, you know." Rowan edged closer to the counter as Gabriel took refuge behind the gumball machine. "Terrible shame what happened to them. You girls are lucky to have each other. You look like your mama, honey, just beautiful. Same exact face, but you have your daddy's coloring. Irish. He was a very fair man, and he had those same lovely eyes. Now tell me, who's this little sweetheart you've got with you?"

She said it so quickly that Rowan didn't register the question until Gabriel tugged on her hand. She turned to him. "Oh—ah, this is, um, my son. I mean my friend's son." She put her foot on top of his and pressed down.

"Ain't that something?" the cashier murmured, smiling. "He don't look much younger than you."

"Foster son!" Rowan blurted. "She's fostering him. Her application was just approved because, you know, you have to pass a background check, so she just got him. Right?" she asked Gabriel. He smiled a little and nodded. Rowan was nodding, too, a deranged puppet with only one string. "Anyway, Ga—he, he's her first placement, and um, she's visiting me. It's important to give back, and I wanted to do it, too, be a foster parent, but I can't because I have a criminal record."

The cashier's face was perfectly blank, her fingers poised over the fresh roll of tape sticking out of the register. Rowan jumped as Gabriel stepped in front of her.

"Hello," he said. His voice was sweet and clear, not at all the way he usually sounded. "It's nice to meet you." The sunlight from the window added golden flecks to his eyes, and his cheeks glowed pink in the late-afternoon air. He had, while standing in the background, messed up his hair.

The cashier melted into a grandmotherly pool. "Sweetheart, you are just ten pounds of cute in a five-pound bag! Tell me, how're you getting on with the new family?"

"Pretty well. My foster mom wanted to visit her other friends today, so Rowan said I could hang out with her." Rowan squeezed his hand, begging him to shut up and give this woman nothing to remember, but he didn't. "We went to the zoo." He sighed, pouting a little. "I'd never been there before."

"Oh, honey," the cashier said, shaking her head. "I'm glad you had the chance to go. That sounds like a nice day. I sure hope things work out for you, darlin'."

"Thank you," he said quietly, looking up at her through his eyelashes.

"We should go," Rowan cut in, tugging Gabriel away from the counter.

"Tell Celia Ruby said hi, will you?"

"I will. It was nice to meet you."

"Nice meeting you," Gabriel said.

Rowan smiled tightly, and they walked out the door.

"Jesus Christ, Gabe," she hissed as they hurried toward the truck. "What the hell were you doing?"

"I was doing a lot better than you were."

They didn't speak on the way home. Gabriel sat pressed against the door, as far from Rowan as he could get. When she pulled into the driveway, he was out of the truck before she cut the engine.

He gave the doorknob three sharp yanks and slammed his palms against the door.

"It's locked," Rowan called, pulling a pebble from the tire.

"I know that!" he shouted, stomping into the yard.

Rowan unlocked the door and went into the kitchen. She could see Gabriel sitting on the back steps, yanking leaves off the basil plants one at a time. She pushed the screen door open with her foot. "Please don't murder my basil. Are you coming in or not?"

"Not if you're going to be mad at me," he said, tearing another leaf.

"I'm not mad at you, though if you don't leave my basil alone, I might be."

Gabriel stalked into the kitchen, making a beeline for the den.

"May I ask why *you* are so mad at me?" Rowan said.

"You don't know?"

"Honestly, I have no idea."

He threw himself on the couch. "How come you don't know what to tell people about me? We've been here a whole month. Celia told you to be ready!"

"Are you upset about what happened in the restaurant? Because it really doesn't matter."

"It does matter!" he yelled. "You acted like I don't even belong to you!"

"You *don't* belong to me."

His anger vanished in an instant, painted over with bright bewilderment. "What?" he managed.

"No, I didn't mean it like that." She sat next to him, but he rolled away, burying his face in his arms.

"Don't touch me."

"I'm not going to. Gabe, I only said that because she took me by surprise."

He sat up, his face red and streaked with tears. "That's not true! You lied so you wouldn't get in trouble! And that's okay for you, but if *you* get caught lying about me, *I'm* the one who gets taken away!" He threw himself on the couch, shoved his head into the corner, and put a pillow on top.

"Gabe…"

He didn't move.

She pulled the pillow off his head and leaned over him; he struggled to push her away, but she was bigger. "Are you going to listen to me?"

He didn't answer.

"Okay, good. You have every right to be angry. I didn't want to think about what to tell Celia about you, so I just didn't think about it until it was too late. The same thing happened today, and that's not fair to you."

"You're crushing me," he mumbled.

She shifted her weight but didn't get up. "You'll live; I'm almost done. The thing is, I was terrified I wouldn't be able to get you here safely. And when it somehow worked out, I was so happy, and I thought you were, too. I figured we could concentrate on that for a little while." She rolled off him and dropped to the floor. "I was wrong," she said. "I'm sorry."

They stayed that way for a long time. The light was beginning to turn the same color as the magnolias, which was Rowan's favorite time of day. Gabriel was so quiet, she thought he'd fallen asleep, but then he spoke, his voice low and broken. "I can't sleep because I'm scared."

She inched closer. "What are you scared of?"

He rolled over and stared at the ceiling, his eyes puffy and damp. "This," he said, waving his arm. "Everything. This whole stupid plan. It's not going to work."

"It already worked. Why would you say that?"

"Because it's true," he insisted, swiping at a tear in the corner of his eye. "I shouldn't have gotten mad at you, because I know there's no reason for me to be here. I've tried to think of one." His breath hitched, and he covered his eyes. "Every night I dream I'm back in the basement, and when I wake up, I know I should be happy, but I'm not. I'm scared someone's going to find out what we did. I'm scared my dad will find me, or Celia's going to call the police, or you'll change your mind."

Rowan ran her thumb over the tears on his cheek. "That's not going to happen," she said, rubbing his forehead; his skin was hot and dry, pulsing with headache and emotion. "No one is going to find out," she whispered. "I promise. Tomorrow I'll sit down and figure out exactly what we need to do, but no matter what happens, no one is taking you away from me. Ever."

Gabriel was quiet. His eyes had slid closed, and before long his breathing grew even and deep. Rowan covered him with a blanket.

The screen door knocked lightly against the wooden frame. Rowan pushed it open and settled on the porch steps. The sun sat low on the horizon, dipping across the trees and turning the pond to liquid gold. The pile of torn basil was drying on the top step. She picked up the fragments one at a time, dropping them into her cupped hand.

The leaves still smelled pungent and green. Her hands would not stop shaking.

CHAPTER ELEVEN

SUMMER MELTED INTO FALL, A FAR GENTLER SLOPE THAN THE BRISK AIR that ferried autumn into New England. The leaves brightened to red and gold, but the warm air stayed far past its welcome. Rowan and Gabriel spent every evening on the porch, burning fragrant wood in the chiminea as they basked in the illusion of chilly nights.

Rowan bought a few odds and ends to put their imprint on the house, but when it came to Gabriel, there was nothing he didn't need. She filled his closet with clothes, ordered him dozens of books, and let him pick out any phone he wanted. They spent an entire weekend marching up and down the stairs with gallons of paint and plastic trays and rollers. It took him forever to decide on a color for his room, but eventually, he chose a rich, mossy green. Rowan honestly thought it looked amazing with the pink carpet, but Gabriel opted for the cherrywood floor hiding underneath. They assembled bookcases, mounted a TV on the wall, and dragged two burnt-orange armchairs up the stairs.

If it was warm enough, Rowan let Gabriel loose in the pond. He was fearless in the water, carefree and unencumbered by pained and fearful thoughts. While he jumped and splashed and dove, she sat on the dock, quietly devouring books on child psychology and abuse recovery and parenting.

Celia had her own opinion on the situation. It included words like *spoiled* and *overindulgent* and *boundaries*. Rowan didn't care. He was thriving. By mid-October Gabriel had gained ten pounds, grown two inches, and turned twelve years old.

Rowan pulled out all the stops for his birthday, obsessed with finding the perfect theme, the perfect decorations, the perfect gifts. She bought a silver cake topper bearing his name, bookmarked dozens of recipes for homemade ice cream, and ordered a set of outrageously overpriced party hats. She was determined to orchestrate joy, create a core memory—a vivid, happy place he could visit or hide. But even though she got the decorations right and he loved his presents, every crucial moment felt lined with thorns.

If Gabriel noticed, he didn't let on—it was always just the two of them anyway, so there was really nothing *to* notice. When they chose their party hats, he made no mention of the six left in the box. He didn't seem to mind when she sang "Happy Birthday" by herself or that every single package in his pile of gifts was from her. He scooped up fingerfuls of frosting, chatting happily as Rowan packed up his birthday cake with only two pieces gone.

Still, he was getting better. The nightmares had stopped shortly after the Ruby debacle, leaving a more liminal version of Gabriel behind. He was happy, but that happiness came with an edge of caution—it was rare to see him truly enjoy anything; he always had one hand raised to protect. One night, just before Thanksgiving, Rowan wandered into the den while he was watching TV. He didn't notice her come in because he was laughing—great big belly laughs that had him doubled over on the sofa. It was an image her brain could not compute, and she spent a good ten seconds trying to figure out what was wrong with him as he giggled helplessly, tears streaming down his face.

It was like she'd never seen him before.

Despite Rowan's private doubts, Celia's frequent protests, and Gabriel's lingering fears, by the time winter ushered in the new year, they had found their balance. They were safe, buried within the confines of the house and untouched by the outside, with no need for anything else. Then, in April, Laine called and turned everything on end.

"You want to come here?" Rowan repeated.

"I'd love it!" said Laine. "My credits are done, and I have nothing to do until graduation. And I miss you. It's been way too long."

Rowan listened in stark terror, twisting her hair into knots.

"I'm in New Hampshire with my parents for another week, so I can fly in straight from here."

She could hardly deny her the hospitality, not after Laine had put a roof over Rowan's head and unknowingly blessed her with a child. After they worked out the details, Rowan sat down with Gabriel and presented him with the most logical plan.

"No way!"

She had him cornered at the kitchen table after luring him inside with the promise of baked goods.

He stared at her with a fork sticking out of his mouth. "Why do you hate me?"

"Gabriel," she said, indicating the pie on the table. "Look at this pie. Fresh rhubarb. Homegrown strawberries. A braided lattice crust. Celia brought one of these to Ruby at the diner, and they've been ordering half a dozen a week ever since. I baked this pie for you because it's your favorite, and I want you to be happy."

He pushed the plate away. "I don't care. I'm *not* staying with Celia. It won't work anyway. My stuff is all over the house."

"Yeah, I know it is, and maybe if you were at Celia's for a week, I could get some of it put away." She snatched the fork out of his hand and picked up the plate, digging into the pie herself. "What am I supposed to tell her? The legal guardian story isn't going to fly. If any of my dead friends were going to leave me a kid, it would be Laine."

"Tell her you're fostering me," he suggested.

"Be a bit awkward to bring it up now, don't you think?"

"When's she coming?"

"Next week!"

"So you have a whole week to think of something," he said with an infuriating air of serenity. He cut himself another slice of pie.

The next day, she turned to Celia.

"I don't know what you want me to tell you, Rowan," she said, taking a sip of iced tea. "You wanted to do this. You swore up and down that you could handle it. This isn't the witness protection program. You can't just disappear and think everyone is going to forget about you."

Rowan pressed her lips together. As much as she hated involving her sister in anything, Celia occasionally had her uses. After weeks of combing even the smallest corners of the internet for any mention of Gabriel's name, Rowan had felt reasonably safe claiming him, but other than his birth certificate, she had no paperwork, no proof, and no plan.

Celia had all three. She'd been Rowan's legal guardian for almost four years, and it was her idea to alter their own documents, changing Celia's name to Rowan and Rowan's name to Gabriel. After a visit to Celia's safety deposit box and an afternoon of forgery, Rowan penned a fake will bequeathing Gabriel to her. Celia borrowed credentials from a coworker with a notary stamp and a penchant for long lunch hours and embossed him into Rowan's care. So far, their scheme had earned them insurance coverage and a pediatrician, but it wouldn't work on Laine.

"Honestly, Rowan, I don't see what's wrong with telling her you're fostering him."

"He's not going to be able to act like a foster kid. He's too comfortable with me, and he's very clingy."

"Yes, he is. And that's your fault. You don't give him any boundaries."

Rowan shot her a look. "Any child who nearly bleeds out at my feet can be as clingy as they want." She paced the kitchen. "It's only a week, Ceil, please. He's very good company. You probably won't even see him that much; he sleeps really late."

"I can't force him if he doesn't want to go," Celia said, staring past her into the yard. "Rowan, is he *driving* your truck?"

Rowan waved her hand. "He won't leave the yard. It's the only way to keep him out of the house."

"He's twelve years old! And the grass—"

"I don't care!" Rowan screeched. "Help me!"

Celia pushed her chair back. "I will help you. But this is Gabriel's home too. You can't just kick him out because he's become inconvenient." She looped her bag over her shoulder. "I have to go; I have a patient at three. Thanks for the pie, though. Peach is my favorite."

"I know," Rowan said, slumping in her chair. She stared out the window as Gabriel steered the truck in wide circles over the lawn, kicking up chunks of dirt and grass with every pass.

———————

A week later, Rowan nudged Gabriel ahead of her down the stairs, fixing his hair as they went. "Tell me the story again."

"I could say it in my sleep."

"Good, see if you can say it while you're awake."

He sighed, hopping the last two steps. "I am a foster child. My father's dead, and my mother's a drug addict."

"And?"

"And you fostered me two months ago while my mom was in rehab. Last week she started smoking meth again, and the courts asked if you would keep me until she's clean. I arrived two days ago. Happy?"

"Yes," she said. "Frankly, I'm not surprised it only took a few weeks with you to get your mother back on the pipe." Celia had been dispatched to pick up Laine at the airport, and they were due any second. "Don't try too hard. You have the easy part," she said. "Just be really sad and pretty. You're good at that." She raced around the foyer, picking things up and putting them down again. "The most important thing is that you *act* like a foster kid. Try to keep your distance; don't hang on me." A horn sounded, and Rowan jumped a mile. "Shit."

She started toward the door, but before she could take a step,

Gabriel grabbed her and hugged her from behind, his arms tight around her neck. "What did I *just* say?"

"Last time for a week," Gabriel said. "I'll miss you."

———————

Laine descended on them like a hurricane. She blew through the door and grabbed Rowan in a fierce hug, nearly knocking her off her feet. Gabriel hung back, but he was swept into the commotion before Laine was even introduced to him.

"I'll show you your room," Rowan said. She picked up Laine's suitcase and lugged it up the stairs before she could start asking questions. "I put you in the round bedroom. The light in there is amazing."

Rowan led her to the very end of the hall. Light had nothing to do with it. She'd chosen the round bedroom because it was really far away from Rowan's and Gabriel's rooms.

"You have no idea how good it feels to be here," Laine said, collapsing on the bed. "My parents were on my last nerve."

"How long did you visit them?"

"Two weeks. It felt longer." She turned her head and smiled. "I can't believe I'm actually seeing you. You look amazing, kiddo, you really do."

Rowan felt her cheeks color because she knew she didn't—not compared to Laine. Gone was the shy, lanky girl she remembered.

Laine brimmed with a confidence Rowan couldn't even fake. Her bronze skin was smooth and flawless, and her black hair had been cropped short to complement her bone structure. "No, *you* look amazing," Rowan replied, lying next to her. "I look like something that went through a meat grinder."

Laine's face fell. "How bad was it?"

Rowan rose to her knees and lifted the hem of her shirt, twisting to show Laine the road map of scars on her back.

"Jesus Christ, Rowan!" Laine gasped, cupping a hand over her mouth. "He's still in prison, right?"

Rowan flopped back down. "For the moment."

Laine shook her head. "I can't believe he didn't get more time. He could have killed you."

Rowan laughed without humor. "Oh, that doesn't matter! His family's loaded. And they're so, so sorry they didn't teach him the difference between right and wrong, otherwise he'd *never* have thrown me through a glass door. He just has a little bit of a temper. It's no big deal." She shook her head. "I'm lucky he got any time at all."

Laine hauled her suitcase onto the bed. "Tell me about Gabriel," she said. "I can't believe you never told me you were fostering. Not that it isn't a great thing to do. I'm just surprised."

Rowan rested her head on her arms so Laine couldn't see her face. "I hope you're not upset he's here. It was kind of last-minute."

"Of course not."

"He's my first placement," Rowan said, privately entering a new level of self-loathing for feeding Laine such bullshit. "He went home to his mother a few weeks ago, but she's on all kinds of stuff. The social worker asked if I would take him back."

Laine shook her head. "I have never seen such an adorable kid, and he seems so sweet. Can you believe people?"

"Not lately," Rowan said, getting to her feet. "Why don't you get settled before we eat? I was planning to barbecue if that's all right."

"That sounds perfect. I think I might pass out for half an hour."

"It'll take me that long to heat up the grill. I'll give you a yell when everything's ready."

Rowan pulled the door closed. Gabriel was waiting outside; she ushered him into his room.

"Where's Celia?" she asked.

"She went to the store; she'll be right back. What did Laine say?" he asked.

"She seemed to take it all in stride."

Gabriel smiled. "See? I told you everything would be okay."

"Oh, Gabe," she sighed. "It's been half an hour. Do you really think this is over?"

Rowan grilled up a storm, fixing fat hamburgers, chicken wings doused in homemade barbecue sauce, and seared greens alongside ears of sweet corn dripping with butter. She was going to let Gabriel try grilling, but the metal fork dangling next to the tongs made her rethink that idea. She put him to work assembling the salads instead, and by the time Laine joined them, there was enough food to feed everyone three times over.

Celia joined them for dinner, and for that Rowan was grateful. Laine had everyone in fits of laughter as she talked about her last few semesters at Amherst, time spent in a shoebox-size apartment with a cat that was not strictly hers but refused to vacate the premises after the previous owners moved away. At ten o'clock they were still lingering over dessert, the night too pleasant to forfeit.

Rowan transferred another slice of cake to Laine's plate. "How are things at the house?" Rowan asked.

"Oh, fine. Thank you again for fixing my shutters. You did a great job."

"From a distance, maybe, but don't look too close."

"Lee told me he donated his crew to help you get them back on the house."

Rowan's heart skipped a beat and then picked up, double time. Gabriel's fingers tightened against his glass. "Yes," she said after a moment. "He did."

"He's the best neighbor—I have a real asshole on the other side. When I got back from Korea, Lee made me an engraved garden stone with my name on it, and—Oh, I almost forgot! Shit, he told me this a long time ago—did you borrow something from him while you were at my house?"

Rowan froze as the ball began to roll faster than she could chase it. "I don't think so," she said slowly. She didn't dare look at Gabriel. "Did he say what?"

"No," Laine said, popping a forkful of cake into her mouth. "He just asked me to remind you that you have something of his."

Gabriel choked and dropped his lemonade. The glass shattered on the wooden boards, sending sugary spikes in every direction. Rowan jumped up so fast, her chair clattered down the porch steps. "Take him in, Celia, take him in!"

Celia was moving before the words left Rowan's mouth. She grabbed Gabriel in a bear hug from behind and lifted him out of his seat. His chest was heaving; his face had gone purple. They disappeared through the back door, leaving Rowan and Laine in stunned silence.

Laine's hand was pressed to her mouth. "What...?"

Rowan bent to pick up the glass, but her hands were trembling so badly, she couldn't bring herself to touch a single piece. "He's... It's asthma," Rowan said, peering into the window. "Celia knows what to do."

Laine gaped at her. "I had a roommate with asthma," she said. "It never looked like that."

"He has it pretty bad. It comes on all of a sudden. I better check on him."

Celia came outside then, visibly shaken. "He needs you," she said to Rowan. "Right now, go."

Rowan flew into the kitchen. Celia followed. "What did you tell Laine?" Celia asked.

"I said he has asthma."

"Good enough," Celia said, pressing a hard nugget into Rowan's hand. "Give him this."

"What is it?"

"Valium, very mild. He was hysterical—I had to slap him."

"You *hit* him?"

"I had to, or he would've hurt himself." Celia pointed to the den. "Go."

Rowan found Gabriel slumped in the recliner looking glazed and blank, hardly the writhing mess she'd expected. She knelt in front of him. "Gabe?"

His eyes rolled vaguely in her direction. When he spoke, it sounded like he was channeling someone else. "He knows."

"He only thinks he does."

"He knows! He's going to find me!"

"No, he won't," she said, smoothing his hair. "Come upstairs."

He didn't respond, but he allowed her to lead him into her room, moving like a zombie. Rowan closed the door and ran to the bathroom for a cold washcloth. "Here," she said. "Come here." She sat him on the bed and gripped the back of his neck, running the cloth over his face. Gradually, he lost the glazed look, wilting against her shoulder.

Rowan held him close and rubbed circles over his back. "Listen to me," she said, trying not to sound like she was convincing herself. "Laine said he told her that a long time ago."

"Then he's been looking for a long time! What if Laine told him she was coming here?"

"She spent two weeks at her parents' before she came here. He can't possibly know where we are."

"She could have told him at any time."

"I'm going to talk to her," Rowan said. "I'll find out exactly what he knows, and then we'll figure out what to do. Even if she told him we're in Oklahoma, it would be almost impossible to find us. I'm not even listed as the owner of the house—Celia is."

"What if he does know?"

"Then we'll leave," she promised, resting her cheek on his head. "We'll go wherever we have to."

"You swear?"

"I swear."

Eventually, Gabriel's breathing evened out, and he relaxed in her arms. "What did you tell Laine?" he mumbled.

"I said it was an asthma attack." She squeezed him tighter and tried to smile. "So throw in a wheeze every now and then, okay?"

He nodded and pulled back a little, swiping his fingers under his eyes. "I'm scared," he whispered.

Rowan pressed her lips to his forehead. "I know." His cheek was red where Celia had slapped him; she rubbed her thumb over the spot. "Celia gave me some medicine to help you calm down. Do you want to take it?"

Gabriel shook his head, resting against her shoulder again. "Can I sleep in your room tonight? Please?"

"Yeah," Rowan said, probably too quickly. Her own fear was immense, bubbling over and burning her chest, but she couldn't let him see it. "Go get ready for bed while I talk to Laine, okay? I'll be right up." The Valium was still clutched in her fist. She eased the door shut and then shoved the pill into her own mouth. She swallowed it dry.

Celia and Laine were in the kitchen when Rowan returned. Celia jumped to her feet. "Is he all right?"

Rowan tried to smile. "He'll be fine. I'll stay with him tonight so I can keep an eye on him."

"Does he get attacks like that a lot?" Laine asked. "That was intense. I feel so bad."

"It's okay, I swear," Rowan said. "We've been through much worse with him, right, Celia?"

Celia nodded. "Call me if you need me, okay?" She gave Rowan a brief hug before turning to Laine. "I hope I'll see more of you before the end of your visit. I look forward to less dramatic evenings." Her smile was so warm, Rowan could see a bit of the Celia it seemed only her patients knew.

When she was gone, Rowan poured herself a glass of wine and joined Laine at the table. "I'm really proud of you," Laine said. "You're amazing with him."

Rowan shrugged, staring into her glass. "I know what it's like." She took a deep drink and tried to smile. "We never finished catching up. What were we talking about?"

"I don't even remember."

"You said something about Lee—he asked you about me?"

Laine nodded. "He just said if I talked to you to tell you that you have something of his, and he wanted to get it back."

Rowan fiddled with her glass. "Did you tell him we were friends?"

"Sure."

Rowan cringed a little. "Did you tell him where I went?"

"What?"

"He didn't ask where I live or anything?"

Laine gave her a weird look. "No…why?"

Rowan pulled her chair closer to the table. "I don't know. He kind of creeped me out."

"Lee?" Laine asked, laughing. "Are you kidding? He's a teddy bear."

"I know, and I'm probably thinking way too highly of myself," Rowan said with a sheepish grin. "But there was something about him—he was always…*there*. It was like he was following me around or something." She took another gulp of wine. "Did you tell him you were coming to visit?"

"No, I haven't seen him lately. Why are you so paranoid?"

"He just gave me the creeps. If he asks you about me again, don't say anything. Tell him we don't talk anymore." The more she said, the worse she felt, but she couldn't tell Laine about Gabriel. If Lee even suspected Laine knew, she'd have a target on her back. "I wouldn't talk to him at all if I were you."

"I'll consider myself warned," Laine said wryly. "Don't take this the wrong way, but he didn't exactly sound infatuated enough to hunt you down."

Rowan shrugged. "You never know what people will do."

They talked for a few more minutes before Laine retired to her bedroom. Rowan walked to the opposite end of the hall. Her room was dark, lit only by a wash of moonlight. Gabriel was tucked under the covers, his face open and expectant. "What did she say?"

Rowan put a finger over her lips and sat next to him. "He doesn't know she's here, and he doesn't know we're here. She didn't tell him anything. In fact," Rowan went on, cupping his cheek, "I told her not to talk to him at all."

"Really?"

"Really. I told you, we're absolutely safe." She dropped a kiss on his cheek. "Go to sleep."

She half expected him to be awake all night, but the shock must have taken a lot out of him. She went into the bathroom to change for bed, and by the time she came out, he was already asleep, his eyelashes resting like feathers against his cheeks.

He was so beautiful, even in sleep. Rowan couldn't imagine how anyone could have it in them to hurt him. She got into bed, replaying Laine's words over and over, and as she did, her fear grew spikes, turning angry and indignant. By the time she fell asleep, she almost wanted Lee to come after her—to find out what would happen if he ever tried to take what was hers.

CHAPTER TWELVE

GABRIEL STARED AT HIMSELF IN THE MIRROR, TUGGING AT THE LENGTH of fabric hanging around his neck. To celebrate the last night of Laine's visit, Rowan announced she was taking everyone out to dinner, and the restaurant she chose was so fancy, it came with a dress code. Gabriel was pretty sure he was wearing more clothes than he'd ever had on his body at once. He crossed the ends of his tie and pulled, which accomplished nothing. He put on a belt instead.

"Are you ready?" Rowan called from her room.

"Do I have to wear a tie?"

"Yes!"

"I can't tie it!"

"I'll tie it—give me two minutes."

Gabriel knew Rowan was relieved they wouldn't have to lie to Laine anymore—at least not to her face—but he could tell, aside from that first horrible day, that Rowan loved having Laine around. He did too. She was funny and full of stories about Rowan. Gabriel had learned more about her in a few days than he had in the past year. The three of them went somewhere different every day. Once, they rented a canoe on Lake Texoma and spent an hour spinning in circles because no one knew how to paddle. It had been an easy week, like a reward for good behavior.

But sometimes Laine noticed things he and Rowan didn't. They were having lunch at an outdoor café one afternoon, close to where the yearly Magnolia Festival was held. As soon as they ordered, Rowan started talking about dessert, the way she always did before the real food came. Gabriel picked up the little tent with the dessert menu and began reading all the specials out loud. He noticed Laine staring at him as he spoke, and when he was finished, she shook her fork in his direction. "Have you always lived in Oklahoma?"

He glanced at Rowan and put the menu down. "Uh-huh."

"You don't sound like it."

Rowan stared at him with wide eyes—for all their preparation, they'd never thought about linguistics.

"Celia does, but not you."

"Celia doesn't have an accent," Rowan said quickly.

"She still sounds different than you do. Maybe it's the cadence or something, I don't know." She turned back to Gabriel. "You talk like you could have grown up on our street."

Gabriel had smiled and shrugged, afraid to say another word.

He was still fiddling with the tie when Rowan came into his room. At first, he didn't realize it was her. He'd never seen her in anything fancier than jeans, but tonight she was wearing a short green dress with thin straps, almost like a ballerina would wear. She had a long piece of matching fabric wrapped around her shoulders. "How do I look?" she asked, spinning in a circle.

"I didn't know you had a dress," he said.

"Wow, thanks." Rowan took hold of the tie and knotted it with practiced ease. She'd bought him the suit that morning, with strict instructions not to outgrow it right away. She was only kidding, but he felt bad—it seemed like he needed new clothes every couple of months. He'd grown five inches since he'd been living with Rowan and was already taller than she was. She straightened the knot. "You clean up good, kiddo."

"Are you guys ready?" Laine asked, coming in. "The reservation—Oh my God!" Rowan smiled and bumped her hip against Gabriel's. "Look at you two! You look like porcelain dolls. Come downstairs so I can take your picture."

They went into the big living room, the one they never used, and Laine arranged them in front of the fireplace. She had a yellow-and-white camera with a rainbow stripe down the middle that spit out the pictures right away; they smiled as the flash lit up the room.

———

The restaurant looked nice, but the menu was so weird, Rowan had to order for him. The three of them were the youngest people there by about forty years, and definitely the loudest. Rowan and Laine got more talkative each time their wineglasses were refilled. For dessert, the waiter brought three different flavors of chocolate mousse in tall crystal columns. Rowan and Laine also ordered tiny glasses of liqueur, and Rowan let Gabriel try little sips of hers when no one was looking. It was rich and creamy, flavored like coffee and chocolate.

Laine raised her glass in a toast. "I've had such a wonderful week," she began. "I'm so glad I got to spend it with the two of you." She turned to Rowan. "From now on, visits are a rule, not an exception. I love you way too much to let another seven years pass before I see you again."

Rowan scooted her chair over and hugged Laine, knotting her arms tightly around her neck. Gabriel wanted to let them have a moment to themselves, but as he started to look away, Rowan's silky wrap slid off her shoulders and slithered to the floor.

Rowan never went swimming with him. She said she didn't know how, but she didn't sunbathe on the dock either or wear anything much lighter than a sweatshirt. Gabriel had never really bothered to wonder why, but when he saw what was hiding underneath that green fabric, his face burned like he had accidentally seen her naked. Her back was a mess of scars, angry gashes that started at her shoulders and disappeared under her dress. They made the marks on his own back look like paper cuts. Rowan caught his expression before he could look away, and she jerked back in her chair, picking up the wrap and pulling it tightly over her shoulders.

Gabriel trailed Rowan and Laine as they left the restaurant with their arms linked, laughing and stumbling and leaning into each other. Gabriel wanted to join them; he wanted to be that happy, but something was tugging him back, a tiny worry only just beginning to hatch. They broke away so Laine could order an Uber, and Gabriel jumped as the sleek fabric of Rowan's dress brushed his hand.

"What's the matter?" she asked.

"What?"

"You look like you've seen a ghost."

"I'm just tired."

"Me too," she said, squeezing his shoulder. "By the way," she added. "Thank you."

"For what?"

She nodded toward Laine. "For this week. For letting her have me for a little while."

Rowan woke early the next morning—too early. The half bottle of wine she'd had at dinner had relocated to her temples, and her head pounded alongside her heart. There was a glass of water on her night-stand; she didn't know if it was a gift from her drunken self or someone else, but she was grateful. The water was warm, barely refreshing, but it pushed some of the pain out of her head and plumped her dried-up veins just enough to help her think again.

The house was quiet, something it hadn't been for days. She went down to the kitchen and shoved two pieces of bread into the toaster, staring out the window into the thick, hazy air.

Laine's voice startled her out of her daze. "Good morning."

Rowan jumped and so did her toast; it was crisp and pouring steam, nearly burnt.

Laine stood in the doorway, a cup of coffee in her hand. "You look like you had a rough night," she said.

"I did." Rowan tried to smile, but her lips shook. Laine had been a force all week, a live wire of confidence and energy, but in that moment, she looked small and fragile in her pajamas and socks, so fine and easily breakable. "You're up early."

"I slept like the dead."

"I'm glad. I was hoping I could talk to you for a minute. Before Gabriel wakes up."

"About what?"

"Not in here," Rowan said. "Let's go outside."

They sat on the porch swing. The air was thick, dripping with moisture and the promise of real rain. "You should come in the fall," Rowan said, staring at the light mist hovering over the pond. "The weather's just beautiful."

"I didn't come for the weather."

"I know."

"What are we talking about?" Laine asked.

Rowan pressed her feet against the boards, rocking the swing back and forth. "Gabriel."

Laine nodded slowly. "I was hoping you'd say that."

"Why?"

"Because I have my own questions about Gabriel."

"Like what?"

Laine shook her head. "You first. What were you going to tell me?"

Rowan took a deep breath. "That's the thing. I *wasn't* going to tell you. But the more I thought about it, the more I knew I just can't send you back without knowing. I can't. I owe you more than that."

"Go ahead. I'm listening."

Rowan clasped her hands together. "Gabriel," she began, "is not a foster kid."

Laine nodded a little. "I didn't think so."

"You didn't?"

"No. I tried to tell myself it wasn't weird that you forgot to tell me something like that. Or that he didn't go to school all week, or that he has such a nice room, or that you two finish each other's sentences, but it is weird, Rowan. It's very weird."

Rowan squeezed her eyes shut. "I know."

"So whose kid is he?"

"He's…he's mine."

"He's yours?"

"Yes," she said. "He lives here. He's mine."

"What does that mean? Did you adopt him or something?"

"No."

"Then where did he come from?"

"Laine, please," Rowan begged. "I couldn't tell you before. I wanted to, I swear, but it was too dangerous for you."

"What does this have to do with me?"

Rowan drew a breath. "Gabriel," she said slowly, "is Lee's son."

Laine paused a moment. "Lee," she repeated. "From next door?"

"Yes."

A small smile crept onto her lips. "Come on…"

"It's true."

"Rowan, I lived next door to him for a year before you got there. I think I would've noticed if he had a kid."

"He was there. He saw you almost every day."

"How come I never saw him?"

"Because you didn't look in the basement."

The flush of pink left Laine's cheeks. "What?"

Rowan stared into her lap, trying to clear the tears from her throat. "Lee kept him locked down there," she whispered. "He was beating him, starving him. He'd been there for years. I don't know what made him start talking to me, but he did. When I found out what was going on, I wanted to call the police, but Gabriel begged me not to. He was scared of what would happen to him." Rowan drew a ragged breath. "I could understand that. So, when I left, I just…took him."

She looked at Laine, her eyes brimming with tears. "We left during the block party. Before I got there, Lee caught Gabriel trying to go out the window. He dragged him back inside and beat him with a barbecue fork. I had to break into the house to get him out. He might have killed him if I hadn't. I brought him to a hotel and sewed him up as best as I could. Then we came here."

Laine's eyes were wide, one hand pressed over her mouth. "Rowan! Why didn't you tell me?"

"I didn't want Lee to think you knew anything. I never even told him we were friends. He thought I was just renting the house."

"What did you tell Celia?"

"The truth. What else could I say? I told her the truth." Rowan gave a brief humorless chuckle. "She acted like I did this horrible, blasphemous thing. There but for the grace of God go I…truer words, huh?" Rowan shook her head. "She didn't think so."

Laine squeezed her hand. "I do."

Rowan nodded, and her eyes spilled over; she tasted salt on her lips. "But, Laine, it's worse than that. What he said to you… I think he knows. He knows I have him."

Laine paled in the gray air. "But that was all he said to me, Rowan. He never asked where you were."

"Then maybe he just thinks he knows," Rowan said, clutching Laine's fingers tight. "Maybe he was trying to see if you'd react."

"I didn't tell him anything," Laine went on in a rush.

"Is that the only time he asked about me?"

"He's mentioned you a few times, but nothing weird. He told me he helped you with the shutters, and he said you always said hello."

"Okay," Rowan said, pulling a breath. "God, I hate that you're going back there."

"I'm glad I'm going back there," Laine said. "Now I can watch him for you."

"No!"

"Why not? I'm right there."

"Laine, I swear to God, do not put yourself in any kind of danger for me. If he—"

"Who?"

Rowan jumped, and so did Laine; her coffee sloshed onto both their laps. Gabriel was standing on the porch, not five feet away. He was sleepy and tousled, but there was fear in his eyes. "What are you talking about?"

Rowan glanced at Laine. "I told her," Rowan said quietly. "Everything."

"Hey, neighbor," Laine said, trying to smile.

Gabriel knitted his eyebrows together. "Hey."

Laine shook her head. "I am so sorry," she whispered. "I'm sorry

I didn't know. I'm sorry I didn't see you. If I had, I would have helped you." She reached over and took his hand. "But I'm going to help you now, okay? I'm going to do everything I can to make sure he doesn't find you."

"What if he tries to hurt you?"

"Impossible. When I was a kid, we used to get bears in our backyard. Mean ones—Rowan can tell you. If I can scare off a bear, I can deal with your dad."

"You swear?"

"I swear. I'll do whatever it takes. I'm so sorry that happened to you." Her voice broke, her eyes bright with tears. "Is it okay if I give you a hug?"

Gabriel nodded and sat next to her, wrapping his arms tight around her neck. They stayed that way for a long time, and Rowan could tell they believed each other, believed that Lee was just a bear they could scare away, that all this would be fine.

Rowan turned so they couldn't see her face, the fresh fear that had taken over the gratitude in her heart.

CHAPTER THIRTEEN

THAT SPRING, AND THAT SUMMER, LEE WAS EVERYWHERE.

He'd arrived with Laine, but he didn't leave with her. He stayed behind, woven into the air in the house, hovering in the corners and flashing to life when Rowan least expected it. He was behind the steering wheel of every white van that passed them on the street. He was the broad back in front of them at the grocery store, the unfamiliar number lighting up her phone. Nighttime surrounded the house with deep hulking shadows, and Rowan could see the shape of him inside every single one.

It was a terrible thing to shift back to fear—to wonder again who might be watching. She'd barely shed Ethan's specter, and Lee's was far worse. Especially since Gabriel could see him too.

He was left wide-eyed and bewildered in Laine's wake. Even that small glimpse of his father was too much to handle. He began having nightmares again almost as soon as she left. Rowan tried to allay his fears like she always did, but something had shifted, and suddenly, she wasn't enough anymore. Maybe it was because he was older now, or maybe it was just harder to lie when he knew what was possible. He woke up crying some nights, begging her to tell him his father wouldn't be able to see him in Laine's eyes.

She wanted to—she tried—but she couldn't. He didn't believe her the way he used to. She could see more than a lingering question in his eyes, and Rowan wasn't entirely sure it was only about his father. For the first time in a year, it seemed like something about Rowan herself had him wondering.

Her concern over Laine's safety, at least, dimmed a little. Not much, but a little. Part of that was Laine herself—she'd returned home angry, not afraid, fueled by white-hot fury that drove her to track every single move Lee made. In May he added another foot of bricks to the wall around his house, and then he disappeared for nine days. When she heard that, Rowan called a home security company and had the house locked down so tight, even Celia couldn't get in without tripping the alarm. A few weeks later, he invited fifteen people over for a barbecue and refused to answer the door when they arrived. The next morning, he knocked on Laine's door with a sack full of corn on the cob and asked if Rowan was planning another visit that summer.

Rowan then gifted Laine with a security system of her own.

But while Lee's behavior was strange, it wasn't particularly threatening. He didn't seek Laine out; he was neither more nor less interested in talking to her, and he was friendly as usual when he did. Sometimes he mentioned Rowan; sometimes he didn't. Rowan almost thought he knew she was listening, acting just weird enough to be newsworthy, still probing Laine for clues.

She could only pray Laine didn't accidentally give him any.

Since she couldn't completely banish Gabriel's fears or her own, Rowan sought distractions. She signed him up for diving instruction, art classes, metalworking, self-defense—filling their days with so much activity, there was no room to worry. At first, she wasn't sure how Gabriel would adapt to a life outside the house—a routine, a taste of normal—but the minute she handed him the reins, he took them. He embraced every opportunity, he never missed a class, and in the time between, he read voraciously. As soon as he got a taste of the world, he began to crave it like food, like air—no matter how much he took in, it was never enough.

"So what," Celia asked Rowan one day, arms folded across her chest, "are you waiting for?"

It was August. Everything was half dead from the heat, parched and dried out under the bleached-white sky. Rowan and Celia were a good three months into this particular fight. "I told you," Rowan said. She dusted paprika over a plate of deviled eggs—tiny white cups brimming with cholesterol. "He's not ready."

"You've been shuttling him around to classes all summer. School will be no different."

"It's very different."

"Rowan, he *wants* to learn—"

"Don't you think I've talked to him about this? He's afraid, Celia. A real school, all those kids—it's too much for him right now."

"The longer you put it off, the harder it's going to be."

Rowan pulled a block of cheese from the refrigerator and sighed. "That's for me to worry about, Celia. Not you."

"But you're *not* worried. At least you're not worried enough, and in the meantime, he's falling way behind. I'm not just talking about academics. He needs to be around other kids. Socialization is crucial at his age."

"Funny," Rowan said, "you never mentioned your degree in adolescent psychology."

"Don't get defensive. I care about Gabriel too. School would be good for him."

"Yeah, well, it's not up to you," Rowan said, grating furiously.

"I don't think it's up to you either," Celia said.

"No, it *is* up to me. I've barely gotten him to the point where he's not a nervous wreck. I'm trying to keep tabs on his father, my nerves are shot—"

"That's because you need help with him."

"I don't need help with him! And I really don't need a bunch of teachers and parents wondering why I'm twenty-three years old with a teenager."

"The older you get, the older he gets. That's not going to change."

"I can homeschool him just as easily, Celia. He doesn't need to go."

"I'm just saying it would be nice if you let him out of this little bubble. Let him make friends, make some for yourself. You could be dating again if you tried."

Rowan laughed without humor. "Yeah, that's a pool I'm itching to jump back into. I'm sure there are hordes of guys just lining up to be with someone who looks tiger-mauled, but I'm really not looking to complicate things any further."

"So don't. But don't hold him back. Kids grow up to resent their parents for far less."

"You have such a vast knowledge of kids lately. I'm really... I'm flummoxed is what I am."

Celia took the cheese away from Rowan. "You're going to lose a finger. Stop being so threatened and get him enrolled. It would be good for both of you."

Rowan held out her hand. "Give me my cheddar."

"Will you think about it?"

"Fine. But I'm not going to force him if he's not ready. Gabe's not like other kids. I understand him."

Celia handed her the block of cheese and sighed. "Let someone else try."

Gabriel threw himself back on the bed and pulled his pillow over his head. This was all Celia's fault. She kept coming over and dropping little hints, making comments about how he should know how to do math and have at least one friend by now. Most of the time, Rowan seemed just as annoyed as he was. He never, not in a million years, expected her to turn on him.

She did.

Rowan tugged at the pillow, but he wouldn't let go; his voice was muffled in cotton and memory foam. "I don't want to."

"Just listen," Rowan said, yanking it free. She'd cornered him before bed, launching her attack seconds before he turned out his light; she was a master at making major announcements when he was in the middle of eating dinner or half asleep. "It won't be like real school."

"Then what it is?"

"You'll have a private teacher," she said. "And another kid your age will come over to help you."

"That's school!"

"No it's not! You won't have to go anywhere; the teacher will come to you. One-on-one. I met with her today, and she's great. She has a lot of experience with kids who are behind."

"Thanks a lot."

"She works with *gifted* kids, Gabriel. She'll figure out what you need to work on so you can get caught up. You won't have to do the usual curriculum. She'll focus on your strengths."

"What if I don't have any?"

"Please," Rowan told him. "You're smart as a whip, and you know it. I hate to agree with Celia, but she's right—you've got to go back to school sometime. This is a happy medium, okay?" she said. "A compromise."

Gabriel was quiet for a moment. "What other kid?" he asked.

"What?"

"You said there'll be another kid."

"She'll assign you a partner—someone to study with and stuff. No big deal."

He dropped his arms over his face. "I don't want to."

The bed lifted as Rowan got to her feet. "Okay."

"Okay?"

"Sure. You don't have to want to. Your teacher's name is Melanie," she said. "Mel. She's coming to meet you tomorrow."

"So that's it?" he asked. "It doesn't matter what I say?"

Rowan kissed him on the forehead and smiled. It was her old smile, the one she used to use when she was fighting with Celia, not agreeing with her. "Nope."

———

Rowan didn't know if it was genuine approval or a reward for obedi-ence, but at some point after Gabriel started school, Celia began coming over regularly, and not just to fight. That autumn she popped in a few times a week, bringing pots of flowers to decorate the porch or a book she thought Gabriel might like. There were three people to celebrate his birthday that year, and they ushered in the holidays together, wrapping presents under the Christmas tree and affixing bright red bows to wreaths made from pine boughs and twists of green wire. Celia hung a framed photograph of Rowan and Gabriel in her living room, and she took care of them for a week when they both came down with the flu in January.

It was a strange turn, unexpected and sweet. Celia's disapproval was usually like a chord that vibrated whenever they were all in a room together, but all at once, that string seemed to have been cut. At times, Rowan thought she looked almost proud.

Since Celia was making an effort, Rowan and Gabriel did too. Her birthday was on Valentine's Day, and they spent a week planning her presents, and decorating, and making the perfect dinner: three courses of her favorite foods and a strawberry-lemon cake covered in pink roses.

Rowan didn't expect a gift of her own that night, but she got one. It came when Celia arrived and Gabriel ran over and hugged her like it was nothing—like she was his real aunt, his own family.

It was the first time Rowan realized how much she wanted that.

The feeling only grew as they ate dinner and talked and laughed—a rising, delicious anticipation that things might just be getting better. That maybe the worst of their worries had passed.

There was no inkling that night. No spark of clairvoyance or even a clue that it was the last time the three of them would be together that way. They were happy. There was so much to look forward to. Winter was winding down, and a bright spring waited just around the corner.

A lot of things waited around that corner.

CHAPTER FOURTEEN

It had been almost two years, and Rowan still couldn't get over the landscape of Oklahoma, the infinite expanse of space. If she stayed very quiet and very still, she thought she could almost make out the curve of the earth beyond the endless flat.

At the moment they were lost, but it didn't really matter. It was Gabriel's first spring break, and Rowan had bought opera tickets on a whim—an admittedly odd choice, but the only thing she could find at the last minute. After his fit of histrionics over the involuntary immersion in culture, she dragged Gabriel to Oklahoma City for a long weekend.

Despite his initial protests, Gabriel seemed to enjoy the performance, or at least he stayed awake for the entire thing, which was more than Rowan could say for herself. Before they left to go home the next morning, they trawled the hotel gift shop and bought Celia the tackiest souvenirs they could find.

But now, after half an hour without a marked road, Rowan was beginning to regret risking an improvised detour through the barren flat that was Oklahoma. She also regretted bringing Gabriel on this trip at all.

"Let me drive," he pleaded for the millionth time.

"No."

"Come on…"

"*No*. Get your feet off the dashboard."

"There's no one out here, so why not?"

"Because I'm not looking to go to jail today. Or the hospital."

Gabriel gazed up at her, blue eyes wide and mournful, pouting a little. This was a fairly recent tactic, one he'd adopted after puberty kicked in and he became cognizant of his appearance. "Please?"

Rowan burst out laughing. "Save it, buddy. I don't care how pretty you are, that's not gonna work on me."

He threw himself back in his seat. "Come on, please? Please, please, please?"

"You know, I really hope this is a temporary hormonal thing," she said, waving her hand vaguely around him. "You have been so whiny lately."

He stared out the window. "I hate you."

"Love you too."

He waited almost a full minute before speaking again. "Five miles."

"Five miles?" she repeated. "Do you have any idea how long that is?"

"Three."

"One."

He did a double take. "What?"

"I will let you drive one mile. But only if you promise, and I mean *promise*—in blood, with your firstborn as collateral—to be very careful and stop bugging the shit out of me."

Gabriel's face exploded into a grin. He threw his arms around Rowan's neck and kissed her cheek as she pulled the truck to the shoulder. "If you see a single vehicle or another human being, I want you to pull over immediately. Do you understand?"

"Yeah, yeah… Do you have any advice?"

"Don't hit anything."

He maneuvered the truck back onto the road and set off at a good clip—apparently all his backyard practice had been worth something. "How am I doing?"

"Fine. Don't talk."

He shook his head. "You are so paranoid. You used to be a lot more fun."

"So did you."

They were about a tenth of a mile from ending their little stunt free and clear when they passed a small smattering of roadside debris. Gabriel managed to steer the truck around the worst of it, but when he swerved out of the way, both right-hand tires rolled over a chunk of metal near the shoulder. It wasn't very big, but when it went under the wheels, the truck lurched in a way that made Rowan's blood run cold. She was still annoyed that he'd called her paranoid, so she didn't comment, but a moment later, Gabriel did. "Rowan?"

"What?"

"A light went on."

She leaned over to peer at the dashboard. "Oh shit…"

"What is it?"

"The tires! Pull over, quick!"

He hit the brakes, jerking the wheel so hard, the truck hopped the shoulder and rolled onto the soft mud of the surrounding field. The wheels skidded in the muck, and by the time they came to a standstill, the truck was perpendicular to the road. Rowan jumped out and ran her hand over one of the tires. A steady hissing whined in her ears, and they stood there, helplessly watching the truck sink deeper into the mud. Within a minute, both right tires were as flat as the horizon.

Gabriel spoke first, and unfortunately, he chose the wrong question. "Do you have a spare?"

Rowan clenched her fists, forcing herself to speak civilly. "Yes," she said. "I have one."

Gabriel took a step back. "Are you mad at me?"

"No, no," Rowan said, holding up her hand. "I'm not mad at you. I'm mad at me. This is my fault." She reached for her phone.

"Who are you calling?"

"Celia, I hope." She tried three times in a row, but the call wouldn't connect—she got nothing but dead air. Gabriel's phone was no better. She wandered a hundred yards down the road in each direction without finding a single bar. Gabriel had dropped the hatch, and she climbed up next to him on the flatbed. "So," she said.

"So?"

"We're stuck."

Gabriel nodded.

"I don't know where we are."

He shook his head.

"We need to find someone to help us."

"There's no one here."

"Yes, that is the problem." Rowan jumped down and began walking across the stretch of grass that separated the northbound road from the south. "I swear, I am not mad at you, but I think it would be best if I sit on the other side of the road for a while. Stay in the truck. If you see someone coming, honk the horn, and I'll come back, okay?"

"Okay."

Across the field, both the asphalt and the metal guardrail were hot enough to take the skin off her legs, forcing her to pace up and down the blacktop. Beyond the guardrail there was a steep ditch, a shocking notch in the scenery that led to a pile of boulders that had probably been there for a million years. It had rained earlier, and the incline was a sheet of mud, slick as an oil spill.

Rowan had plenty of time to contemplate the landscape because she was there for almost an hour before a lumbering station wagon rolled down the northbound side of the road. The driver's reception was no better than hers, but he agreed to call her a tow truck in the next town over.

The mud began to bake as Rowan reclaimed her position behind the wheel. Gabriel retired to the back of the truck and lay there, staring at nothing.

Two hours later they were still waiting.

Rowan had given up on the radio. Every twist of the dial brought either static or evangelical preachers. At one point the squeal of the Emergency Broadcast System blasted through the speakers, but all that followed was more static.

Gabriel was quiet, still lying in the flatbed and probably asleep. She didn't bother to check. Everything was quiet. The silence carried its own presence, like something you could reach out and grab. The sky had clouded, and flashes of lightning cut through the greenish-gray underbelly. No stranger to Oklahoma thunderstorms, Rowan was about to call Gabriel back into the truck when she noticed him standing motionless beside her open door.

He lifted his hand and tugged rhythmically at her sleeve. Tug, tug, tug. "Rowan…"

"Get in. It's going to pour."

"Rowan…"

"This tow truck better get here soon. If we keep the air on much longer, I'm going to run out of gas."

"*Rowan!*"

"What?"

Gabriel pointed behind her with a hand that visibly shook. "What is that?"

"What's what?" she muttered, twisting in her seat. When she saw what he was pointing at, she fell the rest of the way, landing ass down in the drying mud. Gabriel didn't notice.

She stood and walked to the rear of the truck. "Maybe it's a fire."

"I don't think so. It's bigger now."

"It's *bigger*? When did you notice it?"

"Just a minute ago, but—oh God, Rowan, I think it's a tornado."

"It can't be!"

"Of course it can—we're in the middle of Oklahoma!"

Rowan took two steps. "It looks far away. Maybe it won't come over here."

Gabriel looked like he was going to pass out. "We're going to die today," he said faintly.

Rowan jumped into the truck and turned the radio back on.

Gabriel followed, practically climbing into her lap. She tore through the dial until a broken voice filled the cab.

"Tornado warning...Carter...Garvin and Murray counties..."

"I think we're near Ardmore," Rowan said.

"That's Carter."

"Fuck."

"Traveling east, southeast...Lone Grove...Ardmore..."

Gabriel's arms gripped her neck.

"This is a deadly storm. Seek underground shelter immediately."

"Fuck!" Rowan screamed. "What do we do?"

"I don't know!" Gabriel shrieked. "I think we're supposed to lie on the ground."

"We're not lying down in front of that!"

"We can't stay in the truck!"

"Let's look at it again."

"No—"

She ignored him. The funnel was massive. Nothing like the graceful ropes she sometimes saw dancing across flat fields in the summertime. This one looked like a lead pipe hanging from the sky, a churning maelstrom unleashed from a nightmare. Eerie flashes of light colored the underbelly as power lines were snapped from their bearings. Gabriel grabbed her arm.

"Rowan..."

"Shh." She stared at the funnel, willing it to shift to the right or the left.

"It's not moving," Gabriel said.

"Yes it is." She could hear it now, a steady rumble like thunder that never stopped rolling. "It's coming right at us."

"Rowan, we have to get out of here."

"Get in the truck."

"We can't—"

"*Get in the truck!*" She grabbed Gabriel and shoved him across the seat as she jumped behind the wheel and floored the gas pedal. The tires screamed in protest, the flaccid rubber spinning uselessly in the mud. Rowan slammed her hands against the wheel, and the horn blared. "We have to stay here."

"We'll be killed!"

"There's nowhere to go!"

Their hands tangled together in knots; Gabriel managed to get his door open, but the wind slammed it shut, and Rowan threw her legs over his to stop him from jumping out. They were still struggling, trapped in the desperate grip of tug-of-war, when something hit the rear window like a blast from a cannon. The truck lurched forward as the window exploded, showering them with shiny pebbles. Gabriel shoved his door open with his foot and jumped out, dragging Rowan across the seat with him.

They crouched in front of the truck, barely buffering themselves from the hot, whistling air. "There's a ditch across the field!" Rowan yelled.

"We won't make it!"

"Yes we will, just run!"

She didn't wait for him to argue. She grabbed his hand, and they burst into a sprint toward the northbound road. Rowan tried to hold on to him as they took off, but when the hail began to pound, they needed both arms to protect their heads. Visibility dropped to almost zero by the time she made it to the other side of the field, and she had so much momentum, she cleared the guardrail like it was a crack in the sidewalk. She dropped hard, landing on her hip at the edge of the incline. A roaring whine resonated in her ears as the tornado bore down a quarter of a mile away.

She didn't see Gabriel anywhere.

The wind was vicious, sending blinding grit and rain into her eyes, stealing what little vision she had. She screamed into the void, but her voice was swallowed by the storm. *"Gabriel!"*

One second later he hit her like a freight train, and they tumbled head over heels, flying with tremendous speed toward the rocks below.

Gabriel reached the bottom first, slamming his shoulder painfully into a chunk of rock jutting out of the mud. Rowan came to rest next to him after a wild, spinning descent. "Get between the rocks!" she screamed, scrambling to her feet.

He crawled on his hands and knees, wading through the muck until he was between the boulders. There was a long crack in one of the stones—like a giant shovel cutting into the earth. Rowan was still running toward him, her arms outstretched. She was maybe three feet away when her foot went into the water and didn't come out—after that, everything seemed to happen in slow motion.

The mud devoured her foot to the ankle, and she fell. Gabriel reached for her, but he wasn't quick enough to stop her head from striking the boulder with an audible crack. She rolled sideways off the rock, her eyes wide open.

"*Rowan!*" Blood gushed from her head, pouring down her face in bright red streams. Gabriel grabbed her by the arms and dragged her behind the rocks. "Rowan?" he asked, wiping blood from her eyes.

She nodded, still conscious but stunned. She pushed him toward the narrow split in the rock. "Get in there and lie flat."

"No! We won't both fit! You get in. I can cover you better!"

"Please, Gabe!" Rowan pushed him into the crack and stretched herself over him, protecting him from the worst of the wind. Gabriel was wedged tightly between the rocks, but there was absolutely nothing to cover Rowan or anchor her to the ground. He looped his arms around her and tried to hold her head, gripping her as hard as he could as he said the last words she'd be able to hear. "We're going to die."

"No," she said, her voice steely in his ear. "Not you."

Her arms came around him, and blood dripped onto his face. Every raindrop felt like a bullet, and he knew he had seconds, maybe not even that. Gabriel pulled her head closer until he could press his mouth to her ear, saying the same words over and over, even though he knew she couldn't hear him because he couldn't hear himself. He said them anyway, screaming what should have been his last words to her. His throat ached as he begged her to hear. *"I love you, I love you, I love you…"*

But even though he begged and even though he screamed, it wasn't enough. Her arms went lax around him, and her body wilted until she was heavy and still. He pulled her face against his shoulder; her breath was hot on his skin—hotter than the biting wind that pulled the air from his lungs, stealing his voice.

A moment later, everything was still.

CHAPTER FIFTEEN

GABRIEL TILTED HIS HEAD BACK, BARING HIS FACE TO THE ENDLESS blue sky. He was home, finally, stretched out on the dock with his feet in the water. It was a nice day, very bright and very sunny, but he was cold—probably from swimming too long. His hair was wet, and the water dripped against his face and rolled down his cheeks, like tears.

It had been an awful weekend.

"Gabe!" Rowan's voice reached him from the other end of the dock. "I'm coming in!"

He smiled a little and closed his eyes. "You can't swim!" he called back.

"Come in with me!"

"No," he mumbled, even though she was too far away to hear. "I'm cold."

"I'm not waiting for you," she shouted. "I'm going to jump!"

"No." There was another reason she shouldn't be swimming, but it took a minute for his brain to pick it out. "Wait, Rowan, you can't jump! You hit your head!"

"My head's fine. Are you ready?"

"No!" he shouted, scrambling to stand. But he wasn't quick enough. Her feet were already slapping the boards, and she was running way too fast to catch. She flew past him and leaped into the air, making an arc high above the water before she landed with a splash. Gabriel was drenched in the spray, ice-cold drops covering him from head to toe and making him shiver even more. "Rowan!"

She must have been kicking. Water kept splashing Gabriel in the face. It was in his eyes; he couldn't see. "Gabe, hurry!" she shrieked.

"I can't see you!"

"Jump in, I'm right here!"

"I can't—"

"Jump!"

He had no choice. He always followed Rowan. He closed his eyes and jumped.

The water swallowed him whole, and then he was sinking, lower and lower, his chest painful and tight. He kicked upward as hard as he could, groping for the surface. Somewhere in the distance, someone was calling…

"Over here!"

The water went still and smooth above his head. It didn't want to let him out. At the surface, he was already forgotten.

"I got both of them!"

He could see the sky, but no matter how hard he kicked, he couldn't reach it, couldn't find the air. His chest got tighter and tighter and tighter.

"Get his head up. He can't—"

He opened his mouth to scream.

———

"Breathe!"

Gabriel's eyes flew open, and he gasped, staring up at the steely gray sky. The clouds were spitting rain, icy bullets that pounded against his face. The breath he'd pulled wheezed out of his chest.

Rain pooled around his face and flooded his ears. Someone was holding his head up at a painful angle, and there was a heaviness in his chest, a deep, crushing ache. A disembodied voice reached him, but it was like hearing underwater. "It's okay, buddy. I got you. Move faster, guys. It's rising a lot faster."

Booted feet splashed around his head. There were faceless people everywhere he looked, and they were grabbing at him with too many hands to count.

"One, two, *three!*"

He heard a sickening squelching sound, and the weight suddenly lifted. He tried to roll over, to stand, but his body wasn't working, and the ground had disappeared. He looked around, frantically searching for Rowan. She was in the water, she couldn't swim, she needed him, she…

She was lying next to him, half buried in the thin brown muck. One of her eyes was swollen shut. The other lay half-open, a tiny white crescent moon peeking from the underside.

Blood trickled from her head. It made a heart around her face.

"Get him out of there, Dixon!"

Suddenly, the ground grew firm, and Gabriel was hoisted up and out of the water on some kind of plastic board. The hands were back, and they were moving him, whisking him away from Rowan. He tried to tell them to stop, but his mouth wasn't working either; his lips wouldn't make the words. All he could do was scream.

"Calm down, buddy, you're okay." The guy, Dixon, was bright red and panting as he ran through the water and muck, pressing a wad of gauze against Gabriel's forehead at the same time. "I need you to talk to me. Can you tell me your name?"

"I…I…"

The guy pressed harder on his head. "Take a deep breath. Let it out, nice and slow. You're okay."

His chest heaved, and his mouth opened and closed, forming the shape without saying the word. "G-G…*Gabriel*."

"Gabriel, my name is Dell Dixon, and I want you to look at me, okay? Just keep your eyes on mine."

"Ro…" he gasped. "Rowan."

"We're getting her out, buddy. We've got the whole team on it. Is she your sister?"

"Nnn…nnn…" He was so cold, his teeth chattered. His entire body was racked with tremors, and that made it even harder to talk. The cold and the tightness were the only things he could feel. When he tried to move his hand, it hummed like he was plugged into an electrical outlet. He looked down, and his face went colder. His arm, between his wrist and his elbow, had been snapped perfectly in half. A jagged piece of white bone poked through his skin.

Dell tilted Gabriel's chin up. "Eyes on me, okay? You're gonna be fine, I promise."

Another blue uniform arrived with a handful of bags wrapped in plastic. Strips of gauze were wound around Gabriel's head, and Dell finally stopped pushing on him. Everyone else was around Rowan. He couldn't see her; he couldn't see anything.

"No breath sounds."

"Pulse is almost nil!"

"Start compressions."

"Rowan!" he screamed.

"Gabriel."

Gabriel dragged his eyes upward. All he could see was Dell.

"Look at me."

Gabriel's heart was beating out of his chest; he was panting so hard, he could barely speak. "Rowan…"

"She's—"

"Help her!" Gabriel screamed.

"We are helping her. She's okay."

"I want to see…"

"Not yet, bud. They're fixing her up."

"Please!" he begged, his voice barely a wheeze. "Let me see her!"

"Keep talking to me, okay? How old are you?"

"Thir—thirteen."

"How about Rowan, how old is she?"

"Twenty…three…"

"Are you guys related?"

"No, I'm—no. Call Celia…she'll come…" The crowd around Rowan swarmed now, running with boards and bags, and someone was counting.

"They're taking care of her. Don't worry."

"She's dying!" Gabriel screamed. He thrashed against the board, tears spilling down his cheeks. "Please let me see her, please!"

"If you want us to help her, you gotta calm down."

"She can't die! Please don't let her die, please! Let me see her!"

"If you don't calm down, I can't do anything," Dell said, kneeling next to him. "But if you stop yelling and sit tight for one minute, I'll tell them to bring her by on the way to the ambulance. Okay?"

"Look at me and say that." Gabriel wheezed. "Look at me and promise."

Dell looked him straight in the eye. "I promise."

Then Dell walked off and started talking to one of the other paramedics. Gabriel couldn't hear what they said, but they switched places, and now a woman walked toward him. She was sweating, breathing almost as fast as he was. She pressed two fingers to Gabriel's neck.

"Ro—Ro…"

"Shhh, it's okay, sweetie. Dixon said you're working way too hard over here, so let's get you calmed down, okay?"

"No! He said I could see her. He said…"

"Just relax."

There was a quick flash of silver and a pinch, and a minute later, the world went soft around the edges.

He tried to protest, to talk, but his mouth had filled with syrup. "Ro…Rrr…?"

"Give it one minute," the woman said, her voice quieter now. "Just relax. In one minute you won't feel a thing."

It didn't even take a minute. He could still feel her name in his mouth when his eyes slid closed, and just before they did, he caught sight of Dell, still standing over Rowan. Watching him.

———

When Gabriel opened his eyes again, the people and the water and the sky were gone. He was in some kind of room, lying on a bed. It was noisy. He could hear people yelling and crying, and there were lots of beeps and hissing noises. He wished they would shut up. All he wanted to do was go back to sleep. He shouldn't have stayed in the pond for so long.

He was about to drop off again when the curtains rustled, and someone stepped into the room quietly, like they didn't want to bother him. "Gabriel?"

It took a moment for her presence to register on his radar, but when it did, his entire body twitched. Celia was at his side in an instant. She kissed his cheek and took his hand. "Hi, sweetheart," she whispered.

It was one of the weirdest things she'd ever said to him. His reply was slow and thick. "Celia. W-where's Rowan?"

"Shh. She's here."

"There was a tornado. And I tried to hold on to her, but the wind was so bad. I remember ev-everything. These guys came—Ceil, if you see that one guy, can you hit him for me? He m-made me go to sleep."

"Let's hold off on hitting anyone. Those guys saved your lives," Celia said. She smiled, but her eyes were flooded with tears, and when they escaped down her cheeks, she didn't seem to notice. "Just relax," she said, stroking his forehead. "The doctors are going to take you upstairs and fix you up."

"Where's Rowan?"

"She's already up there; she got to go first."

He smiled faintly. "Figures." Celia laughed out loud and then bit her lip. He didn't miss her expression. "Celia?"

She shook her head. "You're going to be fine, okay? Both of you."

He nodded, but his voice was choked. "Will you wait for me?"

"Absolutely."

"And Rowan?"

"I'll probably see her before you're even done."

"Tell her I'm sorry. It was my fault." His breath hitched and something beeped.

"Shh, it wasn't your fault."

"I wanted to drive. I kept—"

"Then there's no helping you," she said, smiling again. "Rowan will probably kill you as soon as you wake up."

The curtain swished aside, revealing a giant of a male nurse, dark-skinned with a wide friendly smile. "Gabriel? My name's Sherman, and I'll be escorting you to the penthouse. You ready to take a ride upstairs?"

"Why?"

"You broke your arm," Celia said gently. "They need to fix it."

"Oh," he mumbled.

"Ready to roll?" Sherman asked.

"I guess so," Gabriel mumbled. "I'm tied to this bed."

Sherman laughed. "You're right about that, my man. This is a hostage situation." He turned to Celia. "If you grab a blue elevator to the fifth floor, there's a waiting area for relatives. Probably more comfortable."

"Thank you," she said. "I've got another one up there already."

"Tough day."

"It is." She kissed Gabriel again and swept her thumbs over the tears pooled beneath his eyes. "I'll see you soon."

Celia smiled at him as Sherman wheeled him away, but it didn't last very long. Just before the curtain closed, he saw her drop to her knees, right in the middle of the empty floor. She pressed both hands against the white tiles and cried.

———————

Gabriel's first moment of clarity was marked by a bunch of loud, high-pitched beeps. He cracked his eyes open and caught a glimpse of Celia's clear green gaze before everything went dark again. "Gabriel?"

"Don't rush him!" someone said sharply.

"I want him to know his family is here!" She touched his arm. "Gabriel?"

Even half-conscious, Gabriel thought it was weird to hear Celia call him her family. He tried to speak, but there was nothing to support the words; his throat felt lined with cotton. He opened his eyes.

The room was so stark white, he had to squint against the glare. Celia's eyes were wide; she looked like she hadn't slept in a year. Gabriel heard the squeak of rubber as footsteps retreated. He swallowed with difficulty. "Ceil?"

"I'm here, sweetie. Don't talk if it's too hard."

That was twice she'd called him that, which could only mean he was dying. A vague sense of self-awareness came over him as he tried to knit his thoughts together. "Am I okay?"

She smiled. "You will be. The operation went well. You woke up in recovery last night, but they gave you something so you would sleep."

Everything was so fuzzy, he couldn't focus, and he felt like there was something he should be focusing on. Celia's eyes were swimming with unshed tears, and as he watched them brighten from green to blue, he remembered who else had eyes that did that. "Where's Rowan? Is she here?"

Celia laid his hand across his chest and held it. "Yeah, Gabriel. She's here."

"Where?"

Celia's gaze drifted to the ceiling. "Gabriel," she said slowly. "I'm going to tell you because you deserve to know what's going on. The doctor doesn't agree with my telling you, but I think keeping you in the dark would be worse. Do you understand?"

Gabriel said nothing. He didn't want to understand. He didn't want to do anything except go back in time and convince Rowan that Oklahoma City was a terrible idea. No one likes opera anyway. He nodded.

Celia squeezed his hand. "Rowan was hurt worse than you were.

I don't know how much you remember, but something must have hit her in the head. It hit her so hard, her brain started to swell. The doctors operated on her to relieve the swelling, but they aren't sure if it worked."

Gabriel swallowed hard. "She hit her head on the boulder," he said, as if this were the piece they needed to fix her. "I saw it." He looked at Celia before the real question tumbled out. "Is she going to be okay?"

Celia squeezed his hand again. "The surgery went very well. They were able to reduce the pressure, and Rowan should have woken up when it was over, but she didn't. The doctors aren't really sure why. Sometimes, when you get hurt badly enough, your body shuts down so you can heal. They think that may be what's going on with Rowan."

"When will she wake up?"

"I don't know. She's only been out for about twelve hours. She's in the ICU, just one floor over your head, and as soon as you're a little bit stronger, you can go up and see her." She hesitated. "There's something else, though."

"What?" When Celia didn't answer, another wave of panic washed over him. "Please tell me."

"It's, um—she broke her leg." Celia stopped again to blow her nose. "The doctors aren't optimistic about it."

"What does that mean?"

Celia took a deep breath. "Her leg is almost past saving. The surgeon was a bit indelicate, but basically, he said he didn't want to risk her life for the sake of cosmetics."

"Cosmetics?"

"Yes. He doesn't believe she'll heal well enough to walk on it again. But if they remove it—"

"Celia, no!" Gabriel said, hating the whine in his voice. "Don't let them do that!"

"Honey, it's not up to me."

"But you know lots of doctors, you—"

"Gabriel," she cut in. "Listen to what I'm telling you. It's more than her leg. If she loses it, we can deal with that. We need to think about what happens if she doesn't wake up."

The words hit him like a slap. Worse than a slap. A speeding car. "What?" he whispered. "Can that happen?"

"Yes," Celia said gently. "It can. That's why it's so important for you to know and be strong for her. The doctors told me I should talk to her, try and give her a reason to come around. I told them if anyone's going to be able to reach her, it's you."

Gabriel shook his head. He felt tiny, insignificant, no bigger than a speck of dust. "What if I'm not enough?"

Celia cupped his face in her hands. "I think you are," she said. "I'm counting on it."

Gabriel wasn't allowed to see Rowan until after dinner, even though he didn't eat. Celia kept one hand on his shoulder as he was wheeled upstairs. When they got off the elevator, she knelt to face him. "You can only stay for about ten minutes. The rules are different up here."

"I don't know what to do."

"Just talk to her. Be positive, say good things. Don't pay attention to the tubes and machines. Just concentrate on Rowan, okay?"

Celia squeezed his shoulder, and he closed his eyes tight until the orderly wheeled him next to the bed and drew the curtain closed.

The light inside was fake and harsh. Bluish-white bars glowed behind dimpled plastic covers and made everything ugly. He looked at Rowan.

She seemed so small, like a little kid in a too-big bed. Her head was wrapped in layers and layers of white gauze, and there were tubes snaking out from underneath the bandages. One of the tubes was taped to her forehead, and it followed a path around her ear, ending somewhere at the back of her head. He ran his finger lightly over her swollen lips and felt a soft exhale of breath.

Her leg hung from wires attached to the ceiling, clamped inside circles of metal that made a halo around it. The metal circles were screwed directly into her leg. He didn't look at it long.

"Hi," he said, taking her hand. It was warmer than he'd expected. "It's me."

Whatever type of immediate response he'd been hoping for, he didn't get it. "I've, um, I've been thinking about you, Rowan, even though no one would let me see you," he began. "And I have lots to tell you. I don't really know how to say it all, but I'm going to try. Celia said you might be able to hear me, so if you do, don't make fun of me when you wake up, because this is hard. I know you'd be better at it than me."

He squeezed her hand and waited to see if she would squeeze back. She didn't. "So, first off, um, I guess I'll tell you that Celia's being really nice to me, and it's weird." He laughed, and his eyes spilled over. "I keep thinking, *I have to tell Rowan she said this or did that*, and then I remember, but this really threw her, I guess. She's good at it though. Being nice."

The cuff around Rowan's arm came to life, puffing and slowly releasing air. The numbers flashed red but meant nothing to Gabriel.

"I'm really sorry about everything," he continued. "I know I was being a pain, and if I'd listened to you, this might not have happened. So I'm sorry, and I love you, and if you wake up, you can yell at me all you want.

"That's what I was trying to tell you when we were under the rocks. I don't know if you heard me or not—kind of like now, but I still want to say it because it's true. I love you. I should have told you before."

Gabriel squeezed her hand again and felt something he shouldn't. He looked down and frowned. "Look at this," he said. "Somebody put your ring on the wrong hand." He tugged the ring off her left finger and transferred it to her right, nudging the band against the plaster encasing her wrist. "I guess they didn't know where it belonged."

He looked at the clock on the wall; the face was dull gray, the numbers oversize. "They'll probably make me leave in a minute, but I'll come back as soon as I can. Just please promise me you won't leave without—Well, don't go at all. Please."

He leaned over and kissed her cheek, resting his head next to hers on the pillow. He was still sitting like that when the orderly came to take him away.

CHAPTER SIXTEEN

THE DAYS RAN TOGETHER. ROWAN DIDN'T GET ANY BETTER, BUT
Gabriel got worse. His arm was on fire, and his whole body hurt like
he had the flu again. At first, the doctors told him that was normal,
but one morning he woke up with a fever so high, he was shivering, and his skin felt like it was inside out. Suddenly, everyone was
worried about him. Celia parked herself next to his bed, and doctors
and nurses marched in and out all day long, taking his blood and
pumping his IV full of different kinds of medicine. Nothing worked.
In the afternoon, some kind of specialist came and took his arm out
of the splint, carefully examining the broken skin and stitches. Two
hours later, Gabriel was wheeled back into the operating room.

He woke the next morning in a sweet milky haze. All the bad stuff
was gone—the pain, the fear, everything. He floated above it. He

still thought about Rowan, but they were good thoughts now. She'd visited him in his dreams and told him she was fine. He believed her. If he wanted to talk to her again, all he had to do was close his eyes.

His room was still busy, but he didn't really care who showed up to poke at him. Everything was soft and warm, and there was nothing, absolutely nothing, to worry about. A man brought him breakfast, and then another man came and asked him a bunch of questions. He said he was from the news. He had a bright light and a cameraman, and he talked about the tornado like it was a big adventure, something out of a movie.

He was shaking Gabriel's hand when Celia walked through the door.

"Hi, Celia," Gabriel said. "My arm doesn't hurt anymore."

Celia didn't look too worried about his arm. She looked mad. "What's going on?" she demanded. Her voice was high and harsh. "Who are you?"

The reporter turned to her with a wide smile. "Camdyn Boyle, *Channel 9 News*. Gabriel was just helping us with tonight's story."

"Story?" Celia repeated. "What are you talking about?"

"We received an incredible piece of footage this morning from a team of storm chasers. They were recording the tornado, and they caught Gabriel and Rowan running from it—"

"I know," Celia said tightly. "They told the paramedics where to find them."

"It's a good thing they were there. You can see Rowan and Gabriel climbing into the ditch. You can *see* the tornado pass over them. Extraordinary. We're airing it tonight, and we wanted to be sure to include an interview with him—"

"What?" Celia shrieked. "You *cannot* interview a minor child without consent!"

Gabriel winced. She sounded really mad. She was clutching a bakery box in both hands, and he was worried she was going to squash whatever was inside. Maybe she'd brought him doughnuts.

The reporter was still smiling. "Of course we can. Gabriel said he was happy to talk to us."

"Gabriel is thirteen years old and heavily medicated," Celia said. "You have no business barging in here, and you do *not* have permission to run that story!"

"Are you his mother?"

"No," Celia spat.

"Where is she?"

"Upstairs," Gabriel mumbled.

Celia turned and stared at him. She looked like she was about to cry or punch someone. "He's heavily medicated," she repeated, clearing her throat. "Anyone can see that. He's gone through two surgeries, and my sister is lying upstairs in a coma. This is not appropriate right now."

"I'm sorry to hear that, but for a story of this nature, we don't need permission. It's of human interest," he said with a small shrug.

"Listen to me," Celia said slowly. "Run the storm chasers' footage if you must, but do not run this interview. Don't mention his name, and don't mention my sister's name. I won't permit it."

"If you're not his mother, you don't have to permit it. I'm sorry, but that's the way it is. You can take it up with the station if you want."

"Oh, I will," Celia growled. "This is not human interest—it's exploitation. I want you out of here right now."

Celia practically shoved them out of the room. Gabriel could hear her in the hallway yelling at everyone. He hoped she wasn't going to yell at him. Her face was bright red when she came back in.

"Gabriel, that reporter," she said, "you talked to him?"

"Uh-huh."

"What did you say?"

"I told him how we hid from the storm. And that the rain almost drowned us. I told him Rowan takes care of me."

Celia put her face in her hands, and all of a sudden, everything didn't seem quite so perfect and puffy and pink.

Heat crept into his chest. "Did I do something wrong?"

Celia lifted her head. "No," she said quickly. "You didn't do anything wrong. They were wrong to try and talk to you, but it's not your fault." She smiled and settled in the chair next to him. "How are you feeling? Are you hungry?"

Gabriel managed to eat half a doughnut and take a few sips of juice. He tried to talk to Celia, but he kept falling asleep, so she said she was going upstairs to see Rowan.

He slept for a long time. When he woke up, it was dark, and Celia was back, sitting straight up in the chair next to his bed. She didn't notice him. The television was on; he could see lights from the screen moving and dancing in her eyes. She had two fingers pressed to her bottom lip.

"Celia?"

She jumped and jabbed at the remote control. All the light left her eyes.

———————

Three days later, the doctors let Gabriel go home. Only he didn't go home—he went to a hotel with Celia, and every passing moment drained a little bit more life out of him.

He'd hated being in the hospital, but at least he'd been close to Rowan. Now they were in a room that was ten floors up and ten minutes away, and that was way too far. Anything could happen in ten minutes, terrible things. He knew that now.

Celia kept trying to make him rest, but he was afraid to go to sleep. At night he stayed awake until his eyelids felt like sandpaper and closed of their own will. Laine called Celia every day to ask about Rowan, and Gabriel talked to her, too, even though he didn't have anything to say. Laine didn't say much either, but it was enough to know she was on the other side of the phone.

Two days after they got to the hotel, Celia was pleading with Gabriel to eat something and counting out his nighttime pills when her phone vibrated on the nightstand. It was late, almost ten o'clock, and Celia hesitated for a split second before snatching it up. Gabriel followed her into the bathroom, sticking his foot into the door so she couldn't close it.

"Hello?" Celia said quietly. "This is she." Celia listened for a moment, and Gabriel couldn't see her face, but her voice got higher and tighter. "Is she all right?"

"Celia?" Gabriel whispered.

"I'll be right there." Celia hung up and ran back into the bedroom, pushing right past Gabriel.

"What's going on?" he demanded.

"It was the hospital. I have to go."

"I'm coming too!"

"No, no, stay here. They didn't tell me anything and—Oh, shit, *shit!* Okay, you can come. Let's just go."

Celia and Gabriel ran out the door and ran to the car and ran every single red light on the way to the hospital. The elevator was empty, but the two of them huddled in the corner, gripping each other. Gabriel's entire body was shaking, and the elevator rang with a high-pitched keening noise that hurt his ears; after a minute he realized it was coming from him.

Rowan's doctor, Dr. Brimley, appeared as the doors slid open. "Celia?"

"Doctor." Celia choked. "Is she—What's going on?"

"Let's go—"

"No!" Gabriel screamed. "Just say it! Tell us!"

The doctor shook his head and smiled. "I promised Rowan she could tell you."

———

Moments after hearing the best news of his life, Gabriel was sent packing to a row of hard plastic chairs while Celia got to see Rowan first. He walked in circles, trying to concoct a speech that would express everything he felt, but there weren't enough words, and the alphabet didn't have enough letters to make new ones. Every emotion he'd held down was bubbling to life, and he felt far too small to stop them from exploding. He clawed at his hair so much, he had to find a bathroom to try and make himself presentable; when he came out, Celia was waiting for him.

"There you are. You can see her now," Celia said. She was smiling, giddy.

"How is she?"

"She's perfect. She's perfect! They have her on a lot of drugs, so she's a little bit out of it, but it's definitely Rowan." Celia smiled and gripped his hand. "She asked about you first thing. When I walked in, she said, 'Jesus, Celia, you couldn't let Gabe come in first?'"

He laughed and grabbed Celia in a fierce one-armed hug. She

pushed him toward the ICU. "I'm going to call Laine. Go ahead—
she's waiting for you."

Gabriel walked toward Rowan's cube in a daze. The white curtains
looked no different, but his hands shook as he pulled them aside.

Right away, he could see she wasn't perfect by any stretch of the
imagination, but just the fact she was awake and looking at him made
her seem that way. Her open eyes shocked him into silence.

"Gabe." Her voice was so hoarse, he could barely hear her, and it
brought a rush of tears he didn't even try to hold back. "Come here."

It was the longest walk of his life, and he took it too fast, stumbling
over his own feet until she reached up and pulled him into her arms.
He was trying to talk, trying to say all those important things, but
instead he broke down, sobbing without restraint into her shoulder.

Rowan said nothing. She just held him as tight as she could,
given the casts and tubes and awkward position. When his breathing slowed, she lifted his chin. "I didn't believe her," she whispered,
sweeping tears from his cheeks. "I didn't believe her when she said
you were all right."

"Who?"

She shook her head and hugged him again, even though moving
so much must have been hurting her. "Do you remember it?" she
whispered. "I don't remember it." He nodded against her neck, and
her voice hitched and cracked. "Were you scared?"

Gabriel nodded again, but he said nothing. There was no way to explain the battering wind lined with razor blades, the way it yanked them into the air like tissues in a breeze. He didn't want to tell her that he'd hoped to die if she did or what it was like to see her lying in the mud. He didn't want to remember the sound. That eerie, hellish roar that would never, ever leave him.

It didn't matter because he couldn't talk anyway. He was crying so hard, it hurt. He could barely catch a breath, but the heavier his chest felt, the more relief flooded his heart. "I was scared you wouldn't wake up." He choked. His voice rose, and he felt something he didn't expect. Anger. It was raw and hot. He'd never been more furious with anyone in his life. "You shouldn't have done it," he insisted. "You shouldn't have covered me like that. Why did you do it?"

Rowan's eyes weren't quite focused. She was looking at him like she was still waiting to hear the question he'd just asked. But then she smiled, patting his cheek with clumsy fingers. "Because you're more important."

"What?"

"I promised you'd always be more important."

"Promised who?"

Rowan's head fell back on her pillow. "Your mother," she said slowly. "When I took you. That night, in the hotel room, I said to her, 'Please don't worry about him. I'll keep him safe. I'll always, always put him first.'" Rowan squeezed his hand and closed her eyes. "Always."

They fell silent. There was a brand-new bouquet of flowers on her nightstand—creamy roses and round daisies in the palest pink.

Rowan opened her eyes and followed his gaze. "Thank you."

"For what?"

"The flowers," she murmured, stretching a little. "The nurse said you sent them."

"No," he said. "Celia probably did."

Rowan shrugged. "Somebody did. God, Gabe, you look terrible."

He laughed, a wild hiccuping sound. "Have you seen yourself?"

"No, but I can feel myself." She touched the stitches along his hairline. "The doctor said I almost lost my leg," she whispered.

"I know."

"I almost didn't wake up."

"I know." Gabriel took her hand. "Rowan, I'm so sorry."

"No."

"If I lost you—"

"You didn't," she murmured, lying back against the pillow. Her eyes slid closed again. "You won't. Ever." She pulled him down next to her. "Don't talk about it anymore. Don't even think about it. Just sit with me. That's all you have to do."

He gave in to all the pain and fatigue and fear he hadn't allowed himself to feel over the past ten days, more tired than he'd ever been in his life. She put her hand on his cheek, and he rested his head against her shoulder.

The flowers stared at him from the nightstand, but he barely saw them. They were only the second most beautiful thing in the room.

CHAPTER SEVENTEEN

ROWAN LAY FLAT ON HER BACK, PLASTIC BOW LOCKED AND LOADED. Spent ammunition littered the floor around the couch. She watched with thinly veiled disgust as Gabriel aimed his bow at the target Celia had grudgingly affixed to the ceiling. His suction-cup arrow missed the center by less than an inch. Even with three-quarters of his arm in plaster, his aim was flawless.

She swore under her breath as he made a tally mark on the score-card. "Use more spit," he suggested.

"I don't want to do this anymore," Rowan said, pitching her bow at him. The chime of the doorbell sounded in the foyer. "*Celia!*"

"I have ears, Rowan!"

"You can't quit now!" Gabriel said, tossing it back. "We said we'd play to five thousand."

"I can't shoot this thing left-handed."

"I'm doing it."

"You're left-handed! I give up. It's over—you win." She shot her last arrow to cement her surrender; it flew straight to the ceiling, struck the target dead center, and held.

They both stared at it. "You would have gotten a hundred for that," Gabriel said. "You want to watch TV?"

"No."

"Are you hungry?"

"We just ate."

He scooted under her leg. "Can I draw on your cast?"

"Later." She heard the front door open, and faint voices traveled down the hall. A headache was coming—they came often now—and she closed her eyes, waiting for the throb. "Why don't you go outside?"

"No. Why? Are you okay?"

"I'm fine."

It was a bold-faced lie, and Gabriel probably knew it. Every movement, every breath, every heartbeat brought one pain or another, and that was very hard to hide. Some were mild, but some had spikes, lurking quietly in her muscles and her bones, waiting for her to move the wrong way.

Rowan had almost no recollection of the tornado itself, nor could she remember much about her first days out of the coma—they rattled around like puzzle pieces in a box. Her first solid memory was of the flowers on her hospital tray: a blushing tumble of ivory roses nestled between pale pink daisies and swirling begonias. She wished she knew who to thank. There'd been no card.

For the second time in her life, she'd woken up in a new body, only this one didn't do what it was told. Her movements were wild and jerky. She could barely use a fork without taking out an eye. Rowan spent two weeks in the hospital, and then she was moved to a short-term inpatient facility for six weeks of rehab. When she was cleared for release, the doctor suggested a home aide, but Celia staunchly refused. Instead, she'd taken a month of family leave and reclaimed her old bedroom across the hall from Gabriel's.

Where Celia summoned her energy, Rowan could not even begin to guess. Rowan had been home for ten days, and Celia got up at the crack of dawn without fail—cooking, cleaning, and caring for Rowan's entire body like it was her own. She kept a running chart of every nap Rowan took, every meal, every headache. She doled out Rowan's pills, helped her get washed and dressed, and hauled her to the toilet at two in the morning without complaint. For the first time in her life, Rowan was grateful that Celia had dumped her back in foster care so she could become a nurse.

Gabriel had barely left her side since the moment she'd come home. He stayed within arm's reach, wide-eyed and slightly stunned, like he'd been handed a newborn baby.

"I mean it," she insisted, pushing his shoulder. "I'm fine. You don't have to sit here with me all day."

"I don't mind."

"I do," she said. "Go outside. Get some air."

He was just getting to his feet when Celia came tearing into the room, her face red and hectic. "Sit up, Rowan, quick. There's someone here to see you." Before Rowan could respond, Celia propped her up on a pillow, tugging at the hem of her cotton dress. "This is too short," she mumbled.

"Find me a pair of pants that'll fit over this cast, and I'll gladly put them on. Who's here? Everyone I know is in this room."

Celia smoothed the end of Rowan's ponytail. "One of the paramedics from the storm—the one who took care of you in the ambulance. His name is Dell."

"*What?*" Gabriel yelped.

"Oh my God, really?" From all accounts, he'd done a lot more than take care of her. Rowan had flatlined twice in the ambulance, and there wasn't a single doctor in that hospital who hadn't regaled her with tales of Dell the Paramedic and the stunning resurrections he'd performed. "*The* Dell, the one who held death at bay?"

"Yes, you may want to thank him for that."

"Why is he here?" Rowan asked, panicked as to why Celia was grooming her all of a sudden.

"He said he wants to meet you. Gabriel, move—go sit in the chair."

Rowan turned to Gabriel as Celia darted out of the room. "Do you remember this guy?"

Gabriel could barely sputter in response. "Why can't *he* sit in the chair?"

A new set of footsteps approached, and Celia returned with their visitor in tow. "Rowan, this is Dell, one of the paramedics who saved you after the storm." Rowan could feel Gabriel's eyes roll without even looking at him. "Dell, this is Rowan, and this is Gabriel."

Dell nodded. "Hello."

"Hi, Dell," Rowan said, smiling up at him. "I'm so happy to meet you."

"It's nice to meet you too."

"The doctors told me how much you did for me," she said. "I'm glad I can thank you in person."

"How did you know where we live?" Gabriel asked.

"Gabriel!" Celia said.

Dell's ears went a little pink. "Actually, he's right, this is kind of against the rules. I hope you don't mind me dropping in, but I—" Rowan didn't hear a word he said after that. Something moved above her head, and she watched helplessly as her hundred-point arrow chose that moment to dislodge. It fell from the ceiling, inches from Dell's nose, and he jumped, batting it away like it was a live insect. Gabriel let out a bark of laughter and slid closer to Rowan. Celia looked like it was taking all her willpower not to physically yank him off the couch.

"Dell, sit, please," Celia said. "I'll get everyone something to drink. Gabriel, come help me," she said pointedly.

Gabriel got the point a little too well. "I can't." He held up his cast. "My arm is broken."

Dell was still standing in the middle of the room, though now he looked like he wanted to run out of the house. He was young, maybe a few years older than Rowan, with sweet brown eyes and a drawl that definitely originated outside of Oklahoma. He was tall enough to dwarf Celia, but his awkward position in the center of the room made him look even younger and very, very nervous.

He was absolutely adorable.

Rowan bit back another smile, and Dell chose that moment to speak. "Rowan," he said. "I never met anyone with that name. Rowan, like the tree."

She blinked. "What?"

"There's a type of tree, a rowan tree. I only know because I took a semester of botany in college." He seemed to run out of steam there.

"I didn't know that," Rowan said, even though she did. "I've never met a Dell either. Dell like…"

"Like the farmer," Gabriel chirped. Rowan glared at him.

"You look great," Dell added, taking a seat in the chair Gabriel would not deign to occupy. "I wouldn't have recognized you."

Rowan laughed. "God, I hope not. The last time you saw me, I was dead."

Dell, to his credit, was unfazed. "Almost," he amended. "I wish I could have seen you in the hospital."

"I'm glad you didn't. My head wasn't working too well. I might have forgotten you."

Gabriel let out a gusty sigh. Rowan reached under her cast and poked him in the hip.

"You look good, too, Gabriel," Dell said. "I don't know if you remember me, but—"

"I remember you," Gabriel said flatly.

"He's a brave kid," Dell said, turning to Rowan. "I've seen grown men go into shock for less, but he fought us tooth and nail. Did he fill you in on what happened?"

Her leg tingled painfully; Gabriel had her practically sitting in his lap. "Yes," she said. "He told me we were hit by a tornado."

Dell's mouth opened, but nothing came out. Celia returned with a tray loaded with cold drinks and cookies. "Don't listen to her, Dell," Celia said, handing him a glass of iced tea. "Sarcasm is the only language she speaks."

Rowan smiled, pleased with her sister's description.

Dell smiled too. "Speaking of the tornado," he said, "we found something of yours that day, and I thought you might want it back."

Rowan looked up in surprise. "You did?"

"Yup. I left it outside. Want to join me on the porch?"

She grimaced inwardly and hoped it wouldn't show. Getting

hoisted in and out of the wheelchair was torture. Gabriel glanced sideways at her, and even Celia looked a little put out. "Let me get her wheelchair, Dell," Celia said. "She's not exactly easy to move."

"Mind if I give it a shot?" he asked.

Gabriel tightened his grip on Rowan's cast as Celia rolled the wheelchair in front of the couch. Dell leaned over and lifted Rowan from Gabriel's lap like she was made of feathers before settling her into the wheelchair in a single smooth motion. For the first time since leaving the hospital, the move was almost completely painless.

Celia clapped her hands. "Good job! That usually takes me at least five minutes, with no small amount of screaming. From both of us."

Gabriel looked very small sitting on the couch by himself. He looked at Rowan, and then he got up and walked out without a word. The front door slammed as Dell took hold of Rowan's chair.

Going over the threshold was bumpy, but Rowan barely noticed because there, parked in the driveway, was her truck, completely intact, with a brand-new rear window. "Oh my God!"

"The whole team chipped in to fix up the window," Dell said. "And we got you a new pair of tires."

"Oh God, Dell. You didn't have to do that."

"We wanted to."

Gabriel stood next to her, stock-still, staring at the truck with his mouth wide open. Rowan leaned over and smacked him on the hip. "I told you we should have stayed in the truck!"

Celia clapped. "Rowan, that's wonderful! You were just saying you wanted to get a new truck for your birthday."

Dell looked down at her. "It's your birthday?"

"Next week."

"Close enough." He tossed her silver key chain—a gift from Gabriel when he'd gone through his metalworks phase—into her lap. "Happy birthday."

———————

Two hours after Dell left, Celia was flitting around the house, practically bursting into song as she brought fresh-cut flowers from the garden and peeled mounds of vegetables. Gabriel sat quietly in the chair next to the couch. Rowan was reading a magazine, obviously occupying a different planet.

"Rowan?" he said.

"Hmm?"

"I don't think this is a good idea."

"Why not?"

"You're still in a lot of pain."

"I'll take something beforehand. Stop worrying about me and go outside."

"We don't even know this guy. Why does he have to come for dinner?"

"I don't know. Celia invited him."

Celia *had* invited him—out of nowhere and without consulting anyone else first. As a result, Gabriel had been forced to remove her from his list of allies. "You don't think this is a little weird?"

"He's nice. He was nice to both of us. Plus, he's really cute."

"He's *cute*?"

Rowan glanced at him. "What is wrong with you?"

"I just..."

"What?"

"I don't like him. I don't want him here."

"Ohhh, I get it," she said, putting the magazine down. "We're jealous there's going to be another man in the house."

Gabriel exploded. "He's not going to be *in* the house! He's just eating dinner, and then he'll leave, and we'll never see him again." He jumped up and grabbed a handful of his hair. "I'm leaving. I'm going. I need to go outside or something."

He ran through the kitchen, shooting daggers at Celia as he charged out the back door. He walked around the pond for an hour, kicking up dust until he heard the crunch of rocks in the driveway. Gabriel ducked behind the magnolia tree and watched as Dell climbed the front steps with a white box in his hand. He knocked on the door and stood there fixing his hair until Celia let him in.

Dell drove a truck too. It was old and beat-up, with blankets covering the seats. The tires were way too big for the cab, which was bright, screaming red, like something Satan would drive. Gabriel kicked the bumper on his way back inside.

Dell was sitting at the kitchen table, leaning his chair against the wall like he owned the place. Rowan sat next to him in the wheelchair, her eyes dancing in the pink light of early evening. She was wearing a blue dress printed with green tropical flowers. Her hair was braided down her back, the twisted strands shining red and gold.

Gabriel's stomach twisted. He stood there for a full minute, watching her laugh at some stupid story Dell was telling, before anyone noticed him, and even then, it was Celia. "Gabriel, can you set out the silverware?"

Rowan smiled at him. "Where've you been?"

"Outside. You told me to go out."

"You're right, you're right. I did. You don't have to get mad."

"I'm not mad," he mumbled, stomping out to the porch, where Celia had set the table like the queen was coming. The tablecloth and napkins were linen, and there was a big bunch of flowers in the middle. Gabriel dropped the silverware on the edge of the table in a clump and sat down. Dell eased Rowan's chair through the door.

She rolled herself next to Gabriel. Her eyes looked sleepy, but her smile was really, really big. Dell took a seat on the opposite side of the table.

"I'm afraid dinner isn't up to par with what Rowan would have put together," Celia said, sticking a pair of tongs into the salad. "She's much better in the kitchen than I am."

"I'm better in other rooms too." Rowan giggled. Celia looked traumatized. Gabriel turned to stare at Rowan.

"Are you okay?" he whispered.

"I'm *great*," she said, loud enough to make him jump.

"Did you take a painkiller?"

"No. I took two."

"So," Dell said as Celia passed him a platter of fried chicken. "Thank you. This is a beautiful house. How long have you lived here?"

"Two years," Rowan said, trying and failing to butter a roll. "This was our parents' house, mine and Celia's. We moved here from Massachusetts."

Dell paused, holding the salad tongs aloft. "All of you?"

"Just Gabe and me. Celia and I used to live in Virginia, but then she moved down here. I grew up in New Hampshire. Just me, not them," Rowan clarified, waving her butter knife.

"And now you live here together?"

"No," she said. The roll slipped from her fingers and tumbled to the ground. "Just Gabe and me."

"And how are you two related?"

"We're not."

The expression on Dell's face might have been funny if not for the free and easy way Rowan was volunteering information. Gabriel looked up and saw Celia frowning at him, jerking her head toward the basket of dinner rolls. Gabriel grabbed one, buttered it as well as he could, and pushed it into Rowan's hand. "Eat this," he said quietly.

"So you and Celia lived in Virginia, and then she moved down here, and you moved to Massachusetts?"

"Yup. Then Gabe and I moved down here together. It's all…it's just so complicated, Dell."

"Rowan, have some iced tea," Celia said, filling a glass and passing it to Gabriel. Dell was looking at him too. Rowan took a clumsy sip, dribbling tea down her chin. "Where do you live, Dell?" Celia asked.

"I'm, uh, in Colbert, but I'm originally from Dallas. I moved here last year, after my mother passed away."

"Oh, I'm sorry," Celia said.

"I'm renting an apartment for now. I'm not really in a position for anything more, but it's just me, so it's fine." He smiled at Rowan. "I live over a bakery. I figured you might be traumatized from all that rehab food, so I brought you some of their specialties."

Rowan smiled slowly. "Ohhh, hear that, Gabriel?" She pronounced each syllable of his name individually. "Careful, or he'll eat it all. I have to bake for him all the time."

"You don't *have* to," Gabriel mumbled.

"This boy takes in a zillion calories a day. God bless the adolescent metabolism, huh?" She lifted her glass in a toast.

Dell blinked. "Um. What grade are you in, Gabriel?"

"Eighth."

He looked at him in surprise. "Really? You look younger."

"No, I don't," Gabriel said, narrowing his eyes. "I'm thirteen."

"He's a *wunderkind*!" Rowan piped up, adopting a German accent all of a sudden. She looped her arm around Gabriel's neck and yanked. Their heads banged together, and while he felt it, she definitely didn't. "Smartest kid you've ever seen. He takes after me. I'm a genius."

There wasn't much to add after that. They finished dinner with a sprinkling of conversation, mostly between Dell and Celia. Gabriel was about to get Rowan some coffee when she yanked him down next to her. "Gabe," she whispered, cupping her hand around his ear. "Do me a favor. Go over there, be *very quiet*, and tell Celia I have to go to the bathroom."

He glanced at Dell. "I'll take you."

"No, you damn well won't."

"I can do it!"

"I don't want you to do it! Just tell her, please?"

Gabriel sat back and heaved a sigh. "She needs to pee, Celia."

"Gabe!" Rowan shrieked.

Celia smiled apologetically at Dell and got to her feet. "Excuse us." She gripped the back of Rowan's wheelchair, glaring at Gabriel. The door slammed shut behind them.

Dell fiddled with his glass, wiping beads of water off the outside. "So. What's Massachusetts like?"

Gabriel narrowed his eyes.

CHAPTER EIGHTEEN

MEL, GABRIEL'S TUTOR, DROPPED BY A FEW DAYS LATER. SHE SWEPT Gabriel into a hug and gripped Rowan's hand. "I'm so happy to see you. When Celia told me, I was just…"

"It was not the vacation we were hoping for," Rowan said.

"I'm not going to stay, but I wanted to talk to Gabriel about summer school. You're going to have a new tutoring partner for a while."

Gabriel looked up, stricken. "What about Flip? I just talked to him."

"Flip's family is going to Italy in July. He'll be gone the whole month."

Rowan was secretly relieved to hear that. Flip was a terror. When they'd first found out Gabriel's peer tutoring partner was going to be Philip Samuels, Rowan half expected a junior accountant in a three-piece suit to show up with a briefcase and a Rolodex. What she got was so far off, it wasn't even funny. He was fourteen, he looked like he'd never seen a comb in his life, and he announced his presence by skateboarding around the perimeter of the porch, moving too fast for Rowan to even catch a glimpse of him through the window. She thought they were under attack. He and Gabriel were partners for less than a year, and in that time, Flip tried to do a 360 on the porch swing, lit an entire roll of toilet paper on fire, and fell off the roof. Twice. Rowan had harbored serious doubts about Flip and Gabriel's compatibility as study buddies, but they hit it off instantly. During their first meeting, they worked on their homework for a grand total of twenty minutes before Flip grabbed Gabriel and his skateboard and pulled them both out the door. Rowan didn't see them for another two hours. When they got back, they were filthy, and Gabriel's jeans were almost as shredded as Flip's, but he had a huge smile on his face. Their homework sessions still gave Rowan a headache.

Gabriel looked enormously put out as Mel flipped through her folder. "Your new partner is…Charlie Murphy," she said. "I know school isn't out yet, but since you guys are going to be partners all summer, I want you to start working together right away. You and I will meet three times a week, from nine to two, and you should be all set to start ninth grade right on schedule. I know you and Flip are supposed to meet tomorrow, but I asked Charlie to come instead. Is that all right?"

Gabriel nodded silently.

"Flip can come over after," Rowan offered.

Mel scribbled Charlie's name and number on a slip of paper and handed it to Gabriel. "In case anything changes," she said, getting to her feet.

"Are you going already?" Rowan asked.

"Yeah, I have some hysterics to deal with. All my seniors have precollege panic."

"If you had another half hour, you could meet my shiny new paramedic," Rowan said with a wry smile.

"You snagged your paramedic? That's talent."

"Wait, what?" Gabriel cut in. "He's coming here again?"

"Just for a little while."

Gabriel jumped to his feet. "What am I supposed to do while he's here?" he demanded.

"Whatever you want," Rowan said, glancing at Mel. "Hang out down here though. He's bringing us brownies."

"Eat them yourself," Gabriel grumbled, sweeping his books under his good arm. Mel and Rowan watched as he stomped out of the room and ran up the stairs.

Gabriel refused to leave his bedroom, no matter how many times Rowan yelled for him to come down. When the doorbell rang, she was stuck. Celia was at the supermarket. "Gabe!" she screamed.

There was no response. She picked up her phone and called him. He answered without saying hello.

"Can you come get the door?"

"No."

"Please? I don't want the alarm to go off."

He let out a huge sigh and hung up on her. Footsteps sounded on the stairs, and the front door opened and shut. A minute later Dell walked into the den alone.

"Hello again," he said, sitting on the opposite end of the couch.

"Hi. I'm normal today, I swear. I didn't even take aspirin."

Dell laughed and leaned back into the cushions. "Don't worry, I understand."

"You were so nice to bring the truck back. I'm glad I didn't scare you off."

"Honestly, I thought it was cute."

A blush creeped over her cheeks. "I don't even remember what we talked about."

"Oh, it was entertaining. How're you feeling?"

"Okay, I guess. Bored."

"I bet." He fidgeted in his seat. "I wanted to tell you something if I could. I was going to do it the other night, but…"

"I was high."

"Yeah."

She held up her hands. "Stone-cold sober. Shoot."

He pressed his own hands to his knees. "Okay. The thing is, I haven't been doing this long. Been a paramedic, I mean. After the storm, we were called in for backup because all the local ambulances were sent to the residential areas. When I found out where you were from, it seemed like fate." His eyes darted up, and he blushed bright red. "Sorry. I said to myself on the way over, 'Don't talk about fate.'" He waved his arms around like he was trying to erase that part of his speech. "Anyway, when they sent us to look for you, I was petrified. I'd only ever really 'rescued' rubber dolls in field simulations. I was the only one with you in the back of that ambulance, and when you stopped breathing, I was breathing *for* you. I was physically putting air from my lungs into yours, your heart started beating under my hands, and now you're sitting here, and I just…it's incredible. I guess I want to thank you for *not* dying on my watch."

Rowan smiled and offered him her hand. After a moment he took it. "The only way I could be more grateful," she said, squeezing his fingers, "is if you'd shown up half an hour earlier in a tow truck."

The next morning Celia sat clawing at her cheeks as she watched Rowan hoist herself into the wheelchair unassisted. Dell had spent two hours teaching her how to get in and out without killing herself, not that she didn't come close a few times.

"You should talk to your physical therapist about having Dell help you out between sessions," Celia remarked as Rowan nestled herself into the seat. "He has a knack for it."

"Shouldn't I ask Dell if he wants to take on that particular headache?"

"I think it's pretty clear he wouldn't mind."

Rowan tried not to smile. She hadn't realized she was so desperate for attention, but she didn't mind the source. As she pivoted back into the chair, Gabriel walked into the room wearing rumpled jeans and a black T-shirt. It wasn't his finest look, but it was the first time in days she'd seen him in something other than pajamas or basketball shorts. "Hey, kiddo. What time is Charlie coming over?"

"He was supposed to be here already," he said, running his hand over his head. He always did that when he was nervous, and Rowan secretly loved it because he looked so cute with his hair messed up. He glanced at the clock above the fireplace. "Maybe he won't come." The minute the words left his mouth, the chime of the doorbell sounded in the hallway. Gabriel deflated a bit. "I'll get it."

Rowan unlocked the wheels of her chair and began another torturous lap around the room. As she rolled back to the couch, Gabriel reappeared in the doorway, a look of absolute panic on his face. His eyes were begging for help or rescue from something Rowan couldn't see. "What?" she asked him. "What's the matter?"

He shook his head, walking into the room like a zombie. After a few steps, a tiny girl with a dark blond ponytail, big brown eyes, and a huge smile bounced in after him. Rowan bit back her own smile as Gabriel gestured helplessly toward her. "This, um, this is Charlie."

Rowan smiled for real. "Hi, Charlie."

A giggle bubbled out of her like water from a fountain. "Hi," she said with a little wave. Since the day Rowan had come home, the air in the house had felt off, tight and tense, like clothes that didn't fit, but Charlie instantly filled the room with a carefree vibe that made Rowan want to laugh too.

Gabriel, however, was unimpressed. "This is Rowan," he said. "And this is Celia."

"Hi, Charlie," Celia said. "Can I get you something to drink?"

"Sure, that'd be great. I had cheer all morning, and it's awful out."

"Sit down," Rowan offered.

Charlie hopped onto the couch before swinging her little sneakered feet. Rowan looked at Gabriel and nodded toward the spot next to Charlie, but he ignored her, slumping in the armchair instead.

Charlie's smile faltered a bit. She folded and unfolded her hands in her lap. "You have a really nice house."

"Thank you," Rowan said. "We kind of inherited it."

"Are you guys brother and sister?" she asked.

Rowan waited for Gabriel to answer, but he didn't. "I'm his guardian," Rowan told her.

"Oh, wow." Charlie's eyes bounced between them. "You're really young," she said to Rowan. "Is that weird?"

"Not really," Rowan said. "I was a teenager myself not that long ago, so I know what it's like."

Gabriel shot Rowan a look that said she did *not* know what it was like, and if she did, she wouldn't be torturing him right now.

"That's really cool," Charlie said. "I'm the youngest in my family by, like, years. My parents had me when they were super old. My one sister is married with kids already. My mom and dad got divorced a few years ago, so now I have a stepdad and two stepbrothers, and my real dad has a girlfriend. They're okay, but it's kind of weird for me."

"I'm sure," Rowan said. "But it can be nice to have lots of family."

Charlie shrugged. "I guess."

"What grade are you in?" Rowan asked.

"I'll be a sophomore in September. At Thornall."

Gabriel sat there, saying absolutely nothing. Charlie kept sneaking looks at him like she'd just won the lottery. Rowan didn't blame her. It's easy to lose the innocent beauty of childhood to adolescent awkwardness, but Gabriel did not have that problem. He was tall for his age, long-limbed and thin without being lanky, with a certain grace that comes from growing up too fast. His skin was smooth and unmarred, and his blue eyes were bright under his mass of messy dark waves.

His face might have been working in his favor, but his personality was not shining. "Gabriel starts ninth grade in September," Rowan said. "Right, Gabe?"

"Uh-huh."

Charlie narrowed her eyes and cocked her head slightly. "Do you go to Waterford Middle?" she asked.

"I'm homeschooled."

Celia returned with lemonade and some blueberry tea cakes Dell had brought over. She set the tray on the table and joined Charlie on the sofa.

"Who do you hang out with?" Charlie asked. "Because you look super familiar."

Gabriel shrugged. "No one, really."

"I feel like I've seen you." Charlie's eyes landed on Gabriel's plastered arm, and she sucked in a gasp that took half the air out of the room. "Oh my God, wait! I do know you! You were in the big tornado in Ardmore!"

Rowan blinked. "How did you know that?"

"His interview came up on my Insta."

"His what?" Rowan turned to Celia, whose face had gone ashen, eyes panicked and pleading. "What interview?"

"It was on the news."

"The…" A blast of fear stabbed Rowan in the stomach, painful and white-hot. Gabriel looked equally stunned, but the only word for Celia's expression was *caught*.

"I know a kid from Ardmore who lost, like, his whole house," Charlie went on. "He posted a bunch of stuff about it. I've only ever seen tornadoes from really far away. My mom always makes me stay inside. It's so cool that you, like, outran one. The video was intense. I saved it."

"The *video*?" Rowan choked.

Gabriel had gone dead white; even his lips looked erased. "I don't—"

Celia stood. "Gabriel, why don't you and Charlie take the drinks and go up to the loft for a while?"

"But—Celia—"

"Take the syllabus Mel left so you can go over it. Go on."

Gabriel stood like a robot and headed for the stairs. Charlie jumped to her feet, practically skipping after him. "I'll carry the tray," she said following him out. "God, I watched that video a million times. I can't believe it was you."

Rowan had one hand pressed against her mouth. She had to; she'd have screamed otherwise. "What the hell is she talking about?" she demanded when they were gone.

"Rowan—"

"*Interview?* As in someone interviewed him and put it on the fucking news? And you *knew* about it?"

"It wasn't my fault!"

"I don't give a shit, Celia—you were supposed to be watching him! How the hell did that happen?"

"I *was* watching him! It was the day after he had surgery for the infection. When I called the hospital the next morning, the nurse said he was still asleep. Someone let the reporter in before I got there, and I threw them out right away. Rowan, I swear on my life, I did everything I could to stop it from being aired."

"This was local news, right?" Rowan asked, trying to keep her voice steady. "I want you to tell me this didn't make it out of Oklahoma."

Celia pressed her lips together. "It was," she said quietly. "But the Associated Press picked it up."

"Why didn't you tell me?" Rowan cried.

"Because you were in no shape to know! I watched him like a hawk the entire time you were in rehab. Nothing has happened," Celia insisted. "It's been nearly two months. He won't be able to find you. The tornado was in Ardmore—"

"That's still a damn big bread crumb!"

"If his father were going to do something, he'd have done it already."

Rowan was barely listening. She grabbed her phone and punched in Gabriel's name. She found the interview in three seconds.

"Oh my *God*, Ceil!" she said, staring at Gabriel's face. He was battered but far from unrecognizable. "He was completely drugged. He could have said anything!"

"I know," Celia said, her head in her hands. "I know. But he didn't."

"You didn't tell Gabriel it aired?"

"No! He barely remembers talking to them."

"Okay," Rowan said, trying to breathe. "Okay. What about Laine? Did she say anything?"

"She wasn't home at the time." Rowan buried her own face in her hands. "She was in New Hampshire with her parents for a couple of weeks, but she has seen Lee every day since she came home. She said he's acting completely normal."

"If he googles his name one time—shit."

"They didn't mention his hometown, just Ardmore."

"And Mercy Memorial Hospital!"

"That's what I'm saying," Celia said, grabbing Rowan's hand. "If his father saw it, he had plenty of time to get to him at the hospital. And he won't call the police. They're going to ask him why he hasn't reported his son missing for two years. Ardmore is fifty miles away. That's a big radius to cover."

Rowan squeezed her eyes shut. "It's still a radius." Tiny stars danced in the darkness, but her mind's eye was filled with flowers: creamy roses, tuberous begonias, and daisies—pale pink daisies, identical to the flowers in Gabriel's picture, the flowers that flooded his mother's lap.

"I'm going to call the security company," she said after a moment. "I want the system upgraded, and I want cameras."

"You have cameras."

"I want more. If they can install them today, I want you to take Gabriel to your house and keep him until after dinner."

"You're in no shape to be left alone."

"I don't care. Please, Celia," Rowan said. "I can get in and out of the wheelchair. I'll be fine. Just do this for me."

"All right," Celia said. "Are you going to tell him? About the cameras?"

"No. Neither are you."

―――――――――

"It's okay," Rowan said, gripping Gabriel's hand. "It wasn't your fault."

"What if he sees—"

"It's old news, Gabe. It's been almost two months. *We* didn't even know about it. And Laine is watching him," she said. "Just like before. If anything happens, she'll tell us."

"He could have gone to the hospital," Gabriel whispered. "You weren't even awake. He could have taken me."

"But he didn't," Rowan said.

"He still could."

"He won't," she said firmly. "I promise."

"Are you sure?"

"Positive," Rowan said, leaning back on the arm of the couch. "It's after midnight," she added. "I want you to get some sleep."

"I'm not going to be able to sleep."

"Just try." Rowan reached for her blanket. "I can't wait until I can go back to my own bed," she said, pulling it over her shoulders. "It's lonely down here at night."

"Do you want me to stay with you?"

"No, no, you won't be comfortable."

"Yes I will. Please?"

"I guess so. Go get your pillow."

Gabriel ran upstairs, and Rowan lay back, listening to the tinkling melody of her butterfly wind chimes on the porch. It was a nice night, but the windows weren't open—they were locked. Everything was. The security company had finished up before dinnertime; it didn't take them long to upgrade the system and install surveillance cameras inside and out. Rowan and Celia's phones were linked to every single one—if so much as a bird flew by, they would know about it.

Gabriel came back down and settled himself on the other end of the couch, burrowing under his own blanket. She was glad he thought it was his idea. They'd both sleep better. "Good night," he said.

Rowan clicked off the light. "Good night."

CHAPTER NINETEEN

ROWAN TEETERED ON HER CRUTCHES, TRYING TO AVOID A TRIP TO THE floor. "This is how I die. I know it."

Dell smiled. "If you want to get back on your feet, you gotta do the work."

"I'd prefer a loaves and fishes kind of miracle," she said "I really appreciate you helping me."

"You're helping me. This is good practice. I've been debating going back to school for physical therapy."

"You should. You're good at it."

As soon as Rowan was mobile enough for Celia to pick up a few shifts, Dell had volunteered to take over as Rowan's therapy partner. He arrived at noon every day, usually toting some new delicacy from the bakery, and spent an hour moving through the exercises designed to strengthen her leg and loosen her torso. The crutches were proving to be a bigger obstacle.

Rowan passed them back to Dell and eased down to the couch. "How's the night shift treating you?"

"It's more interesting," he said, working the handgrip up a notch. "I had a gunshot wound the other night."

"Sniper?"

"BB," he said sheepishly. "Bunch of kids at a bonfire. One of them shot into the woods and hit his friend. He had a BB stuck in his shin. He screamed like someone cut his leg off."

"I envy your exciting life."

"It is that."

"I've been meaning to ask you," she said, frowning at a blister on the heel of her hand. "You're here with me during the day, and you're working until what? Three or four in the morning? How can you keep that kind of schedule?"

"I don't sleep," he said, as casually as a vegetarian would say they don't eat meat.

"You don't sleep?"

"No."

"Ever?"

"Not much."

"Oh," she said after a moment. "You must get a lot done."

He laughed. "Sorry, I know it sounds weird. When my mother

was sick, she needed meds around the clock, so I had alarms set to wake me every couple of hours. After a while"—he shrugged and reached for the other crutch—"I didn't need them anymore."

"You couldn't go back to normal afterward?"

"I tried," Dell said, twisting the screw. "My doctor told me I disrupted my circadian rhythm. I'm used to it by now."

"So the next time I get a craving for those checkerboard brownies in the middle of the night, I shouldn't hesitate to call you?" Rowan asked, smiling.

He replaced the crutch on the floor. "You don't have to hesitate to call me, ever." He held her eye for a beat, and she was suddenly very aware of Gabriel in the next room.

"I shouldn't have mentioned food," she said. "Are you hungry? Gabe!" she called. "Are you hungry?"

Gabriel came in from the kitchen. "I could eat," he said, joining Rowan on the couch.

"Dell?"

"Sure."

"What should we get? You want Chinese?" She poked Gabriel in the side and grinned. "You want some puffy chicken?"

"Aren't you sick of Chinese?"

"What the hell is puffy chicken?" Dell asked at the same time.

"Any vetoes?" Rowan asked.

"Sounds good to me," Dell said. "Do you have a menu?"

"Sideboard in the hall."

Gabriel lifted her hand. His own cast had come off the week before, and his arm was still shriveled and thin. "Your wrist is swollen."

"It'll go down. How's the essay?"

"I need Charlie to read it over."

"How are things going with you two?"

"Okay, I guess. She's smart."

"She's different from Flip, I'll give her that. She hasn't set anything on fire in the bathroom." Gabriel didn't smile. He looked straight ahead, staring at nothing. She pushed his shoulder with hers. "You okay?"

"Do we have to go all the way to Tulsa for your surgery?"

"Well, the hospital is there, so yeah…"

"Why can't you go to the hospital here?"

"They don't do orthopedics. We're only going overnight."

"I have so much homework," he moaned, rubbing his eyes with the heels of his hands. "I don't want to go."

Dell came back in with the menu. "To school?" he asked, handing it to Rowan.

"To Tulsa," Rowan said. "My ankle needs a minor realignment."

"Why can't he stay home?"

Rowan smiled. "Because he's thirteen."

"Oh."

"I'll just sit in the hotel room and get nothing done," Gabriel muttered.

"You've been working nonstop, Gabe. An overnight isn't going to kill you."

"When are you going?" Dell asked.

"Day after tomorrow."

"I can stay with him," he offered. "I'm not on until next week. What do you say, Gabe?"

Gabriel lifted his head. "Don't call me that."

Dell blinked. "There's, um—there's great fishing up in Tishomingo. Maybe we could do something like that?"

"You are a brave, brave man, Dell," Rowan said under her breath.

Gabriel didn't hear her. He was having his own unique reaction to this proposal. "*Fishing?*" he said, as though Dell had suggested they spend the weekend weaving baskets or bathing the elderly. "What for?"

"For...for fish," Dell said, casting a helpless look toward Rowan.

"I'm not going fishing with you. We barely know you."

"Gabriel, enough," Rowan said, palming the top of his head. "Do you want your usual?"

"Yeah."

"Go upstairs and take a break. Your eyes are all red. I'll call you when it gets here."

He shuffled out of the room, and Dell pressed his hands to his knees. "Wow..."

"I'm sorry," Rowan said. "It's usually just the two of us. I think he's a little jealous."

"I'm serious about staying with him," Dell said. "I'd be happy to help."

Rowan shook her head. "That's okay."

"It's no trou—"

"No," she cut in, her voice sharper than she'd intended. She took a breath and tried to smile. "Please don't take it personally. I don't leave him with anyone but Celia."

She braced herself for a follow-up question she wouldn't be able to answer, but Dell just leaned back in his chair. "Would you leave him with Celia for an evening, maybe?"

Rowan tilted her head. "Maybe. What did you have in mind?"

"I don't know...dinner? Someplace without any thirteen-year-olds kicking around?" He recoiled slightly. "Sorry. I didn't mean it like that. I'm just not sure how to go about things when the girl you like comes with a venomous teenage appendage."

"You're doing fine," Rowan said. She kept her face neutral, but what she really wanted to do was call Laine and screech, *He likes me!*

A door slammed above her head, and she glanced up, remembering her appendage. As much as she knew her next words were the right ones, hearing herself say them still felt like a betrayal. "When should we go?"

———————

The light was turning pink, and there had been no rain for days. The pond was as still and even as a sheet of glass. Gabriel lay sprawled across the porch swing, while Rowan sat on the steps, examining her plants.

"I just don't get why he has to be here all the time."

"He's helping me. What's so horrible about Dell?"

"He's here *all the time*. And he creeps me out. He's always staring at me."

"You think he's trying to seduce you?"

"Shut up." He kicked a pebble across the porch and watched it bounce down the steps. "He's always staring at you too."

Rowan turned so he wouldn't see her smile. "Sounds like you're the one always staring at him."

"It's weird. He's weird. He told me he never sleeps."

"He can't. His circadian rhythm is botched," she explained.

Gabriel lifted his arm from his eyes. "What, like locusts? What does that mean?"

"That's cicadas," she said, pulling mint leaves off the stems. "Look how gorgeous these are. I'm having a mojito tonight."

"He's not coming back, is he?"

"No," she said, nibbling on a leaf. The mint was at its prime, sharp and clean. She picked a few stems for drying.

"Thank God."

"But," she continued, "we're going out next week."

"Where are we going?"

She pulled the leaf out of her mouth and looked at him. "I meant me," she said. "Me and Dell."

"Where are you going?" he asked, sitting up.

"Just to dinner."

She watched his Adam's apple bob. "Like a date?"

"Like—yes." She swallowed, too, with some difficulty. "Like that."

Gabriel walked over and sat next to her on the steps. "Why?" His voice was flat and distant, and it broke her heart.

Rowan kept her eyes on the trees; black shapes against the pink sky. "I like him," she said quietly.

Gabriel didn't respond. He plucked a mint leaf from the stem in her hand; she could smell the sharp tang as he crushed it between his teeth. Her shoulder brushed his, and he jerked away.

"Gabe, please," she begged. "I'm not trying to hurt you."

"What are you trying to do?"

"I'm trying to be happy. But we can't…link that, you know? My happiness can't be conditional to your misery. We have to work together. I know you don't like Dell, and I'm sorry I do. I'm sorry. But please don't sabotage this without giving me a chance."

Gabriel looked at her for a long time. Then he got to his feet. A moment later the screen door slammed, and Rowan was alone, mint leaves falling softly from her hand.

"Never again," Dell said.

"Come on, was it that bad?"

"Absolutely. Next time I get to pick the restaurant."

Rowan smiled as the truck bumped along the road. "I can't believe you never had sushi before."

"I'm from Texas," he explained. "Down there we cook our food."

Despite dinner being an exercise in bravery, conversation had been good. Dell seemed looser than he did at the house, and funnier. Afterward they went out for ice cream—tall soft-serve cones that melted quickly, sending sticky rivers down their arms as they fought to keep up.

Rowan licked her finger and rubbed at a smudge on his chin. "You missed a spot."

"Did you just spit clean me?"

She laughed. "Sorry—Mom habit. Gabe yells at me too."

Dell cleared his throat. "Speaking of…I never know quite how to ask, but I have to know. How the hell did you two end up in this situation?"

"The tornado?"

"No, living together. You're what, ten years older than him, you're not related, and you're raising him by yourself?"

"I'm his guardian."

"How long have you been guarding him?"

"I got him when he was eleven."

Dell took his eyes off the road for a beat. "Got him?"

"Yeah." Rowan stretched her arm through the window. The night air rushed by, making her fingers curl and dance. "That rain really cooled everything off."

"So I guess that means you're not telling?"

"Nope," she said, smiling.

"Okay, that's fine. I'll get it out of you eventually." He turned down an unpaved road nearly hidden by the tree line.

"Where are we going?" Rowan asked.

"I'm not telling."

Dell stopped in the middle of a four-way intersection of tire-packed paths, like an X on a treasure map. There was nothing of note in any direction, but the sky was beautiful: inky black, with pinprick stars bright as diamonds on velvet. He got out and dropped the tailgate.

"Are you going to murder me over the sushi?" Rowan asked as he opened her door. "Because Gabe knows we're out. He'll tell on you." She actually wasn't sure if he would. He'd barely spoken to her all week.

He laughed and lifted her onto the hatch. "Not quite. Look up."

She did. A moment later a bright streak lit up the sky, followed in quick succession by two more—flashes of quicksilver darting between the stars. She glanced at Dell. "Is this a fluke, or did you arrange it special?"

"Meteor showers are more common than people think. On nights like this, you can usually catch a few falling stars."

The night was clear and brilliant, with a fat white moon that bathed them in cool, silvery light. Rowan leaned back on her elbows, swinging her feet. The doctor in Tulsa had changed her cast, and the new one was only knee-high. Her thigh was shriveled and gray, but she felt almost normal for the first time in months. She searched the sky for constellations, trying to force the star clusters into the proper shapes. Dell copied her position; she could feel his eyes on her. "Hi," he said.

"Hi."

He traced a line on her arm, brushing a shiny pink gash much older than the tornado. Her new scars were a welcome addition; they blended with the old, and she could pretend she'd only been battered once. "You having a good time? It's your first night out. That's a lot of pressure."

She smiled, her eyes still fixed on the endless night. "I am. Even though you hated the sushi."

"I'm glad. And I did hate the sushi," he said, sitting up.

"Are we going?" Rowan asked.

"Do you want to go?"

She shook her head before she'd decided on an answer. She felt weird, detached, like she was borrowing someone else's life for the night. "No."

Dell feathered his fingers over her jaw. The breeze was cool against her skin, but she felt flushed, feverish even. He kept his eyes on hers as he stroked her cheek, and when he leaned in and kissed her, she was not sorry.

He smelled like cookies and tasted like ice cream. She expected something shy and sweet—a morsel that would leave her wanting more—but the kiss wasn't tender, and she didn't want it to be. When he coaxed her mouth open and slid his tongue over hers, a molten wave of blatant lust traveled upward from the pit of her stomach, stealing her breath in an audible moan. Dell slid off the truck and stood between her knees, gripping her waist and pulling her closer. They stayed that way for an impossible measure of time, kissing fervently, before they broke apart.

Heat bloomed high on Rowan's cheeks. Dell fixed his eyes on hers and ran his hands lightly up and down her back, like he was playing piano. "I've wanted to do that," he said, slipping his finger under the strap of her dress, "for a very long time." The strap slid off her shoulder.

She smiled against his cheek. "How long?"

"Pretty much since the moment I saw you lying on the couch wearing that little white dress," he said, pressing his lips to the hollow of her throat.

"Plus my weight in medical dressings," Rowan murmured.

"I didn't even notice." He lifted his head and kissed her again, holding her so close, she felt like the world could stop spinning and he would keep her grounded. He worked his mouth over hers and gripped her lower back as she began to move against him.

But her memory was too fresh to enjoy it for long. Shadows gathered in the corners of her eyes, dim shapes she couldn't blink away. It was everything old, everything abysmal, her last memory of being touched that way. It was everything she thought she'd left behind.

"Dell," she said, putting a hand on his chest, "I think we better go back."

"Are you okay?"

"Yeah, I'm fine. It's just…I should really get home," she said, trying to smile. "I don't like to leave Gabriel for long."

"I noticed," Dell said, keeping his eyes on hers. "He's a little old for round-the-clock supervision, isn't he?"

Rowan felt herself flush. "If you and I got run over by a tornado, I wouldn't let you out of my sight either," she said, tugging at his hair.

"Good point." He kissed her again, and she could feel him smiling. "So, tomorrow?" he asked. "Sushi?"

"I don't want to torture you," Rowan said.

"Far too late for that."

He helped her back into the truck and leaned in through her open window. His eyes stayed on hers, glistening like amber in the moonlight. "I like you," he whispered.

"I hope so, after all that," she replied, running her thumb over his bottom lip. He had a mesmerizing bottom lip. "I like you too."

Pulling up to the house was like slamming her head into a brick wall. It was too much reality after such a delicious disconnect. Dell cut the engine. "Thank you," she said. "Best first date ever, I mean it."

"Does that mean we're on for sushi tomorrow?"

"We'll see," she said, reaching for her crutches. "It was fun, and we got to make out, but you didn't bring me any checkerboard brownies."

"Noted."

Dell helped Rowan to the porch, shooting quick nervous glances over his shoulder the whole time. "Sorry," he said. "I have a feeling there's a crossbow somewhere with my name on it."

"He doesn't have one, but he's wicked with a BB gun," Rowan said with a smile.

"And we know what kind of damage those can do. I'll call you tomorrow." Dell kissed her quickly and jumped back into the truck. He honked twice as he drove away.

Rowan lurched her way to the back of the house—the keypad for the front door was temperamental, and she didn't feel like giving anyone a heart attack. She was almost to the door when Celia threw it open, nearly knocking Rowan to the ground.

"Jesus, Celia!" Rowan said, hopping on her good leg.

Celia gripped Rowan's shoulder to steady her. "You need to talk to Gabriel."

"What's the matter?"

"He's upset. He's been sitting on the dock for over an hour."

"Celia!" The dock wasn't much more than a stone's throw from the edge of the yard, but Rowan didn't want him there at midnight. "Every single time I leave him with you, he goes rogue."

"I could see him from the window the whole time."

Rowan squinted toward the black water. "Why is he on the dock?"

"I don't know," Celia said quietly. "He barely said a word to me all night. We were watching TV, and I said I hoped you were having a good time. He started crying."

Rowan's stomach dropped. "Really crying?"

"Yes. He wouldn't talk to me. He just ran off."

"Oh God," Rowan said. "I can't—I don't know what to say to him anymore."

"Well, you need to say something. Can you make it down there?"

"I think so."

"Please be careful."

"I'm fine—"

"No," Celia said. "With him."

The path to the pond was nearly invisible in the dark. Rowan's crutches punched holes in the dirt until Gabriel's silhouette revealed itself. He didn't move as her three-legged form clumped onto the dock. He sat at the very edge of the boards, his feet resting on the top rung of the wooden ladder. Rowan eased down behind him with difficulty. "Hey."

Gabriel didn't respond.

"Celia said you've been out here for a while. Are you okay?"

He shrugged.

"Is there anything you want to tell me?"

"No," he whispered.

"Can I talk to you for a minute?"

"Sure," he said, speaking to the water. "I have to listen to you all the time."

Rowan scooted closer and wrapped her arms around him from behind, resting her chin on his shoulder. "I hope this goes without saying"—she pressed her hand against his heart—"but I think you need to hear it. You know I love you, right?"

He twitched in her arms but offered no other response.

"Well, I do," she said quietly. "I love you. And I think it's important for you to understand the difference between how I feel about Dell and how I feel about you."

He seemed to weigh her words. "What's the difference?"

"If Dell left tomorrow," she said, hugging him closer, "and I never saw him again, I'd be kind of upset. I'd eat a lot of ice cream and be in a bad mood for a while, but in general I'd be okay. I'd live. But you, if *you* left, I would be destroyed." She held him tight, rocking back and forth. "I would roll over and die. Can you see the difference?"

Gabriel sat there, still and silent in her arms. "If that's true," he said finally, "if you really care that much, why is he always around?

I mean, I *know* why. I'm not a baby. I just thought…" He lifted his head, eyes fixed on the endless sky.

"What?"

"I thought you'd be on my side," he said. "I know you think I'm jealous, but I—" He stared into his lap. "That's not why I don't like him."

"Why then?"

"I thought that would be enough. If you didn't like someone, I wouldn't let them visit all the time or go places with them or anything. I wouldn't hurt you."

"Gabriel, I'm not trying to hurt you."

"It feels like it." His breath hitched. "You know why I don't like him?"

"No. Tell me."

"After the tornado," he began, leaning his head back until it almost touched her shoulder, "the paramedics got me out first. They put me on a stretcher and carried me away from you. All I could hear was everyone yelling that you weren't breathing, and you were crushed and bleeding." He reached up and gripped her arm with both hands. "I thought you were dead. Then Dell came over and told me they got you out. He said you were just sleeping, and they were fixing you up. So I asked him if I could see you." He stopped, and Rowan tightened her arms around him.

"I knew you weren't okay," he said after a moment, "but I had to see for myself. And when I asked Dell, it was like he didn't even hear me. I kept asking and asking, and finally, he said that if I was quiet, he'd bring you over on the way to the ambulance." Gabriel stopped and covered his eyes, and Rowan would have broken every bone in her body if it meant he wouldn't have to carry that moment alone.

"But he lied," he said. "I never got to see you. He went and talked to this lady, and then she came over and gave me a shot. I don't remember anything after that. I didn't wake up until I was in the hospital. And that means if you died," Gabriel said, choking on the words, "I never would have seen you again."

"Gabe..."

"And the worst part is he *knew* that. He knew you were probably going to die." Tears cut through the smooth skin on his cheek, clean and silver, like the meteors moving across the sky. "Maybe he didn't think I was important enough, or I didn't deserve to see you—and I don't know how you could want to be with someone who'd do that to me."

"I know," Rowan whispered, swiping her fingers over his cheeks. He was shaking all over, and she wanted to tell him she was sorry, that Dell wasn't worth this; nothing was worth this.

She wasn't worth this.

But she didn't have the words, so she just held him, stunned and speechless, the same way she had the night she'd taken him, when he was writhing in pain, and she watched him bleed on the floor. At least then she'd had tools, some idea of how to fix him. Now she had nothing.

"Can you go now?" he whispered, wiping his eyes. "Please?"

"I can't leave you alone. Come inside with me so we can talk."

"No." He shook his head in quick painful jerks. "I already know what you're going to say."

"Gabe," she said, pressing her cheek against his, "did you ever think that Dell might have done that so you *wouldn't* get hurt? That you wouldn't want to remember me that way?" She blinked back her own tears, but her broken voice betrayed her. "You already have to deal with more horrible memories than most people will in their whole lives."

"That's not why. He did it because I'm nothing." His voice, his delivery, was dead.

"What do you mean?"

"I mean I'm nothing to you. Celia's your sister. Dell will probably be your boyfriend. Laine's your best friend. But I'm nothing."

"Gabriel, you are everything."

"Maybe if I said I was your brother or your kid or someone important, he would have let me see you."

"Who cares what Dell or anyone else thinks we are? *We* know. And no matter what happens, he will never be as important to me as you are. Never."

"What good is that if we can't tell anyone? You're not my mom, and I'm not your kid—we're nothing. It'll always be like that. You barely know Dell, but you can already call him something people will understand." Gabriel wiped his face with the hem of his shirt. "I hate him for that." He shrugged loose from her grip and stood on the top rung of the ladder. "I'm tired. I want to go to bed."

"Wait a minute," she said gripping his arm. "If you really hate Dell that much—" She swallowed, but the lump in her throat only burned; it didn't budge. "I'll tell him to stop coming around. But I'm asking you, please, to give him another chance. Just for a little while."

He nodded, dropping his head between his shoulders. She couldn't see his face.

They didn't speak as they walked back to the house. Rowan went to her room, and Gabriel went to his. All the doors stayed closed.

CHAPTER TWENTY

THE NEXT MORNING, GABRIEL SAT SLUMPED OVER THE TABLE, STARING
blankly at his history assignment; he'd read the prompt three times,
and he still didn't know what he was supposed to do. He hated history.
He hated history, and he hated homework, and at the moment, he
hated Charlie. Not for any good reason, but just because she was
there, sitting next to him on the porch and breathing too loud. She
was supposed to be reading his English essay, but her eyes hadn't
moved in five minutes. She wasn't talking either; she was just sighing
a lot and wiping her nose.

"Are you okay?" he asked finally. He didn't really want to know.
He'd barely slept at all, and his head was killing him.

"I guess," Charlie whispered with another sad little sniffle.

"What's the matter?"

She gave him a wobbly smile. "Nothing, it's just—I'm kind of upset about something."

He waited for her to explain what she was upset about. When she didn't, he assumed the conversation was over. "Oh," he said, picking up his pen.

"My school is having this thing."

Gabriel closed his eyes and put the pen back down.

"It's called FreshFest," she said. "The school throws a big party for all the freshman to celebrate the start of summer vacation. The juniors and the seniors have prom, the sophomores have a cotillion, and the freshmen have FreshFest. It's not as fancy as prom, but there's a dinner, and they have, like, games, and you get raffle tickets so you can win stuff. But the thing is you need someone to go with."

"Oh," Gabriel said.

"And I've been talking to this one guy for a while. We're not going out or anything, but I really thought he was going to ask me." She took a deep breath that got caught in her throat. "But then"—she choked—"last night this other girl posted on her Snap that he asked her instead. So that means I'm not going to be able to go."

Charlie's head drooped like a dead flower on a stem. Gabriel saw a drop of water plink on the porch table.

"Oh," Gabriel said. "That's really...wow."

"Yeah," she whispered. "It's on Friday, and there's, like, zero chance of anyone else asking me. I was so excited, and now I just can't believe it."

Another tear landed on the table.

Gabriel sighed; he had no patience for this scene. Worse than the headache, waking up that morning brought several pieces of new information. Rowan was with Dell, obviously, and probably would be forever, eventually forcing Gabriel to be the ring bearer at their wedding or do something equally humiliating. That was bad, but the things he'd said to her were worse. He hadn't planned on telling her every single secret thought he had and crying like a baby. Gabriel could barely look at Rowan this morning—he felt awful and guilty and embarrassed. All of that was too much to process without the added stress of Charlie crying on the porch.

"Gabe!" Rowan's voice shattered the air and made him jump. "Come here for a minute."

Gabriel rose from the table in a stiff, arthritic manner and went into the kitchen, grateful for the distraction. Rowan perched on a stool next to the counter, sprinkling nuts over paper-thin dough layered onto a baking tray. The counter was already crammed with cookies and pastries. She was back to stocking the dessert case at Ruby's diner, which was the most activity she could handle on one leg. She gave him a painfully careful smile that made him want to jam a fork into his eyes. "What?" he asked.

"Come here a sec." She picked up a knife as he shuffled over before making quick, clean cuts through the layers of dough.

"What?" he asked again.

"Did you know," Rowan whispered, "that you are completely oblivious?"

That must have been true because he had no idea what she was talking about. "Oblivious about what?"

Rowan gave him a look. "Seriously? Charlie is practically begging you to ask her to that dance."

"No, she's not!" Gabriel hissed, horrified at the thought.

"Gabe, please. She's dangling a damn hook in front of your face. It's painful to listen to."

"So don't listen."

"Why don't you ask her?"

"*What?*"

"Ask her," Rowan said, handing him the tray. "You've been cooped up for months. It would be good for you. Throw that in the oven for me?"

Gabriel opened the oven and shoved the tray inside. "I don't want to ask her."

"Why not? She's nice, and you guys get along."

"Yeah, she's fine to study with, but I don't want to *date* her."

"It doesn't have to be a date. You can go as friends. If it's a freshman thing, I bet Flip is going."

"I'd rather go with him."

"I mean it," she said, squeezing his hand. "You missed out on so much already. I don't want you to grow up and regret missing anything else."

Gabriel shook his head. "What if she says no?"

"She's not going to say no," Rowan said with the air of someone who'd never taken no for an answer in her life. "Come on," she wheedled. "I'll buy you a nice suit, you'll get a free dinner—it'll be fun."

He threw his head back, gripping his hair with both hands. "Fine. But if she says no—"

"She *won't*." Rowan plucked two chocolate chip cookies from a tray and handed them to Gabriel. "Here. Insurance."

On the porch, Charlie was still slumped at the table, staring blankly at her phone. He stood there for a minute, hoping to be saved, but bombs never just fall out of the sky when you need them. "Charlie?"

She lifted her dripping face and sniffed. "Yeah?"

"Do you…"

"What?"

"Do you want a cookie?"

She swiped at her cheek. "Okay."

He dropped it in her hand. "I was…um…this thing at your school…can you bring anyone?"

"Yeah," Charlie said quickly, staring up at him.

"Even if they don't go to your school?"

"Yeah, it can be anyone. I mean, like, even homeschooled kids can go."

Deprived of his final out, he took a deep breath and spoke to the sky. "Well, if you want—I would go with you. I mean…do you want to go, um, with me?"

Her eyes lit behind the torrent of tears. "Really?"

"You don't have to," he said quickly.

"OhmyGod, *yes!*" she shrieked. "To be honest, I'd so rather go with you anyway. I tried to ask you, like, weeks ago, but I got scared you'd say no." She jumped up and bounced on the balls of her feet. "I'm not trying to be weird. I know we've only hung out a few times, but you're really sweet, and *God*, you're so cute—seriously, my friends are going to die when they meet you. It's probably just, like, a crush or something, but as soon as I met you, I felt like we'd be good together, you know?"

No. He smiled weakly, wondering if anyone else planned to profess their love to him that weekend. "Wow, that's, um—So what do I have to do?"

———————

Rowan watched them through the back window, her heart beating a little faster than she'd expected. She'd call the school and ask about chaperones and safety measures, try to cover all the bases. If she didn't like what they told her, she'd sit outside—keep watch on the parking lot all night if she had to. But she wasn't going to tell Gabriel any of that.

Later that night, she sat in her room and went through all her stretches and bends, doing twice as many reps as prescribed before she folded her rubber bands and put them back in their bag. When she'd called her therapist earlier that day, he was a little surprised by her question, but he gave her his best guess. August. By August she'd be able to bear weight on her leg, but it might take until Christmas before she could walk on her own. She asked if it would help to add extra reps, more exercises, anything. He told her not to push herself. She could get hurt if she pushed too hard.

If he'd told her that yesterday, she would have listened. Now she didn't care.

Rowan reached under her pillow and pulled out a small envelope. It had arrived that morning, stuffed into a larger envelope forwarded from the hospital. She traced the letters on the back with the tips of her fingers.

Gabriel Emerson

That was all it said.

So Rowan had called the hospital, cycling through four different aides and desk nurses before she found the person she needed. He was sorry for the delay, he said. The note had arrived the day after Gabriel's release and somehow gotten misplaced. He hoped it wasn't anything too important.

"Did it come in the mail?" Rowan asked him.

"No," he told her. "It came with a visitor. A man. He wrote it out at the desk when we told him Gabriel had been released."

The man hadn't wanted to leave it, the nurse had told her. But he had to. They wouldn't give him Gabriel's address.

Even though he'd said he was a relative.

Rowan's fingers shook as she lifted the flap for probably the dozenth time. Inside was a piece of white paper with two sentences written in crisp letters:

Glad the tornado didn't beat me to it. See you soon, buddy.

It was bad news, and it was terrifying, but it also meant he hadn't found them. She'd been repeating it to herself like a mantra all day long: *He hasn't found us.*

But a darker voice kept interrupting.

He was looking.

That afternoon, Rowan called a Realtor and asked about putting the house on the market or leasing it—whatever she did would probably be up to Celia as the house was still in her name. While Gabriel and Charlie studied on the porch, Rowan had made a list of possibilities, trying to figure out if it was easier to disappear in a big city or a tiny town. She'd move him to California, Washington, Arizona—as far as it took for Lee to lose his grip.

Rowan turned off the light and sank into her pillow. For now he was as safe as she could make him, but being safe wasn't enough. This life wasn't enough; *she* wasn't enough. Last night, as the water rocked them on the dock, he'd printed all his fears on her heart, and they were worse than she'd expected. Despite the house, despite the pond, despite the miles and miles of open land, Gabriel knew, as well as she did, that she'd done nothing but move him to a bigger basement.

CHAPTER TWENTY-ONE

"C'mon, Ro-Ro, you can do this. We said August was it, crunch time. You take five steps, and I'll talk to the doctor about getting you that skin graft you've been asking for."

Rowan gritted her teeth. Austin Saunders, her physical therapist, was behind her at the parallel bars, gripping the gait belt around her waist. "I know you don't care," she said, "but I'd like to remind you: this hurts like a bitch."

"I know it does, baby doll. I have plenty of metal in my own knee from my football days. Give me five steps, and I'll show you the scars."

"Weak incentive, Austin," Rowan muttered. "Mine are better." Pain shot through her ankle and up her calf as she pressed her foot to the floor, but she managed to take one shaky step. Then another. When she reached the end of the mat, Austin rewarded her with a high five.

"That's how you do it, kiddo—one step at a time."

Rowan tried to smile. Like everything else in her life, baby steps were all she could manage. It had been a long vampiric slog to August—the heat sucked the life out of everything, and Rowan was plagued by a relentless sense of foreboding, like the weight of an endless stare. She was always nervous, always on guard, one eye glued to the steely skies, the other on Gabriel. Laine went back to Seoul for four weeks, so for most of the summer, there was no one to watch Lee. Rowan told no one about his note, refusing to add weight to Celia's guilt or Gabriel's fear. Not when time was so short. She'd hit her first goal—she was on her feet—and even though she was walking slowly, she was walking. A few more steps, and she'd be at the edge of the precipice, ready to grab Gabriel's hand and jump into a new house, a new town, a new life.

And just like the first time, they'd have to jump alone. Celia couldn't go with them. Neither could Dell, and eventually, she'd have to tell him that their bourgeoning relationship wasn't going to get much bigger. The entire summer felt like the calm before the storm, marked by still moments when the air didn't move, the silence was endless, and all the birds disappeared.

Her time with Austin, however, was therapeutic in more ways than one. He couldn't have pushed her harder if he'd known the stakes, and he lifted her again and again and again. Austin didn't mind when she hissed and cursed and groaned, but he never let her wallow, and Rowan found it hard to believe anything bad could happen while she was in that sunny mirrored room.

"So how's life without the cast?" Austin asked, helping her sit on one of the balancing balls.

Rowan stared down at her leg. Before the storm, it had been one of the only parts of her that hadn't been slashed to bits, but now it was just as hideous as her back—a sharp, bony ridge covered in tissue paper skin and puckered with scars, like bites from a single-fanged creature. "Not as itchy," she said, "but the cast was prettier than this mess."

"It won't be a mess for long," Austin promised, setting up a mat for her next exercise. "How's Gabriel doing? I haven't seen him lately."

Austin had treated Gabriel for eight weeks after his cast came off. When Rowan and Celia arrived to pick up him from their first session, they'd found Austin teaching him a variety of football tackles, lifting him and tossing him to the mats like a rag doll. Gabriel loved him.

"He's fine," Rowan said, reaching for her water bottle. "Tired. Summer school was rough; he worked really hard."

"Still got the girlfriend?"

Rowan choked on a laugh as she took a gulp of water. "God, no. That horse never made it out of the gate."

"I thought they were going out?"

"Just once." The ninth-grade blowout had been an unmitigated disaster and cast a cloud of mutual resentment on Gabriel and Charlie's study sessions for the rest of the summer. In retrospect, Rowan had perhaps been a bit too enthusiastic about FreshFest. Even though there was no dress code in place, it was his first social event, and she wanted him to look nice. She ended up putting together an all-black ensemble that was sleek and rakish and made him look like he'd just jumped off a runway. It was a mistake. The girls were *very* interested in getting to know him, and he had to dodge a swarm all night. According to Flip, Gabriel spent most of the dance hiding in the bathroom. Charlie was not pleased, and neither was Gabriel. He had girls calling for weeks afterward. "I think the experience was enough to turn him off dating for a while," Rowan said. "He did win a Switch, though."

Austin laughed. "So I guess his arm's doing okay?"

"It's fine, but it's bent funny now." She crooked her finger to demonstrate. "He says he can't see it, but it is."

"I believe you. Women are masters of observation. Is Dell picking you up today? Or—" He stopped short as the door opened and Celia walked in.

She froze when she saw him, her hand clutching the doorknob. "Oh. I thought you'd be done by now. I'll just wait outside." She turned to leave, but Austin was at her side in an instant.

"*Celia...*" he sang in a warbling falsetto.

"Oh no, please, Austin, not again—"

"You're breaking my heart…"

Rowan bounced on her ball and clapped.

"You're shaking my confidence daily…"

"I'm reporting you, I swear—"

"Oh, Cecilia!" he went on, holding the note. Rowan joined him on the harmony.

"Finish up," Celia snapped. "We have to pick up Gabriel at Flip's on the way home."

"Hold on," Austin said. "Just one more thing, and I'll let you ladies go. You can even help us, Cecilia. She'll need a buddy for this. Is Dell still helping you out?" he asked Rowan.

"Not this week," she said as Austin pulled her up. "He's visiting his dad, but he'll be home tonight."

"Both feet on the ground, Ro-Ro. That's it," he said, gripping her hands. "Dell and I are going to have to have a talk. He managed to charm one of the lovely McNamara girls. Maybe he has some ideas about how I can woo the other." He dropped Rowan a wink.

"Don't sing anymore," she suggested.

"That I can't do. Music is my life. Okay," he said, snapping to business. "Here's the deal, Rowe. You're using your upper body a little too much when you're moving across those bars. The idea is to build up the muscles in your leg, not kill your arms. I want you to work on bearing weight, but you'll need a partner until we get your balance where it needs to be." He looked up. "Cecilia? You want to give us a hand?"

Celia took two steps, moving with extreme caution, and Rowan smiled. Whenever Austin was around, Celia became completely unhinged—she couldn't wrap her head around the fact he genuinely liked her, though Rowan was pretty sure the feeling was mutual. Austin admitted to Rowan that he'd noticed Celia around the hospital long before Rowan's name had shown up on his patient roster. Rowan would bet Celia had noticed him too. Austin could charm anyone within a twenty-foot radius. He had a smile that was both sly and contagious; he'd been a big football star in college ten years back, and he still looked the part. He was well over six feet tall and built like a tank, with deep-brown skin and eyes like polished bronze. Bedroom eyes, Rowan had once told him, much to his delight.

"Okay," Austin said. "I want you to grab each other's wrists like you're doing a basket toss. We were all cheerleaders here, right?" He demonstrated the hold, positioning Celia's hands around Rowan's arms. "Don't hold her up, Cecilia; let her support herself. If she stumbles, guide her *forward*, toward you. Got it? This is going to be a lovely little dance. Are you ready?"

Celia nodded, gripping Rowan's wrists.

"All systems go, Ro-Ro. Walk."

Rowan took a tentative step, hissing through her teeth. Celia stepped back and gently tugged her forward; together they made slow progress across the floor.

Austin clapped—three loud reports that echoed off the mirrored walls. "That's the way to do it, ladies. Good job," he said, easing Rowan back onto the ball. "Start slow. Try to get a few minutes on your feet a couple of times a day, even if you're just standing." Celia looked strange, like she couldn't decide whether to laugh or cry. Austin noticed. "What's up, beautiful?"

She shook her head. "Nothing. It's silly, but that reminded me of when she was a baby. She was late to walk, and I used to hold her hands then too."

Rowan smiled. "Twenty-four years later, and I still can't walk for shit."

Austin adjusted the straps on Rowan's brace. "Okay, baby girl," he said, "you are free to go. Remember, I get you back in two more days, so don't miss me too much."

"Don't tell me. Talk to Celia."

"Rowan! That's not—We're going. Thank you, Austin."

"Are you going to come see me too?"

"What? No, I have to work on Wednesday."

"Dell's bringing me," Rowan said. "Any guesses on how long I'll have to beg rides?"

"Not long. Pretty soon you'll be driving yourself, my dear," Austin replied.

"I can't wait. See you Wednesday," Rowan said, rolling toward the door. She'd started alternating her crutches with a tiny scooter she could kneel on. Austin hated it, but Rowan couldn't resist bringing it to her sessions; it was way too much fun on the polished floors.

"Goodbye, my Cecilia."

"That's not even my *name*, I—Goodbye, Austin," Celia said, letting the door slam behind them.

Rowan glided alongside her. "Wow, Ceil—look at that blush."

"Stop it, or I'm not taking you home."

"That's okay. I bet Austin will. Then I'll invite him to dinner—give him a chance to really get to know you."

"Rowan!"

"What? That's what you did to me."

Celia shook her head as they exited the sharp, cool air into the relentless heat of the parking lot.

———

"Rowan, go," Celia said later that afternoon. "One night out is not going to kill you."

Rowan shifted in her seat. She wasn't supposed to see Dell until tomorrow, but there were flowers waiting on the porch when she got home from therapy. He'd surprised her by taking an earlier flight.

At least he called it a surprise. It had felt like an ambush.

"I'd be fine going to dinner or something, but he lives half an hour away," Rowan said, frowning at the bouquet of pale yellow carnations.

"So?"

"So what if something happens?"

"What do you think is going to happen?" Celia brought a vase of water to the table and plunked the flowers inside. "He'll be fine. Flip is sleeping over. I'll sleep over. Gabriel won't even know you're gone."

"I don't trust Flip," Rowan said. "They'll escape off the roof or something."

"Don't be ridiculous. Go. You've been seeing Dell for three months, and you've never even been to his apartment." Celia lowered her voice. "You two need some time alone. You've both got to be antsy by now."

Heat rose to Rowan's cheeks. "How do you know we never—"

"I just do."

Rowan opened her mouth, but she shut it quickly when Gabriel and Flip wandered in, making a beeline for the refrigerator. "Gabe?"

"Yeah?"

"Dell asked me to come over tonight," Rowan said.

"Okay."

"So I won't be here."

"Okay."

"You don't mind?"

Celia shot her a withering look.

Gabriel glanced at her. "Am I allowed to mind?"

"No," Celia said. "You're not. I'll order you guys whatever horrible food you want for dinner, and—Don't pick him up, Flip. I'm not in the mood for any more broken bones. Don't worry about them, Rowan. Go and get ready."

Gabriel and Flip darted around the kitchen, laughing as they dueled with a broomstick and a roll of paper towels. They weren't truly happy unless they were beating the shit out of each other. Rowan rose slowly from her chair and hobbled upstairs.

When Dell pulled up an hour later, she felt guilty about her reluctance—he'd never seemed so happy to see her. He leaped out of his truck with a giant Toblerone bar from the airport and a bottle of wine. "No cast!" he exclaimed.

"No cast," she said. "But don't look at it—it's ugly."

"Impossible," he said, dropping a kiss on her lips. "You're perfect. I missed you so much."

"I missed you too."

"Now don't go expecting anything fancy," he warned as they pulled out of the driveway. "My place is not big, and I can't cook like you can. I did clean, though."

The bakery was dark when they arrived, but Rowan could practically taste the sugar in the air. She took a deep breath and almost felt full. "This place could give Philosophy a run for its money."

"I can't even smell it anymore," Dell said. "I'm up there," he added, indicating a red door at the top of the wooden outdoor staircase. "Sorry about the steps." He helped her hop upstairs and opened the door.

For all his caveats, Dell's apartment was actually pretty nice. A large bay window mimicked the bakery's storefront, and there was a beautiful woven rug on the hardwood floor. The living room was open and airy, with a blue overstuffed sofa and matching chairs and a small brick fireplace tucked into the wall.

Dell was not a bad cook either. He made grilled chicken stuffed with melty smoked Gouda and fresh spinach, with roasted potatoes on the side. After they ate, he refilled their wineglasses, and they sank to the sofa. Dell threaded his hand through hers, twirling the engagement ring forever perched on her finger.

"Tell me about this," he said.

"What do you want to know?"

"What is it?"

"A mistake."

He examined the stone. "Whose mistake?"

"His."

"Does he have a name?"

"Not to me. Not anymore."

"Why are you wearing it?"

"Because I earned it. His mistake, my ring. He doesn't get to keep what's mine." She twisted it back into place. "It reminds me of more good things than bad."

"Like what?"

She tilted her head and tried to smile. "Like…I got away."

They sat silently, weaving their fingers in and out. "Is that all?"

She looked into his face, his sweet brown eyes. "That's all that's important. That's all you need to know."

But later, pressed skin to skin with their breath coming hard and fast, she realized he needed to know more. As Dell moved on top of her, Rowan moaned in a way that had nothing to do with his hands on her body or his mouth covering hers. She writhed beneath him in panic and desire, praying he wouldn't discover the ridges and bumps and twisting scars—every hideous secret Ethan had left behind. Her hands guided his to what was safe and smooth, but when he tugged her thighs up over his hips, she let out a choked cry she didn't expect. Right before he could do what she thought she was ready to do, a scream ripped from her throat, and she shoved him so hard, he fell to the floor.

His eyes were wide as he climbed back onto the bed. "What's the matter?"

She was crying, sobbing so hard, she couldn't take a breath. Dell dressed quickly. He wrapped her in a sheet and brought her to the kitchen, where the whir of the ceiling fan cooled her skin and slowed her racing heart. He gave her a glass of water, rubbing her hand as she wept and gasped and finally calmed down.

Then she told him. She told him about Ethan and the glass door and the stitches and the staples. And when she finished, Rowan stood in the bright normalcy of the kitchen and let the white sheet pool on the floor, revealing the result of her two-year engagement.

Dell said nothing; her first scared glance revealed tears in his eyes. He feathered his fingers over her broken skin, as though she would feel pain in the tissue long rendered numb. She expected pity and disgust but got neither. His expression vacillated between anger and sadness, and then he took her face in his hands and kissed her—all comfort, no demands. He rescued the sheet from the floor and brought her back to his bedroom, where they then lay side by side until her eyelids grew too heavy to hold open. She woke to a steady thrumming under the floor, mixed with dim laughter and the smell of bread and cinnamon. Dell was wide awake, exactly where he'd been when she'd closed her eyes.

CHAPTER TWENTY-TWO

"I'M SERIOUS, DON'T DO IT!"

"Shhh! It's ringing."

"She's going to kill you!"

"Quiet, he's going to hear—Hello? Austin?"

Gabriel ran his hand over his head and groaned.

"Hey, Austin, it's Rowan. What's going on? No, I'm fine… I know, it looks a lot better already. Yes, I promise I ditched the scooter. I wanted to ask you something. Do you have a minute?"

Gabriel tried to get up, but Rowan grabbed him by the belt loop and yanked him back down. He remained quiet. The last thing he wanted was to be a party to this terrible idea.

"I thought it would be nice to celebrate our progress. I was wondering if I could buy you dinner as a thank-you? I asked Celia to come, too, and… Oh, really? Great!" She grinned at Gabriel. "I thought we could try that tapas place by the hospital, remember we were talking about it? Friday at seven? Okay, see you then. Bye." She hung up the phone and held up her hand. "High five, baby!"

"You are so dead."

"Relax, I left you everything in the will. Now for part two."

Rowan dialed again, smacking Gabriel's hand away when he tried to grab the phone. "Ceil?" she said a minute later. Her voice was shaky, and a tiny sob bled through. "It's me… No, I'm not okay." Her breath hitched. "I just had a huge fight with Gabriel because he wanted to stay over at Flip's on Friday, and I said no, and he said he's sick of me smothering him…"

Gabriel rolled his eyes.

"I know that. I *am* going to let him go, but I really need to get out of the house too. No, Dell's working. You think maybe we could go out to dinner, just the two of us? Okay…yeah, that sounds good. How about the tapas place by the hospital? You want to meet me there at seven? Let's get really dressed up—it'll be fun! Thanks, Ceil, I appreciate it. You have no idea. Okay…bye."

She pitched the phone at Gabriel. He batted it away like it was alive and biting. "You have *no* idea!" she shouted. "Oh, this is going to be *epic*. I'm so excited."

"You're so mean. You're really not going to show up?"

"I'm doing them both a huge favor, you wait and see. Celia's not going to leave Austin sitting there. She's got way too much class for that. And if anyone can budge that stick up her ass, it'll be him."

He shuddered. "Do you have to be so graphic?"

On Saturday morning Gabriel was eating cereal in the kitchen when a car screeched to a halt outside. He put his bowl in the sink and tried to make a quick exit, but Celia caught him by the arm before he could get up the stairs. "Where is she?" she hissed.

"Broken arm, Celia, broken arm!" She let him go, and he rubbed his wrist. "Where is who?"

"Don't you dare!"

"She's, ah…"

"*Rowan!*" Celia screamed.

"*What?*"

"Come down here immediately!" Celia froze Gabriel with just a look. "You stay here."

"I didn't do anything!"

Rowan limped down the stairs, pulling her hair into a ponytail. "What's up? Wow, you look great, Ceil—you're glowing! What's different?"

"Rowan," Celia began, her voice deadly. "That. Was not. Funny."

"What?"

"You *know* what!" Celia exploded. "You call me up in hysterics.

You tell me you're having problems with this one." She flung her arm in Gabriel's direction.

"We made up," he offered weakly.

"I leave work early to meet you, and—"

"Austin?"

"Yes!"

"He likes you. You like him. You'd never have gone on your own. What's the big deal?"

"The big *deal* is that you can't play puppet master with people's lives!"

"Did you have a good time?"

"That's irrelevant."

"Did you?"

Celia threw back her head. "Yes, all right? I did, but that's not the point."

"Austin did too. He just called to thank me." Rowan smiled brightly. "So what are you screaming at me for?"

Celia stared at her. "I'm ordering tests," she said finally. "We cannot possibly be related."

"I tell myself that every day. Have fun tonight. Austin told me he's taking you out again."

Celia's face went beet red. Without a word, she turned and stormed out of the house.

Rowan lurched her way over to Gabriel. Ever since she'd started walking on her own, she moved like one leg was made of clay, too soft to hold her up. "Can I have my due credit?" she asked, holding up her palm.

Gabriel shook his head. "She's really mad."

"That's just her way of saying *thank you.*"

———————

The kitchen was boiling hot, wrapped in an almost visible shimmer. Rowan had to fight her way to the refrigerator, nudge people aside to check the oven, and load tray after tray with food. Her head throbbed. She'd planned her cooking time to the minute, but she hadn't counted on working in a throng. After Dell tripped on the oven door and she accidentally smacked Gabriel in the face with a grill pan, Rowan clapped her hands and made an announcement. "Guys! I love you all, but you need to get the hell out of my kitchen."

The impromptu dinner party was a peace offering—an attempt to smooth things over with Celia, who still refused to confirm any type of relationship with Austin even though she'd gone out with him three more times. Austin, who wasn't bothered by the setup at all, had arrived with a huge grin on his face, bearing wine and flowers. At the moment, he was doing bicep curls in the middle of the kitchen, Gabriel hanging on one arm and Flip on the other.

"What can I help you with?" Celia asked Rowan.

"You can get everyone out of here."

"Okay, we'll—Austin, don't let them do that," Celia said, pulling

Flip off a chair. Gabriel jumped on Austin's back as Celia led everyone into the dining room.

Dell stayed behind. Rowan wiped her forehead with an oven mitt. "Don't think you're exempt, buddy."

He slid behind her, nipping her earlobe. "But I haven't seen you since Wednesday."

"You're the one who insists on going to work every night. Taste this," she said, sliding a spoon into his mouth.

"Mmm…Merlot?"

"Very good. Would you take the appetizers to the dining room?"

"Sure," he said, nuzzling her cheek.

"Tray's over there," she said. "You'll need to physically pick it up…"

He turned her around and cupped her face until she put down the spoon and responded properly.

"Mmm," she echoed, pulling away. "Much as I enjoy carrying on in a ten-thousand-degree kitchen, there are people in the next room."

"Oh," said Dell, with a twinge of bitterness. "Them."

Rowan laughed. "Bring the appetizers out. That'll keep them occupied for a few minutes."

"Good, 'cause I have a surprise for you."

"What is it?"

"Busy!"

Rowan checked on her beef Wellington. She'd laminated the pastry herself, and it was perfect: golden brown and beautifully puffed. She was just about to pull it from the oven when Dell came back into the kitchen. His smile faltered when he saw her. "Rowan, sit," he said, pushing her into a chair.

"What?"

"You've been on that leg too long; you're dragging it. Take a rest for a minute."

"My beef needs to rest, too, or no one's eating."

Austin wandered in, probably spurred by the smell of food. "What's going on, darling?"

"Dell is paranoid, and dinner is burning."

Dell took the Beef Wellington out of the oven as Austin crouched, pressing his palm to the inside of her knee.

"I'm fine," she said.

"You are overextended," he replied. "Your leg and your soul. Where's your brace?"

"In my room somewhere."

"I'll get it," Dell said.

"You'll never find it. Gabe'll know."

"Gabe, Gabe, your go-to man," Austin sang. Rowan thought she saw something flicker across Dell's face, but in the next moment, it was gone. "Gabby!"

Gabriel's head popped around the corner. "What?"

"Be a sweetheart and find Rowan's brace, will you? She's been doing too many cartwheels in here."

Rowan leaned back and sighed. "Okay, you got me sitting, so what's my surprise?" she asked Dell.

He glanced at Austin. "I..."

"Oh, don't mind me," Austin said. "I love surprises. Better than that, I love love. Long as it won't give me nightmares, you go on and give it to her. Pretend I'm not here."

"It's just..." Dell pulled up something on his phone and handed it to her.

Rowan peered at the screen. "Football?"

"Football?" Austin said, looking up.

"In Dallas," Dell went on. "Next week. I thought—"

"Dallas?!" Austin exclaimed. He grabbed Rowan's wrist and stared at the phone. "Where the hell did you get these? They must've set you back—" He stopped short at the look Dell shot him. "Well, that's a very nice surprise," Austin said, subdued. "One I wouldn't mind getting myself if the receiving party isn't willing to enjoy it."

Rowan looked at Dell again. "Football?"

"I booked a hotel. I thought we could make a weekend of it."

"Oh," said Austin knowingly.

Rowan ignored him and looked at the tickets again. "Oh, wait a minute, Dell, no. That's Gabe's birthday."

"It is?"

"Yes, it's on Sunday." She looked at him for a moment. "You knew that."

"Little buddy won't mind," Austin said, bound and determined to be part of the conversation. "Cecilia and I will take him out."

"Mind what?" Gabriel asked from the doorway.

"Nothing," Rowan said.

Austin took the brace from Gabriel and carefully fit it around Rowan's leg. "Okay, peanut, you are off for the rest of the night, got it?"

"Yes, sir. Can you and Dell get the rest of the food to the table?" Rowan took Gabriel's arm and limped into the dining room.

"So what do you say?" Austin asked as soon as everyone was seated. "Are you gonna go or let those precious tickets go to waste?"

"Go where?" Gabriel asked.

"To Dallas," Rowan said reluctantly. "But it's on your birthday, and I'm not—Can we just drop it for now?"

Before Gabriel could respond, Flip leaned over and said something to him in a low voice. Rowan couldn't make it out, but Gabriel went crimson, Austin nearly did a spit-take across the table, and Celia shrieked, "*Philip!*"

"What?" Rowan asked.

"Nothing. It's nothing we need to repeat at the table," Celia said, shooting Flip a look.

But Austin was cracking up, sputtering into his hand. "He said—oh Jesus, Ceil, your face—he said, 'Let her go. I'll get those Thornall girls over here and make sure you get laid for your birthday.'"

Rowan's face flooded with heat. "No one is getting laid for their birthday," she snapped. "I told you I'm not discussing this. Can we just eat, please?"

The rest of the meal was fairly uneventful, save for Flip choking on a glazed almond. After everyone went home and Gabriel was upstairs, Dell pulled Rowan into a hug on the porch. "Come to Dallas with me."

She shook her head. "I can't, Dell. There's no way. I'm not missing his birthday."

Dell put a finger to her lips. "You're not missing anything. You'll be home the next day. Celia and Austin said they'll take him. What's the problem?"

"He's a kid, Dell. How would you feel if your mom missed your birthday when you were fourteen?"

A wave of hurt blew across his face before settling into dull confusion. "But you're not his mother, Rowan."

Her fingers tingled with the unpleasant urge to smack him. "To him," she said carefully, "I am."

"You're not even related."

"That doesn't matter."

"Yes it does! You're like…his babysitter."

"*Babysitter*, are you serious?"

"You tell me!" Dell exclaimed. "Tell me anything. Explain it all. I'm dying to know."

"You don't need to know."

"But I deserve to. You've been wearing that kid like a wet sheet since the day I met you. I ask you questions, and you change the subject. I ask him questions, and he ignores me. You're a nervous wreck if he's not within arm's reach. What the fuck is going on? Why are you acting like he's going to vanish into thin air if you leave him for two days?"

"It's his birthday!"

"I know that now," Dell said shortly. "I didn't do it on purpose."

"I'm not saying you did." She rubbed her eyes and sighed. "Just give me a few days, okay? Let me talk to him."

Dell's face clouded again, but this time it didn't pass. He nodded once and walked down the stairs without so much as a goodbye. After he drove away, Rowan went upstairs to Gabriel's bedroom.

It was dark. The only movement, the only sound, came from the tree branches scraping against the windows. Before she could even find his shape in the shadows, Gabriel spoke. "Go with him. I don't care."

A stream of cool air touched her face. The window next to his bed was open; he'd heard everything. "I do."

"It's not important."

"No, Gabe. It is. It's very important."

It was a long time before he spoke. "Why?"

Rowan sat on the bed and rubbed a circle over his back. "Because you're important."

"Dell doesn't think so."

"Dell has nothing to do with it." She squeezed his shoulder. "I have a present for you," she added. "Don't you want it?"

"You can give it to me when you get back," he said almost inaudibly.

Rowan squeezed his shoulder. "That's not what I want."

"It's what I want. Go."

———————

Rowan stared into her suitcase. It was six o'clock on Saturday morning; Dell was picking her up at seven. Gabriel and Celia were still asleep.

The drive to Dallas was only an hour and a half, but Dell wanted to get there early. Rowan had never been, and he was excited to show her the city. It was good he knew his way around, he'd told her—it would cut down on walking, and they'd have more time to explore. He'd mentioned at least twenty possible destinations and activities and had a place in mind for every meal; he'd even agreed to an upscale sushi restaurant for dinner. Afterward, they were meeting up with some of his old friends for drinks. On Sunday, while Rowan and Dell were at the game, Austin and Celia were taking Gabriel and Flip to an amusement park and then a haunted hayride in the woods. Rowan had Gabriel's favorite dinner and a birthday cake planned for everyone on Monday night.

She flipped through her closet, pulling things out and putting them back. She'd tried to pack the night before, but all her clothes looked wrong—too warm, too thin, too fancy, too casual, too itchy, too tight...

Rowan took out a slinky mid-length black dress, cut low at the neck and edged in lace, like a negligee. She'd bought it almost two years ago, but it showed her back, and she was never brave enough to wear it. All of a sudden, she didn't care. She draped it over the bed and opened her jewelry box, then rooted around until she found what she was looking for: a blue-green pendant hanging from a delicate platinum chain.

The chain was thin as angel hair, and the pendant flashed in the early morning sun. It was a pear-shaped aquamarine, perfectly cut and unadorned with secondary stones. Rowan placed it against the back of her hand and then laid it on top of the dress.

Next to her suitcase, her phone lit up. Rowan picked up the chain and hooked it around her neck before she answered. "Hello?"

"Just making sure you're awake."

"I'm awake."

"Are you excited?"

She stared into the mirror, admiring the shade of blue against her skin. "Very."

"I've already got my stuff in the car. If you're ready, we can go early."

Rowan paused for a moment, her fingers fiddling with the stone. "I'm not," she said quietly.

"You're not ready?"

"No. I'm not going."

———————

An hour later, Rowan still sat on her bed, dress still laid out, pendant still around her neck.

Dell had barely reacted. She'd hoped for anger or disappointment—something she could fight against. She didn't get it. Ten seconds of silence followed her words, and then Dell cleared his throat. He said he hoped Gabriel had a nice birthday, then hung up the phone, leaving her explanation burning in her mouth. Her planned speech wasn't the truth. She couldn't tell him that, but he wasn't interested anyway. The truth had blindsided her to the point of tears—shameful grief over the idea that she'd even considered leaving.

She pressed her hand over the necklace, and her memory lifted her, carrying her back to the first time she'd seen it.

The day before Rowan's twenty-third birthday had been an absolute nightmare. She burned her hand making breakfast, badly enough to blister, and she was in agony the entire day. Following that, she accidentally drove over half her herb garden, broke a shelf that sent two dozen glasses shattering to the floor, and had a pie explode in the oven; the scorched fruit smelled like burning rubber and set off every fire alarm in the house. By nine o'clock she accepted defeat and went to bed, tossing and turning in the warm air until the sheets were damp and twisted.

Eventually, she fell asleep, but she was awoken by a hand on her shoulder. She opened her eyes and found Gabriel sitting next to her on the bed, a crudely frosted cupcake in one hand, and a silver-wrapped box in the other. She blinked against the light of a single candle.

"Happy birthday," Gabriel whispered. The clock next to her bed changed from 12:00 to 12:01 as she watched, her eyes blurry with sleep. "I want today to be better than yesterday." He placed the box on her chest. "Open it."

"Now?"

"Why not?"

Rowan sat up and rubbed her eyes. "Okay."

Her fingers were tired and clumsy as she peeled back the paper, revealing a plain black jewelry box. She eased the lid open and found the aquamarine necklace, pale blue-green and perfect against the velvet. She stared at it for a moment.

Gabriel smiled. "Do you like it?"

"I love it," she said quietly. "It's beautiful. How did you—"

"It reminds me of your eyes—it's the same color, anyway. I couldn't think of anything to get you. Celia tried to help me, but I kept changing my mind. Then I found this, and I thought, if you wear it, you'll always have something that matches you."

They'd been living together for almost a year. Gabriel was twelve. His voice, as he spoke, was just beginning to creak, preparing to shed the first fragments of childhood. Rowan squeezed his hand, extremely touched but not quite understanding. She had a passing familiarity with jewelry, and this was a quality piece. "It's perfect," she said. "I love it. Celia took you shopping?" Rowan couldn't help but wonder where they'd gone—there must have been a hefty loan involved.

"Yeah. Just for the wrapping paper, though. I got a card, too, but I can't remember where I put it."

"Then—where did you get the necklace?"

"I already had it," he said. His eyes were hopeful, shining, and sweetly innocent. "In my box. It was my mom's."

Rowan's heart nearly stopped. "Oh, Gabe," she said, bringing her hand to her mouth. "I can't—"

"What?"

"I can't accept this. You need to keep it."

His expression faltered a bit. "You said you liked it."

"I do, I love it, but you can't give this to me."

"Why not?"

"Because something like this is too precious," she said, fumbling all over her words. "You need to save it. When you're older, you may want to give it to someone really special—"

"I am."

"—someone you really care about—"

"I *am*," he insisted. "I'm giving it to you."

Rowan's eyes filled, and she pressed her lips together. She didn't dare try to speak. Instead she took him in her arms and hugged him as hard as she could, positive she had never loved anyone, never would love anyone, more than she loved him in those first few minutes of her twenty-third year.

———————

By eight o'clock, Rowan could hear Celia moving around across the hall; Gabriel was still asleep. Rowan caught her outside her room and filled her in on the change of plans, and as soon as Gabriel woke up, Celia brought him to her house for the day. Rowan spent the next three hours baking a chocolate cake with pecan caramel filling. She frosted the cake and added caramelized pecans before scripting his name on top. It was agony waiting for Celia to pull into the driveway, but eventually she did, rolling slowly over the rounded rocks. Rowan hurried upstairs and hid in her room until she heard Gabriel go to bed.

———————

"Gabe?"

"Mmph…"

"Gabriel." Like a song, a soft breeze against the side of his neck. "Wake up."

It wasn't real; it was a hallucination. He was dreaming. Something bright was penetrating his eyelids, a concentrated glow that made no sense. Neither did the shape he could see behind it. He blinked. "Rowan?"

She was holding her phone up with one hand and balancing a cupcake in the other. Wax streamed down the twisted blue-and-white candle. The phone's screen glowed. It was midnight. "Happy birthday," she whispered.

He sat up, suddenly wide awake. "You came back?"

"I never left."

"What? Why not?"

"You think I would miss your birthday for a stupid football game?" She put the cupcake on his nightstand and placed a box in his lap. "Open it."

The box was wrapped in baby-blue paper and tied with a red ribbon. Stuck somewhere between shock and confusion, he pulled the ends the wrong way, yanking and tugging until he finally managed to slide the ribbon free. He tore off the paper and reached for the lid, but before he could open it, Rowan brought her hand down on top.

"This isn't your whole present," she said. "It's only what I have so far."

"Okay…"

"I know it doesn't look like much. There's still a lot more to it, but—" Rowan smiled a little, sliding her hand away. "Open it."

He lifted the lid before pushing sheets of red tissue paper aside. The box was full of paper, thick creamy sheets all stapled together. He wasn't sure what kind of present this was supposed to be—his first thought was that she'd done his homework for him. He scanned the pages, but his brain was a foggy mess, and the words…

Things—impossible things—began to click inside his head, and his eyes darted between Rowan's face and the papers in his hand. "Rowan? What does this mean?"

"It's my license," she said. "Everything I finished. The last part was the hardest. I had to have the house inspected, and—"

"Your license to do what?"

Rowan smiled, but her lips were shaking; it was a moment before she spoke. "Adopt you."

Gabriel's face grew hot, along with his stomach and his throat. "What?"

Two tears slid down Rowan's cheeks, bright and startling. He couldn't remember ever seeing her cry before. "So, um, if you want to adopt," she began in a wobbly voice, "the first thing you have to do is get licensed to foster. There are a bunch of steps, but I did it. I got my license, so now we have to figure out some way to, um, separate you from your father—legally, I mean. Once we do that, I can—" Her voice died on her then. She tipped her head back and stared at the ceiling, holding up one finger. "Sorry," she whispered. "One sec."

He couldn't wait a sec. That was too long. Gabriel grabbed her, burying his face in her shoulder, and then they were both crying in hard, loud bursts. "Really?" he managed.

"I just hope it'll work!" Rowan said, her voice hitching between every word. "Austin is friends with a family law attorney. I wasn't really specific, but he told me the criteria, and Celia and I did a ton of research too. The easiest way, I think, is—"

"Shut *up*," Gabriel said, his arms locked around her neck. "This is enough. It's more than enough."

"No it's not," she said, gripping the back of his head. "I'm going to finish. I don't care what it takes. Even if I have to drive back to Massachusetts and force your dad to sign over his rights. I'll do it." She pulled back and cupped his face in her hands. "You are never, *ever* going to feel like nothing again."

Gabriel nodded, his head falling to her shoulder.

"And you're not just getting me," Rowan went on. "Celia will be your aunt. And if we're lucky, she'll end up with Austin."

"I really hope she ends up with Austin," Gabriel said with a watery smile.

"See?" Rowan hiccuped, cupping his face. "I told you I love you. Do you believe me now?"

"I always believed you," Gabriel whispered, even though it was impossible to imagine that she could love him even half as much as he loved her. "I love you too."

She kissed his forehead, resting her cheek on the top of his head. "Happy birthday."

They sat there for a long time without saying a thing. They didn't have to. They just clung to each other, rocking back and forth as the light from the single candle danced around them in the dark.

CHAPTER TWENTY-THREE

On Monday night, Rowan's adrenaline was extinguished. Dell was back from Dallas. He wanted to talk to her.

After dinner, Rowan walked into the den where Gabriel was watching TV. "Sorry, kiddo," she said, flicking the television off. "I'm kicking you out. Dell's coming over."

"Oh, damn." His face fell. "Is he really mad?"

"He didn't sound happy." Rowan pulled Gabriel off the couch. "I sense a breakup."

The corners of his mouth twitched up. "Really?"

"Try not to look so devastated," Rowan said, pushing him toward the stairs. "Watch TV in your room until bed, okay? And if you hear yelling, don't be alarmed."

Apparently, Dell wasn't in a rush to see Rowan either. It was after eleven by the time his truck crunched into the driveway, and Gabriel was already asleep. Rowan told Dell she'd leave the alarm off, but he knocked, which was worse. She shuffled to the door and pulled it open. "Hi," she said quietly.

"Hi."

"Come on in," she said. "How was the trip?"

"Great," he said. "Someone sideswiped me in a parking lot and tore off my driver's side mirror. I got stood up at the bar by all but one of my friends, and my team lost the game. Really a good time."

Her fingers tightened on the doorknob. "Oh."

"Where's Gabriel?"

"Asleep."

"Good. Can we talk?"

"Yeah."

She started for the den, but Dell made a beeline for the staircase. She followed him up to her bedroom.

"So," he began, his voice dripping with false brightness. "Was he surprised?"

Rowan closed the door and sat next to him on the bed. "Yeah."

"I bet," Dell said mildly. "He might've been more surprised than I was."

"I'm sorry," Rowan said. "I'm sorry. I didn't want to hurt you, but I couldn't disappoint him. He needs me too much."

"How much?"

"What?"

"How much does he need you?"

"I don't..."

Dell scrubbed his hand over his face. "I used to date someone with a kid," he said. "Someone else, I mean. Claudia. She had a little girl who was six, maybe seven, I don't remember. I liked Claudia a lot. I hoped it would turn into something serious, but it never did. She was always busy. Her daughter was a handful, and the dad wasn't in the picture. I knew all that going in, and I tried to help her out as much as I could. I babysat, took them to parks, watched Disney movies with them. If Claudia had to break plans because of school stuff or if her daughter got sick, I didn't mind."

"Okay," Rowan said slowly.

"I'm telling you this so you'll know I'm not completely ignorant about raising a kid. It's hard. I understand that. But this?" he said, gesturing to a photo of Rowan and Gabriel on her nightstand. "I'm sorry, Rowan, but I don't understand this at all."

"Dell—"

"I dated Claudia for six months, and in that time, she was never, not once, as overprotective of her daughter as you are of Gabriel. And maybe that's weird on her part, I don't know, but Gabriel's not six. He's fourteen. When I was fourteen, I only went home to sleep. I was out with my friends all the time. I went to school. I rode my bike all over the city. If my parents went out, they left me home—by myself."

"Sounds great," Rowan said. "I was in foster care when I was fourteen. I spent my birthday in the parking lot at school. Laine and I got wasted on a bottle of Boone's Farm, and she sang 'Happy Birthday' over a pack of Hostess cupcakes. Kids don't all grow up the same. I understand you're frustrated with me—I don't blame you—but I have to do what I think is best for him. I'm not apologizing for that."

Dell looked at her for a moment, and then he kicked off his shoes and lay down on the bed. "Come here," he said, holding out his arms.

She hesitated. The right thing, the decent and truly caring thing, would be to tell him now. To cut him loose, to send him away. But it was so late, and he already looked so hurt. She curled up next to him and rested her head on his chest.

"I don't want to fight," he murmured into the top of her head.

"Neither do I."

"But being with you makes me wonder."

"Wonder what?"

"If I'm ever going to be as important as he is."

Rowan could have answered that easily, but he said he didn't want to fight. She leaned over and switched off the light so he couldn't see her face. "It's not a competition."

"It feels like one," Dell said, running his fingers along her arm. "Why are you so scared of him?"

Rowan pushed him away. "I'm not scared of him."

"You're scared of something."

She shrugged. "Maybe I am."

"Maybe I can help."

"No," Rowan said after a moment. "You can't." She leaned in and kissed him. There was no tenderness or intent. She just wanted to end the conversation, but a few minutes later, his hands began to wander over her chest and under her shirt. She pulled it off as Dell's lips traced her jaw and neck, searching for a soft spot to linger.

His breathing picked up as his hands and mouth grew bolder, paying deep attention to every part of her. She slid out of the rest of her clothes and stretched out, watching as he shed his. He crawled toward her from the foot of the bed, and she felt his fingers, curious and searching. His lips brushed the inside of her thigh, and her back arched as he moved both hands between her legs, tugging them apart so he could graze in the space. She eased back, letting him warm her further. Dell didn't hurry. He worked over her like she was something soft and moldable, their rhythm finally perfect, their energies in sync. This time there was no fear, no hesitation. He moved up her body and gripped her thighs, sliding his hips forward until Rowan moaned, full but not sated. They began to rock, deeper and deeper, and she had to grip him tight just to hold on. Her focus narrowed until Dell was nearly gone. She was alone in her body, and it was begging for release. The sensation grew and grew until she couldn't stand it another second, and she screamed into his shoulder as he tensed and then relaxed, both of them boneless and gasping for breath.

She studied his face in the dim light. His cheeks were flushed, his pupils blown wide open. He leaned in and brushed his lips against hers. "I love you."

Rowan wanted to tell him not to. Not to waste an ounce of love or a drop of energy on her because she was a lost cause. Breaking his heart would be a kindness. She'd talked to the real estate agent that morning and said yes, finally, she was ready to do more than just look. She wanted a house, something at the far reaches of the state, in a town small enough to ignore but big enough to hide in. The woman asked her a million questions—what was her wish list, her time frame, her budget? Rowan wasn't making any wishes and would pay whatever it took, but she did have a time frame: January. She'd do a few more months of therapy, let Gabriel finish out the semester, and figure out what to do with her parents' house. She and Gabriel would soak in as much as they could between Thanksgiving and the New Year, fill the house with everyone they loved for as long as possible. January gave her just enough time to plan. Just enough time to say goodbye.

Rowan stared into Dell's eyes. His words hung in the air, vulnerable, expectant, listening. She moved her gaze to the ceiling and tightened her arms around his neck. "I know you do."

CHAPTER TWENTY-FOUR

THE SECOND WEEK OF NOVEMBER BROUGHT AN INTENSE BOUT OF heat—four sweltering days followed by a blast of ice and a sudden blanket of frost. Normally, this was Rowan's favorite time of year, but the chill in the air brought none of the comforts of autumn. She tried to fake it, buying pumpkins and gourds, arranging cornstalks, and baking apple pies. The porch overflowed with fiery chrysanthemums in blazing oranges and deep reds, and the chiminea burned every night, filling the air with fragrant curls of smoked hickory and sweet applewood.

It was a good show, but that was all it was. Her nerves were so raw, they were shooting sparks. Rowan had never had qualms about leaving one life behind to start another. She'd done it before, but this time was different. The house, every room, held a piece of the life she and Gabriel were building together, and the thought of trusting their memories to preserve all that history made her stomach churn.

"You don't look good," Gabriel said to her one night. She was making grilled Brie sandwiches on thick grainy bread, layering the cheese with apple slices and cranberry compote. It was the first food she'd made in a week that wasn't in the shape of a nugget.

"Thanks a lot."

"Well, you don't."

"I'm tired," Rowan said. "It's past my bedtime."

"It's six o'clock. And you took a four-hour nap this afternoon."

Rowan shrugged. "I'm tired," she said again. "I feel like a corpse."

Gabriel took a huge bite of his sandwich. "You look like one too."

Rowan didn't think much about it until the next day. She fell asleep again, this time sitting straight up in a kitchen chair while the breakfast dishes soaked in the sink. When she was awake, her head felt too heavy to hold up, and that scared her. It was too much like her first weeks out of the coma when everything had looked foggy and unreal.

She made the mistake of mentioning this to Celia, who was at the house in thirty minutes flat.

"I don't know," Celia said, whipping around a penlight for Rowan's eyes to follow. Always eager for a patient, Celia had arrived with an arsenal of stethoscopes and blood pressure cuffs and oxygen readers. Celia pushed and pulled at Rowan's arms and legs, hit her knees with a hammer, and had her walk around the room and balance on one foot. "You seem to be working okay."

"I feel like shit," Rowan moaned, flopping back on the sofa.

"You've been stressed for a long time," Celia said. "I think what you really need is a therapist, but go to your regular doctor if you're worried."

"I don't have a regular doctor."

"Why not?"

Rowan stifled a yawn. "I have you. And I must say, you're being extremely helpful."

Celia ignored that. "So the only doctors you have are specialists who won't have an open appointment for weeks?"

"I guess so."

"I swear it's like you're five years old sometimes," Celia mumbled, pulling out her phone.

———————

The next morning Rowan sat on a paper-covered table, shivering in a thin blue gown. Celia had called her own physician, Dr. Stahl, and uttered the magic words: *traumatic brain injury*, which worked as well as a secret knock at an underground nightclub. The doctor came in half an hour early just to see her.

"How long have you been under the weather?" the doctor asked, peering into Rowan's eyes.

"A week or two. I don't really feel sick, just kind of foggy."

"But you're less than a year out from a brain injury," Dr. Stahl said, jotting something down on a clipboard. "You don't want to take chances with that. How often do you see your neurologist?"

"Every eight weeks."

"And?"

"No issues. And all my scans have been normal."

"Good. You're not showing any really worrying symptoms, so this could be as simple as a virus or even holiday stress." Dr. Stahl ran her eyes down the sheet Rowan had filled out in the waiting room. "I can't tell you how many exhausted people I see between Thanksgiving and Christmas. When was your last period?"

"Maybe six weeks ago, but that's normal for me. I have an IUD."

"Fair enough. Let's do some blood work and see what comes up."

A nurse came in to draw blood, and Rowan gave a urine sample. Then she was alone, a wad of gauze pressed to the crook of her elbow. She pulled out her phone. The Realtor had dropped three new listings in her inbox—that made nine total—but Rowan was no closer to a decision. She scrolled through a refurbished farmhouse at the tip of the panhandle, what looked like a log cabin in the middle of the woods, and a bright pink ranch that could probably be seen from space.

Rowan frowned down at the phone. The cabin was cute, but the nearest grocery store was probably two hours away. She was still scrolling when Dr. Stahl came back in. "Rowan?"

"Yeah?"

"Can you lie back for me? Just for a minute."

Rowan leaned back on the padded table, and Dr. Stahl pushed it flat. Then she pressed on Rowan's belly, just below her navel. "Any pain here?"

"No."

"How about here?" she asked, moving to the left and then the right.

"No."

"Great. You can sit up," the doctor said. "Your blood work should be back in a few days, but I ran your urine sample, and I don't think we'll have to wait on the blood."

She paused there. Rowan let out a nervous laugh. "I'm not dying, am I?"

"No," Dr. Stahl said, putting a hand on Rowan's arm. "You're pregnant."

CHAPTER TWENTY-FIVE

ROWAN STOOD AT THE STOVE, MECHANICALLY STIRRING A POT OF STEW as her bread bowls cooled on the counter. She felt entirely divorced from her body—even comatose, she'd been aware of more. Her mind was miles away, still at the obstetrician's office. It had taken her a week to get an appointment, even with Celia's connections, and Rowan had spent every precious moment praying to wake up, praying it was a mistake, praying for a miracle.

In the end, she got one. But it wasn't the one she wanted.

She closed her eyes, and the darkness filled with the fast, flickering spot the doctor had shown her on the black-and-white screen. She'd felt nothing at the sight because that's what it looked like. Nothing. There was no connection, no jolt that it was something she should love.

If the spot hadn't been humming, it could have been a cherry pit, a pearl, a tiny grain of sand. Something safe and innocuous and without the power to tether her to someone she barely knew in a place she'd been planning to escape.

She'd wasted the week waiting. Her inbox filled with seven days of unopened listings from the Realtor, and she ignored every call that came in. Celia nagged her, Dell irritated her, and she'd been biting Gabriel's head off for days. She was afraid to go near him, even to apologize. Across the hall, Rowan could hear Flip trying to browbeat him into going to some kind of live-action horror movie at the high school—apparently the height of entertainment for the teenage sect. She was trying not to listen.

Heavy clouds had moved in, promising a storm by dark. To feign normalcy, she'd invited everyone over for dinner, even though Thanksgiving was a week away, and she'd have to cook for them then too. She hadn't told Dell about the baby. Not yet. He and Celia were due at the house soon, but Austin played a pivotal role at the high school horror show and had plans to be decapitated. Since Austin would be around to watch him, she was hoping Gabriel would give in and go with Flip. She could count on Dell to be clueless, but Gabriel absolutely knew something was up.

"I have to stay here," she heard him say in a voice designed to dodge her ears. "We're having company."

"No you don't," Rowan called. "You can go. Flip, take him, please."

More muffled words, and then the front door slammed. Gabriel came into the kitchen. "I didn't want to go, Rowan. Now he's mad at me."

She tested the potatoes with a fork. "He'll get over it."

"You don't want me here?"

"I don't care where you are, but don't tell people I'm keeping you from doing things when I'm not."

Gabriel stood in the doorway for a long moment. Then he walked up to the stove and stood behind her, so close that she could hear him breathing. "Would you look at me for a minute?" he asked.

She adjusted the flame under the pot. "I already know what you look like."

"Please."

She sighed and turned to face him. "What?"

His eyes were wide and wounded. "I don't know why you're mad at me," he said, "but whatever I did, I'm sorry."

"I'm not mad at you."

"Then can you please stop? All week you've been acting like—"

The front door slammed again, and voices sounded in the hall.

Rowan struggled to keep her own voice steady. "Acting like what?"

Gabriel didn't move. He held her eye stubbornly, painfully, until the hurt on his face melted into confusion. He opened his mouth, and his voice pitched high, curious, genuinely wondering. "What's wrong with you?"

Rowan's own face began to burn, along with the skin on her arm. She jerked away from the stove. Celia and Dell stood in the doorway, silently observing the standoff. Rowan turned quickly, bumping into Gabriel. "Sit down. Dinner's ready."

Gabriel shook his head. "I'm not hungry."

"You still have to eat," Rowan said. "Sit."

Gabriel slumped down at the table. Celia sat next to him, murmuring something Rowan couldn't hear.

"Are you okay?" Dell asked.

"Fine," Rowan said shortly. She ladled stew into a bread bowl. "Gabe, get me some real bowls in case these leak." Something buzzed on top of the refrigerator. It took her a minute to recognize it as her phone; she didn't remember putting it there. "Dell, can you grab that?"

He plucked the phone from the refrigerator and started to hand it to her, but then his eyes caught the screen, and he stopped. "Rowan."

"What?"

In the split second it took her to ask, his face went hard, twisting and morphing him into someone she didn't recognize. "Rowan," he whispered.

"What? Who is it?"

Dell's jaw rippled as he clenched his teeth tight. He could barely get the name out. "Ethan."

"Eth…" A black blizzard swirled in front of her eyes, and she watched it for a minute before she realized she was perilously close to passing out. She reached out to steady herself, and her hand landed on the cast-iron pot still bubbling on the burner. Her skin hissed on contact, but she didn't even flinch.

Make no mistake, Rowe, the next time I call you, you'll be close enough to grab.

She reached out her hand. "Give me the phone."

"No."

Her stomach dropped. "Don't tell me no, give it to me!"

"No." He looked feral all of a sudden, white-hot rage was painted all over his face. He slid his finger across the screen.

"Don't you dare!" she screamed.

"I want to talk to this son of a bitch! He tried to—"

"*NO!*"

"Who the hell does he think he is?"

"Dell, *stop!*"

Dell had the phone halfway to his ear when Rowan pounced. She didn't notice that Gabriel had moved next to her, and Gabriel didn't see her raise her arm to strike. She drew back, and the hot ladle smacked Gabriel's cheekbone with an audible crack. He stumbled backward, one hand over his face.

"God *damn it*, Dell!" Rowan shouted. The phone was still in his hand, the call still connected. Her skin prickled with phantom fingers, and she slammed the ladle to the ground so hard, the handle flew off and hit the wall. "Give me the phone!"

"Dell, hang up," Celia said quietly.

"He's not—"

"Hang up the *fucking* phone!" Rowan screamed, grabbing it out of his hand. Her finger stabbed the screen, and the call ended like a wire had been snipped. "Jesus Christ, Dell, what the hell is wrong with you?"

"I was trying to help!"

"Bullshit you were trying to help! You just told me to fuck off so you could be a big hero. You had no right to do that!" She marched to the back door. "I want you to leave," she said, throwing it open. "Get out. Now."

"Rowan—"

"*Get out!* I am not here for your bullshit, Dell. You do not get to decide what is right for me."

"I'm not—"

"No, *I'm* not!" Her own jaw was tight. "I'm not telling you again. Go. Leave me the fuck alone."

"Oh, I'm going to." He yanked his jacket off the hook so hard, Rowan heard it tear. "I'm going to leave you very much alone until you sort out your shit and grow up, Rowan!"

Dell stormed past her and out the door. The walls shook when she slammed it behind him.

"Rowan," Celia said. "Please calm down."

"Calm *down*? He called, Celia! He's out!"

"Who is?" Gabriel asked.

Celia touched his arm. "Rowan, please—this isn't the time."

"Celia, I can't…" She pressed both hands to her face and let out a hard cry. "I can't take one more thing. I just can't."

"I know," Celia said gently. "I know that, and I'm right here. I will help you."

"You can't help me," Rowan mumbled, fumbling for her phone.

"What is going on?" Gabriel cried.

"It's okay—" Celia began.

"No," Rowan said. "It's not okay, and I don't want to lie to him anymore. He should know what's going on. He should know why he has to live in a goddamned police state!"

Gabriel's eyes were swimming. "Rowan?"

She shook her head. "I tried to keep you safe," she whispered. "But I can't. I can't even keep myself safe."

"What does that mean?"

She turned to Celia. "Will you take him? Please?"

"Take him where?"

"Anywhere," Rowan said, walking out the door. "Just take him. I can't do this anymore."

———————

When Celia took his hand, Gabriel fully expected her to drag him out the door, but she pulled him into the bathroom instead. They sat on the edge of the tub. "Gabriel," she said. "Calm down."

He opened his mouth, but nothing came out. His eyes were streaming, partly because of the pain in his chest. He couldn't pull a real breath. All he could manage were quick high-pitched bursts. "I'm—I'm…"

"You're hyperventilating, and you're going to pass out." She ran a washcloth under cold water and pressed it to his forehead. "Breathe slowly."

"I don't have anywhere to go. She doesn't want me anymore!"

"Gabriel, *calm down*. No words, five minutes. Do you hear me?"

He relented, wilting against her shoulder. Celia moved the cloth to the nape of his neck and rubbed circles over his back until his breathing slowed. She tilted his chin up and probed his cheek. "Does that hurt?"

He shook his head without meeting her eye.

"She didn't mean to hit you," Celia said. "It was an accident."

Gabriel said nothing. He felt like a little boy again, trapped and cowering at the mercy of someone who could hurt him terribly.

At least when his father had done it, he'd told him why.

"Who is Ethan?" he whispered.

Celia drew a breath. "Rowan should tell you."

"She didn't. She won't. You tell me."

She looked at him for an eternity, her hand still rubbing his shoulder. "He was her fiancé," she said finally. "She was going to marry him."

Gabriel lifted his head in plain and painful confusion. "What?"

"I know," Celia said quietly. "I know that may not make a lot of sense to you, but you need to know what's going on. It's the only way for you to understand what happened tonight. But you also need to understand that Rowan does not want you to know about this."

Part of him wanted to scream, run away, hold his ears. But a bigger part of him already knew what she was going to say. "What?"

Celia shifted a little. "Ethan treated Rowan," she said carefully, "the same way your father treated you. That's why she's afraid."

"He hit her?"

"Yes. He went to jail for hurting her."

"What did he do?"

"I don't think I should tell you that."

He stared down at his hands. "I saw her back."

"What?"

"Her back. She has scars, a lot worse than mine. I saw them a long time ago. But she never told me about them, and I never asked. I was afraid to ask."

"Yes," Celia whispered. "He did that to her."

Gabriel swallowed hard, finally meeting Celia's eye. "Why didn't she ever tell me?"

"I don't know. Would you like to ask her?"

He shook his head. "I don't know what to say."

Celia leaned over and hugged him close, pulling him to his feet. "I think you do."

———————————

Darkness came early, and the storm came with it, bringing down power lines less than ten minutes after Celia drove away. Celia had gone upstairs to talk to Rowan before she left, but Rowan never came down, and Gabriel couldn't find her anywhere. After stumbling through every room in the house, he stood in the middle of her empty bedroom, scanning the darkened corners. Lightning flashed under her closet door, and Gabriel tugged it open. All the hangers had been shoved aside to make room for a pull-down ladder, which led to a small open square in the ceiling.

Gabriel climbed the ladder slowly before stepping up into a little alcove that was cramped and pitch-black. Another flash of lightning threw the room into sudden sharp detail, and he saw Rowan, pale and silent, sitting in front of the window.

It was a big window that looked out over the front of the house—a window he'd seen a million times without once wondering what was on the other side. The window stretched from floor to ceiling, and there was a small bench just in front of it that looked like an invitation to plummet to your death. That was where Rowan sat, wrapped in a blanket and staring into the storm.

Gabriel made his way toward her, stepping carefully across the wooden floor. As he got closer, he saw her hair wasn't bunched on top of her head for once. It hung straight down her back, so long that the ends almost touched the bench; a single bobby pin next to her temple revealed an old scar, gossamer now. She looked so different, much more than she should from just one small change. It was like it was the first time he was seeing her, the first time he'd ever seen her.

"I didn't know this was up here," he said, just to have something to say.

The lightning revealed shiny tears on her cheeks. When she spoke, her voice was stronger than she looked, sadder than he expected.

"I know," she said, pressing her palm to the window. The glass clouded around her fingers, and when she pulled away, the ghost of her hand stayed behind. "I'm hiding."

Gabriel sat next to her on the bench. "Are you okay?"

"No. Are you?"

"No."

"I know," she said, swiping a hand across her cheek. "I know." The treetops swayed wildly.

"Rowan," he said, his voice catching on her name. "Why didn't you ever tell me?"

She looked at him, scared, he thought. "Tell you what?"

He reached for her hand, then gripped the engagement ring between his fingers. "This."

Rowan stared down at the ring for a long time. Then she put her hand over his. "Celia told you?"

"Why didn't you tell me?"

"Because you didn't need to know."

"But…maybe *you* needed me to know. I would have understood."

"I don't want you to understand," Rowan whispered.

"Why not?" he asked. "You're acting like I'm a little kid. I'm not that little anymore."

She shook her head and pressed the heels of her hands into her eyes. "I saw your back," Gabriel said. Rowan twitched a little, but she didn't look up. "A long time ago. Celia told me he hurt you. What did he do?"

"He did a lot of things."

"Just tell me one. The worst one."

"Why?"

"Because," Gabriel said carefully, "it might help. You know my worst thing; tell me yours."

Rowan didn't answer for a long time. Then she lifted her head and looked at him with swollen red eyes. "I'm not going to tell you about my back."

"Why not?"

"Because that's not my worst thing." She was silent for another beat. "Still want to know?"

He nodded.

"Okay…God," she said, taking a deep breath. "Okay. Do you remember the night we found the stick-snake in the basement?"

It wasn't a sharp memory anymore, but it was there, jumbled in the chaos of those first few weeks. "Yes."

"Did you ever wonder," she asked, "why I was so afraid?"

"I just thought you were scared of snakes."

"Oh, I am. But that's only part of it. The real reason I was so freaked out is because of one of the first things Ethan ever did to me. You're going to love this. So, one day, we went to the zoo—this was right after we got engaged—and he wanted me to walk through the reptile house. But I said no. I was scared of the snakes. Not scared like I was when you saw me. I just didn't like them, and I didn't want to go in. He was mad because he got mad at me for everything, but he didn't make me go in, and I didn't think too much of it.

"That night," she went on, "I dreamed I was suffocating. It felt so real that I started to panic before I even woke up. I couldn't open my eyes. At first I thought the pillow was over my face, but it wasn't. It was a snake, a boa constrictor, about three feet long," she said, stretching out her arms. "Ethan borrowed it from his friend. He waited until I was asleep, and then he put it on my head.

"I screamed and tried to get it off, but I didn't want to touch it. I can't even tell you how scared I was. I couldn't see anything, and all I could hear was Ethan laughing. When I screamed, the snake got scared too." She lifted her hair to reveal a scar behind her ear, faded but clearly a bite mark. "I guess I'm lucky it didn't choke me to death. After it bit me, I got so hysterical, I passed out on the floor. When I woke up, Ethan was holding the snake, dangling it over my head. He kept that snake for a week, right in the living room. I didn't sleep a single night. I used to lock myself in the bathroom with a pillow and blanket and take naps in the tub. I was so scared he would do it again."

Rowan stared into her lap. "I didn't know what to do. He told me if I left him, I'd have no one. Not Celia. Not Laine. Looking back, I know that was never true, but I really believed it. He made me believe it. In the beginning he was like my savior. I was only sixteen and living with Celia again, and she and I hated each other. He helped me deal with her. He took care of me. He made me feel like he understood me in a way that she didn't, that nobody did. It worked. I thought I needed him." She blew her nose on the tissue clutched in her fist. "Stuff like that can make you kind of jumpy," she whispered. "Even if it's only a stick."

Gabriel didn't speak. He couldn't even open his mouth.

"Sometimes I think he did me a favor that night. Because afterward my mind just shut off. Whenever he hit me or screamed at me or humiliated me, it didn't seem like it was really happening. It was like watching it happen to some other girl, someone I didn't know. I felt bad for her, but she wasn't me. I was long gone."

They sat side by side, silently watching the storm. It too

seemed tired, offering only occasional flashes of clarity and a
steady weeping rain. Fresh tears slid down Rowan's cheeks.
Gabriel wanted to say something, hug her, anything, but he didn't.
She seemed so far away.

"I didn't keep Ethan from you because I didn't think you'd understand. I knew you would. But *I* understand that if you hold on to
things, all the bad memories, they'll kill you even after you get away.
I didn't want that for you. I wanted to save you. But I think I did it
wrong. I think the girl who could have saved you died as soon as that
snake touched her face. I didn't wake up until the paramedics were
trying to get me onto a stretcher with a foot of glass sticking out of my
back, and by then I wasn't the same anymore. You never met me, not
really. I never let you." She smiled, almost apologetically.

"He liked my hair," she said, tugging on a strand. "Ethan. He
never let me cut it or put it up. So, afterward, that was one more thing
I had to hide, you see? I'm still running after all this time." She held
up her hand, brandishing the ring. "I can't take it off," she whispered.
"And I know you're scared right now, I do. But I'm scared too."

"Scared about what?" he asked softly.

"Scared about Ethan—of him finding me somehow," she said,
wiping her cheeks.

"Will he?"

Rowan shook her head. "I called the police in Virginia—that's
where he lives. He's not allowed to leave the state while he's on

probation, and he's not allowed to talk to me at all." She smiled a little. "It's okay," she said. "They'll get him."

"Are you sure?"

"Yes. He's wearing a monitor, so he can't get far. And I'm so sorry I freaked out like I did, but when he called tonight, I knew he was out, and I just... It was too much," she said, cupping his cheek. "I'm sorry."

"When you said you couldn't do it anymore, I thought you'd changed your mind. About me."

"No," she said. "Never. I just have to figure out a way to make it official."

"What has to happen?"

"Murder or blackmail," she said, smiling a little at his expression. "No, I'm kidding—about murder, at least. But blackmail...maybe. I've been thinking about that a lot."

"He'd never do it."

"You don't think? I've got a pretty strong case. I took all those pictures of you. I have the fork."

"You do?"

"It's in my closet. I have fantasies of just showing up on his doorstep with all of it, forcing him to sign you away." Her smile faded as she brushed her fingers over the welt on his cheek. "Jesus," she whispered.

"It was an accident."

"I don't care," she said, her eyes welling up again. "I shouldn't have acted like that in front of you."

"Why not? You've seen me freak out plenty of times."

"I know, but it's different. You're allowed. I just—I think if I had a little time to focus and clear my head, I might be able to figure everything out. But maybe I need more help than that." She shivered, pulling the blanket up over her shoulders. "It's cold up here," she said, rubbing his arm. "Let's go downstairs."

Rowan swung one leg over the bench, but Gabriel stopped her. "Wait a minute—wait." He wrapped his arms around her and held her as tight as he could, tight enough to feel her heart fluttering against his chest. "Don't be scared," he whispered. "It'll be okay."

"I know." When she hugged him back, she covered him in the blanket, too, and he fought back tears because this—just this—felt safe.

Felt like coming home.

After a while, Gabriel pulled back a little. He reached up until his fingers found the pin in her hair. He tugged it free. Then he lifted her hand and twirled the ring around her finger. After a moment he slid it off, too, that final trapping. He let the ring tumble to the floor, a bright flash in the darkness. Gabriel's eyes slid toward Rowan's as it bounced against the soft wood. "Better?"

Rowan nodded.

"Everything's okay," he said.

She tried to smile, but her mouth twitched down, over and over until she brought her hand up to cover it. "Gabriel," she said. "I need to tell you something else."

The way she said it made heat bubble in his stomach, fear of another dreadful unknown. "What?"

Her lips trembled, and her fingers clutched his in a way that didn't comfort him at all. She clung to him like she was asking for courage. "I was planning to break up with Dell," she said after a moment.

"Really?" he blurted. It was too quick. He sounded too happy.

Rowan nodded. "After the news story and everything, I felt like maybe we shouldn't stay here. Just in case."

"What? No—"

"I know," she said quickly. "I should have told you. I've, um, been talking to a Realtor about maybe getting another house, just far enough so that we wouldn't have to worry so much. I knew we couldn't go anywhere until I was better, until my leg healed and I didn't have to go to the doctor all the time. But something happened, and now I don't think we can go at all."

He almost said, *Good*, but he could see that whatever had happened was not good. "Why not?"

She looked at him, and this time she didn't look away. "Because I'm pregnant."

The words hovered in the still silence. Gabriel heard her say them, but he didn't listen. He couldn't. If he listened, they would become real, and it would be true. This could not be true.

He jerked his hand away, leaving hers hanging in the space between them. She looked small and stunned, staring at her empty fingers. "What did you say?"

"I'm sorry. I am so, so sorry."

"How…how?"

"It was an accident."

"But…is Dell…?"

"Dell doesn't know," she said, wiping her cheeks. "He doesn't know. I have to tell him. I should have told him already, but I can't yet. I just can't."

Gabriel stared at her, waiting to be slapped with a reaction: anger, maybe, or his own tears. It was a tremendous relief when neither came. He wasn't ready to know how to feel.

"This doesn't have anything to do with you," Rowan said quickly. She reached for his hands again, gripping him so tightly, it hurt. He was grateful for the pain because the numbness was slipping away. "We're going to do the adoption, and everything will be fine, I swear."

"But…"

"Gabe, please," she whispered. "I know this is horrible for you to hear, and I hate to put any of this on you, but I need you right now. More than Celia and more than Dell."

"Why?"

"Because I love you," she said quietly. "I love you. You're the only thing I've ever gotten right."

Now he was crying, and he hated himself for it. "What does that mean?"

Rowan wrapped her hand around the back of his neck, pulling his forehead down to hers. "Taking you," she began, "was the easiest decision I ever made. I told myself I was going to make up for everything your father did. I was going to give you the best life ever, anything you wanted. I said that to Celia the first morning we were here. And she told me raising you had to be about more than what I could give you. I didn't believe her at the time, but she was right. I had no idea what I should be to you or what you would be to me. All I knew was that it was the first time in my life I ever cared about someone else more than I cared about myself. And the longer I had you, the more important you became. I never thought I could love anyone like I love you." She cupped his cheek. "And you know what?"

Gabriel shook his head.

"It is…the *best* feeling," she whispered. "You mean everything to me, and I am so proud of you." She smiled a little, wiping her eyes. "When I found out about the baby, I told Celia I couldn't do it. And I meant it. But later that night, I looked at you, really looked at you, and I thought…if there is even the slightest chance I might be able to love another person the way I love you—if I can give *you* another person to love—then I absolutely can."

"So you're going to do it?" he asked, his voice cracking. "You're going to have a baby?"

"Yes."

"Are you going to marry Dell?"

"No!" She covered her eyes and took a quick hitching breath. "No."

"When he finds out, he's going to ask you to marry him," Gabriel said, panic rising in his throat. He knew Dell didn't like him—up until now, he'd *liked* that Dell didn't like him. But now it was like he had a timer on his head, pushing him toward some dark, unknown place.

"He's not going to ask me to marry him. We've barely known each other for six months."

"It doesn't matter. I know he is."

"Well, I don't want to marry him, so don't worry about that."

"He hates me."

"He doesn't hate you. He just doesn't understand you. And it's not up to Dell," she said slowly. "You are just as much mine as this baby is. You always will be."

"But the baby will *really* be yours." He choked on tears that burned like poison. "Yours and Dell's."

"And yours!" she said, trying to smile. "Right? We're talking about your sister or brother, kiddo."

"What about everything else, though? It doesn't make my dad go away. It doesn't make Ethan go away. All that's still there."

"And I will handle it," she said. "I had just as much to worry about when I took you—maybe more. Do you really think I had any idea how to take care of you? God, Gabe, I could barely take care of myself. So maybe it's hard right now, but it won't be hard forever. I promise."

He stared out the window, oblivious to the thrashing branches lit by sharp streaks of lightning. "So what happens now?"

"Now we're going to go downstairs," Rowan said, and it sounded like she was trying to convince herself. "We'll go downstairs, and we'll wait for the storm to end. That's all we have to do."

Gabriel's heart felt like shattered glass, and his chest throbbed with a million painful beats. But he managed to stand. He stood and reached for Rowan's hand before stepping carefully to guide her back to the door in the dark.

Later, Gabriel sat on Rowan's bed and watched shadowy raindrops make patterns on her face. She'd fallen asleep on top of the covers. The house was still dark and still cold, so Gabriel brought the blankets from his own bed and tucked them around her. He was more tired than he'd ever been in his life, but it didn't even occur to him to sleep.

The lightning and the shadows played tricks on his eyes. Instead of her dresser, he saw the hulking shape of the furnace in the basement. The ceiling fan turned into the dripping rusty showerhead he had used to try and clean himself. Always at night because there was nothing more terrifying than the thought of a beating without even his clothes to protect him. Sometimes, if he was bleeding, his father would drag Gabriel under the shower with his clothes on, covering him in a downpour of icy shards. Once— and Gabriel honestly believed his father hadn't even meant to—his father shoved him aside, and Gabriel tripped before smacking his head on a metal pipe sticking out of the floor. It had opened a gash that sent blood pouring down his face, far more than a bloody nose or a split lip. He remembered the way his father had knelt next to him, his face almost scared. But it didn't last—a minute later he hauled Gabriel up by the back of his shirt, dumped him under the shower, and turned the water on full blast. Gabriel writhed and slipped and threw up on the floor as his father watched him flop around in grim fascination. After a while, Gabriel gave up and rested his head on the cement, his eyes fixed on the rusty water swirling down the drain.

That had been one of his worst nights. And it wasn't because of the pain or the blood or the freezing-cold floor—it was knowing his father was waiting to see if he would die.

The barbecue fork was on his lap, still wrapped in plastic and sealed in tape. He'd found it in Rowan's closet, exactly where she'd said it was.

But he hadn't found the note there—the note written on a piece of paper that said *Mercy Memorial Hospital* in an envelope addressed to him. The one Rowan had kept for months and months without saying a thing. He'd found that in her top dresser drawer.

Glad the tornado didn't beat me to it. See you soon, buddy.

Gabriel picked up the fork and ran his fingers over the plastic-covered tines.

He was glad too.

CHAPTER TWENTY-SIX

SUNLIGHT STREAMED THROUGH THE WINDOW, BRINGING TINY RAINBOWS in the beads of water that hugged the glass. Rowan rolled over. She was buried under Gabriel's comforter, but she didn't remember him covering her, or even falling asleep.

"Gabe?" The bathroom door was ajar, the light off. "Gabriel?"

The scent of coffee hit her nose. She swung her legs off the bed and padded downstairs. "You should have woken me up, I—" She walked into the kitchen and froze.

Dell was at the counter, pouring coffee into a mug. "Good morning."

"How did you get in here?"

He looked at her, a small smile on his lips. "Through the door."

"No, how did you get past the alarm?"

"It wasn't set. And the back door was unlocked."

Rowan started a little, remembering the power outage. "Oh."

There were two bakery boxes on the counter—one was open and full of doughnuts, the other still tied with red-and-white string. Dell handed her a cup of coffee. "I wasn't sure if you would talk to me if I called. Are you okay?"

Rowan nodded, fiddling with a strand of hair. "Where's Gabriel?"

"I haven't seen him, but I didn't look," he said. "I'm sorry about last night."

She pulled a doughnut from the box without meeting his eye.

"Did you get my note?"

"What note?"

"Here." Dell brought the other box over to her—a sheet of white paper was tucked under the string. "Checkerboard brownies. I dropped them off last night. I didn't think you'd be up to dealing with me, so I left the box by the door. It was in here this morning."

"Gabe must have brought it in," she said, moving toward the back door.

"Where are you going?"

Rowan ignored him. She stepped onto the porch and circled the house, the wood soft and damp under her feet. Her truck was still in the driveway, and her clay pots still lined the steps. She'd forgotten to bring the plants in before the frost, and the mint and basil had shriveled to blackened corpses. The air was cool, but that wasn't what made goose bumps rise on her skin. She went back to the kitchen. "You didn't see him at all?"

"No."

The whole house felt cold, deserted—she'd felt it the moment she'd woken up. "How long have you been here?"

"An hour? I thought—"

Rowan didn't wait for him to finish. She went upstairs to Gabriel's room and threw open the door. His bed was unmade, and clothes were scattered around as usual, but it had the same empty air as the rest of the house. She yanked his dresser drawers out one at a time before she even knew what she was looking for. A blank space on his mirror caught her eye. One of his pictures, the one Laine took of Rowan and Gabriel in front of the fireplace, was missing—the circle of tape was still stuck to the glass. She ran back to the kitchen.

"Rowan?"

"Hang on," she said, grabbing her phone. Gabriel's line went straight to voicemail. "Shit."

"What's the big deal? He's probably—"

"No, something's wrong," she said, dialing again. "Call Celia. Tell her I—Denise? It's Rowan, how are you? Good, listen, I'm sorry to call so early, but Gabriel's not over there, is he? Okay…what about Flip? Oh, that's right, I forgot." She laughed, not even approaching her normal voice. "Could you have Flip call me when he wakes up? Thanks, Denise…bye." She turned back to Dell. "Did you get her?"

"She's just going into church."

"I have to call Austin."

"Calm down."

"Don't tell me to calm down! Where the hell is he?"

"Did you check his room?"

"Of course I checked his room."

Dell went up there anyway, scanning the inside of Gabriel's closet and the top of his dresser. "Is anything missing?" he asked Rowan.

"The picture of us on his mirror," Rowan said, pointing to the tape.

"That could have fallen off."

"Jesus Christ, Dell," she said, storming past him. In her room, she flung the blankets off the bed and even peeked her head into the alcove over her closet. There was nothing. She stood in the middle of the room, their conversation in the attic ricocheting inside her head.

Dell watched her from the doorway. "What are you looking for?"

"I don't know," she said. "I don't know."

The words had barely left her mouth when her eyes fell on the jewelry box sitting in a patch of sunlight on her dresser. It was a ballerina jewelry box, one of the only things she had from her childhood. Celia had brought it over shortly after Rowan moved into the house. When she gave it to her, Rowan wound it up, but time had rendered both the music and the dancer frail and weak. The tiny pink figure had twisted in painful jerks to the croaking peals of "You Are My Sunshine."

Now there was no music and no dancing. The domed lid was open, the ballerina still. Rowan could see a flash of blue winking in the pale light. Her aquamarine pendant dangled over the edge of the box, a piece of white notepaper threaded through the chain.

Rowan,

There's something I need to do. I'll be back soon. Please don't worry. I promise I'm safe and I'll be careful. I love you.

Gabriel

Celia and Austin made the thirty-minute trip in fifteen.

"Rowan, think!" Celia said, pacing the kitchen. "Where would he go?"

"I don't know! Don't you think I would tell you?"

Celia picked up the note. "Gabriel wouldn't just take off. What time did you see him last?"

"It must have been after midnight. There was no power, so we were talking in my room. When I fell asleep, he was right next to me."

"I don't think we should overreact," Dell said, hell-bent on being irritating as well as useless. "He left a note."

"Oh, in *that* case—"

He held up his hands. "I just don't think you need to get hysterical. He's not five years old. It says he'll be back."

"Then why won't he answer his phone?" Rowan demanded. "Why did he stop sharing his location? Why didn't he just tell me where he was going?"

"Fine," Dell said. "If you're so worried, call the police."

"No!" Rowan and Celia yelped at the same time. Austin raised an eyebrow and led Celia into a chair.

"I don't know if the cops would consider him a runaway," Austin said, rubbing Celia's shoulders. "He did say he'll be back, and it's only been a few hours."

"Forget the note," Rowan said. "He only left it so he could get a head start."

"Did you check the cameras?" Celia asked.

"The storm knocked everything out."

"Let's be logical about this," Austin said. "Kid's fourteen. There aren't many places he could go. Did he have money? A bank account, debit card, anything we could check?"

"He has a savings account, but he can't withdraw from it without me."

"What about cash?"

"Just his allowance."

"How much is that?"

"Enough."

"How much is enough?" Celia asked.

Rowan mumbled her answer, and only Dell heard her. "*What? A week?*"

"I put half of it in the bank!"

"That's not an allowance—that's a salary," Dell said. "My first job didn't pay me that much."

"I'm sorry, okay?"

"I don't know, Rowe," Austin said, shaking his head. "If he's got enough cash to travel, he could get pretty far."

"Yeah, but to go where?"

"I don't know, but the longer we talk, the harder it's gonna be to find him. I'm going to take a ride, have a look around," Austin said, swinging his keys around his finger. "You want to join me, Dell?"

"Thank you," Rowan said, equally grateful to have Dell out of the house. The minute they were gone, she grabbed for her phone. "I have to call Laine," she said. "If Lee—"

"You'd know if he'd been here."

"I don't know anything anymore."

But Celia was right; according to Laine, Lee had been home all weekend, repaving his driveway. As relieved as Rowan was, she'd half hoped for some kind of clue, anything to go on. Rowan called her cell provider next to ask about tracking his location, while Celia pulled up every cab company within twenty miles.

Rowan was sitting on hold when the text from Austin popped up.

It was a photo of a bicycle, an orange-and-black mountain bike with wide tires and flat handlebars. Austin probably knew it was Gabriel's because he had gone with Rowan to pick it out. She'd wanted to get Gabriel a present for finishing eighth grade, something to celebrate the end of summer school. Gabriel took care of that bike like it was made of glass. Austin and Dell found it locked to a metal bench at a bus stop nearly ten miles away.

Three different buses stopped at that line, the woman at the transit authority told Rowan. Those three buses covered a dozen stops each before arriving at the main depot, where he would have been able to find a bus to take him to a train, or an airport, or pretty much anywhere.

Rowan thanked her and hung up. Then she made one more call.

Austin was right—the police didn't share her sense of urgency, and they didn't show up right away. Celia, Austin, and Dell sat with her while she waited, all four of their phones set in the center of the table like a bundle of kindling that refused to light. It was late afternoon by the time the doorbell rang, plenty of time to come up with a million what-ifs that were far scarier than the risk of giving birth in prison for kidnapping, forgery, and lying to authorities.

Later that evening, Rowan sat on the porch swing, cocooned in blankets as the darkness swirled in front of her eyes. Her phone was in her lap, unlit and silent. The text messages she'd sent Gabriel, dozens of them, were still unread. She'd called him more than fifty times and filled his voicemail with panicked pleas until the box would listen to her no more.

Talking to the police hadn't been the nightmare she'd expected, but it also did nothing to allay her fears. Far from being led away in handcuffs, she could have flat-out told Officer Menkin that she'd been harboring an abducted child for all he seemed to care. He'd arrived with sharp eyes and brisk intentions, but the minute Rowan produced Gabriel's note, his interest morphed to irritation without skipping a beat.

"You said he was missing."

"He is missing," Rowan said. "No one has seen him since last night, and he's not answering his phone."

"But he left a note saying he'll be back soon?"

"He's fourteen," she said. "*Soon* is twenty minutes, not twelve hours. I'm afraid something happened to him."

"We've already reached out to hospitals," Celia added.

The officer scanned the page again. "Does he have a history of running away? Drug use? Alcohol?"

"No."

"Do you have reason to believe he's in danger?"

"I just told you—"

"We found his bike at a bus stop ten miles from here," Austin cut in, settling his hands on Rowan's shoulders. "And we know he's got cash on him."

Officer Menkin glanced at him and finally summoned the energy to ask a few helpful questions. "You said he's how old?"

"Fourteen."

"What does he look like?"

"He's tall for his age, about five seven, maybe a hundred and twenty-five pounds. Fair skin, dark brown hair, blue eyes. I have pictures," Rowan said, reaching for her phone.

"Birthmarks? Scars?"

"He has a scar running along the right side of his hairline and another one on his left eyebrow. There's a surgical incision on his right arm, and he's got scarring on his lower back..." She trailed off as Officer Menkin stared at her, the tip of his pen pressed to the tablet.

"Why's he so beat-up?"

"He was injured earlier this year," Rowan said quickly. "In the Ardmore tornado."

"Ah," the officer said, nodding. "That was a bad one. Friend of mine lost his house. You said he left early this morning?"

"I think so."

"Did he take anything?"

"His phone, his bike, and at least one change of clothes, far as I can tell."

"How was he acting when you saw him last?"

Rowan hesitated. "He was upset."

"About what?"

She glanced at Dell. "I told him we might be moving." Dell's eyes fell on her for far longer than a glance. "And he didn't want to go."

"I'm willing to bet he's hunkering down with one of his buddies to cool off."

"I already called his friends. They haven't seen him."

"Doesn't matter. Kids that age cover each other's asses. When I was thirteen, I hid out in a friend's basement for three days after my parents got divorced. His folks didn't know a thing."

Rowan gritted her teeth. "No one has seen him."

"All right," the officer said, snapping the tablet closed. "I'll get him into the database on my end and send his description to the Department of Transit. I can't tell you not to worry, but I have a feeling you won't be waiting long. Nine times out of ten, runaways come back on their own within a few days. Especially the younger ones. Keep up with his friends, other family members, anyone you can think of. If he shows up, give me a call. I'll be in touch."

After he left, Celia and Austin decided to canvass the area again, but Dell stayed behind. Rowan was boiling with nervous energy, running around the house and inventing chores that didn't need doing. He sat at the kitchen table and watched her rearrange the refrigerator, sweep and mop the floor, and pick up the phone to call Gabriel. Again and again and again.

"Sit down," Dell said as Rowan wandered around the room sending another barrage of texts to Gabriel's number.

"I don't want to."

"You should. Why don't you have a drink? Have a glass of wine. It'll calm you down."

"I can't," Rowan said automatically.

"Why not?"

She paused her fingers against the screen. "I don't have any wine."

Dell's eyes followed her around the kitchen—they had been doing so all night. He'd been staring at her since Officer Menkin walked out the door. "Can I ask you something?"

"No, Dell, you can't ask me something. Don't ask me anything right now."

"Were you going to tell me you were moving?"

She slapped her phone on the counter. "We're not moving. It was just something I was thinking about."

"Then why was he upset?"

"Do you really want to pick a fight with me right now?"

"How am I picking a fight? I'm just asking you—"

"And I'm *telling* you that now is not the time. Just leave it."

"Okay," Dell said. "But if you're really worried about him, it's also not the time to be keeping secrets. Maybe think about that."

"Maybe you'd rather not be here," Rowan said tightly. "You're obviously very concerned."

"Stop," Dell said. "I am concerned. I'll be here until we hear something."

That had been hours ago. They didn't hear anything.

Rowan sat in the swing, her mind churning in a childish catcall of disbelief. She kept trying to reassemble their conversation in the attic, but she couldn't—it had shattered into a million broken pieces she couldn't fit together.

There was anger in the chaos. Not at Dell's indifference or the policeman's apathy, but at Gabriel himself—for sacrificing his safety for emotion, for not believing her. It was like he'd run off with her legs, her hands, her heart—dangling them just beyond her reach while giving her a new heavy thing to hold.

Please don't worry. I promise I'm safe and I'll be careful. I love you.

Rowan jumped, the blankets pooling on the porch. She lifted her head so quickly, the swirling shapes scurried away, leaving no comfort in their wake. Her eyes grew sharp as his intentions dawned, as did the understanding that he *had* told her, right from the beginning.

From the moment she'd taken him, Gabriel had surrendered his own legs, and hands, and heart. She'd taken all his burdens onto herself, kept them locked up tight, and then she threw that box wide open and showed him exactly how heavy it was. She'd laid out every fear and given him crystal clear instructions.

What has to happen?

Murder or blackmail...

In her room, Rowan wrenched open her dresser drawer, her fingers rooting for the hard edge of the envelope she'd tucked into the seam of the wood.

I have fantasies of just showing up on his doorstep...forcing him to give you up...

She opened the closet and groped for the plastic-wrapped fork that had spent the past two years gathering dust in the corner.

It was gone.

Her phone trembled in her hand as she pulled up her photos. Rowan had set up a shared album the night Gabriel and Charlie went to the dance, with strict instructions to take lots of pictures that night. Gabriel had uploaded only one: a grinning selfie from the bathroom with Flip scaling the walls of a stall in the background.

Now the album was full. Gabriel's face, impossibly young, swollen and mottled with purple bruises. A half-deflated air mattress on a concrete floor. A bare showerhead dripping rusty water.

The next picture came to life. An eleven-year-old Gabriel reciting his name as he stood in his cement prison, beaten, emaciated, and more terrified than Rowan remembered. Too small, too weak, too young to even think about fighting back.

I'm not that little anymore.

Blood roared in her ears, and for a split second, her eyes went dark. Every fearful thought vanished as she was invited into soft oblivion, a place that was quiet and peaceful and safe.

Then she ran out of the room and took the stairs as fast as she could, eyes and mouth wide as she screamed for Celia.

CHAPTER TWENTY-SEVEN

———

GABRIEL PRESSED HIS FOREHEAD TO THE WINDOW AND STARED INTO his own glass eyes. He'd been trapped in a squashed little seat for hours, and his back and legs ached. He wanted to put his feet up, but the flight attendant had already yelled at him once for that, even though no one was sitting next to him. It didn't matter. The tiny screen on the seat in front of him had a countdown to landing, and it was only forty more minutes to Albany.

Albany was as close as he could get, but it was close enough. He figured he could take a cab from the airport to his father's house. He'd already taken one all the way from the bus station to the airport in Oklahoma City. It was a two-and-a-half-hour ride, but he would have spent five times as long getting on and off buses to go the same distance. The only reason he went to the bus station in the first place was because he hadn't wanted to call a cab at the house—Rowan would have thought of that.

Aside from being cramped and freezing cold, he didn't mind the plane. He could turn off his phone without feeling guilty about ignoring the stream of calls and voicemails and what felt like hundreds of texts.

The hardest part of this whole mission was believing how easy it was. The taxi driver had asked him no questions aside from where he was going, and neither had the ticket agent at the airport; when the boarding pass landed in his hand, it felt like an electric shock, rendering him blissfully numb. He'd had to switch planes in Atlanta, but the stop was only an hour and a half, and it gave him a chance to sit down and eat.

The only bad part had been giving his backpack to the woman at the ticket counter. It never occurred to him that he wouldn't be able to bring it on the plane until he was in the ticket line, face-to-face with a giant sign that asked: ARE YOU TRAVELING WITH RESTRICTED ITEMS?

The sign showed pictures of things like scissors and matches. He had an eighteen-inch barbecue fork. He had to assume the answer was yes.

Aside from that, he'd made most of his decisions without thinking. Thoughts had no place in action; Rowan had taught him that. He tried to channel her energy, the way she focused on beginnings and endings and ignored everything in between. *Don't think, don't hesitate, just move.* It worked. He made it all the way to Albany, and he'd barely had a coherent thought since he'd stormed out of the house with that blood-caked fork and almost nothing else. Back at the house, wrapped up in plastic and hidden in the closet, it had still been his father's weapon. Now it was his. He was ready to use it.

Gabriel wasn't sure what he was going to say when he got to his dad's—he didn't even know if he was afraid or angry. All he knew was that Rowan was both, and she had been for a long time. He thought he'd let go of every fear and every secret, but he hadn't. He'd just handed them to her, walking away a little lighter every time.

But his father was too heavy for either of them to carry, even if they did it together. So Gabriel was going to get rid of him. The how didn't matter. He'd worry about that later.

———————

Gabriel's initial plan had been to worry in the cab, but he fell asleep instead, an unfortunate detour that slashed his strategy time from an hour and a half to thirty seconds. The cabdriver had to shake him awake, and Gabriel was only half-conscious when he stumbled out of the overheated, coconut-scented air into full darkness. He'd forgotten that November in New England was very different than November in the South: at home it was cool; here it was freezing. The icy air helped him forget for a moment that he was standing in the middle of the street, thirty feet from his father's house.

He stared at the house, waiting for some inner pull of familiarity, a link to the past version of himself. There was none. Only a brick wall and strands of Christmas lights and a window tucked into the foundation. He'd expected a flood of memories: the sound of his father's hand striking his skin or the stale smell of beer and peppermint perpetually on his breath. There was nothing.

The windows in the house next door burst to life with pale golden light. Gabriel didn't wait. He ran to the door before pounding on it with the flat side of his fist. A figure approached, morphed by the thick rippled glass. The door opened, and Laine's brown eyes blinked three times. "Gabriel?"

"I need to come in," he said, pushing past her. "I'm sorry, I—"

"What are you *doing* here?" She tried to hug him, but his arms refused to leave his sides. "Are you all right?"

"No," he said shortly, moving into the warm glow of the kitchen. He sat at the table and then stood, picking up a rolling pin and spinning it in his fingers. "You can't tell Rowan I'm here, okay? Promise you won't?"

"Honey, she's worried sick about you. We have to call her."

"No!" he barked, louder than he meant. "Please."

Gabriel could feel Laine's eyes on him as he turned and began to move magnets around on the refrigerator. "Sit," she said carefully. "Have you eaten? I can make coffee—"

"No, no, no," Gabriel said, dropping into a chair. "Coffee's on the list."

"What list?"

"The list, the list, the Foods I Don't Like list," he said, drumming his fingers on the tabletop. "Rowan made the list. It's on our refrigerator, but that's okay. I don't need to write it all down for myself, right? I—"

Laine laid her hands on his. "Gabriel? Breathe."

He stopped, pressing his palms against the wood. "I'm sorry."

"It's okay. You're okay. Is Coke on the list?"

"No."

She poured him a glass and sat. "How did you get here?"

"I flew," he said, taking a noisy gulp that hurt his swollen throat. "To Albany. Then I took a cab here. It was easy. But I used up all my money, so I don't know how I'm going to get back."

"Why did you leave in the first place? Rowan loves you so much, honey."

Gabriel began to wander the kitchen again. He couldn't hear things like that. It made everything harder to ignore. He turned suddenly. "You know she's pregnant, right?"

Laine sat back in her chair. "Is that why you left?"

"No," he said, listening to his shoes squeak on the tiles. "I left because there's something I need to do."

"You should have talked to her. She would have helped you."

"She wouldn't have helped me with this." He met Laine's eye for the first time. "My father went to the hospital after the tornado. I was already gone, so he left me a note—I have it in my bag if you want to see. It sounded like he was coming for me, like he was going to hurt me. But I never got the note. Rowan did. She was hiding it from me so I wouldn't be scared. She told me all about Ethan and about the baby, but she didn't tell me about that."

"She didn't want to upset you."

"She should have! She's treating me like a baby, and I'm not a baby. That note was for *me*." His head felt too heavy to hold up, and he let his chin fall to his chest. "Everything was getting better," he whispered. "We were getting better. She was going to adopt me."

"She's still going to do that."

"She can't. Not unless my father gives me up. That's what she told me. That's why I'm here. I can't do anything about the baby, or about Ethan, or any of that, but I can do something about my father."

"Gabriel, no…"

"Don't tell me no! I came all this way, and he's going to listen to me. He has to." He reached inside his backpack and pulled out the plastic-wrapped fork.

Laine paled. "What is that?"

"Evidence. He used it on me, and now I'm going to use it on him. Look." He turned and lifted his shirt so Laine could see his back, the long scars that matched the tines. "It still has my blood on it. And I have more. If he doesn't leave us alone, I'll tell the police what he did to me. I have proof. I'll tell them everything."

"You can't do that! He hurt you before—he could do it again. He's dangerous."

"So am I."

"Gabriel," Laine said, holding up her hands. "Please call Rowan. At least let her know you're all right. She is absolutely sick about this."

"Not until I can tell her she doesn't ever have to worry about him again. I owe that to her." His eyes boiled with sudden tears. "I owe her a lot."

"Do you really think she would want this?"

"No, but she deserves it. She's done so much for me. And some of the things she does aren't about taking care of me or keeping me safe. She does them just to make me happy."

"Like what?"

"Little things. Like, she wakes up early every morning just to make me breakfast, even though I told her I can make it myself. And the first time she went grocery shopping after we got to Oklahoma, she asked me what kind of ice cream I liked. When I told her I didn't know, she came home with about twenty different flavors. She said I had to try them all to find my favorite so she'd always know what to get me." He laughed, and the lump in his throat dissolved as his eyes spilled over. "God, we had ice cream for months. She did a lot of things like that. She writes *Love, Santa* on all my Christmas presents," he went on, wiping his cheeks, "even though I'm too old. She stayed up with me when I had nightmares, she takes me to the doctor when

I get sick, and when that tornado came, she almost died because she pushed *me* in between those rocks."

"Gabriel?"

"I want my father to know that," he went on, clenching his fists. "I want him to know I could hurt him. I think I could even kill him. This will be the last time he ever sees me, and I'm going to decide how it ends. He does not get to take away my ending."

Laine touched his shoulder. "Gabriel, please—you're very upset. You need to rest. Just promise me you won't do anything tonight. Stay here, get a good night's sleep, and we'll talk about everything in the morning."

He swiped a hand across his nose. "Will you help me?"

Laine paused—he couldn't read her expression. "I'll try. For now just go upstairs, take a nice hot shower, and try to relax. I'll order something for dinner and make up the spare room for you."

"You won't tell Rowan?"

"I won't tell Rowan. Don't worry. We'll figure everything out in the morning." This time when she hugged him, he hugged her back, in real gratitude, before slowly climbing the stairs.

CHAPTER TWENTY-EIGHT

ROWAN'S PANICKED SCREAM BROUGHT EVERYONE TO THE FOYER. DELL was two steps behind Austin, but Celia got there first. "What's the matter?!"

Rowan stumbled down the stairs as fast as her leg would let her. When she reached the bottom, she didn't even try to avoid colliding with Celia. Her phone flew out of her hand and skidded across the hall. "I know where he is—I—"

Celia grabbed her by the shoulders. "Did he call you?"

"No. He's going to Massachusetts." She choked. "He took the fork and the pictures—"

"The fork?" Dell repeated.

"He's going to see his father!"

"Are you sure?" Celia asked. When Rowan didn't answer, Celia shook her. "Rowan! Are you sure?"

"Yes. The fork is gone."

Rowan saw Dell turn to Austin, as though expecting camaraderie in his confusion, but there was none to be had. "Rowe, do you want me to call the police back?" Austin asked.

"No! If they find out—"

"If they find out what?" Dell asked. "What is going on?"

Celia sat on the stairs, but it looked more like a collapse than a decision.

Rowan couldn't even catch a breath; she was doubled over with one hand pressed to her chest. "He'll kill him," she managed.

Under the table, Rowan's phone began to ring. Rowan scrambled across the floor on her hands and knees and snatched it up. "Gabe?"

"Rowan, it's okay, he's here—"

"Laine? Is he okay?"

"Yes, he's fine. He's—"

"Are you sure? How did he get there?"

"He flew into Albany and took a cab the rest of the way."

"Tell him I'm coming," Rowan said. "Keep him there. I need—"

Laine's voice flowed through the speaker, low and soothing. "Rowan, I have him. He's safe. Please take a breath."

Rowan dropped next to Celia, the phone trembling in her grip. "Let me talk to him."

"I sent him upstairs to get cleaned up. I promised him I wouldn't call you, and I don't want him to get upset."

"Oh God...did his father see him?"

"I don't even think Lee's home," Laine said after a pause. "His van is gone."

"Laine—" Rowan glanced up. Dell was staring holes through her, his eyes neither relieved nor concerned. He looked wholly confused, bordering on furious. "Hang on."

She crossed the hall to the sunroom, swinging the French doors closed for the first time since they'd moved in. "Dell's here," she whispered.

His voice reached her through the doors. "What the hell is going on?"

Celia, softer. "You need to ask Rowan."

"God, I am so sick of all this head-spinning bullshit," he spat. "She's not going to tell me. I've been trying to find out about this kid for months."

"There's a reason she couldn't. Wait until she comes out."

"Laine," Rowan whispered. "What does he want to do?"

"He wants to talk to his father."

Rowan sucked in her breath, even though she expected nothing less.

"He showed up brandishing a goddamned spear. He said he thought he could kill him."

"He's not scared?" Rowan asked.

"He didn't sound scared. What difference does it make?"

Rowan was quiet for a moment. "Laine, do you know any of the police around there? Anyone you could ask for help without saying too much?"

"You're going to let him go over there?"

"He'll do it anyway. I had him on lockdown, and he got away from me the minute I looked away. If he's determined enough to fly across the country, he'll walk next door. We have to make sure he's safe. Do you know any cops?"

"No."

"Fuck...okay. Shit."

"If he stays outside, I'll be able to see him the whole time."

"Lee could grab him in two seconds. You cracked a rib picking up a medicine ball in gym class."

"That was not my fault—it was way heavier than it looked."

"Well, I can't see you tackling him to the ground. I'm sorry, I love you, but it's true. The best you could do is call the cops, and that's not good enough."

Laine was quiet for a moment. "What if I had help?"

"Who?"

"I have a friend...kind of. His name's Guillermo—Guy. He works in private security, and he's an absolute unit. If I asked him to help me, he'd show up armed and ready in a second. I know he would. We're on good terms."

"How good?"

"Very. Like, as-of-last-weekend good."

"Could you hide him somewhere?"

"I don't think he should hide. I think he should be right outside. I'll have him pretend to work on my car or something. If he's in the driveway and Gabriel is in Lee's front yard, he'll be fifteen feet away. I can't guarantee Lee won't do anything, but the odds are better that he won't if someone's right there. And if he does, Guy could absolutely tackle him to the ground."

Rowan was quiet for a moment. "Laine. Listen to me. Gabriel is… This is my life we're talking about."

"I know," Laine said. "I'll do whatever I have to do."

Rowan stepped through the French doors into the foyer. Celia was still sitting on the stairs, and now Austin was, too; she had her head resting on his chest. Dell stood in front of them.

"Laine is going to keep him with her tonight," Rowan said.

None of them moved. The words hung in the air as though they were still waiting to be heard. Dell stared at her. The question in his eyes was crushing, a mammoth in a room already stuffed with elephants.

She didn't know what to say. So she put her phone into her back pocket and walked away.

About three seconds later, she heard footsteps. Dell followed her into the kitchen. "That's it?"

"For now," Rowan said, filling a glass with water. "We're going to try and fly him home tomorrow."

"Why did he go there? Why can't he see his father? Why isn't he *with* his father?"

Rowan looked at him. An expectant silence stretched between them like a cord, one end attached to the seed in her belly. She put down her glass and motioned toward the back door. "Come outside."

They went to the porch swing; the blankets were still on the ground from earlier. Rowan picked one up and shook it out without saying a word. "Well?" Dell asked.

"What do you want to know?"

"I want to know about Gabriel! God, I feel like I'm in the fucking Twilight Zone. Where did he come from?"

"I kidnapped him," Rowan said immediately. To her horror, a bubble of laughter followed that statement. She clapped a hand over her mouth.

Dell glared at her. "You know what? Forget it. After all this, you still want to feed me ten lines of bullshit—"

"No, wait!" she cried. "It's true. It's absolutely true."

"You kidnapped him?"

"Yes."

"Why?"

Rowan pressed her lips together. Then she sat back and began to recite what sounded like the biggest line of bullshit of them all. She told him why, and she told him how. She walked him through every link, from Laine to Lee to Gabriel. And when she was done telling him, she pulled out her phone and showed him.

When he reached the last picture, Dell stared at it until the screen went dark. Then he cleared his throat and handed the phone back to her.

"Do you understand?" she asked quietly.

Dell's eyes were wide. "No."

"What don't you understand?"

"How you could possibly get away with that."

"It wasn't easy."

"Does anyone else know?"

"Celia, of course. Laine. Austin." She grimaced at the wave of hurt that blew across Dell's face. "I didn't tell him," she added in a rush. "Gabe did. He wanted him to know."

"Why?"

"Because," she said quietly. "Austin loves him."

Dell stared into his lap. "Why would he go there?" he asked. "If his father is as bad as you say he is."

Rowan tilted her head back. "When someone hurts you for a long time," she said carefully, "and you get away, you don't just stop being scared. It doesn't matter how safe you are. It's not like a switch. Ethan is a thousand miles away, and I'm still scared of him." Her voice rose and broke.

Dell reached for her hand, weaving his fingers through hers.

"The fear just stays. You don't always think about it, but it's always there. I've been trying to protect him from his, and that was a mistake. He has to deal with it." Rowan wiped her eyes. "Did I scare you away?"

"No."

"Do you want to know anything else?"

"Is there anything else?"

Rowan stared into her lap. She shook her head without meeting his eye. "No."

———————————

Gabriel slept for twelve hours without a single dream. When he stumbled downstairs in the morning, Laine was in the kitchen, pouring orange juice into a glass. There was a plate of blueberry waffles on the table.

"I'm sorry they're frozen," Laine said, handing him the juice. "I mean formerly frozen. I would have made them fresh, but I don't have a waffle iron. Or ingredients. And I don't know how to make waffles." She sat across from him. "I hope none of this is on your food list."

"No, you're good. Thank you," he added.

"You slept well."

"I didn't think I'd be able to."

Laine took a sip of coffee. "How do you feel?"

"I don't know yet."

That wasn't really true—he felt like he'd been split into two chunks. The part of him that was thinking about his father felt almost giddy, like a one-man surprise party. He wanted to run over there right now, this second, just to see the look on his face.

The part of him that was thinking about the basement was terrified.

"Do you still want to talk to him?" Laine asked.

"Yes."

"I'm going to help you," she said carefully. "But you have to agree to every single thing I say. If you don't, you're not going to see him. If you go anyway, I'm calling the police, and we will all have much bigger problems to deal with. Got it?"

He lifted his chin. "I'm going over there alone."

"You're going to listen to me first."

———

Gabriel crossed Laine's lawn. He'd agreed to her rules, and she'd agreed to wait on her steps, even though he really didn't want an audience. And it wasn't just Laine. Some guy was there, too, fiddling with something under the hood of her car. Gabriel asked Laine if she could move them both to the street, but she said a mechanic who made house calls was too valuable to piss off.

He stopped at the foot of the walkway. The fifteen hundred miles it took Gabriel to get to this spot weren't as long as the stretch of stones in front of him. It felt wrong to walk up to the house, because he'd never really walked away from it. Six years ago his father had carried him inside. It was a long drive to get to the new house, and by the time they did, Gabriel was almost asleep. He remembered being desperate for bed and excited about his new room; it was a special room, his dad told him. Just for him. Then his father carried him in. Gabriel hadn't left that room until three years later, when Rowan carried him out.

It felt really, really important that he walk this time.

Inside the house, a door slammed.

His father was home.

Gabriel took one step, and something inside him seemed to break. He didn't walk up the path—he ran straight up the stairs to the front door.

He raised his fist and knocked.

Another door slammed. He heard footsteps pound the floor. Then a voice.

"Who is it?"

It was and it wasn't his father. Gabriel recognized him immediately, but he sounded so *old*; there were far more than two years in that voice, and that alone nearly sent him running.

But he didn't run. He had a new voice, too, and he wanted his father to hear it. "It's me."

Silence. A long, long silence that stretched like taffy. There was fear in that silence, and it took him a moment to realize it wasn't coming from him. He knocked again, louder this time. "Open the door. It's me."

Another beat. Two. Then there was a scrape of metal on metal, and before Gabriel could decide whether to stay or run, his father stood behind the screen door.

He looked exactly the same. Exactly. Gabriel took two steps back and cursed himself for showing fear so soon.

But his father looked scared too. "Gabe."

Gabriel swallowed. He'd imagined this scene a million times, but now it was live, and someone had snatched the script out of his hands. He said the only thing he could think of. "I bet you want to know where I've been, huh?"

The ghost of a smile touched his father's lips. "I know where you've been." He unhooked the latch. "Come in."

Before he could get the door open, Gabriel walked back down the steps. It wouldn't be the first time his father had pushed him down the stairs. "Come out."

Another smile, a little longer this time. "All right."

Gabriel took a few more steps back, trying not to hurry. He'd promised Laine he wouldn't get close enough to grab.

But his father was keeping his distance too. He didn't even come down the stairs. He eased himself down and sat on the top step—painfully, Gabriel thought. "So tell me, Gabe," he said, stretching his legs. "What have you been up to?"

"You just said you know."

"I know where you've been. Next time you run away, maybe don't go on national news."

"You still didn't find me."

"No," he agreed. "The hospital wouldn't tell me. They wouldn't tell *your father* where you were. That's impressive. You two must have come up with quite a story."

"I bet you were glad I got hurt."

His father shrugged. "I wasn't surprised. That's what happens when you run away from what you deserve."

Gabriel's hands balled into fists. "I didn't deserve it."

"No? That bitch tell you that?"

"Don't call her that."

"She let you come here all by yourself?"

"She doesn't know I'm here."

"That's my brave boy."

"And I'm not staying," Gabriel said, meeting his father's eye. "I came to tell you something and to ask you for something. A favor."

"I really don't think I owe you any favors."

"I don't think you'll mind this one."

"Go ahead."

Gabriel straightened to his full height, which usually felt much taller. "I want you to give me up," he said.

"Give you up?"

"Yes. Legally."

His father threw his head back and laughed.

Gabriel didn't flinch. "It'll be easy. Just say you can't take care of me. Say you sent me away on purpose. You'll finally be rid of me."

"Why would I do that?" his father asked. "For *her*?"

"No. For me."

"Oh no, Gabe, I'm sorry. I mind that very much."

"Why?"

"Because you belong to me. I don't give a shit how long you've been gone or who you've been with. Blood is blood."

"You don't have to tell me about blood." Gabriel unshouldered his backpack. "I have something to show you."

Something—not quite fear, but close—flickered in his dad's eyes. Gabriel pulled out the plastic-wrapped fork and pointed it at his father. "This is my blood," he said, examining the pointed tines. He turned the fork over and showed him the handle. "And these are your fingerprints. That's all part of what I wanted to tell you."

His father blinked a few times. "What are you telling me?"

"This has nothing to do with the favor. That's just an ask. What I'm going to tell you is not a choice; you're just going to do it."

"And what is that?"

"If you don't leave us alone," Gabriel said slowly, "I will tell the police what you did to me. I will tell them everything, and I can prove it all."

His dad smiled. "How about this? I go to the cops first and tell them that a little bitch named Rowan McNamara kidnapped my son and brought him all the way to Okla-fucking-homa. How does that sound?"

"Two years ago, Dad. Two years. You made a mistake keeping me locked up like that. You should have at least sent me to school or something because then you could have reported it. But if you do it now, the police will wonder why no one knew about me. Or why you waited two years to tell anyone I was missing. And if they find me, I'll tell them why she took me." He pointed the fork at his father. "If we get one more note, if we get one more threat, or one more message from you, I will tell. Leave us alone and we're even. I keep the fork. But," Gabriel said, "if you want to be really sure, you can give me up like I asked. If you do that, you get the fork."

His father stood. Gabriel didn't move. "You think you can blackmail me?"

"It's not blackmail. You just have to leave us alone," Gabriel said.

"Like you left me alone?"

Gabriel blinked. "What?"

His father walked toward him. "You left me alone," he said slowly. "The day you killed your mother."

"I didn't—"

"You killed her, and you killed yourself. You're both dead. The only difference is that you got up, and she didn't."

It sounded like the same crazed rambling he'd heard during every single beating, but something was different—his father had never sounded sad about losing him. Ever.

"Do you remember yourself before that day?" his father whispered. "Or do you just remember her?"

Gabriel opened and closed his mouth. There were tears, actual tears, welling in his father's eyes. Gabriel had hurt him and wasn't sure how. "No," he said quietly. "I don't. You could have told me."

"I couldn't even look at you. You killed her. You are dead to me." A tiny piece of clarity, of humanity flickered in his father's eyes, just barely. "What do you want, Gabe?"

"I want to know why you kept me in that basement," Gabriel said, willing his voice not to shake.

"It made me feel better."

"Hurting me made you feel better?"

"Yes." His father smiled down at the cobblestones. "There are no words," he said, "for how much I hate you. She never should have been there. It should have been you."

Gabriel took a deep breath and wedged his fingers into that crack. "Then how come you won't let me go?"

His father took a step toward him. "It was really something to come home that night," he said. "You know that? You left a lot of blood on the floor."

Gabriel took a step back. "I'm glad."

His dad smiled a little. Another step. "Give me the fork."

"No."

Another. "Give me the fork," he repeated. "If you don't want to get hurt, and you don't want her to get hurt, give me the fork."

Gabriel clutched it tighter. "Do you promise to leave us alone?"

"Give it to me."

"She loves me. She wants to adopt me," Gabriel said. "And I want her to. We can't do that unless you give me up."

"I don't really care what you want."

"You used to."

His father's eyes went dark. "Give me the fork," he said quietly, "and I will leave you alone."

Gabriel stared at the stretch of grass over his father's shoulder. He saw tiny chips of paint dancing in the breeze around his own ghost and Rowan's, the way she used to be. She was different now, not as fearless, not as brave, and it was his fault she'd been scared for too long. All he wanted was to bring her back. So he bent, slowly, keeping his eyes on his father's face. He put the fork on the ground at his feet. Then he turned and walked away from the house for the first and last time.

CHAPTER TWENTY-NINE

GABRIEL CIRCLED THE BLOCK TWICE BEFORE GOING BACK TO LAINE'S. The mechanic must have been testing out her car, because he drove around the block, too, starting and stopping and backing up. Gabriel barely noticed. Both his body and his mind were thrown by the sudden arrival of the very last buried part of him, and he needed to breathe.

He'd never seen these streets or the trees or the houses, but he knew what they sounded like, and he wanted one chance to say goodbye to the things he used to hate. A school bus rumbled past him. It stopped at the corner, and four kids about his age got out, laughing and jostling each other on the other side of the street. He stared at them, wondering if they were the screamers who rode their bikes all day long and yelled at the ice cream man. They were carrying backpacks, like he was, weighted down with books and homework and laptops. Even though his was empty, he knew it was much, much heavier.

Laine was sitting on the steps when he got back, wrapped in a giant fuzzy coat. He only had his sweatshirt. It hadn't occurred to him to be cold.

"Come inside," she said, reaching for his hand. "It's freezing."

He followed her through the door and into the living room. There was a fire dancing in the tiny brick fireplace, and he sat on the couch in front of it. Laine disappeared into the kitchen. She came back a minute later with a mug of something and pressed it into his hands. "Did you get to say what you needed to?"

Gabriel shrugged.

"Are you okay?"

He nodded and took a sip from the mug—hot chocolate.

"You don't look okay."

Gabriel stared into his cup. "I feel like he died," he said. "Or like he never really existed, like I made him up."

"I think you're in a little bit of shock." She touched his forehead like she was checking for a fever, and as she pulled back, he caught her hand and held it. He felt like he'd float right through the ceiling if he didn't. His entire body seemed loose, untethered to anything real.

"He said he'll leave us alone," he said. "And I think I believe him."

Laine gripped his fingers. "Do you want to call Rowan?"

"In a minute."

She paused. "Do you need a hug?"

He nodded—he didn't trust his voice to speak. She'd already done way more than he deserved, but in that moment, he was just grateful to have anyone with a pair of arms next to him. She wrapped him up, and they sat there without moving. He didn't fall to pieces or cry or laugh or feel vindicated or relieved. He didn't even think about his father. He just let himself be there, on the couch in a room Rowan had once been in, holding on to the person who'd saved her life so she could save his.

It was a very long time before he spoke. "Thank you."

"I wish Rowan were here for you, sweetie," Laine said into his shoulder. "I feel like a poor substitute."

"You're not."

"Why don't you call her? Let her know you're okay."

"You already did, didn't you?"

"Of course," Laine said, pulling back. Her eyes were wet, but she was smiling. "She was on the phone with me the whole time you were over there. Did you really think I'd listen to you?"

He smiled, too, but it died on his face when he looked at his phone, at all the messages he'd ignored. Calls and voicemails, dozens and dozens of them. Texts from Rowan, Celia, Austin, Flip, Mel, Charlie. Even Dell. He was hit by a horrible wave of guilt, and he couldn't believe he'd waited more than thirty seconds to tell Rowan he was okay.

She answered on the first ring. He knew she would. "Gabe?"

"I want to come home."

In the end, he flew home by himself. He had no doubt his father meant what he'd said, but that didn't mean he wanted to hang around to find out. Rowan booked him on a direct flight out of Albany at six o'clock the next morning.

Laine drove him to Albany as soon as he hung up with Rowan, and they stayed in a hotel near the airport. After the whirlwind of the past two days, plus waking up at four a.m., Gabriel fell asleep almost as soon as he got on the plane, and by the time he opened his eyes, the pilot was announcing their descent. He was still groggy when he walked out of the gate. Everything looked blurry around the edges; he couldn't sharpen the corners enough to convince himself it wasn't a dream.

But then he saw Rowan. She was standing alone, bright and clear in front of the airport's big glass window. He got his feet under him and started to run, dodging people and winding lines and rolling suitcases. He didn't stop until his arms were around her, his legs almost too weak to hold him up, and Rowan clutched him, her wet cheek pressed against his, saying the same thing over and over.

"I've got you. I've got you."

It was dark, and the house was quieter than it had been in days. Gabriel was in bed, and Rowan had a feeling he'd be staying there for a while. He hadn't let go of her the entire way home, for two and a half hours, but he didn't say much. She hadn't let anyone press him—he'd talk when he was ready.

Rowan poured a glass of red wine and walked into the den. Dell was on the couch, the last member of the search party. Everyone had stayed for dinner, which was less of a meal and more of a free-for-all on whatever odds and ends were floating around in the fridge. Options ranged from a southwestern frittata to dino nuggets. Afterward, Celia and Austin went home to sleep, but Rowan had asked Dell to stay.

"Finally having that drink?" Dell asked as Rowan sank next to him on the couch.

"This is for you," she said, handing him the glass. "Thank you for staying."

"Is Gabriel asleep?" Dell asked.

"Knocked out cold. I'm going to call his doctor tomorrow and see what kind of therapist she can recommend. If he thought he had to do this for me, I'm not doing a very good job."

"You're doing an incredible job," Dell said, smoothing her hair back. "He wouldn't have gone if you weren't."

Rowan shrugged. "It's time to delegate, I think. He needs more than just me."

Dell smiled. "Having second thoughts on the whole parenting thing?"

"No," Rowan said quietly. "Not at all."

Dell rubbed her hand. "Did the lawyer call you back? About Ethan?"

Rowan nodded. "They confirmed the call with his phone records, and the GPS got him going over the state line. It's a parole violation just for him to call me, and since he showed intent to come here, they're holding him again until the board meets."

"That's good."

She shrugged. "It's better than nothing. I wish I had it in me to take him on. Gabriel seems… I don't know. Kind of purged, I think. But the thought of seeing Ethan again…"

"Maybe Gabriel needed it," Dell said. "And maybe you don't."

She fell silent. Dell cupped her cheek and pressed his forehead to hers, kissing her so softly, Rowan could barely taste the wine. His thumb traced her skin. "I really want you to be okay."

"I know."

"And I feel like you've been so…*angry*, lately," Dell whispered. "I know this sounds bad, but it's a relief to know why."

Rowan pulled back—time was getting short. "Dell…Gabriel kind of waylaid this, but there's something I need to talk to you about."

"You're not moving, are you?"

"No," she said. "It's not that. With everything that's happened, I feel like we've been together for a lot longer than we have. But we haven't. It's only been six months, and honestly, I know I can be a lot to deal with. And I know Gabriel can be a lot, and you don't love having him around, so I won't blame you if you're not altogether thrilled about this."

Dell smiled without joy. "Sounds like a breakup."

"It's not," she said, fixing her eyes on his. "I'm pregnant."

His smile didn't die; it was more like it fell off his face. "What?"

"I only found out last week. I should have told you right away, but I didn't even know how I felt about it—"

"What do you mean you didn't know how you felt?" Dell exclaimed, gripping her cheek. "Aren't you happy?"

"Yes, I am, but there's a lot to think about."

"Oh my God, Rowan!" Dell said, a wide grin taking over his face. "I can't believe it!"

"Dell, this is complicated. It's not just about us. There's Gabriel—"

But Dell wasn't listening. He grabbed her in a crushing hug and then eased her down before pressing his hands to her belly. "Did you go to the doctor? Is everything okay?"

"Everything's fine," she said, trying to smile. "I'm due at the end of July."

He leaned in and kissed her, then buried his face into her shoulder until Rowan didn't know if he was laughing or crying.

"I thought I was losing you," he said, his lips moving against her neck. "I really did, but now—oh my God, I'm so happy. We're going to be fine. We're going to be great. I love you so much."

Rowan hugged him back. It had taken her a long time to decide how she felt about the baby. But she still didn't know how she felt about Dell.

CHAPTER THIRTY

GABRIEL GOT SICK ALMOST IMMEDIATELY AFTER COMING HOME. HE woke up with a fever that spiked at night, and his head ached so badly, Rowan put up blackout curtains to keep the light out of his room. When his fever refused to break, she bundled him up and took him to the doctor, who diagnosed him with a viral infection, likely brought on by stress and unauthorized air travel.

The bug only lasted a week, but he was out of commission for Thanksgiving. Rowan had to cancel on everyone, and the four-course meal she'd planned turned into a small roasted turkey and mini batches of mashed potatoes and stuffing and fresh cranberry compote. She and Gabriel ate in front of the TV without even changing out of their pajamas, took a four-hour nap, and then woke up and had dinner all over again. That night they watched holiday movies and devoured pumpkin and apple pie right out of the dishes balanced on their laps.

It was the best Thanksgiving she'd ever had. Rowan vowed to do all the holidays the same way, but the very next day, Celia arrived with the news that Christmas was going to be an absolute shit show.

"You want to have a cocktail party," Rowan repeated. "On Christmas Eve."

"Right."

"After all this, everything that just happened… You don't think it's a good idea to let everyone chill for a while?"

"It'll be fun," Celia said. She'd arrived at the house with boxes full of vintage lights, ceramic decorations, and antique Christmas ornaments that went against Rowan's entire holiday aesthetic. "We'll do a buffet, get all dressed up. What do you think?"

"I think you're out of your mind. Who throws a party on Christmas Eve?"

"You need it. So does Gabriel. This will be a good chance to relax."

"We did relax—yesterday, in our pajamas. Why can't we do that again?"

"Because it's unsociable," Celia said. "Christmas is a celebration."

"How many people are you inviting to this thing?"

"About thirty—I have a list."

"You want me to cook for *thirty* people? I haven't even started decorating yet."

"If you don't want to cook, we'll get it catered."

"That still sounds like a lot of work," Rowan said. "And a hideous disregard for your pregnant sister."

"It won't be," Celia promised. "We'll serve appetizers and dessert. That's it. You can be in charge of the cocktails."

"I can't even drink!"

———————

When Dell came over on Sunday, Rowan was sitting at the table, poring over the list of obscure holiday drinks that Celia had sent over and trying to figure out where the hell she was supposed to find Szechuan peppercorns. "Can I help you with anything?" he asked, dropping a kiss on her head.

"Yes," she said, handing him her phone. "There's a bunch of hideous Christmas stuff in the den. Throw it away, and then call Celia and tell her this party is a horrible idea."

"It's a great idea! I've never been to a cocktail party."

"That's because it's not 1955. I've never even heard of half this shit—what the hell is a Mary Pickford? And I'm not making milk punch. People are going to be throwing up all over the place."

Gabriel came into the kitchen to dump his sandwich crusts in the garbage. "Is the pie all gone?"

"Yes, but there's a ton of ice cream," Rowan said. "How's your head?"

"Better."

"What's wrong with your head?" Dell asked.

"He was sick," Rowan told him slowly. "Remember? That's why we had to cancel Thanksgiving…"

"Oh, right. Sorry."

"Can Flip come to the party?" Gabriel asked, standing on the back of Rowan's chair.

"He's already coming," Rowan said, crossing squid ink off the list. "His parents are, too…oh God," she moaned. "Flip. That means we can't have any candles, and I'll have to make virgin cocktails, too. I hate this."

"Give the kids soda in a wineglass. They won't care," Dell said. "Make a list of whatever alcohol you need, and I'll go to the wholesale place by me." A car crunched over the driveway. "Austin's here," Dell said, hopping up. "We're going to do the lights."

"Don't put up too many!" Rowan said. "I don't want to spend a week taking them down."

Dell walked out, and Gabriel began to mound ice cream in a bowl. "Can me and Flip try the drinks if we only have a little?"

Rowan pressed her forehead to the table. "Flip and I…" she mumbled.

———

In addition to the normal holiday melee of gifts and cookies and trees, Rowan helped Celia cook, set up tables, and arrange a buffet line in the dining room, all while scrutinizing her body for even the slightest hint of a change. On Christmas Eve, she stared at herself in the mirror, smoothing her dress over her hips. She was eleven weeks pregnant, but aside from the circles lining her eyes, she looked the same as always. Her leg was still shriveled, and her belly was still flat.

Rowan stood by the door, taking coats and directing people around the house. She knew about 5 percent of the assembled guests, and within a few hours, the event looked less cocktail and more fraternity.

"Celia, who are these people?" Rowan yelled over the music, elbowing her way to her sister.

"Some friends from church, some from the hospital."

"They are *wasted*," Rowan said, rescuing a bottle of vodka perched atop her petit four platter. "I spent all day spicing persimmon and making winterberry spritzers, and they're playing beer pong on the dining room table."

"Maybe they don't get out much."

"It's almost midnight," Rowan said. "Which means Christmas is here and they need to go home."

Celia smiled at her. "Where's Dell?"

"He could be passed out anywhere. I don't know."

"I think he's on the porch," Celia told her. "Why don't you go out for a minute and get some air?"

Rowan weaved her way through the crowd, one hand clasped

protectively over her abdomen. The front door flew open to admit a group of smokers, and through the haze, she spotted Dell on the porch swing. Her exit was blocked by a cardiac intern and the church secretary groping in the foyer, but she managed to squeeze through.

"Merry Christmas," Dell said in response to the twelve chimes that sounded as she stepped through the door. The air was brisk and thin, leaving vapors trailing with every breath. Rowan sat next to him, and he wrapped his arms around her shoulders. "You should have a coat."

"It's hot in there," she said, kicking off her shoes. "We're going to be opening presents knee-deep in beer cans."

"I'll clean up, don't worry."

Christmas music poured from the open windows, slow and beautiful. The porch was lit with thousands of white lights—he and Austin had worked on it for two days.

Dell rose from the swing. "Dance with me?"

Rowan let him pull her to her feet. They moved slowly to the music, the air full of burning wood and laughter. "You've had a hard time lately," he said.

"Uh-huh."

"Lots of surprises."

"Yeah."

"I wanted to surprise you too," he said, gripping her arms.

"With what?"

"Your Christmas present. It may be a little early, but I couldn't wait any more."

"What is it?"

Dell smiled at her. "It's coming."

The boards thudded with footsteps. Celia came around the corner, pulling Gabriel by the hand. She was smiling, but Gabriel's face was painted with a million questions. A minute later Austin appeared, too, but Rowan couldn't read his expression. "Dell?" she asked.

He took a step back, and she watched in complete and abject horror as he sank to one knee and held a tiny box aloft. He cracked it open, revealing a glimmer in the center she couldn't focus on. "Rowan—"

"Dell, wait, please get up!"

"I was so happy when you told me about the baby. I know it's not something we planned, but I love you. I love you so much, and I want you to be with me, forever." He took her hand before she could say a word and slid the ring onto her finger. "Marry me?"

"Dell, please," she cried, trying to pull him up.

"I'm not doing this because I have to," he said. "I always knew I wanted to be with you." He pressed his hand to her belly. "We belong together. This proves it."

She cast a helpless look toward her sister, but Celia was still smiling, though it was starting to wobble around the edges. Gabriel had a hard crease between his eyes; he looked like he wanted to run off the porch. Austin had his face in his hands.

"Rowan?"

"Dell, can they leave, please?" she whispered.

"What?"

"Can you guys give us a minute?" she said, louder. She squeezed her eyes shut, and a moment later, their footsteps faded. "Dell, sit down, right now."

The first twinge of fear flickered in his eyes. "What's the matter?"

She sank onto the swing. "I appreciate the gesture, I do, but..."

"The *gesture*? It's not a gesture. I love you. We're having a baby together."

"That doesn't mean I'm ready to marry you."

"So you're saying no?"

She stared down at the porch. "Yes," she said quietly. "I'm saying no."

He tilted his head back, eyes on the sky. "Is it because it's too soon?" he asked. "Just tell me that," he said thickly. "It's not because you don't want to. It's just because it's too soon."

Her lips trembled; she couldn't manage more than a whisper. "No."

Dell looked at her for a long moment. Then he got to his feet and took a stumbling step forward. He put his hand out to steady himself and knocked a ruby-red globe from the wreath above her head. It hit the swing and shattered, the bright shards falling soundlessly to the ground. When he spoke, he didn't sound anything like himself. "You won't even think about it?"

Rowan's fingers were clumsy, smudging the tears on her cheeks. "If I weren't pregnant, would you be asking me to marry you right now?"

"Maybe not tonight. But soon. I told you I'm not doing this because I have to—"

"After seven months?"

"Yes," he said, defiance flashing in his eyes. "I was thinking about it."

"You're completely ready to marry me? And become a stepfather?"

"Gabriel's not—"

"He's not what?"

"I'm ready to be a father to *this* baby!" he exclaimed. "If we're going to raise a child together, we should at least try to be together!"

"That doesn't mean we have to get married!"

"Why not? Why won't you think about it?"

"Because I don't *want* to be with you!"

The words were a fist she didn't mean to throw, an invisible punch that brought real tears to his eyes. She wanted to snatch them out of the air. "Dell—"

He pulled the ring off her finger and shoved it into his pocket, letting the box fall to the ground. Then he walked down the porch steps and got into his truck without a word. The tires didn't spin on the rocks; he backed out slowly, almost like it was hard for him to see.

Rowan didn't move after he drove away. She sat there and stared at the red glass littering the wooden boards. Shining fragments as jagged and raw as a broken heart.

Rowan sat on the swing until the last guest filed out. Carloads of people left to continue the party elsewhere or go home to sleep it off. When the last car drove away, Rowan walked inside. Gabriel and Austin were trying to deal with the pile of debris that was the dining room. "Don't worry about cleaning up, Austin," Rowan said. "Can you give me a minute? I need to talk to Celia."

"You got it, sweetheart." His tone was easy; he'd heard everything. "Tell Ceil I'm going to her place. If you need anything, you call me, okay?" He kissed her cheek, swung his key around his finger, and was out the door before she could respond.

Gabriel walked over to her, but she shook her head before he could say a word. "Go to bed," she whispered, squeezing his hand.

He nodded. She bumped her lips against his cheek and pushed him toward the stairs. As soon as he was out of sight, she walked into the kitchen. Celia was piling dishes next to the sink.

"Great idea, Ceil," Rowan said quietly. "Big party to keep me distracted, midnight proposal. Was that the plan?"

"It wasn't a plan," Celia said, her voice just as quiet.

"Yes, it was," Rowan spat. "You knew the whole time!"

"And?" Celia asked, turning to face her. "Was I supposed to stop him?"

"Yes! You were! At least from doing it like this. Do you think I wanted to turn him down in front of everyone?"

"But you did."

"Was I supposed to say yes just so I wouldn't hurt his feelings?" Her voice broke, and hot, angry tears slid down her cheeks. "What about my feelings? Do you care about me at all?"

"Yes, I do," Celia said, slapping a dish towel down on the sink. "I have spent the last twenty-four years caring about you, which is why it is so hard to watch you make mistake after mistake. And this is a mistake, Rowan. It's a big one. Like it or not, you and Dell are going to be tied together for life. You had a stable relationship. You were *happy*. You could have at least given him a chance."

"I don't love him," Rowan said. "I was always honest about that. He said those words, but I never did. It would have been a lie."

Celia smiled a little and shook her head. "You're *living* a lie," she said. "You haven't noticed the kind of damage it's done to Gabriel? You don't have the slightest idea how lucky you were to get him back. Dell offered you a chance to have something true, a *real* life. One that would have been good for the baby and for Gabriel."

"How come they matter," Rowan asked, her voice barely a whisper, "but I don't?"

"Rowan," Celia said, looking her straight in the eye, "I told you the day you brought Gabriel home that being a parent, being a mother, would mean putting yourself last. You should have thought, for one

minute, about what stability would have done for him. For all of you."
Celia opened the basement door and took her coat and purse from
the hook on the other side. "I hope you have some kind of a plan
in mind for raising two kids on your own," she said just before she
stepped outside. "Because I am tired of dealing with your messes.
And I'm not going to help you with this one."

CHAPTER THIRTY-ONE

LIKE THANKSGIVING, CHRISTMAS WAS A QUIET AFFAIR. AFTER CELIA left, Rowan spent the entire night cleaning, moving through the house like a robot. She swept and mopped the floors, threw out trays of food still in their metal warmers, and tossed heaps of garland on top. By morning, there wasn't a single shred of the party left. When Gabriel came down, she lit the fireplace because the house seemed so cold. They put on music and opened their presents under the tree, and it was miserable. Austin came by around noon with another stack of gifts for Gabriel, but Celia didn't even call. Neither did Dell.

They didn't call the week after either. Or the week after that.

Austin was the only one still talking to everyone, and he made a valiant attempt to mediate the situation, but it was useless. Seven days after the new year, Rowan drove to the medical pavilion alone and lay quietly on Dr. Marsh's exam table, listening as a watery thud filled the room.

Later that afternoon, Austin came by to help Gabriel with algebra. Rowan stared out the window as they worked; the yard looked harsh and frozen without a comforting buffer of snow. "I guess Celia's back to hating me, huh?"

Austin shrugged. "I'm not gonna lie, she doesn't like you very much right now... Nope, nope, order of operations," he said, tapping a piece of scrap paper. "You gotta multiply before you subtract." Gabriel groaned, erasing furiously. "I've been trying to tip the scales," Austin went on, "but apparently the two of you have other beefs that go way back. If it's any consolation, she looks as bad as you do."

"Wow, thanks," Rowan said, handing him a cup of coffee.

"I'm not trying to bum you out, but really, you look terrible. Aren't you supposed to glow by now?"

"I don't know. I never got a schedule."

"Ceil's worried about you."

"Celia's worried about Dell, not me," Rowan said, walking to the sink. "Although, considering he's the one who left me here to gestate his spawn, I—" A high-pitched hum in her ears stopped her.

Austin glanced up. "You okay?"

"Yeah. I got up too fast."

He stood and took two steps toward her, but he looked really far away. "Sit down. You're white as a sheet."

Rowan's grip on the kitchen sink went lax; she tried to raise her hand and ended up poking herself in the eye. "I…" she managed, before a million black dots invaded her vision.

Time passed, but she was not part of it. Her cheekbone throbbed against a cool surface. Austin's voice reached her through wads of steel wool.

"Now, Celia!" Then: "It's okay, buddy. She'll be fine." She felt herself being lifted and carried. Her eyes opened as Austin placed her on the couch. Gabriel dropped onto the floor next to her. Austin said, "Take it easy, Rowe. Your sister's on her way."

"Why?"

"Because it took a nice dramatic move to screw her head on straight, so good job. How do you feel, any pain?"

"No," she said, checking to see if that was true. "Do you think the baby…?"

"Nah, you didn't land hard. It was more of a slither. Keep her company," he told Gabriel. "I'll be right back."

Gabriel put his hand on her forehead, the way she always did when he didn't feel well. "You're not hot," he said, and she almost smiled. "Are you okay?"

"I think so."

"Why'd you pass out?"

"Because they don't call it a delicate condition for nothing," Austin hollered from the kitchen. He came back in and handed

Rowan a glass of apple juice. "Down the hatch, kiddo. A little bit of sugar goes a long way."

Twenty minutes later, Celia swept in. Austin caught her at the door, and they had a brief whispered conversation. Rowan couldn't hear them, nor could she read Celia's expression. Gabriel squeezed Rowan's hand as Celia walked toward the couch. "Are you all right?" she asked.

"I'm fine."

Austin cleared his throat. "That Christmas tree is getting to be a fire hazard. Why don't we take a little break?" he asked Gabriel. "You can help me haul it out." Gabriel followed Austin to the door. "I'll be within shouting distance," Austin added. "So if anyone hits anyone else, you'll have me to deal with. That's all I'm gonna say."

"I'm not trying to interrupt your precious grudge," Rowan said when they were gone. "I didn't plan this."

"I never said you did. And I'm not holding a grudge."

Rowan laughed. "Oh my God, really? Tell me, how have we been getting along these days?"

Celia fiddled with the hem of her skirt. "I've been talking to Dell."

Rowan felt a twinge at his name. "Is he okay?"

"He said if it weren't for the baby, he'd move back to Texas."

That hurt. Dell had hated living in Texas; he'd told Rowan that between his parents' divorce and the death of his mother, it was like a huge reservoir of bad memories. Rowan took a deep breath and stared at Celia. "I hate you like this."

Celia blinked. "Excuse me?"

"I thought we were past this, and now we're doing it again. Fighting like strangers. Tell me how you really feel."

"I think you know how I feel."

"Where's your loyalty?" Rowan challenged.

"I have no *loyalties*. I'm sick about this for both your sakes, it's just—God, Rowan, how could you do that to him?"

"I was honest with him. I can't help how I feel. It's not his fault, but it's not mine either." Rowan's eyes dropped to the rise of her abdomen.

Celia followed the path of Rowan's gaze. "You're starting to show."

"I had another ultrasound. The doctor let me listen this time."

"What was that like?"

Rowan closed her eyes. The rapid thump that filled the room had surprised her. It was the most triumphant feeling of her life, even more than escaping with Ethan's ring on her finger—something else she got to keep. This was more than pretty, and the first giddy anticipation of what was to come echoed alongside it. "It was perfect."

———————

Rowan spent the next few weeks wearing a path in the floor between her bed and the couch, fascinated and terrified by the way her belly grew, while her phone remained silent. She ate because she had to, slept when she could, and made lists: things she needed to do before the baby was born, things she needed but would never get to start the adoption—all the steps necessary to unfuck her entire life. It should have been thera-peutic, but putting those impossible tasks to paper just made them look worse. She was content to wallow all winter long, but Celia and Austin shattered her solitude by buying her and Gabriel tickets to the hospi-tal's annual Valentine's Day benefit—in a barn, of all ridiculous places. Since Christmas, Rowan had eschewed social gatherings, but it was also Celia's birthday, which made the invitation harder to refuse.

Rowan tried to envision what Valentine's Day in a barn might look like, and it was a good thing she did. Had she not mentally prepared herself, she would have run away the minute they stepped through the door. The barn had been cleared of hay and other animal-related items, but they couldn't do a thing about the smell. The air was stifling, layered with notes of candle wax and manure. The party committee had dressed the space in strands of red lights, miles of foil hearts, and enough space heaters to create the bloodiest fire hazard Rowan had ever seen. The minute they got there, Gabriel ran off with Austin, and Celia pulled Rowan to a table overflowing with paper hearts and cookies dipped in red sugar.

"Drink something," she said, pushing a glass of pink punch into Rowan's hand. "I don't like the temperature in here for you."

"Why did I have to come here again?"

"Because you haven't left the house since Christmas. Your life isn't over. Don't act like it is."

"We'll have to agree to disagree on that. I'm going over there," Rowan said, gesturing with her cup. A cluster of chairs was set up near a photography area, where couples could have their picture taken inside a giant red heart chalked on the wall—with or without the addition of two baby pigs. The option of swine in a romance-themed photograph made Rowan love the local color of Oklahoma all the more. In the span of an hour, she saw the pigs pee on three different people, and she had a front-row seat for the drunk, diapered Cupid, who was expelled from the festivities shortly after.

At a quarter after nine, Austin bumped and nudged his way over. Gabriel had joined her by then, overheated and bored out of his mind. "Do me a favor, peanut," Austin said. "Go grab your sister and keep her near the dance floor, okay? Just for five minutes, don't let her go anywhere."

"Okay, what—Jesus Christ, are you having a heart attack?" His chest was pounding like a jackhammer against her shoulder. "Are you okay?"

"I'm delightful. Now go get her."

Rowan assumed something birthday related was about to happen that Celia was going to hate, but she and Gabriel gamely captured Celia near the edge of the dance floor. Sure enough, the chords changed, and the band launched into a cover of "Cecilia" that was slow and quite lovely. "I'm guessing this is for you," Rowan said.

Celia flushed. "Did Austin…?"

"He just said to keep you here—what's the matter?"

"I'm scared."

"Oh, shut up, you love it."

The band reached the first bridge. Rowan barely registered the lyrics as she pointed out another pig-pee victim to Celia, who wasn't listening either; her eyes darted around the room as though she expected Austin to descend from the ceiling.

"Oh, Cecilia…I'm down on my knees…I'm begging you please to…"

"Marry me."

The music stopped, and the entire room fell silent. A spotlight landed on Celia. Austin knelt on the stage with a microphone, holding a small box in the air.

"Happy birthday, my Cecilia." Rowan wouldn't have believed it if she weren't looking, but his hand shook. "I got you a ring, but if you want it, you have to take me too. What do you say?"

Celia stood frozen in slack-jawed silence. Every single person in the barn was watching her.

Rowan gave Celia a helpful shove, and she began to move slowly through the crowd, following the spotlight like it was the only thing holding her up. She climbed the steps and stopped in front of Austin.

There was barely a sound in the room—even the pigs were quiet. An anonymous voice suddenly boomed, "Well?" and the tension was broken.

There were hoots and applause, and when Celia shouted, "Yes!" into the microphone, her voice shaky and unreal, Rowan grabbed Gabriel around the neck and burst into a mishmash of laughter and tears. Celia and Austin embraced as the band picked up where they'd left off, the light shining on the two of them as they moved together.

Gabriel grinned at Rowan. "You didn't know?"

"No!" Rowan laughed and wiped her cheeks, trying to ignore the tug of loss pulling on her heart. She took a deep drink of punch, focusing on the rainbow foam of sherbet melting on top. When she lowered her cup, she saw Dell staring at her from the opposite end of the room. He walked toward them, and Gabriel's smile died. Rowan was suddenly cautious, scared even. "Dell?"

Dell didn't speak. He just took her hand and led her to the middle of the dance floor, amid a sea of people whose hearts were pressed together.

"I'm supposed to be on cleanup," Dell said, putting on his coat. "But I'm taking you home instead." His voice wasn't exactly friendly.

"Thanks. Um—Celia and Austin said they'll take Gabe."

He nodded tightly; they were both reeling in the aftermath of unmitigated joy, and it was a painful reminder. She climbed into his truck without a word.

The road rose ahead of the bouncing headlights. Rowan rested her hand on the rise of her belly. "I didn't know you'd be here."

"Celia told me you were coming."

"I was hoping to hear from you. I didn't think you'd want me to call."

"I didn't. I had a lot to think about." He paused for a beat. "I quit my job."

"You did?"

"Yeah. I thought that after taking care of my mom, it would be the perfect thing, but it's not for me. I'm going to go back to school, try for something a little more life centered. But don't worry about money."

"I'm not. I'm happy for you."

Dell nodded. In the next breath, he was pulling to the side of the road, and she remembered the last time he'd done that, the night they'd had sushi and ice cream and watched shooting stars in that empty X in the woods. "I have something to say to you."

Rowan's heart thudded with a quickness. "Okay."

He met her eye. "I am," he said, "so sorry."

She jammed her fingers in her haste to unbuckle her seat belt, and the minute she was free, she leaned across the gearshift, wrapping her arms around his neck. "Please don't be."

"I am," he said, shaking his head against her shoulder. "You were right, and the more I thought about it, the more embarrassed I got. I wanted to tell you, I just—" He took a deep breath. "I'm sorry. I've been calling Celia to check on you every day."

"I know," Rowan said, gripping him tighter. "I know."

"From the minute I met you, I was obsessed with making sure we ended up together. I never saw your situation for what it was because I didn't want to. I just kept telling myself it was fate that I met you, that I saved you, that it would all work out because it was meant to be, but it wasn't," he said, pulling back a little. "It was just my job."

"It was more than that."

"Maybe," he said, tilting his head back against the seat. "But it still wouldn't have worked. You and me. The timing, everything was off. We were always a little bit off." He swiped at his eyes and then turned to smile at her. "Wow," he whispered, pressing his hand to her belly.

"I know."

"How are you feeling?"

"I felt the baby move the other day," she offered.

"Already?"

"Yeah. Everyone says you only feel it a little in the beginning, but I felt it a lot." She laughed a little, wiping her eyes. "I couldn't wait to tell you." She rested her hand on top of his. "My twenty-week ultrasound is next month. They can tell us if it's a boy or a girl…if you want," she added. "I'm okay with being surprised."

"Me too," Dell said softly. "I'll be there."

Rowan smiled, but her lips shook. "I'm really glad you want to," she managed. "I was afraid—"

"Not on your life." He caught her eye for a moment. "Is Gabriel excited?"

"Yeah," said Rowan carefully. "He is."

"I think he'll be a great big brother."

Rowan let out a breath, releasing the last bit of fear hiding in her heart. "I think so too."

CHAPTER THIRTY-TWO

"You gotta…no…"

"Why are they getting stuck?"

"They're not—you're flipping them too soon. Wait!" Rowan said, grabbing Gabriel's wrist. "Wait until they get bubbly. Then you can flip them."

Gabriel poked at the melted butter with his spatula. "This is not fun."

"Wait until we get to dessert," Rowan said. "After a batch of macarons and a couple of chocolate soufflés, you're going to be begging to make pancakes." She nudged him aside so she could get the muffins out of the oven. Celia and Austin were on their way over with top secret wedding intel.

Gabriel frowned at the griddle. "If I learn how to cook, you're going to make me do it all the time."

"Yeah, of course I am. You can flip those now."

A voice sounded from the porch. "Rowe?"

"It's open!"

"Ha! I did it!" Gabriel exclaimed as Austin stepped through the back door carrying a box of doughnuts and a jug of orange juice. "How do I know when the other side's done?"

"They'll get puffy. Hello, my brother-to-be," Rowan said, giving Austin a hug.

"Hello, my dear. Doughnut?"

"Thank you," she said, taking the box.

Celia came in from the living room, carrying a white binder the size of a kite.

"What the hell is that?" Rowan asked.

"My wedding planner. And your mail," Celia said, dropping a stack of envelopes and a squashy brown mailer on the table.

"You're going to lug that thing around until July?"

"Yes. Sit down—you, too, Gabriel."

"I only have four pancakes done," Gabriel said. "And two of them aren't in one piece."

"Just sit," Celia said. "I want to talk to you about the wedding party."

"We have a severe sibling imbalance," Austin added.

"Oh no," Rowan said.

"Austin has five brothers," Celia told them.

"You have *five* brothers?" Gabriel said.

"And the scars to prove it."

"I can't come up with that many bridesmaids, so we decided we're just going to have a best man and a maid of honor."

"I'm sure that won't piss anyone off. Who's the lucky brother?" Rowan asked Austin.

"I don't know yet. I'm picking him out of a hat."

"Then there's you," Celia said to Gabriel.

"Me?"

"Of course!" Celia said. "We can't leave you out."

His cheeks went pink, and Rowan smiled.

"I had an idea," Celia went on. "I don't know if you'll want to do it, but it would mean the world to me."

"What?"

"I know it's a completely antiquated, patriarchal concept, but I really hate the idea of walking down the aisle by myself," Celia told him. "How would you like to give me away?"

"*What?*" Rowan cried. "He's going to give you away?"

"I hope so."

"I've never been to a wedding. What does that mean?" Gabriel asked.

"You'll be the one to walk me down the aisle. And when the minister asks, 'Who gives this woman in marriage?' you'll say that you do."

Gabriel flushed a deeper red. "That sounds like a big deal."

"It is," Celia said.

"Are you sure you want me to do it?"

"I wouldn't ask anyone else."

Gabriel was quiet for a moment, and then his face broke into a grin. "Thank you, Celia," he said, getting to his feet. "Of course I will."

"I don't know," Rowan said as Gabriel gave Celia a hug. "I think if anyone deserves to unload you, it's me."

"I'd pay to see that," Austin said, leaning back in his chair. "It would be quite the spectacle."

"That's exactly why I didn't ask her," Celia said. She cupped Gabriel's face in her hands and smiled.

"So, to sum up, you're having an outdoor wedding in July," Rowan said, "in Oklahoma. Your maid of honor will be nine months pregnant, and you're going to have a fourteen-year-old walk you down the aisle."

"What could possibly go wrong?" Austin asked.

"I can't think of a thing," Rowan said.

"Is anyone going to eat my pancakes?" Gabriel asked.

Austin and Gabriel divided up the shredded pancakes, while Celia cracked open her wedding tome and began a running monologue about dress cuts and fabric and color schemes. Rowan wasn't ready to fight about any of that, so she flipped through the mail Celia had brought in—utility bills, ads, bank statements. She picked up the big brown envelope and squinted at the return address: THE LAW OFFICES OF WISNIEWSKI AND ALLEN.

"What is this?" Rowan asked no one in particular.

Celia looked up from her white book. "What's what?"

"This," Rowan said, yanking at the pull tab. "It's from a lawyer."

"Did you and Dell talk about custody arrangements?"

"Yeah, a little, but we didn't say anything about getting lawyers."

"You should have," Celia said.

"Dell didn't even tell me…" Rowan said, pulling a pile of papers free.

The first page was full of bold black print with an interlocking *A* and *W* splashed across the top. Her eyes were too eager to be slow; they ran the length of the page grabbing words and phrases at random.

…please be advised…

"Why would Dell get a lawyer?" Gabriel asked.

"Because he's smart," Celia said, nibbling on a muffin.

"Call my buddy again," Austin said. "He's family law; he'll help you out."

…terminated parental rights…

The words blurred and scurried along the page.

…please refer to enclosed documentation to initiate…

Rowan lifted the next page. It was signed by three different people, sealed with a notary stamp. Her legs turned to pipe cleaners, and when she tried to sit, she almost missed the chair.

Celia grabbed her arm to steady her. "Rowan? What does it say?"

Rowan shook her head and looked at Gabriel. "Come here," she whispered.

"What?"

Rowan walked over, nudging him aside so they could share the chair. She pushed the paper into his hand. "Read it."

"Is it bad?"

"Just read it."

Gabriel glanced around the table. "I," he began slowly, "Lee Emerson…oh, God, Rowan!" He dropped the paper and shoved it away. "What is this?"

"Keep going!"

The paper shimmied and danced in his grip. "I, Lee Emerson… as, um, as the father of Gabriel Emerson, age fourteen, of the sex male, born in Wareham, Massachusetts, on October eighteenth, do hereby…um…voluntarily and unconditionally surrender Gabriel Emerson…"

Celia's hands flew to cover her mouth. Gabriel slumped sideways into Rowan—she had to wrap her arms around him to keep him upright.

"…to the care and custody of…" He squeezed his eyes shut, his voice barely a whisper. "Rowan McNamara."

"*Fuck* yeah!" Austin shouted.

Rowan let out a strangled cry that felt like laughter and sounded like a sob. Gabriel threw his arms around her, burying his face in her neck.

"Wait, is that for real?" Celia asked. "How?"

"Gabriel asked him," Rowan managed. "When he went there. He stared him down like a fucking badass and *asked* him."

"And he actually did it?"

"There may have been a minor threat involved," Rowan said. Gabriel's arms tightened, and Rowan barely had room to speak. "Hey, Austin?"

"What's up, baby doll?"

"I need a lawyer," she said, still laughing and crying and rocking back and forth. "Can you call your buddy for me?"

That night, after Gabriel was asleep, Rowan climbed into the tiny alcove above her bedroom. It was dark, but it didn't take her long to find the engagement ring Gabriel had pulled from her finger months before. The stone was still brilliant, still glistening with an icy shine that had never, not even for a moment, warmed her heart.

Once the initial shock had worn off, Gabriel had told Austin and Celia about the fork, his own painful talisman, and the way he'd used it to set them free. It was one of the only details he'd shared about that day, even to Rowan. For the most part, he chose to carry his final moments with his father alone. But as happy as she was, she could still feel her own tether pulling tight, and she knew she couldn't bear to be wedded to Ethan, however tenuously, for a minute longer.

Violating parole had landed him back in jail, and even though it might not be for long, it was enough. She wasn't going to run, and she wasn't going to be afraid. Her life was hers, he had no place in it, and she wasn't going to give him another moment of her time.

Rowan changed her phone number the next day. She wiped every picture, every text, every missed call clean, and then she went to the post office with a tiny package bearing Ethan's name and said goodbye to him for good.

CHAPTER THIRTY-THREE

THE HOUSE HAD FALLEN TO CHAOS. IT WAS IMPOSSIBLE TO MOVE WITHOUT bumping into food or flowers or garment bags, and every few minutes, the air lit with pops of blinding light. The brunch Rowan had laid out that morning was soggy and untouched; the caterers wouldn't let anyone in the kitchen while the cake was being decorated, and that project was on hour four. Celia's wedding planner was a roving siren, his screams flowing from room to room. Rowan just managed to extricate herself, taking respite in the foyer where she sat huddled at the bottom of the staircase, gnawing on a bagel. She was supposed to be upstairs helping Celia get dressed, but she wasn't entirely sure she'd walk out alive.

The front door burst open to admit two white-shirted waiters balancing stacks of trays, the harpist with a fistful of sheet music, and Laine, dragging a massive suitcase behind her.

"Oh, thank God!" Rowan shrieked, hoisting herself off the steps. "I didn't think you'd make it in time!"

"Me neither," Laine said, wrapping her in a hug. "We had to circle the airport for an hour, and then my Uber driver got lost. Jesus, look at you!"

Rowan grinned as Laine pressed both hands to the globe of her belly. The baby kicked in greeting. "Flight was bad?"

"Twins," Laine said with a grimace. "Three years old. Right in front of me. One of them was a puker."

"It's not much better here."

Gabriel's voice echoed down the hall. "I'm not wearing this tie, Rowan. I don't care what Celia said."

Rowan pulled Laine into the back room, where Gabriel was trying to hook his cummerbund. "Where'd everyone go?" she asked him.

"To the tent. Hey, Laine," he said, hugging her.

"Hey, Houdini. What's wrong with the tie?"

"Look at it," he said, producing the offending item from his pocket. "It looks like an Easter egg. And I wouldn't mind so much, but everyone else gets to wear black."

"If you value your life, you'll shut up and put it on," Rowan warned. "Austin!"

"Peanut!" Austin exclaimed, coming into the room. He took a swig from the tumbler in his hand. "Don't tell Ceil, okay?"

"Can I have it?" Gabriel asked.

Rowan swatted his hand away. "Austin, I'd like you to meet Laine, my best friend in the whole world. Laine, this is Austin."

"Nice to meet you," Laine said, holding out her hand.

Austin didn't even glance at it. He stared at Rowan, looking absolutely crushed. "I thought I was your best friend."

"You're my best male friend."

"Hey!" Gabriel said.

Laine withdrew her hand and stared at the three of them. "You're marrying Celia?"

"That I am, and I'm sorry, but I don't shake hands with Rowan's best friends," he said, pulling Laine into a hug. "I've heard a lot about you, kiddo. *Best* doesn't even begin to cover it."

"I've heard a lot about you too," Laine said, smiling. "Although I guess I haven't been paying attention. I was expecting someone a little more..."

"Neurotic?" Rowan asked.

"Lame?" Gabriel offered.

"Subdued," Laine said. "You are a very pleasant surprise. I'm so happy for you both."

"Thank you." Austin turned to Gabriel. "How come you get to wear a blue tie?" he asked, giving it a tug.

"You want to trade?"

"Yes, I do."

"Don't you dare!" Rowan said as Austin pulled the blue tie from under Gabriel's collar and tossed him his black one.

"I like the blue," Austin said. "Pastels make me glow."

"Celia's going to kill you."

"She'll be lost in a haze of love. She won't even notice."

"You better count on that haze." Rowan took Laine by the hand and pulled her toward the staircase. "Celia's been biting my head off all day."

"Is Dell coming?"

"He's sitting at your table."

Celia was in Rowan's room, struggling with a pair of elbow-length gloves. "Did you see the florist?" she asked.

"No, but I saw flowers. Say hi to Laine."

"I'm not going to tell you never to get married," Celia said, hugging Laine. "Just don't have a wedding. Everything's going wrong."

"Nothing's going wrong, and everything looks beautiful," Rowan said. "It's not even that hot today; you should be on your knees thanking God."

"You look gorgeous, Celia," Laine put in.

She did. Her hair fell in sleek, old-timey Hollywood waves past her shoulders, the color rich and dark against the creamy ivory of her gown. It was Rowan who'd eventually found the dress, after half a dozen trips to different bridal shops. It had a sweetheart neckline with fine, sheer lace extending all the way up to her throat. The high cut was perfect for Celia, who had the height to make it work, and it added just the right amount of modesty to suit her. The hairdresser had woven a cluster of tiny roses into her hair, perfect blossoms in cream and deep red.

Rowan adjusted one of the roses and smiled. "Your boobs look fantastic in that dress."

Celia shook her head. "Get dressed."

Rowan's dress was a silky flowing shift in the palest shade of aqua—the same color as Gabriel's tie—with thin, barely there spaghetti straps. Laine pulled her shoes from the box. "Red?"

"Contrasting jewel tones," Rowan said. She glanced at Celia, who'd drifted to the window. "See? They match Celia's flowers."

"I love it. I never would have thought of that. Celia? You okay?"

"Yes, I just—Rowan, do you feel all right?"

"I feel great."

"You're not going to go into labor during the wedding, are you?"

"If I do, I'll keep it to myself," she promised. "Are you ready?"

Celia's smile trembled at the edges. "I guess so. I'm glad you wore that necklace; it's perfect with your dress."

"Oh, I almost forgot," Rowan said. She reached behind her neck and unhooked the clasp. "Borrowed," she said, pressing the aquamarine pendant Gabriel had given her into Celia's hand. "And blue."

Celia nodded, gripping the necklace tight. "Perfect."

Dearly beloved, we are gathered here, in the sight of God, to join together this man and this woman…

The late-afternoon breeze was warm and light as Rowan made her way down the white runner studded with ruby petals. The yard was lit with people and flowers and an energy she hadn't known, not once, in the entire time they'd lived there. She was ready to cry before she even made it to her spot, where she was pulled into a hug by Austin. She took her place, and the music shifted. Everyone rose as Celia and Gabriel appeared around the bend of ivory chairs, their arms and hands linked, faces alive and bright and beautiful.

Today we celebrate the love and commitment with which Austin and Celia begin their lives together.

When they reached the arch of flowers, Celia kissed Gabriel's cheek and joined Austin in front of the minister. Rowan's face was streaked with tears. Gabriel took her hand.

"Who gives this woman in marriage to this man?"

Rowan's eyes lit on the bright chain wrapped around the base of Celia's bouquet. Gabriel followed her gaze to the flashing pendant dangling below the deep-red roses. He smiled at Rowan, and they both stepped forward.

"We do."

Rowan looked out over a sea of faces with a proud, scared smile. She caught Laine's eye, saw her broadcasting support. Ruby from the café smiled from the middle row. Her name matched her lipstick and the bow on her hat. Everyone watched as Celia and Austin took their oath—as they swore to do, to have, to be.

"You may kiss the bride."

Austin leaned in, grinning wickedly as Celia's eyes pleaded for control. He didn't listen. This was their moment. He kissed her, *really* kissed her, lifting her right off the ground as the yard thundered with cheers and applause.

Gabriel shouted into Rowan's ear, "Hold out your hand!" He tugged on her wrist, and she extended her hand, palm flat.

Gabriel slapped it. "Good job."

Knives clinked against crystal, everything twinkling under a galaxy of white lights. Rowan stood between Celia and Austin, a microphone in one hand and a glass of shimmering grape juice in the other.

"Welcome, everyone, and thank you for coming on what I'm sure you'll agree was *extremely* short notice to share this day with Austin and Celia. I say 'short notice,' but that's not really true. When something is inevitable, there's no point in wasting time, and the minute I saw the two of them together, I knew it was only a matter of how much time they were willing to waste.

"For those of you who don't know me, I'm Celia's sister, Rowan. Celia and I are pretty light on family, which means there is a *lot* of love for Austin in this room." There was wild applause, and one of

Austin's five brothers let out a whoop. "However, if you'll indulge me for a moment, I'd like to talk about Celia first." Rowan handed her glass to Gabriel and gripped Celia's hand.

"I love my sister. I know that seems like an obvious statement, but up until recently, it wasn't something I ever thought I'd say. When we were growing up, we were the only family we had, and we hated each other for it. We were too different. So we put up walls, and we hid behind them for a long time. It wasn't until..." Celia squeezed her fingers, and Rowan smiled. "It wasn't until we started to be tested that we understood what it meant to have that connection. And no matter how badly we neglected it, it was still strong enough to keep us together. Even when we didn't want it to. Celia is my hero. I'm here to tell anyone who doesn't know it yet that she's a very good person to have on your side."

Rowan's eyes started to fill, and she was really missing champagne as she turned to Austin. "As for this guy, he was my brother from the word *go*. And I take full credit for the fact we're even standing here today, because this one"—she tapped Austin on the head—"was too scared to ask Ceil out, and she was way too scared to say yes. I had to do a little bit of legwork to get things rolling. Celia was so mad. She told me the next day that I can't play puppet master with people's lives." Rowan looked over at Gabriel and smiled. "But I think sometimes it takes the people who really love us to show us the right strings to pull. They're the ones who see how beautiful we could be if we just let the right things in. They want that for us, even if it doesn't always seem that way.

"Austin threw us all for a loop when he came into Celia's life, and I'm so grateful he did. I want to thank him for that. For being bold and bright and hilarious and wonderful. For loving my sister with his whole heart and lightening her up just a little bit." Rowan turned to Celia. "And I'd like to thank Celia for recognizing the things that are true and the things that are important. For being wise, even when it meant not being popular, and for turning herself into someone who's hard to be away from. I love you both. Celia, I hope you find nothing but joy in your new family, but please, please don't forget your old one." Celia whispered something to Gabriel and kissed the top of his head. "And Austin, I wish you a lifetime of blue ties." She retrieved her glass from Gabriel and held it high. "To Celia and Austin."

The chime of glass on glass filled the room, and Celia took Rowan into her arms. "I should have vetted that speech. You ruined a very expensive makeup job."

Rowan laughed. "That is so great."

"Yeah, for you," Celia said, smiling as she wiped her eyes.

"No, for both of us. God, Ceil, can't you see how great that is? That means after all this, somewhere along the way, we did something right."

CHAPTER THIRTY-FOUR

THE SUN SAT LOW ON THE HORIZON, BUT THE MERCURY WAS SIMMER-ing when Rowan padded outside and joined Laine on the porch swing. Temperatures had soared in the days following the wedding, leaving a dense, heavy silence that seemed to stretch for miles. Nothing called and nothing answered.

"You're taking your life in your hands out here," Rowan said, sinking next to her.

"I can't help it. I love a porch. How do you feel?"

"Horrible," Rowan said, wiping at the sweat beaded along her hairline. "I had some contractions today."

"Why didn't you say anything?"

"I called the doctor. She said it's normal."

"You should lie down."

"I'm fine. Thank you," Rowan added. "For staying with me."

"I love it here."

"I just hope the baby comes before you leave. How goes the tiny sweater?"

Laine regarded the tangle of silvery-gray yarn in her lap. "I think I should have started with something easier. Since I don't actually know how to knit."

"Dell does," Rowan said, trying to stretch her back. "His mom taught him when she was sick. He made me a hat and a scarf last fall. I wore them all the time."

"I know," Laine said, winding the yarn into a ball. "He told me."

"When?"

"He stopped by this afternoon. Right after you fell asleep." Laine stuck the knitting needles into the ball. "He tried to help me, but I don't seem to have the knitting gene."

"Me neither. It's our privileged upbringing. What else did you guys talk about?"

"Not much." Laine paused for a minute. "He's really nice."

"He said the same thing about you." The back door slammed against the house, and Gabriel's feet pounded the porch. He flew past them down the stairs. "Where are you going?"

"Swimming," he called.

"Not by yourself—"

"Flip's coming!"

On cue, a car pulled up in the front of the house, and Flip tumbled out in a red bathing suit. He tore down the path after Gabriel, the two of them kicking up clouds of dust in their wake. Denise waved at Rowan through the window.

"Shit," Rowan muttered, smiling as she waved back. "That's worse than him going alone."

They watched as Gabriel and Flip ran down the dock and cannon-balled into the water, dotting the early evening sky with a million glittering drops.

"He's so happy," Laine said.

"Do you really think so?"

"My God, Rowan, look at him. It's like he's a different kid." She waited another beat. "Did you do it?"

Rowan nodded. "My attorney filed the petition two weeks ago."

"How do you feel?"

Rowan pulled in a deep breath and blew it out. "Terrified," she admitted, resting a hand on her belly. "But the odds are good."

"What happens next?"

"He stays with me. I was worried about that, but my lawyer said it's in Gabriel's best interest—he called it a kinship placement. If the petition is approved, we'll get a court date to finalize, and it should be pretty quick. There's no one to contest the adoption, so…"

"So that's good." Laine tapped Rowan's knee. "You did good. And it is in his best interest. He's getting a whole family. Celia adores him, and Austin obviously does too. He has friends, he'll have a brother or sister…"

"And he tolerates Dell," Rowan said, smiling. "Which I'll take." She was quiet for a minute. "I wish I knew why he did it."

"Lee?"

Rowan nodded.

"I don't think there was any love lost there."

"At first, I thought the same thing. Gabriel threatened him to leave us alone, so maybe he was just scared, but now I'm not sure. I think if he was scared or angry or whatever, he would have tried that much harder to get him back—just to win, you know? And then I read this article about how parents put kids up for adoption out of love, not hate, and that made me think of something else."

"What?"

"When we ran away, Gabriel took this big box of pictures with him," Rowan said. "It was pretty much all he took. All of his mom. But a few months after we got here, I was dusting in his room, and I found another picture—he had it taped to the bottom of his lamp. It was him and his dad at a baseball game. They're wearing matching jerseys and hats, and Gabriel is holding up a ball. He's sitting on his dad's lap, and they both have the biggest smiles…" Rowan shivered in the heavy air. "That picture, after knowing what happened to them, was just… I had to sit down. It was the creepiest thing I've ever seen. But I remembered it after we got the paperwork, and I keep thinking that maybe it was *that* guy who let me have him. The one who used to love him. Maybe he stuck his head out just long enough to give him that."

"Does that make you feel better?" Laine asked.

"Good enough," Rowan said, nodding. "I keep wondering if I should tell Gabriel."

"Maybe he already knows."

"I hope so." Rowan turned to Laine and tried to smile. "My other kid is telling me I better eat. I'm not cooking in this heat, but we can order something. Are you hungry?"

"Not really. Dell brought me a ton of stuff from the bakery, and I—What?"

Rowan stared at her. "He brought you stuff from the bakery?"

"Uh-huh. We were talking about it at the wedding."

"Was there a brownie?" Rowan demanded. "A huge one that looks like a checkerboard?"

"Yeah—how did you know?"

She shook her head. "Forget it."

Rowan went to bed before dark, but her sleep was too light and too broken to count. She felt a painful quickening unlike those that had come before. She dozed on and off, but her entire body hummed with an energy she couldn't tamp down—even her dreams seemed to vibrate. Every so often there was a strengthening embrace that lasted until she almost opened her eyes. In that hazy dream state, she couldn't be sure if there was real life to the kicks and rolls in her belly or if her mind was just playing with ghosts.

Then she felt something else—a fiery clamp that took hold and would not let go. She woke with a gasp, pressing her hands to the hardening globe of her abdomen. This was real pain, and it felt productive—a squirming ball thrashing and kicking deep in her gut. The pain rose and rose, and then it fell, leaving her limp and breathless on top of the covers.

The aftermath was dark and very still. The corners in the room were too sharp. It was like being trapped in the silence before a scream.

———————

Gabriel sat straight up in bed. There was a nightmare waiting behind his closed eyes, but that was a constant and wasn't what woke him. He could hear talking downstairs—the front door opened and shut, and then creaking footsteps passed his door.

"Rowan?"

But it was Laine who appeared outside the doorway. "It's okay. Go back to sleep."

"What's going on?"

Laine stepped into the room; there was just enough light to see her smile. "The baby's coming," she whispered. "Dell took Rowan to the hospital."

"*Now?*" Gabriel scrambled with the sheets, trying to get to his feet. "Is she okay?"

"She's fine. She went into labor just after midnight. Dell and I have been sitting with her all night."

"Why didn't anyone wake me up?"

"There's nothing you can do."

"Can we go to the hospital?"

"It's five o'clock in the morning," Laine said.

"So?"

"So they won't even let us in. She's fine, I promise. Dell's with her, and he'll call if anything happens. Go back to sleep."

"I'm not going to sleep! I want to be there when she has the baby."

"Oh, honey," Laine said, shaking her head. "No you don't."

Rowan fought and bit and clawed at Dell's shirt for four hours before she caved and got an epidural. She was exhausted. Her water had broken before they'd even left the house, and the contractions that followed were incredibly strong and even more erratic. She couldn't brace herself for the pain. It kept sneaking up on her, and after a while, she set every muscle to stone in constant anticipation. Every time she'd managed to get comfortable, she'd been racked with another contraction, curling as tight as a boiled shrimp.

The anesthesiologist arrived with a terrifying array of syringes and wires, but Rowan didn't feel a thing when the needle sank into her back. A delicious sensation of *nothing* flowed through her belly and down her legs, and she fell into a deep, dreamless sleep as soon as her head landed back on the pillow.

It felt like minutes before she heard voices swim up, and she couldn't make out all the words. It was almost like she'd fallen into another coma. Dell's voice was the first to break into Rowan's consciousness. "At least let me get it started for you."

"No, I can… Damn it!"

"I don't know how I feel about Dell being the most accomplished knitter in the room," Austin said.

Rowan cracked open her eyes. Dell sat with Laine, painstakingly showing her how to loop gray yarn over the needle hooks. Celia stood next to the nurse, holding a pitcher of ice chips, and Gabriel and Austin played cards on the floor.

The nurse examined a long strip of printed paper. "Back to the land of the living?" she asked.

"When did everyone get here?" Rowan asked.

"Hours ago," Austin said, dropping a card. "We were hoping for a pre-baby blowout, but frankly, you're very boring."

Gabriel was off the floor and next to her bed in a flash. "Are you okay? Does it hurt?"

"Not at all." That wasn't entirely true. Her belly was calm, but she felt a deep, aching pressure that was very familiar and not at all welcome. "How long was I asleep?"

"Long enough to get your strength back," Celia said, squeezing her shoulder.

"And I hate to kick the family out, but I need to check you," the nurse said.

Austin got to his feet. "Come on, kid," he said to Gabriel. "You are running on empty, and I'm buying lunch."

"You haven't eaten?" Rowan asked.

"He won't. And he's been up since you left," Laine said.

"Jesus, Gabe, go eat. If you pass out, it's going to ruin my day."

"I'll come too," Laine said, stifling a yawn.

"I'm sorry to be a pain," Rowan told the nurse when they were gone. "But I really need to go to the bathroom. And I'm not doing it on a bedpan. I'm just not."

The nurse eased her back. "Well, that tells me everything I need to know, but let's see where we are." She poked around, and Rowan sucked in her breath, but she got a smile in return. "Guess what?"

Rowan clutched Dell's hand. "I don't have to go to the bathroom?"

"Nope. Let me get the doctor."

Dell smoothed her hair back and pressed his lips to her forehead. "You're doing great."

"I'm scared."

"Don't be. I'm right here."

The curtain swished aside, and Dr. Marsh came in. "No fan club?" she asked, pulling on a pair of rubber gloves. "Last time I was here, it looked like your entire family was going to witness the miracle of childbirth, like it or not." She felt Rowan's belly. "Are you ready?"

"No…"

The doctor smiled. "Try to relax, breathe with it. Your body knows what to do."

"I'm glad one of us does."

Dr. Marsh positioned her feet in the stirrups. "When I say push, take a deep breath, keep your chin to your chest, and bear down. Don't stop until I tell you to breathe."

"How do I know if I'm doing it right?"

"You'll know. Are you ready?"

Rowan nodded. Celia took hold of her leg, and Dell moved to the other side. "What can I do?" he asked.

"You can stand there," Dr. Marsh said. "Here's a contraction, Rowan. Are you getting the urge to push?"

Rowan squeezed her eyes shut and nodded, wishing she could lie. The pressure was alive now, a wriggling, squirming entity fighting to get out.

"Okay, Rowan. Push!"

She pushed out of necessity, not agreement; her body gave her no option to disobey. The doctor counted, and Rowan kept pushing and pushing, whether she wanted to or not. Celia and Dell held her legs as the pain moved lower, igniting a fiery agony that turned the contractions into a fond memory. The doctor turned to Dell. "Want to see the baby's head?"

"No!" Rowan gasped. "Look at *my* head."

Celia ran to the foot of the bed instead. "Oh! Oh my God, Dell, look!"

"Dell, if you care about me…"

Dell squeezed her foot. "I'm not going anywhere."

"Keep it going, Rowan, baby's right here."

On the next push, she felt a tremendous release, and Celia let out a loud whooping shriek. Before Rowan could register anything, Celia grabbed Dell, and the doctor placed something warm and wet on Rowan's chest.

Dell leaned over her. "It's a girl, Rowan! It's a girl! Open your eyes, look at her!"

She cracked her eyes open and found a tiny face with a wide steely gaze staring into hers. "Oh my God."

"Would you like to do the honors?" the nurse asked Dell, handing him a pair of scissors. Her voice lifted above the baby's cries as he cut the cord, lilting, like a prayer. "That's the first spark of life, right there. All her breaths are hers from now on."

Celia hugged Rowan. "That was amazing. That was the most amazing thing I've ever seen, and I've delivered babies before." She ran around the bed and hugged Dell too. "I'm going to go find everyone. I'll be back."

"Why don't you have a little moment, just the three of you?" the nurse said once everyone had been washed and stitched. She laid the baby, now swaddled and wearing a tiny pink cap, in Dell's arms.

"Seven pounds, one ounce," the doctor announced. "And perfect. Congratulations."

"Do you know her name?" the nurse asked.

"Poppy," Rowan said, tracing the sweet curve of the baby's nose. "McNamara-Dixon." Dell's mother's name had been Poppy. When he'd mentioned it, Rowan loved it so much, she hadn't even offered an alternative.

The nurse penned the name onto a small white card and tucked it into the bassinet. "Congratulations," she said, slipping out the door.

"God, look at her," Rowan said as the baby pursed her tiny lips and yawned. "She looks just like you."

"No way," he said, running his fingers over a tiny tuft of golden hair peeking out from the cap. "She's all you."

Rowan unwrapped the baby to count her fingers and her toes. Dell captured one tiny foot, rubbing it between his thumb and forefinger. Then he caught Rowan's chin and pressed his lips to hers for just a moment—the span of three heartbeats. She smiled, and he straightened, clearing his throat. "I'd like to call my dad if that's okay?"

"Of course," Rowan said, tucking the baby's arms and legs back into the blanket.

"Do you want me to send anyone in?"

She started to say something, then changed her mind. "They can all come in."

Rowan expected a rush of drumming footsteps, but it was quiet after Dell slipped out the door. The baby let out a sigh, freeing one fist from the blanket and waving it in the air.

"Rowan?"

She looked up. Gabriel was standing in the doorway. "Gabe."

"Dell said you wanted me to come in first."

Rowan smiled, cradling the baby closer. "I did," she admitted.

He walked to the bedside. Rowan scooted over to make room. She was starting to feel a bit like she had after the tornado, which was saying something. Gabriel sank to the bed beside her. "This is your sister," Rowan told him. "Poppy."

Gabriel smiled down at her. "She's so small. I didn't think she'd be so small."

"Here," Rowan said, leaning toward him. "You have to hold her."

"Oh, no, Rowan, I don't know how."

"Bullshit, I've seen you hold lots of things," she said, settling her in his lap. The baby opened her slate-blue eyes, staring up at Gabriel.

He returned the gaze, his own eyes moving over her tiny face. Rowan watched as they took each other in: her proudest achievement and the potential in his arms.

"So?" Rowan said, adjusting the blanket. "What do you think?"

He shook his head, eyes bright. "She's my sister…" he said slowly. "I'm her brother."

"Sounds good, right?"

"Yeah," he said. His smile was huge, but his voice was choked. "That's something…"

"Something what?"

"Something I'll never have to explain," he said, still smiling. "It's something everyone will understand."

CHAPTER THIRTY-FIVE

THE TRUCK FLEW ALONG A RIBBON OF ROAD THAT SPLIT THE FLAT fields into dusty squares of land. Rowan, Dell, and Gabriel were in the front. Poppy was asleep between Austin and Celia in the back. It was a bright, cool September day, but Rowan wasn't fooled. The summer had claws, and it kept sending surprises. Two weeks after Poppy had come home, a tornado warning jerked everyone out of a dead sleep and sent Rowan and Gabriel running for the basement, Poppy in Rowan's arms. The storm passed through the field behind the house, but the resonating whine made it sound like it was right on top of them. The three of them huddled in the basement for hours, well after dawn lightened the sky. When they finally went outside, they found half a tree in the pond, and Rowan's flower bed had been torn to shreds—only her mint and basil plants survived.

The leaves had been stripped, but the roots were still tight inside the ground.

Next to her, Gabriel was quiet. He had been all day. Rowan nudged his shoulder. "Are you okay?"

He nodded.

Rowan squeezed his knee. Ten minutes later, Dell pulled up in front of a redbrick building, and everyone filed out onto the blacktop. There were other people milling about—tired people with anxious eyes and screaming toddlers. They were dressed in everything from cutoffs to chinos, and Rowan flushed, wishing they'd dressed down. Her white sundress and Gabriel's suit cast a beacon they didn't want as they slowly climbed the stairs and went inside.

The lobby was dark and cool, and it looked darker fresh out of the sun. Dell carried Poppy, smiling with his cheek pressed to hers. Celia and Austin brought up the rear, hand in hand.

"Austin!" Corey Palovik of Palovik Family Law came barreling down the hallway. He'd played college football with Austin, and on their first meeting, he'd told Rowan all about how it was his touchdown that destroyed Austin's knee. Austin took a tackle meant for Corey and hit the ground hard enough to crack his helmet. They'd been so concerned about his head, no one had noticed his leg was bent the wrong way. He pulled Austin into a one-armed hug and then turned to Rowan and Gabriel with a wide smile. "You guys ready? Excited?"

Rowan nodded. "Very."

"Questions before we go in?"

"Can anything happen now?" Gabriel blurted out.

"Everything happens now."

"No, I mean can anything go wrong in there?"

Corey smiled. "Not unless one of you changes your mind. This is very straightforward. We'll ask a few questions, the judge will talk to you both, and then all three of you will sign the papers. Piece of cake."

"I told you," Rowan murmured. "The hard part is over, so don't be nervous."

"You will still have the honor of being one of the most interesting adoptions I've ever handled," Corey said, pushing open a big wooden door. "You two go up front. Everyone else take a seat."

Dell, Poppy, Austin, and Celia filled the first bench. Rowan and Gabriel walked between the two tables set up in front of the judge. Rowan took Gabriel's hand and held it tight. The judge smiled at them as Corey sat behind the table.

"Good morning," she said. "Rowan McNamara?"

"Yes."

"Gabriel Emerson?"

Gabriel cleared his throat. "Yes."

"Are you both ready?"

Rowan squeezed Gabriel's hand. "We're ready."

"Perfect. Then it's time to call to matter the adoption of this young man. Let's get started."

FIVE YEARS LATER

"You got it, I can tell. I don't even have to taste them."

"Humor me." Rowan slid her spatula under a brownie and turned it over to Dell, licking chocolate off her thumb. "Well?"

Dell took a bite, held up one finger, and swallowed. "Perfect."

"Really?"

"Perfect checkerboard brownies. You're going to drive them out of business. I bet they sue you."

She threw a dish towel at him. "It's an homage. And you are so full of shit. There's no way you could tell without tasting them."

"Says you," he said, glancing at his watch. "I didn't realize it was so late. I better leave to get Poppy."

"Gabe's picking her up on his way home." Rowan pulled two more trays of brownies out of the oven. "I'm putting these out tomorrow."

"They'll be gone before noon."

The entire house smelled like chocolate and butter and brown sugar. Rowan wore the scent to work every day at four in the morning and back home again at noon, early enough to get a head start on whatever she could bake for the next day. When she had first begun developing her menu, Dell pointed out she was not-so-subtly stealing ideas from his old stomping ground. Rowan had suggested he shut up and make himself useful by being the taste tester for all her experiments.

He smiled as he took in Poppy's preschool artwork, a thousand colors decorating the refrigerator. "Is Gabriel excited about graduation?"

Rowan peeled the parchment away from the edge of the brownies. As soon as the adoption had been finalized, Gabriel started regular high school, and it was like the world burst wide open overnight. He loved it. He'd seemed almost bewildered by the idea of being happy on his own, of relishing an experience that was only his. He took as many AP classes as he could, and earned half his associate's degree by the time he graduated. Now, one year and thirty credits later, he was graduating again. "Yes," she said after a moment.

"Is he going to OU for his bachelor's?"

"I—he's not sure yet. What time does Laine get in?"

"I'm picking her up at six."

Rowan smiled at his expression as she gathered her hair into a ponytail. "And?"

"And what?"

"I want details! What'd she say when you asked her?"

"She said yes."

"I know that, but what did she *say*? How did you do it?"

"Do you have to know everything?"

"Hell yeah, I'm top brass. I was promised maid of honor fifteen years ago."

"Not by me."

Rowan rolled her eyes. "Laine's going to tell me anyway."

"Then you have something to look forward to."

It had been Laine's idea to open the bakery in the first place. In January, Poppy came down with a cold that turned into bronchitis, and a few days later, Gabriel was sick too. The week they were out of commission happened to coincide with a scheduled visit from Laine. At that point, she and Dell had been seeing each other for more than two years, flying back and forth every other month. Rowan and Laine sat in the kitchen one afternoon while Gabriel and Poppy were passed out in front of the television. Snow battered the windows as Laine watched Rowan pull tray after tray out of the oven. "Why are you making so much stuff?"

"Because I've got two whiny patients to deal with."

"Not just now. You're glued to the oven every time I'm here. What do you do with it all?"

Rowan shrugged. "Donate it. Send it to Poppy's preschool. I do birthday cakes for anyone who asks. It relaxes me."

"You should sell it," Laine said, biting into a chocolate croissant. "You'd make a fortune."

Rowan waved her away.

"I'm serious," Laine insisted. "Gabriel's graduating. Poppy will be in kindergarten in September—I think it would be nice to have something of your own."

Rowan smiled and forgot about it until a month later when Dell called to tell her about a bakery for sale in the town proper, with a brand-new kitchen and a month of paid utilities. She brushed it off until Laine went over her head and told Gabriel, who immediately dragged Rowan to see it. They spent an hour in the kitchen, mesmerized by the stainless steel surfaces, and then drove to the real estate office. Within three months she drafted a business plan and took out a commercial loan, and Dell came over every day to help her with the menu. The bakery had opened for business at 6:00 a.m. four weeks earlier, with Rowan and two other sleep-deprived people manning the shop. They were busier than she'd ever thought possible, and she already had ads out for additional staff.

Her phone rang as Rowan flipped another pan onto a rack. "Who is it?" she asked Dell.

"Celia."

Rowan grabbed the phone. "Hey, Mommy," she said.

"Please don't call me that."

"Why not? Another month, and it'll be true."

Celia and Austin had tried desperately for a baby following the wedding. Celia had confessed to Rowan that they'd been trying even before the wedding. After two years and two rounds of IVF, they called it quits, too nervous to take a chance at that stage of the game. Then, right around Thanksgiving the autumn before Celia's forty-second birthday, a routine examination turned up a pregnancy nearly three months along.

"Three months, Celia, are you serious? Three *months*? You're a nurse. What the hell did you think was going on?" Rowan said.

"I thought I was going through early menopause or something! I have no idea how this happened."

"You had sex, and you didn't use anything."

"Shut up."

All her tests had been perfect, and the baby, a boy, was due in less than three weeks. Celia and Austin had been fighting over names for months. Rowan couldn't wait.

"I went to the doctor today," Celia said. "She said the baby's measuring big."

"Are you surprised? You and Austin are both ten feet tall. Did you decide on a name yet?"

"No. Austin said you have to see a baby before you can name it."

Rowan laughed. "Dell's here."

"What about Laine?"

"Tonight. Are you sure you don't want to come?"

"I'd love to, but I can barely walk. Is Poppy home yet?"

"I'm waiting for them now."

"Go ahead then. But do me a favor and make sure Gabriel doesn't suggest any more names to Austin. They both have bizarre taste."

Dell was by the window when Rowan came back into the kitchen. "When did you get a tree house?" he asked.

"Don't even mention that tree house. Gabe put it up just to give me a heart attack. They're home," she said as Gabriel's car rolled in between the packed ruts on the lawn, too narrow to fit in the truck's grooves.

A minute later, Poppy tore into the kitchen, a sheet of white card stock in one hand. "Hi, Mommy!"

"Hi, baby!" Rowan said, scooping her up. "How was school?"

"Good, we made jewelry. Want to see?"

"Of course I do," she said. "Look, Daddy's here."

"Daddy!" Poppy yelled. Dell lifted her from Rowan's arms and spun her around. "Come see my tree house!" He let her pull him out the door, Poppy a golden flash in the afternoon sun. She had hair to rival Rowan's, the same cacophony of colors falling in a bright cascade to her waist, but her sweet brown eyes held none of the indecisiveness of her mother's.

Gabriel shuffled through the kitchen door, a tiny red backpack slung over one arm and his laptop under the other. Finals were brutal; he was putting in almost as many hours as Rowan. He usually went to bed the same time she left for work, his late nights morphing into her early mornings. "How are you even awake right now?" he asked her. "I feel like I had a lobotomy."

Rowan took Poppy's backpack from him and pushed his hair back. "You look like it too." He dropped his laptop on the table and sank into a chair. "Want a brownie?"

"I want a nap," he said.

"Do you have a lot more to do?"

"I'm done," he said, stifling a yawn. "My last test was today."

"So I'm going to be up in the middle of the night all by myself? You're not going to make me coffee at three in the morning?"

"No, I'm going to be comatose at three in the morning," he said, resting his forehead on the table. "Is Laine here?"

"She will be. Tonight."

"I'd take a nap, but I'm pretty sure I wouldn't wake up."

"She's not coming until after six, so you've got time. I'll wake you up."

Poppy kept Dell occupied for nearly an hour before Rowan saw them again. When they came back, Dell was holding out his hands, and Poppy was laughing, dancing around his legs. "Do you do that to everyone?" he asked.

"What did she do? Is it the sap?"

Dell nodded and held up his hands.

"She does it to everyone. That tree sprang a leak, and it hasn't stopped dripping."

Poppy tugged on Rowan's arm. "I made this for you," she said, holding up a strand of rainbow beads mixed with tiny charms.

"It's beautiful! I'm going to put it on right now. Why don't you go get out of your school clothes? Aunt Laine's coming tonight, and we're going to have a party."

Poppy dropped her voice. "Mommy, did Daddy tell you they're getting married, and I get to carry the flowers?"

Rowan laughed. "Yes, he did. That's why we're having a party. Go on up, but Gabe's asleep, so be really quiet, okay?"

Poppy paused, a tiny smile curling her lips. "Did *you* tell Daddy that Gabe—"

"Shh, shh, shh!" Rowan said, pressing a finger to Poppy's mouth. "Secret, remember?"

"Okay, okay," she said with an eye roll that was all too familiar. She ran out of the kitchen, feet pounding the stairs. Rowan turned to Dell, who was drying his hands.

"It's never quiet here," she said.

"I can see that," he replied, taking a seat. "So…secrets, huh?"

"You've got them; I've got them." She smiled as she fastened the beads around her neck. "Everyone's got them."

It was late, well past midnight, when Rowan and Gabriel went outside and sat on the porch swing. Poppy had been in bed for hours, and Laine and Dell had just driven away, even though they had their own guest room upstairs. Rowan had taken the time to make the room distinctly personal to them. Nothing was spare in her life, not anymore.

The air was chilly, more like fall than spring. "Are you cold?" Gabriel asked.

"I'm in front of an oven all day. This is divine."

"I'm happy for Laine and Dell, I really am," he said.

Rowan nodded, breathing in the smoky scent that traveled on the air every night. Fireplaces didn't burn out until March, and then the bonfires took over, clean fires that took the chill right out of the air. In the mornings there was a dampness that was far from unpleasant, a sense of turnover that rose right out of the ground. The fire and the earth dominated in spring, as much as water and wind ruled the summer. "Me too," she said, staring into the dense darkness.

She must have been still for a while, because when Gabriel nudged her with his shoulder, it didn't feel like the first time. "What's the matter? You're a million miles away."

"Sorry, I'm just… I'm counting the days."

"Stop. We said we're not doing that."

She swallowed against the lump in her throat. The one that grew the day Gabriel got his acceptance letter. It hadn't left since. "I can't help it."

"I'm not going far."

"Yeah, California's real close."

"It's just a plane ride. Maybe I'll hate it."

"I hope not," she said, resting her head on his shoulder. The breeze carried the sweet scent of herbs to her nose from the tiny potted plants that had turned into long boxes of lush greens lining the porch railing. "I hope you love it."

Rowan meant it; she really did. But the words did nothing to comfort her. She was not going to love driving to the airport at the end of August, and she didn't even want to think about the years he'd be gone. He was majoring in art history at Stanford, just as his mother had. Rowan and Poppy were the only ones who even knew he was going. Between Laine and Dell's engagement and Celia and Austin's baby, he hadn't wanted to steal anyone's thunder.

"If I do hate it, can I come back?" Gabriel asked.

"You better come back either way," Rowan said. "Before you move to Paris to open up galleries and appraise lost masterpieces and I never see you again."

"I love these imaginary lives you dream up for me. They get better every day."

"I'm sorry," she said, rocking the swing back and forth. "Just let me be sad for a little while. I've had you for eight years. This is hard for me."

"Eight years," Gabriel said. "I never…Jesus."

"You never what?"

"I never counted, I guess."

Rowan felt a jolt because she'd never really counted either. Putting a number on it solidified something that had been shapeless in her mind, just a concept, never a truth. Their lives were not imaginary. They had brought each other to life, and they had every reason to expect more. When she looked at Gabriel, she could see everything that had changed and everything that stayed the same. The things that had healed, even if they weren't pretty, and the pain and blood they'd given to reach this here and this now. As she rested her head against his shoulder again, she thought about those years as the sum of their parts, defined by protection and pain, longing and loss. The journey didn't matter now, none of it did, because everything in her life was real—something she hadn't even allowed herself to hope for. And in the calm air, under a wash of moonlight cutting through the darkness, she found she didn't need anything more.

READING GROUP GUIDE

1. Why do you think Gabriel was so insistent that Rowan not call the police or social services to rescue him from the basement?

2. Do you agree with Rowan's decision to kidnap Gabriel? What do you think you would have done in that situation?

3. How would you describe Rowan and Celia's relationship? Does it feel like a typical sister relationship?

4. Why do you think Rowan was adamant about not telling Gabriel that she, too, had been abused?

5. In what ways did the tornado and its aftermath change each of them—Rowan, Gabriel, and Celia?

6. Why do you think Gabriel reacted so strongly to Dell's appearance in their lives?

7. Why do you think Gabriel's father ultimately agreed to sign away his parental rights to Rowan?

8. What role did Gabriel play in reuniting Rowan and Celia? Do you think they would have reconnected in the same way if Gabriel weren't in the picture?

9. At what point do you think Rowan morphed from being Gabriel's guardian into being his mother?

10. Gabriel seems to save Rowan just as much as Rowan saves Gabriel. Discuss the ways in which this is true.

11. In some ways, found family can have more of an impact on one's life than family by blood. How does this show up in the book? Do you have found family in your own life, and if so, what role do those people play?

A CONVERSATION WITH THE AUTHOR

How did the idea for this book come about?

This novel is the first piece of fiction I ever wrote, and boy, did I have a lot to learn. It's difficult to remember exactly how the story came to me because I got the idea for it when I was a teenager—around Gabriel's age, in fact. At first it wasn't much; I had this recurring image of two people running from a tornado. It kept popping into my head, the two of them tearing across a field and hiding in a pile of rocks. Then I got to wondering about their relationship, why they were out there, and it didn't take long for Rowan and Gabriel to burst into life. They arrived fully formed and ready to talk, and I never had any qualms about telling their story, even though it seemed *very* odd. (Even to me!)

As I grew older, I pieced together more and more of their journey, and I finally sat down and started writing it shortly after my daughter had been born. It was, hands down, the most fun I've ever had in my life! I was completely in love with the characters; they were so real to me, and I'm extremely proud of them. I know there is no story that hasn't already been told, but this one was a real oddball to me, and I just loved diving into every nook and cranny of Rowan's, Gabriel's, and Celia's lives. My house is a bit of a shrine to this book. If I had to cut a line that I loved, I would have it embroidered onto a sampler, frame it, and hang it in my kitchen. I still have notes I jotted down when I was fourteen years old, which is kind of cool.

Tell us about the process of writing this book.

Oh lord…it was a journey and a half! The most notable thing about this book has to be its initial length: 264,000 words. For scale, it was published at around 98,000, so tack on an extra book and a half to get the idea. I think part of that was just me enjoying the characters so much and letting them run wild. And I'm honestly glad I did because it really helped me come to terms with what worked and what didn't. Obviously, having such a huge book led to a *lot* of editing, but I even loved doing that. I would sit to write every night after my daughter went to sleep, and I had to force myself to stop by 3:00 a.m., otherwise I would have *happily* written all night. As it was, I'd still wake up at 5:30 and dive in before I left for work. I had a very chill admin job at the time (thanks, Gregg!), and when it was slow, I would edit what I'd written the night before.

I also did a ton of research. I dove back into my psych books and learned as much as I could about adolescent psychology, breaking patterns of abuse, and working through trauma. At the time, my husband worked for a community center and managed dozens of teenagers. I spent hours chatting with them over the course of a year to try to get an authentic voice for Gabriel. Rowan, I could handle, but getting Gabriel right took a bit more work. Some things turned into an inside joke for me—a good example of that is Flip. I could never get Flip and Gabe to sound as authentic as I wanted them to on paper, which is why, despite his many antics throughout the story, Flip never utters a single word.

Who is your favorite character in this book and why?

Celia, without a doubt. When you think about the story from her perspective, it's a whole different animal, and I'm not just talking about Rowan and Gabriel's effect on her life but what she went through as a teenager herself. I really enjoyed tailoring Rowan and Gabriel's relationships with her based on only what they knew. To Rowan, and to the reader at first, she is a villain, someone who upended Rowan's life at very crucial junctions, but if you flip it around and look at what Celia went through, it's much easier to respect what she had to deal with. Here is someone who lost her parents as a young teenager, was yanked out of a cushy life and placed in a group home, and is dealing with a very angry sister who has no memory of what they lost. Gabriel's perception of Celia is heavily colored by Rowan, but in the end, he comes to love her for who she is. I think when we initially meet Celia, she is a very lonely person who is still punishing herself for a lot of her decisions. Her arc, I believe, is the strongest of all the characters. I really had no plans for Celia and Austin to have any kind of relationship, much less fall in love, but I am so happy he fell for her. She deserved a happy ending as much as Rowan and Gabriel did.

What was the hardest scene to write?

I would have to say the scene in the attic when Gabriel finally learns the truth about Rowan's own abuse. I wanted that scene to read like a raw nerve, and I spent a lot of time trying to understand what those moments must have been like: Gabriel discovering how little he knows of someone he loves so much, and Rowan realizing she has come to lean on Gabriel far more than she'd intended. I read a lot about emotional incest while I was writing this book (i.e., when a parent depends on their child for emotional support that should come from another adult), and I think Rowan really made a concerted effort *not* to lay her burden on Gabriel. When he finds out, it's such a jarring moment for them both—sad, of course, but also beautiful. There is absolutely no doubt about the depths of their love for each other, and the reality of that really slaps them in the face. I wanted Rowan to remain clear in her role but allow herself to acknowledge that she is who she is because of what she experienced and that Gabriel deserved to see her. He, in turn, had to grow up a lot during that scene. I really hope that readers feel it as deeply as they do.

What kinds of research did you do for this book? Did you learn anything new or surprising?

I talked a bit about the more serious research I did above, so I'll share what I learned about tornadoes! I'm a weather nut, I always have been, and as I said, the tornado was the first scene I envisioned. I wanted it to be very cinematic, but I ended up getting caught up in the logistics of literally outrunning a tornado. I had to do *math* (perish the thought!), and I did a bit of field research as well. After looking up tornado speeds based on size, I went to the high school track by my house, ran a quarter of a mile like my life depended on it, and timed myself to see how long it took and how strong a storm I could realistically use. I've never felt closer to death in my life—suffice it to say, I'm *not* a runner—but I did feel a little better about putting Rowan and Gabe in front of an EF3.

What's your advice for new writers?

Do not, and let me repeat, *do not* give up on a story you believe in. This book was written ten years ago. I wrote it, edited it to death, and was signed by my agent with it, but despite our very best efforts, it did not sell. To say I was crushed does not even begin to cover how I felt; I was *devastated*. It took me weeks to stop crying and finally push on, and I eventually came to terms with the fact this wasn't the book. Fast-forward seven years. *After We Were Stolen* had sold, and I had a call scheduled with my editor, Erin, about a potential second book. I had a panicked chat with Melissa, my agent, because even after ten years, I was still madly in love with this story, and I was trying to decide if I could handle the risk of another heartbreak. We decided to throw it into the mix. I did a quick cleanup, wrote a fresh synopsis, and held my breath…and that story ends with the book in your hands. You never know what opportunities are around the corner. Fight like hell.

Do you ever get stuck while writing? How do you work your way out of it?

All the time! Pardon me for being crass, but mental constipation is just as miserable as the physical version. I'll share a really strange tip that works for me. When I'm writing, I keep a Word document where I have a running Q&A with my characters. If I get stuck, I ask them to help me. "Gabe, why are you acting like this?" or "Rowan, what are you going to do about that?" I type out whatever comes to me as fast as I can, with no thought in my head. It's incredible how often it works, and I get some really great character insight out of it.

There's one example of this that always stuck with me. In an earlier draft of this book, Gabriel's basement setup was a little bit different; he slept on a rolling cot with rails, almost like a gurney (I cut that for being too creepy). When they got to the house, I kept finding myself writing scenes where Gabriel fell out of bed, and I didn't know why. So I asked him. It immediately came to me that he was used to having a narrow bed with railings, so he kept rolling out of a regular bed. I know it sounds a little odd, but I swear by it!

ACKNOWLEDGMENTS

I love to read the acknowledgments after finishing a novel. I'm always impressed by the authors who spin poignant and beautiful thanks to the people who helped them along the way.

Unfortunately, I'm more like my dog, running around in a hyperactive frenzy of love and jumping on everyone's legs.

With that said, please accept my most sincere, if ineloquent, thanks.

To my agent, Melissa Sarver-White, the first person to love this book as much as I do. I will never, as long as I live, forget our phone conversation after you read this manuscript. I can tell you now, I was *running* in circles around my living room during the entire call, trying to sound somewhat competent and not at all out of breath. I may have (i.e. definitely) burst into song after we hung up. Thank you so, so much for taking a chance on me (and for being as utterly weird as I am).

To my editor, Erin McClary, for helping me breathe new life into this story (and for being a *very* good sport along the way). I was terrified I wouldn't be able to pull it off. Terrified. I can't tell you how wonderful it was to get an email from you, after six weeks of the most intense editing of my life, that said, "I LOVE THIS BOOK!" Your enthusiasm and support are palpable, and it is so much fun to be on this journey with you by my side.

And thank you to Cheddar for being the best boy when we went out to dinner!

I love working with Sourcebooks. Every member of every team is a pleasure, and their dedication to their art is clear. Massive thanks to Anna Venkus, whom I adore. I wish I could put you in charge of every aspect of my life, because you do not miss a beat. Thank you for your attention, for your care, and for delivering joy with every email.

Thanks and a big hug to Manu Velasco for your kind and thoughtful edits. Your eye for detail and sensitivity is unmatched, and I appreciate you more than I can say. Additional thanks to Jessica Thelander for making sure every detail was perfect!

To art director Heather VenHuizen—I cried when I saw the beautiful cover you created. It *is* the book. A million and one thanks for your stunning work.

To my wonderful friends and fellow wordsmiths at the Woodbridge Writers' Group, Elaine Tweedus, Shannon Quinn-Schneck, Susan Brown-Peitz, Angela Pryor, and Joshua Pryor. You are all so brilliant, and it is my honor to write alongside you. You're also the most patient group of people on planet Earth. (I'm pretty sure you've listened to me read three or four different variations of this story without complaint, bless you all.)

To Neal Padte, Andy Bagnall, Jim Morey, Jessica Morey,

Patrick Kelly, Ashley Powell, Karen Powell, Jin Hee Kim, Kelly Schnorrbusch, Abena Okyere, Maggie Burns, Lori Mongon, Richard Wlodarczyk, Daina Figueroa, Fran Gesek, Lois Griffin, Laura Brown, Kathy Sager, Christine Bridge, and my Friday daughter, Mackayla Stillwell. I love you all, and I am so blessed to have such wonderful people in my life. Thank you for coming to my events, sharing my excitement every step of the way, and offering unconditional love and support.

My deepest thanks and appreciation to Lisa Tortorello-Gilligan who was with me when it looked like this book was never going to be published and still refused to give up on it. I am so grateful for your wisdom and support.

To my mother, Deborah Beyfuss, who rallied an entire congregation to support me and introduced me to so many wonderful people. Thank you for being there through everything and sharing every high and low. P.S. I truly believe it was you, and you alone, who brought gingham back to the '20s.

To my sister, Amanda Gaynor, who is my sounding board for *everything* and the only person I can call up and say, "What was that thing we were talking about two years ago? You know, about that guy from that show, who was kinda tall?" You always know. Every time. Additional kudos to you and Keenan Gaynor for giving me the pure joy that is Grace and Declan.

To my husband, Brandon Powell. You already know everything

I could possibly say. I love you so much. You're never gonna get that Best Buy Rewards card.

To my daughter, Tess Powell, the most self-assured and badass sixteen-year-old I know. You're going to do incredible things. It probably makes me a terrible mother, but I kind of love that you got called down to guidance because your stories for creative writing were so demented. That's my girl!

To my brother, Daniel Beyfuss, and my father, Paul Beyfuss. My only regret is that I can't share this with you. I miss you so very much.

Finally, to my readers, old and new. Thank you for walking through my worlds. I hope you enjoyed every step of the journey.

ABOUT THE AUTHOR

© Electric Love Studios

Brooke Beyfuss is a freelance writer who lives in Woodbridge Township, New Jersey, with her husband, daughter, an incredibly hyperactive dog, and three cats. She graduated from Rutgers University with a BA in psychology and comparative literature and has written extensively on some wonderfully wild topics. Her debut novel, *After We Were Stolen*, was featured in *Bustle* magazine, presented at the 2022 Kansas Book Festival, and selected as a fall 2022 Hoopla Book Club pick. You can follow Brooke on social media @brookebeyfuss or visit brookebeyfuss.com for news and events.

A fire. Her escape.

And the realization her entire life has been a lie.

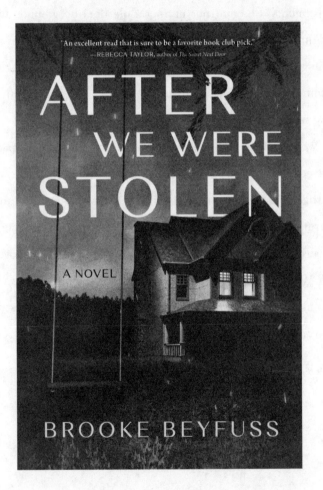

"An excellent read that is sure to be a favorite book club pick."
—REBECCA TAYLOR, author of *The Secret Next Door*

AFTER WE WERE STOLEN

A NOVEL

BROOKE BEYFUSS

When nineteen-year-old Avery awakens to flames consuming her family's remote compound, she knows it's her only chance to escape her father's grueling survival training, bizarre rules, and gruesome punishments. She and her brother Cole flee the grounds for the first time in their lives, suddenly homeless in a world they know nothing about. After months of hiding out, they are arrested for shoplifting, and a shocking discovery is made, resulting in the pair being separated.

Avery is alone and desperate. She is uncertain if her "parents" survived the fire and is terrified to find out. But when the police investigation reveals there may be more survivors, Avery must uncover the truth about the fire to truly be free.

Suspenseful, emotionally charged, and deeply thought-provoking, *After We Were Stolen* delves into the idea of families—those we're born into and those we make—resilience, and the lengths a cult survivor will go to finally be free of her painful past.

For more Brooke Beyfuss, visit: **sourcebooks.com**